Something Beyond the Sky

Siri Mitchell

D0059435

HARVEST HOUSE PUBLISHERS

EUGENE, OREGON

Cover by Garborg Design Works, Minneapolis, Minnesota

Cover photos © Rafal Dudziec/istockphoto.com; Wayne Chambers/istockphoto.com; Sang Nguyen/istockphoto.com

Published in association with the literary agency of Alive Communications, Inc., 7680 Goddard Street, Ste. #200, Colorado Springs, CO 80920

This is a work of fiction. Names, characters, places, and incidents are products of the author's imagination or are used fictitiously. Any resemblance to actual persons, living or dead, or to events or locales, is entirely coincidental.

SOMETHING BEYOND THE SKY
Copyright © 2006 by Siri L. Mitchell
Published by Harvest House Publishers
Eugene, Oregon 97402
www.harvesthousepublishers.com

Library of Congress Cataloging-in-Publication Data

Mitchell, Siri L., 1969–
   Something beyond the sky / Siri L. Mitchell.
      p. cm.
   ISBN-13: 978-0-7369-1637-0 (pbk.)
   ISBN-10: 0-7369-1637-7 (pbk.)
   1. Female friendship—Fiction.   2. Air Force spouses—Fiction.   3. Married women—
Fiction.   I. Title.
   PS3613.I866S66 2006
   816'.6—dc22   2005018230

Printed in the United States of America

06   07   08   09   10   11   12   13   14   /DPS-CF/   10   9   8   7   6   5   4   3   2   1

To Trenna Hart, for friendship

Acknowledgments

To Carolyn McCready and Terry Glaspey, for seeing potential in this project. To my agent, Beth Jusino, for seeing potential in me. To Kim Moore, for never settling for the second-best word or a "good enough" explanation. To Carolyn Peters, for loving her job. To Sandra Schulthess, Michelle Barrette, and Kathy Dawson-Townsend, my ESEP '96–'98 sisters: three women I would never have met had it not been for the Air Force. To the sisterhood of women of Nu Chapter of Alpha Xi Delta sorority, my home away from home. To Sarah Beyer, who allowed me to interrogate her about flying. To SMSgt. Roger Dubois, 434 ABW/HC, who graciously answered my questions about getting married in Germany. And to the WriteHands who answered questions fainter hearts would have dodged.

Roster of Characters

Anne Bradley, newly graduated business major from the University of Washington and newly married to Will Bradley.

Will Bradley, second lieutenant in the U.S. Air Force. He works in public affairs.

Rachel Hawthorne, newly married to R.J. Hawthorne following a whirlwind romance in Europe.

R.J. Hawthorne, captain in the U.S. Air Force. He pilots an AC-130 gunship. The AC-130 is commonly used in special operations.

Karen Bannister, married to Kevin Bannister. Although she has a degree in nursing, Karen stays at home.

Kevin Bannister, first lieutenant in the U.S. Air Force. He works as a civil engineer.

Beth Bennett, married to Marc Bennett. A graduate of the U.S. Air Force Academy, she worked as an aeronautical engineer for the U.S. Air Force. As a captain, Beth resigned her commission and stopped working soon after her twins were born.

Marc Bennett, captain in the U.S. Air Force. He works as an aeronautical engineer. He is also a graduate of the U.S. Air Force Academy.

~

Four roads begin at four points of a compass. They traverse different terrains, weather different storms, and pass through different towns. For one moment in time, they meet at an intersection and the four become one. Who is to say that they do not swap identities and choose to continue in a different direction altogether?

~

Officers' Spouses' Club Has Record Year

We are pleased to announce that the Bullard Officers' Spouses' Club enjoyed their most profitable year in history. The scholarship drive, boosted by a booth at the OSC Christmas Bazaar and the gala Silent Auction, brought in unprecedented funding. Fourteen scholarships were presented to members of our Air Force community at the club's final meeting.

Mrs. Pritchard, honorary president of the OSC, gives much of the credit to this year's food committee. Beth Bennett, food committee member, passed the credit to the rest of the group. "None of us had met prior to the formation of this committee, and none of us had ever been a part of an Officers' Spouses' Club. We came from different states, different backgrounds, and different religions; we joined the food committee for different goals and different reasons. But we soon learned that first impressions are often wrong, and that, when given a chance, the most unlikely people can become friends." She believes that friendship, food, and fun were the perfect ingredients for a profitable year.

CHAPTER 1

Nine months earlier

⁓

*M*rs. William Bradley," Anne deciphered from the calligraphy on the outside of the envelope. She lifted a slim eyebrow. "For me?"

"It came to my mailbox at the office yesterday. I forgot to give it to you last night," Will said over the buzz of his razor. He frowned into the mirror as he pulled his chin up to shave his neck.

She opened it. "Mrs. Pritchard and the Bullard Air Force Base Officers' Spouses' Club cordially invite you to attend a Welcome Tea." She watched her husband wander into the bedroom. "Are they serious?" she asked him.

"What?" He was keeping one eye glued to CNN as he pulled on his pants.

"I said, are they serious?"

"About what?"

"The tea."

"Probably. When is it?"

She consulted the card. "Bullard Air Force Base Officers' Club. Two o'clock, 10 September. I didn't think they still did things like this. Does this mean I have to wear white gloves and a little hat?" she asked, prancing around the room in her bathrobe, nose high in the air, flashing the long legs he'd always admired.

"Come here, you!" he opened his arms. "I'm sure it's just like one of those sorority teas you always had at the university. All the alumnae come, everyone talks, and no one drinks any tea." He caught her around the waist for a hug.

"Will, have you noticed that people have a strange reaction when I tell them my name?" It had been bothering her since she'd arrived in town the previous month.

"Not especially. What do you mean?" He nuzzled her long neck.

"Everywhere I go on base, when I introduce myself, they repeat my name back to me. Like I'd said it in some foreign language." She gave her husband a playful push away from her neck. "I'm serious."

"Don't worry. They just can't believe I'm married and off the market. My exploits from last year are legendary. Had to do something with myself while you were finishing school."

Anne just laughed at him. "Do you know how glad I am that I married you, Lieutenant Bradley?" she asked, tickling his ear with the invitation.

"I think I need to be reminded, Mrs. Bradley."

"Is it really necessary that I go?" asked Rachel, looking at her husband over the top of her sunglasses. She didn't feel like attending a tea. The wives in R.J.'s squadron had not been easy to relate to. To be fair, she wasn't used to socializing with people her own age. But still, she couldn't imagine being trapped in a room full of them.

"Rachel…" he began helplessly as he squirmed on the lawn chair. It nearly fell off the tiny cement patio that extended from their apartment. He loved her even more than he loved flying. A look from her dusky eyes and toss of her glossy black hair could shoot him down faster than any missile.

"Okay, I'll go, I'll go." She folded up the *International Herald Tribune* she'd been reading and reached for the *Financial Times*. "It's just that teas are so *passé*."

"Basically, Rachel, the way it works is when the general's wife asks you to do something, you nod and smile."

"But *tea?*"

"I'm sure they'll have coffee."

She shook her head as she scanned the newspaper. After scanning the international stock quotes quickly, she took a furtive peek at R.J. from over the top of the peach-colored paper. *I have to tell him. The sooner I tell him, the sooner I'll know. Okay. One for the money…*

This was a matter of honor. "One for the money" was sacred; she had never before violated the incantation.

Two for the show.

She took a deep breath.

Three to get ready, and—

R.J. squinted at his watch and then leaped to his feet. "Got to go. I'm five minutes late. Just do me a favor and RSVP, okay?"

"Fine." She blew a kiss to him as he closed the sliding glass door.

Next time. The next chance I get, I'll tell him. This time didn't count. I never got to four.

Her eyes narrowed to slits as she cursed herself. "Coward."

Rachel shook a cigarette from a mother-of-pearl cigarette case and lit it with an ivory inlaid lighter. She took a puff and closed her eyes, listening to the slosh of the water in the pool. She could almost imagine she was poolside at her favorite hotel in Greece. Except it wouldn't be this humid. And the pool would be much larger.

She decided to call New York. She picked up the cell phone that always lay close at hand and dialed a number she'd memorized when she was six.

"Conrad," the voice at the other end answered.

"Hello."

"Rachel, *chérie,* it's good to hear from you. Do they have running water and flush toilets down there?"

"They have cellular service. And internet connections."

"Life as a Southern belle. Something new to add to your résumé."

"Don't count on it. I've only been here a week."

"I still have the papers. Have you told him?"

She exhaled with violence. "No. I'm such a coward."

"You have to tell him."

"I know. I'll do it."

"Why don't you bring him here so I can meet him?"

"Because I don't think he's quite up to it yet."

"Is he treating you well?"

"Yes! I've never been better taken care of in my life. Trust me."

"So tell him."

"I can't, Conrad. I just can't." She was near tears. *Stop being so ridiculous.*

"When are you coming back?"

"That's why I called. I had wanted to come on the tenth, but I won't be able to. I've obligated myself to something here."

"That's fine, *chérie.* I'll look forward to seeing you when I see you."

"You've sent the reports?"

"They're coming to you express this morning. The company guaranteed before noon."

"*A bientôt.*"

"A spouses' tea? I never thought I'd be on this end of things." Beth

shook her head and bent, once more, to pick up óne of the twins'
toys. When she and Marc had moved into the house the year before,
it had been plenty big. But that was before they had known the full
implication of having twins. And their toys, which also had twins. They
needed more room.

"You don't mind much?" asked Marc.

"I don't mind at all." She smiled, avoiding his eyes. "You know that.
I still feel the same way I did before I got out. I can't imagine going to
work every day and leaving these two characters behind."

"Okay," he said, kissing her upturned lips and then her freckled
nose. "I'll see you tonight."

"Tonight."

The fact was that she did miss being in the Air Force. Especially when
the toys were dropping to the floor like bombs. But she still clung to her
belief that being a mother to the twins was more important than being
a captain in the Air Force. Captains were, after all, a dime a dozen. She
ran a hand through short sandy hair before she realized it was covered
in goop from breakfast.

She glanced at the clock. One of the twins had been running a high
fever, which meant that it was just a matter of time before the other one
would be too. She waited until just before 7:30 and then dialed the base
clinic. Answering machine. She hung up.

She pressed redial until 7:50, trying to get through to the
appointments desk. *It would be so much easier if I could just take them in
to sick call. They'd be seen right away without question.* She sighed. Life
as the spouse of an active-duty military person had its privileges as well
as its drawbacks. You didn't have to report in for those early morning
emergency phone-tree drills, but you couldn't push your way into the
hospital without an appointment, either.

She rinsed the dishes and crammed them into the dishwasher with
the phone clamped between her ear and shoulder. She pressed redial
again.

One of the twins started to cry, and so Shelby, their boxer, started
to bark.

"Active-duty military or dependent?" The voice startled her. She'd
been hearing busy signals so long she'd grown used to them.

She snapped at Shelby to get her to lie down. Obediently, the dog
sat and then walked her front feet forward until she was lying on the
floor. Then she let out a heavy sigh and put her head on her paws.

"Hello?"

"I'm sorry. Dependent." Beth still had to overcome her automatic "active-duty military" response. She'd been gung ho military for the past nine years of her life. Four at the Air Force Academy and five years as active-duty Air Force. Old habits are the most stubborn.

"And what is the nature of the appointment?"

One of the twins gave a sudden shriek of rage.

Beth turned around to see her sons throwing their sippy cups at each other. "I'm sorry. I'll have to call back." She slammed the phone down on the counter and then bellowed at the twins. "I hate this life!"

Surprised, they paused in midfight, their tiny gooey mouths forming perfect, small *O*s.

"...and Kevin brought home an invitation to some tea I'm supposed to go to," Karen said, weaving the telephone cord through her fingers.

"How nice." Karen's mother was speaking from halfway across the country. Pots clanged in the background, and Karen could hear the sound of running water. She felt a pang of longing for her mother's bright, sunny kitchen filled with cookie jars and a jungle of plants.

"I hate going to things like this. I won't know anybody."

"But just think, Karen, you will afterward."

She hated it when her mother looked on the bright side of things. "I suppose." She sighed. "I'd better go. Kevin should be home soon, and it's our nickel."

"I'll call *you* next time. When's the tea?"

Karen squinted across the counter at the card. "September tenth."

"Enjoy!" Her mother's last words were meant to be an encouragement. So how come it felt as though they'd been talking about a trip to the dentist?

Karen unthreaded her legs from the stool and walked into the living room of their house on base. Plopped onto the couch. She stared at the sun-numbed world outside. All was still. Not one pine needle trembled. Not one shadow stirred. It was too hot out there to do anything. Too humid to even breathe. Inside, dinner was ready and the house was clean. Every moving box had been flattened and stacked in the carport. She let her eyes wander around the sparsely furnished room. There was nothing left for her to do.

Except get pregnant and have a baby. And God knew they were trying.

She gritted her teeth as she asked herself the timeworn question: *Why?* They'd been through all the tests. The doctors swore there was nothing wrong. It was embarrassing. They were LDS, they'd been married for seven years, and they didn't have any children.

It wasn't embarrassing; it was humiliating.

She could feel herself tensing up over it again and told herself to relax. That's partly why Kevin had chosen this assignment when he'd been told he couldn't stay in Utah.

"Bullard's on the ocean," he'd said, "and it's warm most of the year. Like a tropical paradise. All you'll have to do is relax…"

And hurry up and start having kids, Karen had thought to herself, filling in the blank he'd left.

It's not my fault. And it's not his fault. It's no one's fault, but it's definitely a problem. We're good LDS.

Then that voice that she could never quite silence spoke again: *It is your fault; you know it's your fault.* She got up, walked into her room, and picked up her hairbrush. Drawing it through waist-length auburn hair, she counted a hundred strokes, forcing her thoughts away from self-condemnation to concentrate on the count.

She drew on a sweater against the chill of the air-conditioning. Sliding two fingers underneath her watch band, she checked for tightness. It seemed snugger than yesterday. She pinched herself at the waist. *I have to stop eating so much ice cream.*

Kevin kept insisting that she'd get blown away in a windstorm.

Yeah, right.

CHAPTER 2

*H*ello." Rachel answered the cell phone at the first ring but continued to read through the thick sheaf of documents on the desk in front of her.

"Hey, it's me," said R.J. "Can't talk right now, but meet me at the O Club tonight."

"O Club?"

"The Officers' Club. On Fridays they always have free pizza."

"Sounds great, R.J." She was glad he couldn't see her eyes roll. "What time?"

"Five thirty."

"Where?"

"The O Club. On base." The connection was broken and the phone went dead.

Rachel frowned as she glanced at her watch. It was already 4:30. "Honestly!"

She separated the mountain of paperwork in front of her into separate piles, and then she slipped them into plastic accordion folders before turning off the light. She paused in the doorway before shutting the door. She scowled at the dark brown doors of the closet and the caustic moss green carpet. *Only three more months. I can't wait to leave!*

She was happy to be living with R.J., and she was grateful to belong to someone, but her first impression of his apartment had lasted.

R.J. had thrown open the door and the earth-toned colors had been underwhelming. The fake wood paneling was brown; the shag carpet was green. The '70s wood Venetian blinds were orange.

"I never really decorated because I'm not here much."

She'd patted his arm. "That's okay. I was thinking of something a little larger and brighter anyway."

After walking into the bedroom, she rolled back the door of the closet and then swished through her wardrobe. *Officers' Club...it's probably some sort of gentlemen's club where the guys play poker and pool.* She settled on a backless black crepe tuxedo jumpsuit, and then she added a small rhinestone spiked satin purse and black strappy sandals.

Without much time left for her shoulder-length hair, she scraped it back into a half ponytail, leaving several locks loose to fall onto her forehead.

A spritz of perfume, a touch of lipstick, and she was off.

Rachel liked two things about Bullard Air Force Base. It was on the ocean, and someone saluted her every time she drove onto base.

"Did you see that?" she'd asked R.J. the first time she'd gone to base.

"What?" he'd asked.

"That man, standing in the middle of the road."

"The gate guard?"

"It looked like he saluted."

"He did. They always do."

"Why?"

"Because of this," said R.J., pointing to the sticker on the outside of the Alfa Romeo's windshield.

"What is it?"

"Base sticker. Let's them know you belong here. You can come on base whenever you want. You have to slow down at the security gates, but they'll just wave you through unless there's an ID check going on."

"Do they salute all the cars?"

"Only the ones with officers' stickers. They're blue."

The Alfa Romeo purred up to the front gate and she was saluted onto base. She asked the gate guard for directions to the O Club. The Alfa wasn't the most expensive sports car she'd ever owned, but she loved driving it. And it was an import. It had been R.J.'s before she'd convinced him to buy something else for himself. He bought a pickup, but she hadn't minded. She now had exclusive rights to the sports car. And like all of her accessories, she wore it with panache and nonchalance.

She found an empty shaded parking space under one of the anonymous trees that had become a display stand for Spanish moss. In a practiced maneuver, she drove past and then, putting the car into reverse and spinning the steering wheel, she backed into it. In her opinion, there was nothing worse in a convertible than a sun-cracked dashboard.

Following the sounds of music and laughter, she found her way to what she assumed was the Officers' Club lounge. In front of her and down several steps was a horseshoe-shaped bar extending from the back wall of the room. The same shape was repeated above it, by a wooden glass rack suspended from the ceiling. At the very front, dangling from a short rope, hung a brass bell. To her right, past a dozen tables and an assortment of brown leather captain's chairs on wheels, a long buffet table held a stack of plates and an assortment of pizzas.

More of those tables and chairs were nestled against a waist-high wall in front of the bar. Beneath the wall, the floor plunged five feet and held another dozen tables. The front wall of the lounge was composed of windows which presented a floor-to-ceiling view of the bay.

Officers in camouflage uniforms congregated around the bar, caps stuffed into their lower pants pockets. Rachel's eyes swept past them. She was looking for R.J. He wouldn't be wearing camouflage. He'd be wearing a flight suit.

After she'd walked down the first set of steps, she realized there was an alcove off to her right. And that's where she found R.J., at a pool table, in the middle of a set with another captain. He kissed her and then offered her the cue. "Want to play?"

"Sure." She turned to the other officer. "You don't mind?"

He shrugged. What was it to him if R.J. wanted to let his wife lose the game for him?

She chalked the cue and took her time studying the table.

R.J. began to explain to her what was required, but she shook him off. "I'm quite capable, thank you."

She bent down and, with a deft shot, made the six ball jump over the eight ball. Miraculously it hit both the two and the four into their pockets.

Their opponent whistled through his teeth and then laughed it off as beginner's luck.

"No," Rachel contradicted. "Years spent playing in Monte Carlo."

With three more shots, she cleared the table.

She and R.J. high-fived.

"You're a hustler!" his friend accused Rachel.

"Maybe," R.J. retorted, "but she's my little hustler." He draped an arm over her as they left to go to the bar. "I didn't know you could play like that!"

Rachel shrugged. "One of my secret lives."

R.J. shouldered a hole for them at the bar. "Hey, guys. This is my wife, Rachel."

Rachel smiled. "Hello."

R.J. introduced the people in his squadron. Some of them she recognized by their names, some by face. But there were some she'd never met. They all looked at her as though she were an exotic cat. They were fascinated, but guarded, unsure whether or not she was dangerous.

The wives of the other pilots and navigators began to join the crowd. Then the knot of camouflage-clad officers gave way to those dressed in flight suits. And soon, Rachel herself was pushed to the fringes. She found herself sitting at a small table with several of the wives she recognized from a squadron event the week before. Kate, Ellen, and Natalie were obviously familiar with each other, and they seemed ready to include Rachel in their conversation.

"What's your weight limit, Rachel?" the redheaded Kate asked in an animated voice.

"I'm sorry?"

"What's your weight limit?"

"Your limit," Natalie enjoined. "For me, it's 120. For Ellen, it's 130. She's tall."

"I'm sorry, but I don't understand what you're talking about."

"R.J.'s *weight limit*." Kate was looking at Rachel as though she were dumb. "Ricky says that women over 120 pounds repulse him."

Rachel blinked, and then she lifted her eyebrows in amazement. "So, just out of curiosity, what would he do if you ever weighed more than that? Or if, heaven forbid, you ever got pregnant?"

The three women fell silent.

"So you don't have one?" Kate finally asked.

"I would never marry a man who would impose a weight limit." Rachel tilted her head and fixed her eye on Kate. "What's your weight limit for Ricky? I'd say there's nothing more unattractive than a man carrying around a spare tire." Rachel pushed her chair away from the table. "Excuse me. I need to find R.J."

"We'll see you at the tea, right?"

"R.J., do I have a weight limit?" They were the first words Rachel had spoken during the drive home.

He slowed the car to a stop at the red light before responding. It was too hard to carry on a conversation with the Alfa's top down. "What are you talking about?"

"I thought it was a squadron thing, to have a weight limit for your wife."

R.J. wrinkled his nose.

"So you've heard of it?"

"Well, sure. But I think it's stupid."

"Why? Lots of other wives have them."

"If you married someone because you care about how they make you look, then I can see how a person would be worried about weight. But if you married someone because you care about her, I don't see what weight has to do with it. So the bottom line is no, you don't have a weight limit."

Rachel rewarded him with a breath-stealing kiss.

"I can pull over. Right now, if you want," R.J. said when he could speak. He looked at his wife in a wonder-struck daze. He still couldn't believe he had the fantastic luck to be married to her.

They'd met in Paris.

He'd been on leave from Ramstein Air Base in Germany and had decided, with the help of a couple of his crew members, to take a trip to Paris. It was a tradition that the crew took leave together when they were away from home.

"*All* the girls in Paris have legs up to here," they'd said. "And the accent. How could you *not* fall in love? And it's springtime," they'd reminded him. "I love Paris in the springtime," they'd begun singing.

He'd agreed then because he couldn't stand to listen to them anymore. "Fine. We'll go to Paris."

Paris was incredible. He fell in love with the city the moment he saw the Arc de Triomphe at the end of the Champs-Elysées. And he'd fallen in love again that night on Montmarte, by the big white church on the hill. He'd ducked into a hole-in-the-wall bar with his crew for drinks.

"Who's drinking what?" someone had asked.

"Beer," was the unanimous reply.

"You can't have beer," R.J. argued with exasperation. "We're in *Paris*. We're drinking wine."

"Fine. If *we're* drinking wine, then *you're* doing the buying."

So that was how he'd come to be standing at the bar next to a girl with the longest legs he'd ever seen. She had black hair. It hung straight across her shoulders, but from the way it fell, he could tell that the haircut had probably cost at *least* $30.

He wished he'd paid more attention in his high school French class, but he remembered the basics. *"Bonjour."*

She looked over at him.

"Comment vous appellez vous?" he said, asking her name. It wasn't the greatest pickup line he'd ever used, but at least it was in French.

"Rachel. I'm an American. Do you have a light?"

He'd taken the wine to the guys at the table, borrowed a lighter from his buddy, and then turned right around and gone back to the bar. "I'm R.J."

"Does it stand for something?" she asked.

"Richard Jarrett."

"R.J.'s better," she said, finally smiling. "Where are you from?" she flicked her ashes into an ashtray.

"Montana. But I'm in Germany right now. How about you?"

"New York."

"What do you do?"

"Absolutely nothing. I'm frivolous."

"Are you studying in Paris?"

"No. I'm living here. I graduated from NYU two years ago."

"Working?"

"No. Not really"

"Okay…" he said, shrugging.

"Don't give up now."

"You're not a student and you're not working. So what do you do all day?"

"Whatever I want."

"What are you doing tomorrow?"

"I don't know yet."

"Want to be my tour guide?"

She paused before answering. Turned to watch his friends at their table in the center of the room. One of them was laughing like Pepé Le Pew; the others were egging him on. "I'm not good in groups."

"That's okay. We'd be alone."

She smiled.

They spent the next two days together exploring Paris. She took him to Notre Dame, the Eiffel Tower, and the Louvre.

He took her on the metro.

They'd spent the afternoon jammed elbow-to-elbow with other tourists viewing *Whistler's Mother* and Manet's *Olympia* at the Musée d'Orsay. Then they'd jogged past Gauguin and Picasso, taken a deserted set of stairs back to the ground floor, and fled the building. They found themselves in the middle of the plaza in front of the museum.

"Where's the nearest taxi stand?" Rachel was beginning to walk toward the avenue that bordered the Seine.

R.J. caught her elbow. "Let's just take the metro."

"Why?"

"Because I have ten metro tickets in my wallet and I haven't used any of them."

She looked uncertain.

"It's no big deal—and besides, it's got to be close to rush hour. You've ridden before, right?"

"No, I haven't."

He pulled a city map from the back pocket of his jeans. "Let me just look at this and figure it out."

Rachel crossed her arms and watched the crowds push by on the sidewalk.

"Okay, I've got it. We have to go…" He consulted the map again and then started walking. "This way. We'll take the metro two stops. And then I think we should do one of those boat cruises."

"*Bateaux-Mouches?*"

"Yeah. Have you ever been on one?"

"No."

"So that's what we'll do." He stepped aside to let her pass before him on the tiny sidewalk. Then he realized they were passing a pizzeria. "Wait. Let's get a pizza and we can take it on the boat. What's your favorite?"

"Shrimp and feta."

"For *pizza*."

"Shrimp and feta."

He couldn't believe it. Seafood on a pizza? "Rachel, I'm a meat-and-potatoes kind of guy."

She shrugged. "Get two."

The pizzeria didn't have shrimp and feta, so they settled for extra pepperoni.

Ducking down into the metro, pizza in hand, they choked on the sudden clammy air in the tunnels. "We could take a taxi," Rachel suggested.

"Come on." R.J. took her hand, pulling her down the tunnel.

Up ahead of them a musician wrung *Comme d'habitude* out of his saxophone without any apparent enthusiasm. They passed a woman with a baby, begging for coins. R.J. followed signs for the RER rail system, taking them deeper underground through a series of snaking tunnels. They passed a man selling magazines. And then they came abreast of an accordion player.

The musician saw Rachel and stopped playing to doff his cap. Then his fingers, magically awakened, broke into a seductive gypsy-sounding tune. R.J. smiled and threw him a coin.

The train arrived just as they reached the quai. A bum got in behind them and sprawled on a seat. One door down, a different accordion player got on just as the doors shut. The bum and the accordion player smelled R.J.'s pizza at the same time. And as Italian music drifted from the instrument, the bum told Rachel he'd dance with her if she would give him the pizza.

"Mais non, monsieur. Ce n'est pas neccessaire," she said with a perfect accent.

"Mais oui, pour la plus jolie femme du monde," he took her hand and jerked her into a tango as R.J. howled with laughter.

They got off at the next stop, leaving the accordion player and the bum to split the pizza.

After the boat ride, R.J. escorted Rachel back to the Ritz.

It was the sort of hotel that had discreetly imposing valets standing on the sidewalk and a menacing bodyguard next to the door. R.J. wasn't sure he would have attempted to go inside if Rachel hadn't walked right around the valets, up the stairs past the bodyguard, and through the revolving doors. When they stepped out, they didn't step into a typical hotel lobby. It felt more like a back entrance. But beyond it, they could see an opulent hallway, with a colonnaded extension to the right and a long colonnaded hall in front of them.

He had to hurry in order to keep up with her as she strode ahead down the hall. Quick glances to the right revealed a huge oval staircase that spiraled down to the ground from what looked like five floors above. Soon after, they passed by the lobby that he would have placed at the entrance to the hotel.

She led him right and then left down a long corridor lined on both sides by glass cases filled with jewels, designer clothing, bags, art, and other displays that advertised for the luxury merchants in the area.

"The Gallery of Temptation," Rachel commented as she dragged him down the hall.

At the end they turned right and then immediately left, almost before R.J. could take in the fish tank at the end of a small sitting room in front of him. It was overhung with a striped drape, which was supported by spears protruding from the wall.

Rachel glanced at her watch and then grabbed R.J.'s hand and tugged with urgency.

He tore his gaze from another staircase that marched majestically up to the floor above them. It seemed as if there were staircases everywhere.

She retraced her steps and then came to a stop beside him. "There won't be any room left if we don't hurry." She grabbed his elbow and propelled him around the corner and through a nondescript wood door.

Immediately the scent of cigars assaulted R.J. He breathed deeply, as if it were the finest of perfumes.

"This is the Hemingway Bar. Wednesday night is cigar night. Do you want me to pick one for you?"

R.J. nodded. The bar was small. Very small. The main room was about the size of his apartment's living room, and the bar took up a good third of it. The rest was filled with small circular tables and leather armchairs. Pictures of what R.J. assumed was Hemingway decorated the walls. Off to the left and up a few steps was a small alcove that held several additional tables.

And that was it.

After Rachel finished rolling and smelling a selection of cigars, she chose one for R.J. and they claimed the last remaining table. He tried to recall what he had learned about the Hemingway mystique in his high school English lit class, but he gave it up and succumbed to luxurious blue smoke and Rachel's enchanting eyes.

After he'd finished his cigar, and Rachel had finished her Platinum Bullet, pulling all the petals from the rose that had topped it, she invited him up to her suite. He tried not to get his hopes up. Tried not to be too eager in accepting the invitation.

"This is nice," he said, settling into a plump Louis XVI armchair in her suite's sitting room.

Rachel smiled as she retrieved a stack of papers from the fax machine. She struck the bottom edge against the desk to align the pages and set them down in a pile. Then she walked over to an end table and pulled open a drawer. It contained a car radio-looking stereo that she turned on for classical music.

"You must have gotten a good deal on the rates." To R.J., the furniture and the tapestry on the wall appeared to be antiques, but he assumed that the hotel bought their chairs and beds by the hundreds from a reproduction furniture company. It probably wasn't as nice as it looked.

Rachel was opening the door to a cabinet.

"The couple that rode up the elevator with us looked like they were worth a million bucks. Did you hear them? 'Oh, darling,'" he mimicked, "'I absolutely must have that diamond necklace. Nothing else goes so well with the Carlo Malucci gown I bought this morning.'" He shook his head in disgust. "There's nothing I hate more than rich people. I'm not a democrat or anything, but what's the use? There should be limits. What could a person possibly do with five million dollars that they couldn't do with one million?"

Rachel had her back turned to him and was pouring two tumblers of Armagnac. "So what should be the limit?"

"I'm not stingy. If some people have the ability to make money, good for them. But really, beyond ten million, what's the point? I have no respect for people like that. What do they know about real life?"

Rachel's hand shook. The Armagnac bottle clinked the edge of the glass. "*Zut!* I spilled."

R.J. pulled a handkerchief out of his pocket and leaned over to offer it. "Here."

Rachel wiped up her mess and handed him a glass. "To Paris?"

"To Paris."

Rachel perched herself on the fainting couch at the end of the room.

They sipped from their glasses and exchanged smoldering looks.

"Why don't you come over here and kiss me?" She patted the edge of the couch beside her. She turned to put her glass on an end table and when she straightened up, he was beside her. "You don't waste any time, do you?"

Rachel seemed to enjoy kissing, but she refused to let him do anything else.

"I'm not that kind of girl," she said, pushing him away when he tried to take her hand to lead her to the bedroom.

"Then what kind *are* you?"

"The kind that drives you crazy. The kind that makes you bite your nails and roll around at night instead of sleeping." She smiled and ruffled his black hair.

"You couldn't even be tempted into becoming the other kind?"

"Not even, you big hulking bear," she said firmly.

Eventually, he gave up and went back to the hotel his buddies were staying in. But she was right. He *did* bite his nails and he *didn't* sleep that night.

CHAPTER 3

⌒

*A*nne watched from the balcony as Will drove down the road, brake lights blinking once, twice, three times as he slowed at the intersection. *I love you too!* She waved until he turned the corner. It was so pleasant outside.

She looked through the glass doors into the dining room. Her thank-you notes, gift list, and address lists were piled in heaps on the table, still waiting.

She pulled a face and looked back out past the road and into the dunes. The sea oats were waving a greeting in the breeze. *Twenty thank-yous and then I'll go for a run on the beach.*

She looked back at the table.

Okay, 15. A classic motivation technique: promise reward for work well done.

She stretched before walking back inside.

A latte sounds really good. One latte and then I'll start to write.

She measured coffee and packed it into the filter basket, noting that she was running low. *I'll have to find a Starbucks soon.*

Finally, after having exhausted her strategies for procrastination, she settled into a dining room chair, took a note card from her pile, and started to write.

> Dear Mr. and Mrs. Smith, thank you so much for the lovely vase. Will likes to surprise me with flowers, and your gift showcases them perfectly. We're so glad you were able to attend the wedding and share in our happiness. Liffsbury is beginning to feel like home. It's much sunnier than Seattle, but I wouldn't say that's a bad thing! Will is enjoying his job, and I'm beginning the

search for one. In the meantime, I'm keeping in running shape and finishing unpacking. Hope all is well with you. Thank you again for your gift.

Anne reread it to herself. *Not bad. Of course, I haven't started looking for a job yet, and I've finished all the unpacking...but, hey, allowances should be made when you're writing 200 letters.*
She crossed the Smiths off the list. Only 143 to go.

An hour later Anne yawned and uncrossed her legs. She got up from the table and paced around it twice before going into the living room and throwing herself onto the couch. Her eyes scanned the ceiling, taking in the chandelier that was made from the steering wheel of a boat. Her lips curled into a smile.

From visiting the homes of Will's friends, she knew it was a Liffs- bury rule that at least one room in every home had to be decorated with a beach theme. In their case, it was two: the powder room and the living room.

Will had gotten a great deal on the furnished condo from a couple that was divorcing. It had been strange living amid other people's things; but Anne had grown used to it. The furnishings weren't quite her style, but they had everything they needed. Her eyes swept the walls, deciding that they were coral pink in the morning light. In the evening, they looked peach. She'd never known there was such a color before moving here.

She turned her head and looked through the counter/bar into the kitchen. There, everything was navy and tan. Downstairs, the master bedroom was sea foam green and the guest bedroom was decorated in hunter.

She had a feeling she knew why the previous owners had divorced: everything for them had been fifty-fifty. The husband had probably never gained anything unless the wife lost something, and vice versa. The most valuable advice she and Will had gotten from their marriage counselor was that marriage is a 100 percent, not a 50 percent proposition.

She yawned again and grinned at what a quirky little place they had. The entrance and the bedrooms were downstairs, and the living room, dining room, and kitchen were upstairs. But the location couldn't have been better. The ocean caressed the beach a hundred yards from their door. Anne started from her reverie. If she planned on running, she needed to do it before it became too hot. She got to her feet and collected her coffee mug from the table.

In straightening her piles of thank-you notes, the invitation to the Officers' Spouses' Club Tea reappeared. She rolled her eyes, still not thrilled at the idea.

But, if I miss it, Will would probably kill me.

She put the mug in the sink and then thumb-tacked the invitation to the corkboard by the phone.

I can't forget!

Jogging along the beach was absolute torture. It wasn't because of the sand or the incline or the water. It was the heat. And the humidity.

Take it slow, girl. You're not running any races. Go for distance, not time. Deep breath. Knees up.

After 20 minutes she was exhausted.

You'll be fine. This is not your climate. You'll adjust. Just have to run earlier in the morning before the sun heats everything up. Tomorrow's another day, she told herself as she trudged up the stairs and into the condo.

Stretching out her legs in the lukewarm shower, she talked herself into cheering up. *One thing's for sure in this state: The sun'll come out tomorrow! But tomorrow, I'll be ready for it.*

She dried off, put on the coolest clothes she owned, and went upstairs to look at the paper.

"Come on, *Liffsbury Times*, please give me some good news." The employment section was three pages long, most of it devoted to tourist-related industries. Restaurant and hotel staff positions dominated. The personnel section had three job announcements, but two were the same as the previous week's. Anne circled the new announcement and transcribed the address onto her yellow legal pad. She'd send a cover letter and résumé out after lunch.

She flipped through the rest of the paper. Spent some time reading the Op-Eds. What she read surprised her. The pieces debated local or national politics, but they all mentioned God or faith as though they had a part to play in the debate. The authors of those pieces would have had their pens confiscated in Seattle.

Yes, she believed in God. Yes, she was a Christian. Then how come it made her uncomfortable to read about God in the paper? Why did she have the feeling he didn't belong?

Beth shifted Andy to her other knee and held out a hand toward his brother, Josh. If she could just coax him over to the couch, next to her, then she could contain him. She wouldn't have had to work so hard, but the clinic was running half an hour behind schedule.

"You okay, sweetie?" She brushed a cheek against Andy's damp forehead.

He snuggled into her shoulder and wrapped chubby arms around her neck.

She couldn't help it, but the times she most liked her boys and the times she felt most competent as a mother was when they were sick. Normally, they were more than she could handle. She felt as if she were constantly cleaning up behind the two tiny human tornadoes she called her sons.

"Josh? Why don't you bring that book over here? You can read it to your brother."

Toddling over, he pulled himself onto the couch and held the book up to her.

"You want me to read?"

He nodded, sucking two of his fingers.

"Why don't you take those out of your mouth? You don't want to be sick like Andy, do you?"

Josh complied and then reached out the wet hand and hit his brother's leg.

Andy started to wail and kicked back, catching Josh in the mouth.

"Mrs. Bennett?" a nurse called.

Beth disentangled Andy's arms from her and settled him on her hip. "Josh. Stop crying. You know you're not supposed to hit your brother. Can you carry this bag for Mommy?"

"Mrs. Bennett?"

"Coming!"

Beth shepherded the twins through the doctor's appointment and then herded them into the pharmacy's waiting room. Had the medical industry been efficiently organized, they'd automatically provide double prescriptions to the parents of twins. Without a doubt, Josh would come down with the same bug that his brother had within three days. And she'd spend another half hour on the phone making an appointment with the doctor and another hour in the clinic's waiting rooms.

Look on the bright side. It's not like you have to do this on your lunch hour and then hurry back to work.

It was already noon. They'd have to have lunch on base. Otherwise, Beth faced certain mutiny from the backseat.

"How would you two like to go through the drive-through on the way home?"

"Hambugger!" Josh yelled.

"How about you?" she asked the listless child in her arms.

He just tightened his grip around her neck.

"It'll be real quick, honey. I promise. Then we'll get you home to sleep."

"Mrs. Bennett?" the pharmacist's airman assistant called.

Beth fumbled in her purse for her military ID card. "Andy? Why don't you let go of Mommy for just one minute so she can go get your medicine."

He began to whine.

"Okay, sweetie."

"Mrs. Bennett?"

"I'm coming!"

Beth balanced Andy against the wall and her hip as she searched through her purse. "I'm sorry. I must have left it with the doctor."

"I can't give you your prescription without an ID."

"I have a driver's license."

"I'm sorry, ma'am."

"But you know I had to have it to see the doctor. And there's no way he'd have written me the prescription without it."

"I'm sorry."

Beth had never pulled rank in her active-duty career, but she wished she could now. "It's going to take me five minutes to get my things together and another ten to get to the clinic and then back here. Please."

"I'm sorry, ma'am."

She realized it was pointless to argue. "Okay. I'll be back."

It was only then that she realized Josh had disappeared.

She found him half an hour later when she heard a page for the mother of a lost little boy.

"Josh, it was very naughty of you to leave without Mommy. Do you understand me?" She glared at him via the rearview mirror. Of course he understood. He just didn't care. "Joshy!"

"Mommy?"

"It's very dangerous for you to wander around without me."

"Hambugger?"

Beth gripped the steering wheel even tighter. The last thing she wanted to do was reward Josh's errant behavior, but she couldn't face having to scrounge around the fridge for lunch. She just didn't have the energy.

Once they got home, Josh busied himself by making a train on the floor out of the food containers while Beth put Andy to bed.

"Are you sure you aren't hungry?" she asked Andy as she placed him in his crib.

Andy shook his head.

Beth measured out his medicine. "This is to make you feel better. Wouldn't you like that? Can you open your mouth for Mommy?"

Andy opened wide and swallowed, and then made a face as the full force of the cherry flavoring hit him.

Beth patted his pillow. "Lay down right here, and when you wake up, you'll feel better." She pulled a blanket over him and smoothed his hair. "Mommy loves you."

"Wuv Mommy," he whispered.

She shut the door quietly behind her.

"Mommy, Mommy, Mommy!" she heard Josh yell from the kitchen.

"Joshy, we have to be quiet. Andy's sleeping." She turned the corner into the kitchen and couldn't believe her eyes. Their hamburgers and French fries had all been flattened into the floor. At least what was left of them. Shelby had already helped herself to most of the fries.

"Joshua Bennett, what have you done?"

"Train smash," he illustrated as he cheerfully stomped on what was left of their food.

Beth served him a bowl of cheerios for lunch and let him add as many teaspoons full of sugar as he wanted. Why not? There was no way to make the day any worse. Josh ran circles around the living room for half an hour before he used up the extra energy. It was only after mopping the floor and putting away their lunch dishes that Beth realized the house was silent.

Uh-oh. Never a good sign.

Beth found Josh flat on the floor in the middle of the room, sucking his thumb and rubbing his nose with his forefinger.

She stroked the unruly curls on his forehead for a moment before lifting him into her arms and then laying him in his crib for a nap.

She sat at the computer, aimlessly surfing the internet until she was sure Josh would stay asleep. After 15 minutes, she rose and went into her bedroom, knelt at the foot of the bed, and pulled out a large plastic box filled with scrapbooking materials. And then another one.

She was working on albums for the twins, and she was only four months behind. She knelt between the boxes, a hand on each lid. She usually enjoyed the spare moments she spent with the scrapbooks. It supplied her with much-needed perspective. Helped her to be more patient with toddler foibles when she remembered that short months ago they couldn't even talk. Walk. Or eat with utensils. And viewed from the pages of the scrapbooks, her life looked exciting. Fun. Organized. Who wouldn't want to be the mother of twins?

She shoved the boxes back under the bed.

Maybe some other time. She stifled a yawn. Some other time when she had more energy.

She pushed up to her feet and went into the living room, intending to let Shelby out to run in the backyard. But Shelby was curled up on her pillow, snoring, and suddenly, curling up with a pillow seemed like a very good idea.

Marc woke her when he came home.

"Hey, Sleeping Beauty."

She started and looked around wildly before she focused on Marc, squatting in front of the couch, his face just inches from her own.

"Where are the boys? Is Andy okay?"

"Just got him," Marc let Andy climb out of his arms. "Are you all right?"

"I'm fine. I was only asleep for a minute."

"Relax. No need to rush dinner."

Dinner? She'd fallen asleep around 2:00. It was already time for dinner? She slumped back into the couch. How could she not have heard Marc come home? Shelby always went into a welcome-home routine that could be heard over the car engine.

"Is Shelby okay?"

Marc kissed her forehead. "Just stay there. We can make some spaghetti, can't we boys?"

"Pusghetti!" Josh yelled.

Beth watched as Marc ushered them into the kitchen. Then she closed her eyes and slept.

Five o'clock.

Karen followed the minute hand as it leaped from 4:59 to 5:00. She watched the second hand sweep its rotation and saw the minute hand leap again. She shivered and sat up, burrowing into their puffy couch and rubbing her arms.

Kevin should be home soon. Then he'll ask and I'll have to tell him.

Something at the edge of the couch caught her eye. A ladybug. She put a finger down in front of it and the insect crawled onto it. She brought it close to see the cheery polka dots.

"Ladybug, ladybug, fly away home. Your house is on fire and your children are gone." She always wondered if it meant that the children had turned into ashes, if they'd run away, or if they'd gone to college, graduated, and found jobs. She opened the door and extended her arm into the bright, sizzling sunlight. The ladybug caught the wind and flew away as Kevin drove the car into the carport. She smiled to herself.

Kevin, walking up the sidewalk, misinterpreted the smile. "Karen, you mean—?" His face was transformed by a joyful grin. He engulfed her in a hug.

"No, Kevin. I started today."

"Oh. I'm sorry," he set her down with a jar. "I thought—"

"No."

Why does he still keep hoping? It's been seven years. She felt an unreasonable anger at the man she had married. *Calm down. Relax.*

She tensed her hands into fists and then abruptly released them. Forced herself to smile. "Maybe next month."

"These are for you anyway." He whisked a bouquet of coral-colored roses from behind his back.

"What a surprise! Thank you." She stood on tiptoe to kiss his cheek.

He's only done this every month since we've been married. Maybe this is the problem. Maybe the one month he forgets will be the month I'll actually be able to say I'm pregnant.

The beginnings of hot tears pricked her eyes.

I bet I'm the only wife on earth whose husband brings her flowers the day her period's supposed to start. Dear God, I just want to be normal.

He bent to pick up his briefcase and stood aside to let her go in first.

She felt a pang of guilt as her gaze swept his classic features, as she looked into his clear blue eyes. *I don't deserve him.*

He planted a kiss on her nose. "Don't worry. It'll happen." He gave her a playful pat on the butt with his briefcase. "What's for dinner?"

"I forgot to ask you how the Enrichment Night was last night," he said as she dished up their plates.

"Fine."

"You met some people?"

"Yes. Lots. They were very nice." And had immediately made her feel guilty. Not that they had meant to. Most of the women her age had at least two children by now. One had five. She always felt left out. Everybody talked about their kids, what their kids were doing, or what kinds of colds they were passing to each other. What was there for her to say?

"So what did you do?"

"They talked about decorating. Easy projects with sheets. Some of them didn't even involve sewing." She described the drapes, slipcovers, and headboards the demonstration had covered.

"Are you sure you're full?" Kevin asked as he pushed his plate away. "You didn't eat very much."

"I wasn't very hungry."

"You need to eat."

"I *do* eat. I'm just not usually hungry at night. And besides, I sample when I'm cooking dinner."

"I worry about you." He covered her hand with his. "I love you, you know."

Karen smiled at him. "Thanks. Did you get enough?"

"Plenty."

"I've been called to teach the 12- and 13-year-olds' Sunday school class."

"That's great! A calling. Why not?"

"Why not. Why don't you watch the news while I clean up?"

He handed her his plate and then reached for the salad dressings and butter tray. "I'll carry these in first."

Kevin put the leftovers in plastic containers while Karen rinsed the dishes and put them into the dishwasher.

He held up an invitation card. "Where do you want this?"

"What is it?"

"The invite to the Officers' Spouses' thing."

"Put it on the windowsill above the sink. That way I won't forget about it."

She finished the cleanup in about five minutes. The two of them hardly made enough mess to keep her busy.

"Let's watch the news together." Kevin took her hand as they passed from the kitchen through the dining room and into the living room.

She huddled in the big brown and orange-striped recliner as he stretched out on the couch.

He looked across the room at her and winked. "Come snuggle with me."

She gathered her hair and tied it in a knot to keep it out of the way and then lay down beside him.

He plucked at her sweater. "Are you really that cold?"

"It's freezing in here with the air-conditioning."

"Tuck yourself in between me and the couch." He shifted his body forward.

She rolled over him and behind his back.

"Give me your hands."

She wriggled one arm up from under him and he took the other under his arm, cupping both hands in his. "You should have gangrene with hands this cold. Your blood can't be circulating into them. Are you sure you're not part reptile? Maybe I married Karen Bannister, Queen of the Gila Monsters."

"You're weird." Karen closed her eyes and rested her head in the hollow between his shoulder blades.

"Well, at least I'm handsome."

And you married a mouse. Why did you marry me?

"How was your day?" Marc asked Beth.

"Fine."

"Really? Josh told me he'd been a bad boy."

"Did he?" Beth eyed her demon child, who smiled at her angelically while he tried to shove spaghetti up his nose.

"What happened?"

"He went AWOL on me at the pharmacy. I couldn't find him anywhere. They had to page me."

"Where was he?"

"Playing in the toilets."

"Josh," Marc said with a frown. "What do you do when you go someplace with Mommy?"

"Stay wif Mommy."

"That's right."

Beth didn't think it was appropriate to feel like strangling your own child, but she could hardly keep her hands from twitching.

"Then we stopped by the drive-through for hamburgers and fries. And while I was putting Andy to bed, Josh stepped on them all."

"Train smash!"

"He was playing trains."

Marc couldn't keep himself from smiling.

"It's not funny!"

"Of course it's not."

"There are some days when I would gladly sell all three of you to the circus."

"No, you wouldn't. You love us," Marc insisted.

"No, I don't."

"Of course you do. We love Mommy, don't we, boys?"

"Wuv Mommy," Andy cooed, opening his arms out toward her. "Wuv Mommy."

"*I* love you, Mommy." Josh smiled, exposing a mouthful of un-chewed spaghetti.

Beth smiled in spite of herself. "Josh, baby, please chew your food before you swallow. Do you remember how to do that?"

"Want me to do the dishes?" Marc asked.

"No. Why don't you watch the boys for me?"

"Your wish is my command." He kissed her on top of the head. "Who wants to go for an airplane ride?"

"Me, me, me," Josh sang.

"Let's go." He grabbed his sons with muscular arms and carried them away into the living room.

Beth sat, surveying the damage.

This is not worth it. I gave up a job I loved for a job I hate.

Being a mother had brought out the monster in her. She used to think she was a good, kind, decent person. Now she knew it had all been an illusion. She'd heard it said that there was serenity to be gained in self-discovery. She'd only found misery. Ignorance of her true character had been bliss, and she much preferred that fool's paradise to the enlightened nightmare she was trapped in.

Please, somebody wake me up.

CHAPTER 4

◡

*A*fter dinner Anne and Will took their customary walk on the beach. Between slogging up and down sand dunes and working with each step to pull out or plant a foot in the sand, they worked up a sweat. Anne took her flip-flops off and carried them in one hand while she held onto Will's hand with her other. The sand was still warm, but not near the scorching temperature it always was under the midday sun.

They made their way up to the boardwalk and then over the dunes, pausing at the top to enjoy the last lateral rays of yellow light before the sun turned orange and then red and dove into the ocean.

For a while they dodged the waves that washed up onto the beach. Then they climbed an empty lifeguard chair and settled in to watch the sun's last scene of the day.

Will cuddled Anne into his arms. "This is Will Bradley, live from Liffsbury, bringing you the day's best sunset."

Anne smiled. Will could never resist an opportunity to practice his profession. In fact, they'd met when he'd done an article on her for the university paper. It was her junior year, and as captain of the women's track team, she was the spokesperson, the one the paper contacted first to interview.

She'd received his message at her sorority, having just run down fraternity row through Seattle drizzle that clung to her eyelashes and gave her kaleidoscope vision whenever she'd blinked. She'd asked Amy, the sorority member on phone duty, if the menu for dinner had been posted.

"On the mirror," Amy replied over her shoulder as she dashed to answer the doorbell.

"Teriyaki chicken, rice, peas, salad, and cheesecake." Anne nodded her approval and then fished a phone message out of her pigeonhole mailbox.

"Will Bradley, the *Daily*, 543-2700." She checked her watch. He'd called just ten minutes earlier. Maybe she could still catch him.

The phone on the first floor was busy, but a couple of the lines into the house still looked to be free.

She climbed the stairs to the second floor.

Busy.

The phone on the third floor was free. Closing herself into the closet they called the phone room, she dialed the number. She traced the initials scratched into the bulletin board as she waited for someone to pick up.

"Will Bradley."

"This is Anne Hopkins. I'm returning your call?"

"Great. Thanks. The *Daily* wants to do an article on the track team; it's been such a fantastic year. I wanted to know if I could interview you for it. A personal angle is more interesting than just doing a recap of all the meets."

"Sure. When did you want to talk?"

"Tonight? I'm sorry—I know it's short notice, but I'm tied up the rest of the week and I won't be in town this weekend."

"I've got a meeting at seven that will probably go until nine."

"I could meet you after. Just tell me where."

"Do you know fraternity row?"

"I know where it is."

"We're all the way at the end. Tudor-style house at the corner of Seventeenth and Fiftieth. You'll have to cross Fiftieth to get there. It's 1616 NE Fiftieth."

"Is there a secret knock or anything to get in?"

She heard the page at exactly nine o'clock.

"Anne Hopkins?"

She ran from her room out into the hall. Answered it after the third repetition.

"You have a guest downstairs."

Guest was the sorority code for a guy. If she'd been told she had a visitor, she would have known to expect a girl.

She went back to her room. "I might not be back 'til after ten," she warned her roommate.

"Where are you going?" Lisa asked from the top bunk.

"Interview for the *Daily*. About the track team." Anne stripped off the dress she'd put on for her meeting and pulled a colorful Peruvian wool sweater over her head. Buttoned up her jeans.

"It's raining," Lisa warned without even looking out the window. It always rained in Seattle in the early spring. Anne put on thick wool socks before slipping into her Birkenstocks.

She stopped halfway down the last flight of stairs to take a peek through a small window in the wall. The only guy she could see was a fraternity boy. Blond-haired and clean-cut, he was wearing the frat-rat uniform: navy sport coat, white shirt, khaki pants, loafers. The guy she'd talked to from the paper hadn't seemed like a fraternity boy, hadn't had that "Hey, baby" tone in his voice. Someone's new boyfriend? Had to be. Maybe Will had wandered into the dining room.

As she took a right at the bottom of the stairs, she heard her name called from the left.

It was the fraternity boy. "Anne?" he asked, holding out his hand.

"Will?" she said, shaking it.

"That's right. Do you want to talk here?"

"We don't have to. Where did you come from?"

"The dorms."

"Then let's go somewhere halfway between. That way you won't have to walk as far to get home."

"Café Allegro? It's open 'til 10:30. Not that I'll keep you that long."

"Let's go. I like to get out of the sorority after meetings anyway. Too much moaning and groaning afterward. Umbrella?"

"I left it outside."

They walked down the front steps and the walkway before descending to street level.

He saw she was already holding her hands inside the sleeves of her sweater. "Don't you want a coat or anything?"

"I'm fine."

As they crossed the street, it began to rain in earnest.

"Here," said Will, offering his arm.

Anne began to protest, but then decided he was right. "Thanks." She slipped an arm under his elbow. She hadn't noticed how tall he was until she realized she was standing up straight. Usually when she shared an umbrella with someone else, she had to hunch.

They'd begun the walk down Seventeenth Avenue: fraternity row.

Music boomed as they passed the frat houses. Random whoops and disembodied laughter escaped from the windows.

"Too bad they drink so much. Some of them might actually be smart," Anne commented.

"Looks like we'll never know."

She smiled.

"Mind if I check my facts while we walk?"

"Go ahead."

"Anne Hopkins. With an *e*. Twenty. Junior. Business major. Went to Mercer Island High School."

"That's right."

"Any specialty in the business field?"

"Human resources."

"You were state champion in the 800 meter in high school."

"Yes."

"How long have you been running?"

"Since junior high. Not much in the way of organized track until then."

"What do you see as your chances in the Pac-10 this year?"

"I think they're excellent. And it's not that the other teams are weak. Stanford will be tough, but our team's never been stronger."

"People are predicting this will be your best year at the University of Washington. Any particular reason why?"

"All the spinach they've been feeding me?" she said with a laugh. "I don't know. I've been training harder this year, but in some ways I haven't been taking it as seriously, either."

"What do you mean?"

"It's not quite the matter of life-or-death that it was last year. There are other things that have more priority." She paused. "Please don't print that."

"I won't."

They separated to avoid a huge puddle that filled a gap in the sidewalk.

"I'm graduating next year. I still don't know what I want to be when I grow up."

"Does anybody?"

"Only the lucky ones."

"What do you *think* you want to do?" he asked.

"Work for a personnel department somewhere. That's what I've studied for."

"Do you want to stay in Seattle?"

"I wouldn't mind. It's home. I like Seattle, don't you?"

"Sure."

"Are you a senior?"

"Yes."

"Communications major?"

He confirmed her suspicions. They waited for the light at Forty-fifth to turn, and then they crossed the street and entered the university campus. They walked down silent Memorial Way through a tunnel of sycamore trees. Passed the ultra-simple 1960s-style structure of the Burke Museum on their right. And the multi-turreted, cupola-topped French chateau fantasy of Denny Hall on their left.

"What are you planning to do when you graduate with a degree in communications?"

"Join the Air Force."

"Are you ROTC?"

"Air Force ROTC."

"So you'll be a pilot?"

"No. I'd like to get a job in public affairs."

"They have PR departments?"

"Sure. Whenever you hear, 'A spokesperson from the Air Force confirmed/denied blah, blah, blah,' that's coming from an Air Force PR person."

"Where would you work? The Pentagon?"

"Hopefully not. Not yet, anyway. If you go there before you're a colonel, you're just a coffee boy."

"Oh. I'm really not very military-oriented. What do you start out as? Private?"

"As an officer. A second lieutenant. You have to have a college degree to be an officer. There are three ways to be one: Go to the Air Force Academy for four years, get into an AFROTC program at a school like this one, or go to OTS."

"Anytime now, when you stop speaking in code, I'll understand what you're trying to tell me."

"Officer training school. It's a 12-week course. If an enlisted person gets a college degree and is young enough, they can get selected to go to OTS. Or if you missed out on AFROTC in college, you can apply for OTS too. Once you become an officer, you start at second lieutenant. After two years you become a first lieutenant, and then in two more years a captain. Almost guaranteed."

"What's next?"

"After about eleven years total, you can be considered for major. And if you're selected, then after four more years, you're considered for lieutenant colonel."

"Then?"

"Then colonel in four more years."

"General?"

"Four more years. Brigadier general, major general, lieutenant general, and then the four-star: general."

"Four kinds?"

"Be my little general. Brigadier, major, lieutenant, general," he said, counting them off.

"So you'll be a second lieutenant. Do you get to choose where you go?"

"I can ask, but they don't have to listen to me."

"Where will you ask to go?"

"Bullard. In the South."

"Why?"

"Voted best base in the Air Force two years running. Why not?"

"So you're a quality kind of guy."

He shrugged. They'd cut through the alley behind Magus Books and gone through the parking lot to reach Café Allegro. It looked like a back entrance to a restaurant, but that was part of the charm. He closed the umbrella and moved to open the door, but she'd already done it.

"Would you like something?" Will offered.

"I'd love a latte, but I don't drink caffeine while I'm training. If they have some herbal tea…?"

She found a table in the front room. It was noisier there, but they wouldn't be disturbing those who were trying to get some serious studying done.

He bought the drinks and brought them to the table. He took a sip of his coffee, drinking it black, before sitting down in a chair.

Anne cupped cold hands around her mug of tea and blew a depression into the middle of the liquid.

"I'm just going to write down what you said on the way over." Will plucked a pen and small notebook from the pocket of his jacket.

"Was it important?"

"Maybe."

After he'd finished, he probed the motivations that kept her running. Asked her to recount the high moments of her career. She enjoyed the chance to think about running. To put words to feelings she had never before paused long enough to describe.

"Have you ever thought about the Olympics?"

"Only until I saw the results from last year's world competition. I can't compete at an international level. Not even at a national level. I'm fast, and this has been a good year for me, but after next year, that's it. All the training in the world can't compensate for top-notch ability. At least in competition. What I'd really love to do is train for a marathon."

They talked about her personal goals. And then there were no more questions to ask.

"Thanks," he finally said. He leaned back into his chair and looked into her eyes. "I enjoyed getting to know you."

She looked right back into his. "Maybe we can get together again. So I get the chance to know you."

His eyes swept over the angle of her cheekbones and across the stretch of smooth skin to her mouth, and then back to her espresso-colored eyes. "I'll walk you back."

"I'm the fastest woman in the state. I can run back."

"But I wouldn't be doing my civic duty if I let you."

"That's not only silly, it's a waste of time."

"Please. I'd worry about you all night, and I'd probably call at three o'clock in the morning just to make sure you made it back safely."

"All right, all right."

They walked back up Memorial Way to Forty-fifth in silence. The streetlamps glowed eerily in the dense drizzle. The plaques on the stone pylons at the entrance to the university transmitted dull reflections of the lights from passing cars.

"So what's your life like outside of the paper and studies?" Anne asked.

"On Tuesdays I go to The INN."

"Really? I've never seen you." Anne attended the college-age youth group at University Presbyterian as often as she could. Some nights there were nearly 1000 people.

"Dorm people have to stick together." He paused and slid a glance in her direction. "I'm sorry. I didn't mean it in a bad way."

"Greeks are people too. But I guess we do have a tendency to dominate. I'm speaking at FCA this week. Fellowship of Christian Athletes. Why don't you come?"

"I'm not really into organized sports. I lift weights."

She nodded.

"And I jog."

"Where?"

"Anywhere. Around the campus. Down to Green Lake."

They crossed Fiftieth. Reached the front of the sorority house.

"Any particular time of day?" Anne asked, leaving the shelter of his umbrella.

"In the morning. I like to be the first one up."

"Me too. Do you run down Ravenna Avenue?"

He nodded.

"What time?" She really didn't know why she was being so pushy. She preferred to run alone.

"Around six."

"If I see you, can I run with you?" *Do I have no shame? I am the women's champion in the 800 meter. He should be begging to run with me.*

"Sure."

She walked up the steps to the house.

"Thanks," he yelled from behind her, "for the interview."

She threw a wave over her shoulder as she bent to put her key in the keyhole.

Anne's alarm rang at 5:45 the next morning. Lisa pulled her pillow over her head and burrowed farther into her blanket. Anne slid from her bunk, brushed her teeth, and then pulled her hair back with a scrunchie. She returned to her room. Felt in the dark for her running tights. Pulled them on. Put a fleece sweatshirt on over her jogging bra.

She was stretching against a tree in the median on Seventeenth Avenue when Will ran up. It took a few seconds for him to gather the breath to greet her. Twin patches of red stained his cheeks. He was wearing black running tights and a black long-sleeve zip-neck top.

"Hey. I just need one more minute."

"Take your time. I'd hate to have you pull something."

True to her word, she stretched another minute before she felt limber enough to run. Will was jogging rings around the trees.

"Let's go!" Anne jogged toward the road, setting the pace.

They traded the lead as they ran.

She came to hate it when he jogged in front of her. She couldn't concentrate. Before she could help herself, she'd be watching his shoulders, and then his back, his butt, his calves. He had too nice a body. She forced herself to speed up and pass him.

He began to hate it when she jogged in front of him. He couldn't keep himself from watching the way her body moved. It was fascinating. And dangerous. He sped up to pass her.

It was on their third morning run that he suggested running together. "So we can pace ourselves better."

She quickly agreed to his suggestion.

They'd both sighed with inward relief.

"Penny for your thoughts."

Anne's lips curved into a smile. She tipped her head up to give him a kiss. "I was thinking about how we met."

"About how you refused for years and years to go out with me?"

"No. That must have been your other girlfriend. Seems to me it was more like, is he *ever* going to admit that he likes me?"

"You knew I liked you."

"No, I didn't."

"Yeah, you did."

"Well, maybe from putting all the clues together, but certainly not from anything you ever said!"

"I was trying to be subtle."

"You were scared."

"Absolutely untrue. That's defamation of character. I would sue you if I didn't love you."

Anne snorted.

They had never talked much as they ran those spring mornings, and he never let on that running with her meant anything to him.

"See you tomorrow," she would always yell as he jogged back to the dorms.

"Sure," he would call back.

Sure, she repeated to herself one morning. *What's "sure" mean anyway? "Sure, I love to run with you?" Or, "Sure, I guess that's fine." What a jerk! We've only been running together every day for three months. It's not like I have to run with him. It's not like I have to run with anyone.*

She decided to skip the next morning and run later in the day. Just for spite.

She got up at quarter to six anyway and crept downstairs to see his reaction. When he didn't see her on the corner, he ran up and down the sidewalk in front of the house for a few minutes. Then he ran to the median on Seventeenth and did laps for a while up and down the center. At 6:30 he finally looked at his watch and glanced at the house. Then he turned and jogged back toward campus.

Anne grinned in triumph.

She decided to skip the next day too.

He found her after The INN that night. "Are you feeling okay?" His hazel eyes searched her brown ones.

"Are you?" It was hard for her to keep a straight face.

"Of course. Why?"

"You look anxious. Is there anything wrong?"

"That's what I asked you."

"I'm fine. Why?"

"You didn't show up the last two mornings. I thought you might be sick or something."

She frowned and looked him up and down. Then she crossed her arms in front of her. "Would it hurt you to say that you *enjoy* running with me?"

His face flushed.

"Would it hurt you to say that you *like* me? Even a little?"

"Let me walk you home." His eyes were trying to warn her of something.

She disregarded the message. "I told you before that I'm the fastest runner in the state."

"I *want* to walk you home."

"Fine," she said, turning and heading for the door. At first she made her way slowly, purposely taking time to say goodbye to those she knew. But then she put her hands in her pockets and suddenly made a dash for the exit, just to see what he would do.

He caught up with her outside as she turned the corner of the church. He pulled at her elbow, spinning her around, and then he kissed her.

And she smiled.

"Anne," he breathed, pulling at her braids as he hugged her to his chest. "I didn't want to fall in love with you. I'm leaving this summer for Bullard. And the reason I asked to go there was that I heard it's a good place to meet women."

"Maybe it is. For *other* people." She wrapped her arms around his waist.

"What are we going to do?"

CHAPTER 5

~

*B*eth was trying to hurry. She could already hear the twins stirring in their cribs. She needed to get dressed. She ransacked one of her dresser drawers for a pair of denim shorts before reminding herself that she was supposed to go to the OSC tea. So she opened the door to her closet and selected one of several knit print dresses. She pulled it over her head and stepped into a pair of colorful flats. Whatever else Marc had to say about her, he couldn't call her high maintenance. She didn't wear much jewelry. Usually all she had on was a simple pair of pearl earrings Marc had given her, and a white gold U.S. Air Force Academy ring she had earned that with lots of sweat and a few tears.

She didn't see the point in spending a lot of time or money on makeup or hair products that would only marginally improve her appearance. She had never been and would never be pretty. She was condemned to be cute until her dying day. And that suited her just fine.

Except on days like today.

She sighed, finger-combed her curly wet hair, and stuck out her tongue at herself in the mirror. She had no right to complain. She was short and sturdy, but not in an overweight sense of the word. She was athletic. And until the twins were born, she'd had no hips to draw a tape measure around. Of course with twins, she'd felt like Stretch Armstrong during her pregnancy, but she'd bounced back into shape. Except that now she had hips. Not very big ones. But large enough to make her look like her mother.

Tears pricked her eyes for a moment. She couldn't believe just a passing thought would bring tears after ten years.

She sniffed and crooked a finger under each eye.

There. Now I'm happy I don't wear mascara.

She sniffed again. At least she didn't cry buckets anymore. That hadn't happened since the academy.

She smiled as she thought back to her academy days. She and Marc hadn't had a very promising beginning. It had all started at basic cadet training. Marc had been one of her cadet trainers. She could still remember the hot, hard Colorado sun of July. She could remember the insecurity of being on the lowest rung of USAFA life. Swearing to herself that she'd make it and trying hard not to wonder if she wouldn't. She remembered the fear, and she remembered when it turned into bitter determination.

If it had been at any other moment, she might have been more forgiving of Marc's blunder. As it was, he appeared in her life at the worst possible time.

"You know what you are, Cadet Brown?"

"No, sir!"

"You're a maggot," informed Cadet Marc Bennett.

"Yes, sir!"

"You know why?"

"No, sir!"

"Because maggots are the lowest form of life with the potential for flight." Cadet Bennett saw Cadet Brown's cheeks blaze.

"Yes, sir!"

"Look at you, Cadet. You call that a shoe shine?"

"No, sir!"

"You call that standing at attention?"

"No, sir!" Cadet Beth Brown drew her shoulders back even farther and pushed in her chin even more, producing two extra chins to add to the two already present.

"You're pathetic, Cadet. Your own mother would be ashamed of you," he yelled, glowering at her. He thought he detected the gleam of a tear.

"No, sir!"

"I said, your own mother would be ashamed of you!"

"No, sir!"

"You just cost your squadron 20 push-ups, Cadet!"

The squadron dropped to the floor and punched out 20 push-ups. Then they jumped to their feet and stood at attention.

"Cadet Brown, you're an embarrassment to your entire squadron. You call those push-ups? Call your mother and get her to come take you home." Cadet Bennett had turned on his heel and was searching the cadets for a new victim when Cadet Brown dared to answer him.

"She's dead, sir! Died last month, sir! Four June 1996, sir!" She spit out the words with tears streaming down her face.

"And then she said her mother died last month." Cadet Bennett groaned as he lay on his bunk bed in his room in Sijan Hall.

"No way, man." His roommate was lying on his own bunk, flipping through the pages of the latest Victoria's Secret catalog.

"Yeah. So what do you do then?"

"Got me, buddy."

Marc's hands were clutching at his copper hair. "What should I do?"

"What do you mean, what should you do?"

"I mean, should I apologize or what?"

"What do you think she'd say?"

"I don't think she'd *say* anything. I think she'd try to kill me."

"I wouldn't do anything. She's a freshman, right?"

"Yeah?"

"And you're a junior. So what does it matter?"

It mattered. Marc thought about the situation for a long time.

His roommate finally interrupted his thoughts by throwing the catalog across the room to him. "Irina. Page 16."

Cadet Brown and Cadet Bennett avoided each other for the rest of the year. It was easy to do. She was a freshmen; he was a junior. They weren't supposed to fraternize anyway.

Cadet Brown turned out to be one of the better cadet trainers the next year, after the three-degrees—the sophomores—took over training from the upperclassmen in the late fall. Her shouts didn't end in shrieks like most other girls'. She never let her voice get that high or loud. She got up close to the cadets' faces. Close enough that they could count the freckles on her nose. And she practically whispered. It didn't seem to matter that she was a woman. It didn't matter that she was only 5'4". She could make even the men cry. And her specialty was the athletes. The tough guys.

Cadet Bennett watched her work a squadron one afternoon in silence. A Fury at work.

"Dismissed!" she finally announced.

He breathed a sigh of relief, surprised to find he'd been holding his breath.

"The point isn't to make them *all* cry, Cadet. It's to tear down their barriers. And the ultimate goal is to be able to build them up again. On a foundation of real confidence."

"You would know, wouldn't you?"

"How could I have known that your mother had just died?"

She looked at him. Her brown eyes held no forgiveness.

"If it hadn't been that, it would have been something else that broke you. Or someone else."

"Too bad it was you."

"Too bad." He was sorrier than she knew.

Cadet Brown was a hard woman to get along with. Any sympathy that had been shown her the previous year had long ago expired. It wasn't that her classmates couldn't depend on her. She always did exactly what she said she would. She just didn't seem to expend any emotion doing it, and she didn't show an interest in anybody. She didn't do any favors for anyone, and as a result, no one did any favors for her. In an environment where it was expected that cadets cooperate to graduate, she worked twice as hard because she worked alone. At first it was by choice, but it soon became necessary.

No one wanted to be around her.

It didn't come as any surprise to her when she overheard herself being talked about. It was in the bathroom.

"Who's your roommate this semester, Sue?"

"Brown."

Beth knew the voice. *That would be my roommate, Susan Walling.*

"Oh. Well, at least it's only for a semester."

"I guess."

Thanks, Susan.

"You can come study in my room if you want."

"I might. Thanks."

The funny thing was, Cadet Brown didn't give a rip. About anything. She earned a 4.0 grade average. She carried a commendable athletic performance average and a respectable military performance average. And she earned her jump wings the summer between her freshman and sophomore years by spending half of June free-fall parachuting through the bright blue Colorado sky.

And she didn't feel a thing.

Until spring semester.

I'm going to be an aero engineer. She'd made the decision at the end of fall semester. And she was starting the new year with purpose. *This year is going to be different.*

Then she walked into her first class of the first morning of the year and received the worst surprise in the world.

"I'm going to arrange the seating in alphabetical order," the instructor, Captain Lewis, announced.

A silent groan moved through the room. It manifested itself in the sudden crossing of arms and rolling of eyes.

"Adams, Andrews, Bennett, Brown, Campbell..." the captain continued reading the list as the cadets took their seats.

Cadet Bennett turned around in his seat and looked straight into Cadet Brown's furious eyes. "Hi."

"I thought you were a senior."

"I am."

Captain Lewis explained the goal of the course and the method of grading. "Your final grade will depend, in large part, on the outcome of your final project. The projects will be done in groups of four. Just count off down the rows. So, the first four of you will be together. Then the next four, and so on."

"Howdy, partner," said Bennett, turning again to look at Brown.

She didn't even smile.

Fine. I'm going to have fun in this class with or without you.

The group decided to meet in the Sports Bar after dinner that evening for an organizational session. Or for drinks, depending on personal opinion.

"Hey, fellas," Marc said as he joined the other guys: Cadets Adams and Andrews.

"Hi."

"Hey."

"Where's Brown?"

"Who knows? It sucks that she's in our group," Andrews said.

"Why?"

"She doesn't cooperate, you know?"

"Maybe she's just got a bad rep," Marc said, willing to give her the benefit of doubt.

"You haven't had her in a class before. Just wait."

"Here she comes," Adams warned.

"Hi," Beth said.

Andrews and Adams nodded.

"Hi," Bennett said. "Beer?"

"No," she said, sitting down.

"Okay. Well, it looks like our project is to make some sort of vehicle for a six-year-old girl. She has muscular dystrophy and can't hold herself in a sitting position. Her parents want something that will keep her safe and allow her to be mobile."

"So what's the POA?" asked Andrews.

"We need specifications and a proposal. Then we need to locate suppliers and start the acquisitions paperwork. The project is supposed to simulate the entire development process. Anybody have any good ideas?" Bennett asked.

"Do we have to do the whole thing ourselves?" Adams didn't even want to begin to think about that possibility. "Do we have to actually weld a car together and stick a motor in it?"

"Not if somebody's already figured out how to make what we want," Bennett explained. "My little brothers had some electric cars when they were six. Maybe we could use something like that as a base."

There was general agreement.

"I think we should talk to this girl's parents and see what it is exactly that they want. Take some measurements. I'd hate to end up with something she wouldn't fit into," Beth said.

"I'll call them," Bennett volunteered, "and I'll see when we can go over."

"So, can everybody go over to Melissa's this evening?" Marc asked in class the next week.

"Sure," Andrews replied.

"Yeah," said Adams.

They all turned in the direction of Brown. No one was surprised when she shook her head. "I can't." She had lacrosse practice.

That was the beginning of the end of the group's good graces toward Cadet Brown. When Beth said, "I can't," what they heard was, "I won't."

Several weeks later, there was a knock on Beth's door.

"Come in." She didn't look up from her computer. It was probably for Sue. No one ever came to see her.

"I wondered how it's going with the design," she heard Marc say.

Beth whirled in her seat to face him. "Why? Don't you think I can handle it?"

"I just wanted you to know that if you need help or anything, I'm here."

"I don't need help. You can leave."

"Not everybody's the bad guy. Why don't you let someone help you?"

"I promised my mother that I would work hard to make her proud. That's the only thing she ever made me promise her. I can do it fine by myself."

"*Yourself* isn't what this place is all about. It's about learning how to help everybody else! And you'd help yourself out if you'd defrost a little bit and let people like you."

"Like who? Who'd want to like me?"

"Me."

"Yeah?"

"Yeah!" He turned on his heel and left, slamming the door behind him.

The last month of class, Marc didn't say a word more to her than he had to. It almost made Beth feel bad, especially when they were putting the finishing touches on the chair. He joked around with Adams and Andrews, but not with her.

And then the day arrived. In spite of herself, Beth discovered she was nervous. And not for her grade. She hoped that Melissa and her parents wouldn't be disappointed; it meant so much to the quality of the little girl's future.

She was a dark-haired pixie with cherry red lips that seemed always to be smiling. Her parents pushed her up to them in a conventional wheel chair.

"Hello. It's nice to see you all again." Melissa's mother was smiling at the group.

"This is Beth Brown. She wasn't able to make it last time," said Marc, taking charge.

"Nice to meet you, Beth."

"Hi, Melissa," said Marc, squatting to her level. He tousled her hair. "Let's see how it works!"

Beth's eyes welled up with tears as she watched him pick up Melissa and place her in the chair. He took her hands and curled her fingers around the controls. He put her through the motions of how the chair worked. He watched with endless patience as she tried it out, cheered as she began to operate it on her own.

Beth wiped a tear from her eye. *He's a nice guy. And he's been trying hard to be nice to me too.*

Marc, looking in her direction, caught her wiping the tear. *Forget it. She's made it clear more than once exactly how she feels about me.*

Beth floated through her classes the rest of the day, buoyed by the little girl's smile. She went to the Sports Bar after dinner. The long semester was almost over. The project had been a success. She deserved a drink.

She ordered a Coors Light. Took it to a small table in the middle of the room.

Around her cadets talked and laughed. Played beer games. Shared their lives. She thought of Marc again, his hands wrapped around Melissa's. She took a sip of beer. In the midst of the end-of-semester camaraderie, she'd never felt so alone.

Maybe this is the guy.

He made me cry.

So he made you cry once—two years ago.

She took another sip of beer. *What if he's not interested in me?*

You're interested in him. She closed her eyes and pushed the thought away. When she opened them, Marc was sitting across from her.

"Hi," he said.

"Hi."

"Just saw you sitting here. You shouldn't have to sit in a bar by yourself."

"I seem to have made a habit of doing a lot of things by myself."

"And whose fault is that?" He took a sip of his beer.

"You were good with Melissa today."

"I like kids. I have two little brothers. Twins."

"Really? How old?"

"Eight."

"I don't have any. Brothers or sisters."

"I know."

"Really. What else do you know?"

"That your dad died when you were six. That made me feel *really* bad."

A corner of Beth's mouth turned up in a smile.

"That you spend breaks at your grandparents'."

She raised a sardonic eyebrow. "They're the only people who seem to like me."

"I think you'd like my brothers."

"Really?"

"I think so," he said nodding.

"Well, they probably wouldn't like *me*."

"Oh, I'm sure they'd think you're even better than Jenny Hillsdale," he said, playing with his coaster. He looked up at her. "That's who all the third-grade boys are madly in love with."

"Thanks. I guess."

"Do you have a weekend pass?"

Beth nodded.

"I think you should come home with me this weekend."

"Where's home?"

"Golden."

"I'd hate to break your brothers' hearts when I leave on Sunday."

"Then you'll just have to come visit again."

Beth would always be grateful that the next words out of her mouth were, "I'd like that."

"What are your brothers' names?" she'd asked Marc as they drove from the academy in Colorado Springs to his parents' home in Golden.

"Travis and Trevor."

"Are they identical?"

"Nope. Travis' favorite ice cream is cookies and cream, and Trevor's is chocolate chip mint."

"Thanks for the tip."

"No problem."

"I'm really sorry for the past two years."

"If you promise to be nice to me from now on, I'll accept your apology."

"Thank you." She smiled.

"Does it hurt very much?"

"What?"

"Smiling."

In spite of herself, she laughed. "Have I been that terrible?"

"Pretty much."

"Well, it was nice of you to search for the decent person hiding inside the monster."

"Stop. You're embarrassing me," he said, smiling and looking not at all uncomfortable.

After about an hour and a half, Beth saw a "Welcome to Golden" sign and began to get nervous. What on earth was she doing?

Marc drove his car up into the driveway of a normal-looking home that was in the middle of a normal-looking neighborhood. After parking the car, he insisted on carrying both their bags up to the house.

"Mom?" he yelled, opening the front door.

Beth saw a room filled with country-inspired furnishings. Heard the unmistakable bleeps and blurbs of a video game. Smelled the tantalizing aromas of cookies baking.

"Let's find out where everyone is."

Beth followed him from the entry into what she supposed was the family room.

"Hey, aardvarks!" Marc called to his brothers.

"Marc!" they said, tearing their eyes from the TV screen.

They tried to tackle him, but he fought back, capturing them in headlocks. He turned them around to face Beth. "There's someone I want you to meet. This is Beth. Say hi."

"Hi."

"Hi."

"This one on my right is Trevor."

"Hi, Trevor."

"And this one on my left is Travis."

"Hi there, Travis."

"Are you Marc's girlfriend?" asked Trevor.

"He's never brought any girls over before," said Travis.

Marc released them and they went back to their game. "Where's Mom?"

"In the kitchen."

"You've never brought a girl home to meet your family before?" she asked as she followed him through the house.

"Nope."

"Why not?"

"Because the one I had my eye on would never talk to me, that's why."

Beth had the grace to blush.

"Mom?"

"In here," came the muffled reply from the pantry. "Is that you, Marc?"

"Yes, ma'am."

"Could you come in and reach something for me?"

"It's the only reason they let me come home," he said to Beth. "To get things off the high shelves for them."

Marc disappeared into the pantry while Beth looked around the kitchen. Every available inch of counter space was covered with cookies. Thumbprints, sugar cookies, chocolate crinkles, snickerdoodles, peanut butter, and other more exotic varieties.

Marc reappeared, a container of unsweetened cocoa in his hand, and a woman as short as Beth under his arm. She had straight, shoulder-length white-gray hair and bright blue eyes that were looking straight at Beth.

"Mom," said Marc, "this is Beth Brown. She's a cadet too."

"Nice to meet you, Beth. Sorry about the kitchen. The twins have a bake sale at school on Monday. I said I'd make cookies," she explained, wiping her hands on her apron. "So."

"So she made my favorites, chocolate crinkles; Trevor's favorites, snickerdoodles; Travis' favorites, peanut butter; her favorites, these walnut-jelly things—"

"Thumbprints," his mother interrupted.

"And...Dad's favorites?"

"The sugar cookies."

"And now she's going to sell them all," he said, shaking his head.

"You can sample. I have to get all this cleaned up before we can eat dinner anyway."

"We can help," volunteered Beth.

"Great," said Marc. "My mother raised me to be polite and always do what my guest wants to do. My guest wants to clean."

"You know what would be better? Why don't you call and order some pizzas and go pick them up for me...or are you tired of eating pizza?"

"It always tastes better at home. Hey, aardvarks!" he yelled. Beth followed him as he went into the family room and picked up the phone. "What do you want on your pizzas?"

"Pepperoni."

"Extra cheese."

"Beth?" he asked as the phone at the other end began to ring.

"I like anything."

Marc ordered three large pizzas and hung up the phone. "They said it'll take about 45 minutes. Friday night rush. Are you hungry? Thirsty?"

Beth shook her head.

Trevor cheered as he won the game. Travis groaned and flopped backward onto the floor. He contemplated Beth from his upside-down perspective. "Do you want to play?"

"I don't know how."

"It's easy. I'll teach you."

With an eight-year-old cheering for her, how could she refuse?

Travis was true to his word. It was easy and he did teach Beth how to play. Beginner's luck, however, couldn't compete with the hours the eight-year-old had spent playing the game. Beth gave him five minutes of challenge and then ceded to his expertise.

"Play again. You almost got to the second level."

They played for half an hour before Marc made them get in the car to go pick up the pizzas.

"Do you guys kiss and stuff?" Travis asked from the backseat as they were driving to Pizza Palace.

"Are you kidding? And risk getting girl germs?" said Marc, looking at him from the rearview mirror.

"Come on," urged Trevor. "If she's your girlfriend, you *have* to kiss her. Right?"

"Says you."

"Jenny Hillsdale says she only likes fourth-grade boys," Travis informed them.

"She says we're too immature" said Trevor. "So we were just wondering…you're old and you have a girlfriend, so you must have to kiss her. We've never really watched anyone kiss before. Could you just do it once so we could learn how?"

"It's just like chewing," said Marc while Beth tried not to laugh. "Why don't you ask Mom and Dad for a demonstration?"

"It's gross when parents kiss," said Trevor, gagging.

"Who wants to see Mom and Dad kiss?" complained Travis. "Come on, Marc. Please."

"Why do aardvarks need to know how to kiss anyway? That's what I want to know," said Marc, parking the car.

"It's not like we *need* to know, but it's just one of those things that might come in handy sometime, if Travis ever wanted to walk Jenny home or anything like that," said Trevor.

"It's not like I'd have to kiss her or anything. I could just tell her that I know how."

"If they're going to learn, they might as well see a master in action," said Beth, throwing her influence to the twins' side.

The boys cheered as Marc looked at her in amazement. He cleared his throat. "Okay?"

She nodded.

He smiled as he placed a hand softly around her neck. "You guys watching?" he asked, his eyes never leaving Beth's.

The boys both nodded, their eyes round.

They watched as Marc and Beth's heads moved closer together, as they looked at each other and then closed their eyes. Their lips met.

They couldn't have noticed Marc's fingers disappearing into Beth's hair or Beth's hand clutching his arm. And they couldn't know how the tenderness of Marc's kiss made Beth's heart do a slow cartwheel. They did, however, see the tear that trickled down her cheek.

"I didn't think girls were supposed to cry when you kissed them."

"And it's not like chewing. It's more like blowing bubbles."

The brothers flopped back into their seats.

"Okay. Thanks. You can stop kissing now."

"We get it already."

When they got back to the house, Mr. Bennett was home. He was tall, nearly Marc's height. They both had the same easy manner.

"So. Where are you from, Beth?" Mr. Bennett asked as he was separating pizza slices.

"Oregon."

"Now tell me this, do you people say Or-y-gone or Or-uh-gun?"

"Or-uh-gun."

He nodded. "And what do you call yourselves? Oregonites?"

Beth laughed. He was so earnest. "Oregonians."

"I've heard it's a beautiful state. Never been there myself."

"Is that where your parents live?" one of the twins asked.

"No. They live in heaven. My dad died when I was six and my mom died just before my freshman year."

"Must have been tough," Mrs. Bennett said.

"It was."

Marc squeezed her hand under the table.

"Where'd you guys meet?"

Beth answered before Marc could. "We have a class together this semester."

They all watched a Disney movie, munching cookies and drinking milk, before the twins were sent to bed. Mr. and Mrs. Bennett followed.

"Make sure Beth has towels and anything else she needs," Mrs. Bennett called from the stairs.

"Okay, Mom. Goodnight."

"Night."

"Do you need anything, Beth?" Marc asked from the floor. He was still sprawled at her feet next to the couch. He hadn't moved since the movie ended.

"Yes. I need you to come up here and be with me."

He got up, but he didn't join her on the couch. He walked over to a cupboard, opened it and pulled out a blanket and a pillow. He sat down at the far end of the couch and put the pillow behind his back, punching it into the curve of the arm.

"Come here," he said, stretching his arm along the back of the couch.

Beth curled into his side and he spread the blanket over them.

He kissed the top of her head and began stroking her hair. He'd always admired her hair. It was short. It was cute. He decided that he liked running his fingers up the back of her head where it was cut close. "I'm glad you came here, Beth. You don't know how many times I've dreamed of this."

"Don't talk," she said, turning to him, putting an arm across him, and nestling into his chest. "There's lots of time to talk. Could you just be with me?"

He guessed that some dreams do come true. He sat with her until she fell asleep on him around midnight. He stayed, watching her sleep, until two. Then he carried her upstairs to the guest room. She woke up when he was trying to cover her with the sheets.

"Marc?" she croaked.

"Yeah?" he bent close to hear her.

"Thanks." Her eyelids fluttered once and then went slack.

He pulled the comforter over her and kissed her cheek. "You're welcome," he said, closing the door behind him.

He walked down the hall to his own room. He thought about Beth for an hour before he was able to sleep. Then he dreamed about her.

"Mommy! Mommy!" The twins were chanting her name in a way that told her they'd been calling her for a while.

Beth quickly pulled the comforter over the sheets and beat the pillows together to fluff them. Then she threw them back on the bed, flicked off the light, and went to get the twins out of their cribs.

They don't train you for stuff like this at the academy.

CHAPTER 6

◡

*K*aren kissed her finger and touched it to Kevin's lips. She knew he couldn't be seen kissing her in uniform. No public displays of affection allowed. It wasn't part of the image. Or maybe it wrinkled the uniform too much.

"What time does it start?" Kevin asked.

"At two." Karen tried to smile.

"Have a good time?"

"I'll try."

"We'll meet back at my building at 4:30."

Karen watched him drive away, dreading going inside. She'd never joined the OSC at Hill. They lived so far from base, and she had been so active at church that she'd never given it serious thought. She looked down at her lavender skirt and white shoes. She never knew quite what to wear to things like this. At least in college she'd had a roommate to ask.

Several women passed her. They were talking and laughing together.

Maybe it's like Mom says. Maybe I'll meet some people at this tea. Maybe I'll know someone after this is over. It's only two hours. I can survive anything for two hours.

Beth gave a final glance at her boys. It was only for two hours. How much trouble could they get into? Thank goodness for the base drop-in day care. She just wished she could ditch the tea and drive down to the beach and sit on the sand for two hours.

She immediately felt a twinge of guilt. She smiled at the day care teacher. "I'll be back in a couple hours."

"Okay, Mrs. Bennett. We'll be fine."

Josh and Andy had already commandeered the giant building blocks. She would have waved, but they didn't notice her leaving.

Anne backed her car into a parking space under a tree. She put up the sun visor and then checked her lipstick in the mirror. Smiled.

Good. None on the teeth.

Popping a mint into her mouth, she grabbed her purse and shut the door. She turned and almost collided with the woman who had pulled her car into the space beside Anne's.

Anne put a hand on the woman's arm to steady her. "I'm so sorry."

"I'm in such a hurry I didn't even notice you were there."

"Are you going to the Officers' Spouses' tea?"

The woman nodded.

"Me too. Do you know where it is? I've never been to the Club before."

Rachel's drive across the bay was pure pleasure. The Alfa loved the chance to run, and the wind was kicking the water into peaks. The Officers' Club had been built on a rise that overlooked the bay. At its feet lay a private stretch of officers-only beach. A private dock had steps that connected directly to the restaurant.

I'll have to talk to R.J. about getting a boat. And water skis.

She turned up the volume on her Mozart CD.

Now there was a man who liked the sun.

She turned a pale wrist to look at her watch. It was 2:10.

Right on time.

Her cell phone rang as she drove onto base. "Rachel speaking."

"*Chérie.*"

"Conrad! *Ça va?*"

"*Et vous?*"

Rachel bit her lip. She knew Conrad was going to ask if she'd told R.J. She decided to distract him with news of the house instead. "I went to look at the house yesterday. The room I shipped from Paris is perfect. And the furniture maker who copied the couch in the Louvre did a magnificent job; they sent me a digital photo. The couch should be shipped and on its way by Friday."

"Have you told him?"

"I'm sorry, Conrad, I'm having trouble hearing you. I think we'll be able to move in three months."

"*Splendide.* And have you told him?"

"About the house? Not yet."

Conrad tut-tutted over the phone. "*Courage, chérie*. It's time."

Rachel sighed. "I know. I just need to find the right moment to do it, okay? Trust me."

"*A bientôt.*"

"*Ciao.*"

Rachel parked the car in a shady spot and sat for several minutes wondering how she was going to tell R.J. the things she needed to. She'd never lacked courage before.

In anything.

She'd para-skied in the Alps. She'd driven a car in the Monte Carlo Grand Prix. She'd even danced once in Tahiti at a '20s party *à la* Josephine Baker, although that probably wasn't worth remembering.

She'd done most of the things other people only dream of doing, but she'd done them all with her grandparents at her side. They had been adventurous but protective. She'd had a broad range of experiences and a liberal upbringing, and she'd done it all beneath the radar screen of the media. In part because her family was from old money; the media had lost interest in her ancestors in the 1800s. But it was also partly because she hadn't associated with people her own age. She didn't go to the big parties, didn't hang out in the Hamptons in the summer or Miami in the winter.

And she'd never been on a date, at least not on one that hadn't included her grandparents. Not until she'd met R.J.

It had always been her plan to ask her grandfather's opinion on marriage partners when she got to that point in her life. She even had a theory that he had chosen someone for her before he died. The fact that she hadn't been overrun with suitors after her grandparents' death had confirmed her suspicions. That's when she'd begun her solo tour of the world.

She thought that eventually her grandfather's choice would meet up with her—she'd never assumed him to be an American. But as the months passed and he never presented himself, she had to face the truth: the person her grandfather had chosen obviously hadn't thought her worth choosing. She began to catch herself doing increasingly stupid things. And after the table-dance in Tahiti, she'd flown straight to Paris and checked into the Ritz. Three weeks later, she'd met R.J.

Her grandfather, who had prepared her for anything, who had always planned everything, had failed her at one crucial point. She had all the experience the world could provide in business, vacationing, and personal amusement, but she didn't know anything at all about relationships.

Why couldn't she just open her mouth and tell R.J.? Because she had no way to predict what he might say.

Beth watched the room fill up with women. She wondered if any of them, like her, had once been active-duty military.

I miss my job. I'm missing out on real life.

Put a cork in it. You are not. You know where you can find sympathy? Between syphilis and something else in the dictionary. Her lips quirked as she thought of her grandfather. She could almost hear his voice. Her eyes began to tear.

She busied herself with the information packet. She knew she'd have to sign up for a committee. No way to get around it. And she didn't have the excuse that she didn't know how the military was. She'd pick one that looked as though it wouldn't be too much work. Like the food committee. More than likely the Officers' Club would cater the parties. Once the menu was chosen there probably wouldn't be much work.

"Anne Bradley," Anne replied to the woman staffing the registration booth.

The woman with the nametags and information packets found Anne's. "And?"

"It's just me. Anne Bradley."

"*You're* Anne Bradley?"

"Last time I asked my husband."

"I'm sorry. It's just...my husband works with your husband. Will?" Her eyebrows asked the question.

"Yes."

"Well, it's nice to meet you, Anne. The packet has some information about services available on base. It also has a list of this year's committees with a description of their duties. We encourage each newcomer to sign up for at least one. It helps in meeting people and making Bullard seem more like it's your home."

Rachel observed Mrs. Pritchard's speech from just inside the doorway. If she wasn't running a meeting, this was the way she preferred to attend one. As a nonparticipant.

"Excuse me."

A cold hand on Rachel's arm made her jump. She nearly choked on her cigarette.

"I'm sorry," the petite middle-aged woman was saying, "but we don't allow smoking in the Officers' Club."

"Would you happen to have an ashtray?"

"No."

"Or anything at all that I could put it out in?"

The woman frowned as she considered the problem.

Rachel took a teacup from the table beside her and ground her cigarette into the bottom. "I apologize."

"You aren't here for the tea?"

"Yes, I am."

"What's your name?"

"Rachel Hawthorne."

The woman shuffled through the box of remaining packets and then selected one. She tiptoed back to Rachel. "This one's yours. The committee choices are in it. It's not required that you join one, but it's highly encouraged."

Rachel listened until the speech was over. Mrs. Pritchard concluded by urging everyone to sign up for a committee, assuring them that meeting dates and times would be formed according to group members' preferences. Rachel found an empty chair and sat down to open her packet. She supposed R.J. would want her to sign up for a committee. One meeting a month couldn't be that bad. She'd just look for something that sounded fun.

Food committee. That was the one.

Karen looked around the room as people began to talk. When it became apparent that no one was going to come over to talk with her, she began to shuffle through her information packet.

She plucked out the list of committees.

I need to do something. Anything. I'm bored out of my mind without anyone to talk to all day.

She scanned the committee sign-up sheet. The food committee. That looked like it might be fun.

If nothing else, I can cook.

She checked off the "no preference" box when she was asked to indicate on which days and at which times she could meet.

Anne had found an aisle seat so she would have room for her long legs. If she could just find an indoor track, she could take care of the running problem. After Mrs. Pritchard had finished, she let her glance travel around the room, taking in the groups of women chatting and laughing. She'd figured the OSC was probably just a sorority for grown-ups. The committee list confirmed it.

I should probably sign up for one. When I find a job, I can always back out. I'll just pick one that looks easy to wiggle out of.

Her eyes scanned the list.

Food.

She'd just make sure someone else signed up to do the cooking.

CHAPTER 7

*W*hy did you marry me?" R.J. asked.

Rachel rolled over to face him, laying her head on her elbow. "I don't know, really. It wasn't because you're handsome, even though you are. It wasn't because you're kindhearted and honorable, even though you are. It wasn't even because you're a good kisser," she said, letting the words hang between them.

"Even though I am," he said, after he'd finished proving it.

"Even though you are. I don't know. There was something about you that I couldn't let get away. I guess I just felt like it." She turned onto her back, positioning to enjoy the Saturday morning sun that had snuck between the blinds and the window frame.

"Then are you ever not going to feel like it?"

"What do you mean?"

"Am I going to come back from a TDY someday and find you permanently living at the Ritz?"

"You're still not over that?"

"I still have nightmares about it."

She turned onto her side to cup a hand around his chin. "Poor baby."

The last day R.J. and Rachel had spent together in Paris hadn't been long enough. He had to leave for Germany on a 2:30 train. She went with him by metro to Gare de l'Est.

She watched him take her hand to his lips at the quai. "I am really going to miss you."

"Then don't let's say goodbye. Say what the French do: *au revoir.* 'Til we see each other again."

"Will I see you again?"

"Of course you will."

"When?"

"When do you want to?"

"Now. Come to Germany with me."

She looked into his brown eyes and then smiled. "Okay."

He crushed her in a hug before letting her go. She called the hotel to make arrangements for her things.

"Did everything work out?"

"Of course. It's the Ritz, isn't it?"

They had a wonderful month in Germany before R.J. was deployed, despite the fact that Rachel insisted in staying in a hotel room by herself.

"But where are you going?" she asked as they cuddled in a corner booth at the restaurant in the Officers' Club, three days into her stay.

"I can't tell you."

"Why not?"

"Because I can't."

"Who am I going to tell?"

"You never know. Leaky lips sink ships. All that stuff."

"Just give me a hint."

"I can't. Trust me."

She looked at him a long moment. "Fine, but this is boring. What do you want me to do when you go?"

"What I want you to do, isn't, unfortunately, what you can do. You can't come with me this time."

She slumped toward the table and pushed a book of matches around for a while. "I guess you could always marry me if it would make you feel better about the whole thing."

"What?" he said, not believing his ears.

"Don't be an idiot. I'm asking you to marry me."

"Are you sure? Isn't there anybody you have to ask? Parents? I haven't even met your parents. What're they going to think?"

"My parents died when I was three. I lived with my grandparents until they died two years ago. They all died in boating accidents. Isn't that an odd coincidence?"

"No friends you want to come?"

"I told you, I do whatever I want."

"I don't even know how to get married in Germany. I guess we could talk to the chaplain at the base chapel..."

"Let me take care of it. I have to do something when you're flying around all day."

"Married—? Are you sure?"

"I am. But you haven't even said yes yet."

"Yes!"

Rachel spent the next three weeks on her cell phone, trying to gather the information the German civil authorities required to perform a civil marriage. She located her original birth certificate and had R.J. do the same. Completed affidavits and had them notarized. Built a coalition of the powerful and influential to help push the marriage application through the higher court in Zweibruecken.

And three weeks later, just one day before R.J. was deployed, they were married. Rachel wore a white sheath dress she'd bought at a store in Kaiserslautern. It was something that looked plain and simple, but when R.J. sneaked a look at the price tag, he almost choked when he saw it was the equivalent of over 5000 American dollars. She wore a wispy white scarf around her neck that trailed down her back to the ground.

"I got you these," said R.J., presenting her with a bouquet of roses just before the wedding. They were white.

"White are my favorites."

The gathering was small. There was only his flight crew to witness the event, but they gave a lusty cheer as the new bride and groom kissed. R.J. and Rachel might have been brother and sister; they both had black hair and the same dramatic good looks.

R.J. watched as Rachel penned her name on the documents: Rachel Augusta Porter-Smith. "Last time I'll ever write that."

"You want to take my name?" he asked, surprised at the lump he felt in his throat.

"I'm your wife now, aren't I?"

They spent the night in a castle along the Rhine. The next morning R.J. flew off. Rachel watched until she couldn't see his plane anymore, and then she stared at its condensation trail until it evaporated. She spent Sunday alone in her old hotel room.

She missed R.J. more than she thought she would.

On Monday she decided to tackle the military world. R.J. had said she'd need some sort of identification card and that it would look like a driver's license. She followed signs to the base from the autobahn.

Where would I find an identification card? Surely there must be an information desk somewhere.

A guard at the entrance stopped her. "ID, ma'am?"

"I don't have one, but I need one. I just got married."

The guard directed her to the Visitors' Center. There, they signed her onto the air base and gave her a pass for her car and directions to the Pass and ID Office. She found the building without any problem and walked up to the information desk.

"May I help you, ma'am?"

"Yes. I just got married to an Air Force captain over the weekend. He had to leave base to fly somewhere. He won't tell me where, and he won't say when he'll be back. But he said that I needed to get an identification card."

"So you're a dependent?"

She pursed her lips. "Not really. We don't share bank accounts or anything."

"But you're married to an active-duty Air Force officer."

"Yes."

"Okay, all I need to see is the marriage certificate."

"Marriage certificate. I left it back at the hotel. Sorry."

"Well, who married you? Was it a chaplain on base or a German official?"

"German."

"You don't have the marriage certificate, and the ceremony was performed off base."

"Yes."

"What squadron is your husband in?"

"Squadron?"

"Airlift, Aeromedevac, Ops Support? What kind of planes does he fly?"

"I don't know. Planes that fly somewhere he won't tell me about."

"Warthogs? Eagles? Falcon? Hercules? A-10s, F-15s, F-16s, C-130s, AC-130s?"

She shrugged and lit a cigarette.

"Cargo? Fighter? Tanker?"

"I don't know."

"I'm sorry, ma'am, but we don't allow smoking in here."

They stared at each other for a long time.

The clerk frowned. "Okay, let's try this. What's your husband's social security number?"

"I don't know that either."

"Ma'am, I would love to help you, but you're not making it easy for me."

"I'm sorry. I wish I could help you. Isn't there anything you can at least start for the ID card? Picture? Something?"

"No. The picture gets put on the actual card by computer. If you have your passport, *that* would be something."

She fished it out of her purse in triumph.

The sergeant flipped through it with a low whistle. "You've sure traveled." He copied Rachel's passport number and her name onto a piece of paper.

"It's Rachel Augusta *Hawthorne* now."

"Yes, ma'am, but I can't write that until I see something official about it. Frankly, ma'am, I believe your story, but without the marriage certificate, we can't do anything for you," he said, handing back her passport. "And by the way, I wouldn't show this to anyone. Brazil? Thailand? Tahiti? It makes you look like a drug dealer."

After leaving the Pass and ID Office, Rachel drove straight back to her hotel in town and started packing. She left a message for anyone trying to reach her room. "Tell them that I'm at the Ritz Hotel in Paris," she said to the desk clerk in perfect German.

"Ritz Hotel, Paris. Do you have the phone number?"

Rachel had it memorized.

She'd been in Paris a week before she took a phone call from anyone.

"Don't you love me anymore?" was the first thing R.J. could think to say.

"Of course I love you. I thought that had already been decided."

"Then why are you at the Ritz?"

"Because they wouldn't let me have an ID card on base, and I didn't want to stay in rainy Kaiserslautern when it was sunny in Paris," she said, perching the phone on her shoulder so she could light a cigarette.

He swore into the phone. "Why didn't they let you have an ID card?"

She exhaled the smoke. "They kept asking me all these questions, like what your social security number is and what squadron you're in and who married us and things like that."

"And?"

"And I didn't know. I tried. I'm sorry."

"Will you come back?"

"Where are you?"

"At Ramstein."

"I thought you'd be away for months from the way you were talking. How long will you be there?"

"For another week."

"And then?"

"And then I'm done with Germany and we're flying back to Bullard."

"Where's Bullard again?"

"In the South. It's where I'm assigned."

"Can I go back to Bullard with you?"

"No, you'll have to take a commercial flight. I have to fly the government's plane back. Come to Ramstein. I'll buy you a ticket from here back to the States and we can meet up at Bullard."

There was a long pause across the airwaves.

"What about this. I'll come to Ramstein for the week. You'll fly your plane back and I'll come back to Paris and take a plane from here."

"Whatever. Will you please just come back?"

R.J. picked her up at the train station in Kaiserslautern the next morning.

He watched from the bed as Rachel unpacked her suitcases. She tossed her wallet and passport next to him to keep them from getting mixed up with her clothes.

R.J. picked up her passport and started thumbing through it.

"You've been to Thailand?"

Rachel nodded. "I thought it would be interesting to see."

"And Mexico?"

She nodded again.

"Brazil?"

She shrugged.

"Tahiti?"

"Will you stop?"

"And a million other countries. Why did you go to all these places?"

"Because I felt like it. Haven't you just wanted to go somewhere and do something?"

"Not really."

"Look, maybe it's hard for you to understand, but when your grandparents, your whole entire family, just disappears in one day... when your only friends have been their friends and none of them come around anymore because Grandfather and Grandmother are gone… what are you supposed to do? It's too lonely if you stay in one place by yourself all the time. So I traveled."

"But you always go back to the Ritz."

"It's because they all *know my name*. It's almost like they care," she said, trying to hide the hot tears streaming down her face. It still hurt that her grandparents were dead. It hurt so bad she couldn't talk about it.

"Hey," R.J. said softly, getting up from the bed to put an arm around her shaking shoulders. "It's okay. I'm here."

"But only for a little while, and then you'll go away too."

And there was nothing he could say, because she was right. He was a pilot.

"But I'll come back."

She smiled and tried to sniff up the last of her tears.

R.J. beat Rachel back to Bullard by two days. She had taken a plane from Paris and then a charter from New York to Bullard. She had insisted that she needed a day to tie things up in New York City.

He shook his head as he waited at the terminal for her. So far it looked as though she had champagne tastes and he, unfortunately, had a beer budget. But she was the best thing that had ever happened to him. If she charged a little too much to their credit card, it was something he'd just have to deal with.

He sat up straighter as he saw a small plane glint against the vivid blue of the sky. It was right on time. Waiting at the terminal door, he saw her walk down the steps. She paused as she reached the ground, readjusted her shoulder bag and tossed her hair. *She looks just like a movie star. And she's my wife!*

He greeted her with a kiss that lasted a full five minutes.

"You might as well hit me over the head and drag me to your cave," she smiled with twinkling eyes. "You're going to have to carry me after that kiss."

He obeyed with a flourish, depositing her gently in his Alfa Romeo. They drove along the ocean, the wind whipping their sun-kissed hair.

"I do have nightmares," R.J. was saying. "Sometimes the Ritz even kidnaps you and holds you for ransom."

"R.J., face it, you're stuck with me. I married you. I love you. They're decisions I already made; things I've already committed to. Do you really think I'd waste time and energy rethinking them? I made decisions with the information I had at the moment and now they're part of my history. They can't be changed. They're givens."

"Givens?"

"Assumptions."

"Like…?"

"Market conditions remain stable. The sun is the center of our solar system."

"So I'm a given. I don't know whether to be flattered or insulted."

"Don't you know the definition of a given?"

"No."

"It's a truth that will never change throughout the scenario involved."

"So the short answer is, 'No, there will never be a time when I decide to leave you'?"

"Don't be an idiot. I said I love you!" she yelled, hitting him with her pillow.

"What was your major in college?" he asked after he'd confiscated the pillow.

"Finance."

"Finance?"

"It was what my family expected," she replied, biting a fingernail.

"Do you ever think about God, Rach?"

"No. I'm not convinced he thinks about me."

"But what if he does?"

"Do you think about him?"

"Sometimes. Mostly when I'm flying. You have to do something up there. But this is the thing: What if the sky isn't the limit, Rach? What if there *is* something out there?"

"What if there is?"

"If there is a God, then maybe it wouldn't hurt to find out about him."

"Which God? Of which religion?"

"Here's what I've been thinking. Most religions but Christianity tolerate other thoughts and other religious ideas, right?"

"Right."

"So if you go with the most exclusive, you're okay with that religion, plus you're okay with all the others, right?"

"I guess."

"So I'm thinking Christianity's the way to go. You're covered all around."

"Maybe." She kissed his neck and then took a tiny bite at his earlobe.

"But today is Saturday. Let's not think about it right now. There are other, more important things to do."

Anne and Will still hadn't decided on a church. There hadn't been anything wrong with the previous week's, but it just hadn't felt right. This would be the fifth church they'd tried since Anne had joined Will at Bullard.

"Ready?" he asked, glancing at his watch.

Anne was giving herself a final once-over in the mirror that hung on the back of their bedroom door. "You have the Bible?"

"Got it."

The church service started at 11:00, so they arrived ten minutes early.

"Mercedes to the right and BMW to the left," Anne commented. "Looks just like Mercer Island back home."

Will smiled. "Then we should feel at home, right?"

Anne wrinkled her nose at him.

"Hey. We'll give it a chance, okay?"

"Okay."

Will held the door open for Anne and then got stuck holding it for several families who had been right behind them.

Anne waited for him inside the door in the air-conditioned foyer. She tried to catch the eye of one of the ushers to say "good morning," but no one looked at her.

Will, finished with door duty, came inside. Momentarily blinded by the contrast of the outside sun with the dim building, he walked right past Anne and up to the man handing out bulletins.

"Excuse me, have you seen my wife?"

The man shook his head.

In the meantime, Anne had joined up with Will. "Here I am."

"I'm sorry. I must have walked right past you."

"That's okay. It seems as if today's my day to be invisible." She shook her head at the usher who offered her a bulletin. "We're married. We'll share."

They chose a pew in the middle of the church on the right side of the aisle.

After singing several well-known hymns and one that no one seemed to know, the assistant pastor invited the congregation to greet each other. Will and Anne turned together to greet the people sitting behind them.

"Al Bentley," said the man, extending his hand toward Will.

"Will Bradley. It's nice to meet you."

"Good to meet you. And your friend…?" he asked, turning toward Anne.

"This is my wife, Anne." Will smiled and placed his arm around Anne's waist.

"Your wife! Well, it's nice to meet you too."

As the congregation finished with their greetings, Anne took a moment to look around. She estimated that there were about 400 people. Four hundred white people and one black person: her.

The preacher was interesting, although it took both Anne and Will several minutes of interpreting his accent before they understood what he was saying.

Will cleared his throat after he had negotiated the car out of the parking lot and onto the busy street that passed in front of the church. "Well?"

"I don't want to try a black church and I don't want to try a white church. I just want to go to church. Is that so difficult? Is that asking too much?"

"It wasn't that bad."

"It *was* that bad. I'm starting to get a complex. Did you see how surprised Mr. Bentley was to hear that I was your wife? He didn't know what to do."

"He was just embarrassed. That's all."

"No, Will. It wasn't all. I was the only one out of the whole church."

"The only one what?"

"The only black person."

"There weren't many at the church we went to in Seattle, either."

"But it's different here."

"Different, how?"

"In situations like today, I feel like I offend people."

"Listen, I'm sorry. When the situation is reversed, I feel that way too."

"But how often does that happen?"

"Here? A lot more often than it used to. I'm not a completely insensitive male. We're in this together."

Anne sighed, and then leaned across the seat to kiss him. "I know. I can usually handle it, but I'm just so tired. I know you can understand, intellectually, what I'm saying, but you don't know how I feel. How much it hurts."

Will held her close and began to hum their song, "Say You, Say Me."
"Together, right?"

"Together."

"You know one church we haven't tried? The chapel on base. How
about next week? I'm sure it will be a little more cosmopolitan."

Beth woke with a start from a nap on Sunday afternoon. Without
even opening her eyes she could tell it was past time to start dinner. Her
eyelids were no longer lit with the brightness of the day, and her body
was cool from the roof's protection from the sun.

She stirred against Marc. He rolled over and captured her with an
arm. She tried to be still, but the harder she tried the more fidgety she
became. There were too many things that still had to be done before the
weekend was over, and Marc could watch the twins and give her the
freedom to get at them.

Slipping under his arm, Beth tried to quietly leave the bed, but a
spring gave her away with a squeak.

"Stay," Marc muttered, without moving a muscle.

"Shhh. Keep sleeping. I'll wake you when dinner's ready."

Beth looked in on the twins and verified that they were still sleeping.
What she enjoyed most was watching them sleep. Her frustration and
anger dissipated, and she was left in awe. They really were beautiful
children.

She started at a trot for the kitchen, trying not to notice the disaster
of the living room. Shelby woke at her presence and looked up with
intelligent eyes from her pillow in the corner.

Beth ran a hand through her hair. "Look at this, Shelby! I don't
understand how I can clean this place from top to bottom on Friday,
and in two short days it looks as if some giant came and tipped the
house upside down."

Shelby blinked.

"They say if you do a job right the first time, you don't have to do it
again. That's not true, is it?"

Shelby heaved a sigh and rolled onto her side.

"It's an impossible battle to win." Beth shook her head, determined
not to look at the mess anymore, and went into the kitchen.

It seemed as if she'd spent the entire morning cleaning dishes and
putting pots away, but there they were again, waiting patiently in the
drying rack and soaking in the sink. With a scowl, she yanked the plates

and bowls from the rack and pushed them into the cupboard, and then she scoured the pots and put them in the newly vacated rack.

Beth opened the pantry and waited for something to inspire her. Why was it that no matter how many times she thought she bought enough cans and boxes of "just-adds," all she ever saw were things like green olives, stewed tomatoes, and orange Jell-O? She reached for a box of spaghetti before she remembered that she'd reached for the same box of spaghetti just the night before.

She turned to look over her shoulder at the fridge magnet advertising Pablo's Pizza. Pablo's had great two-for-one deals. But this Friday, as usual, they'd had pizza.

Another glance at the pantry revealed a box of macaroni and cheese hiding in the corner. She snatched it. She'd cook up some hot dogs and tater tots and mostly everyone would be happy.

She looked out the window and into the backyard as she filled a pot with water.

The yard.

She'd been so busy on the inside of the house all weekend that she hadn't even thought of the outside. She had a tray of pansies in the garage that she'd wanted to put in the flower bed. Not to mention the weeding that needed to be done around the camellias. And the lawn.

She glanced at the clock. Four thirty.

They ate at 5:00. Capturing the twins, cleaning them up, and getting them to bed afterward would take until 7:00. *Forget about mowing the lawn.*

The thing about buying a house in the area where everyone wanted to live was that the neighborhood covenants were restrictive. Sure, there were reduced membership fees at the golf club and discounted rates at the dock, but there were also strict rules on things like mowing your lawn. Only between 8:00 AM and 7:00 PM. Of course, the people on the neighborhood boards were retired colonels and generals who had all the time in the world to mow *their* lawns. Or have them mowed for them by someone else.

Why on earth had they bought a house where everyone wanted to live when they didn't play golf, didn't own a boat, and couldn't mow the lawn when they wanted to?

Beth leaned against the counter and watched the water begin to boil.

Weekend is a big misnomer. Weeks never end. They just run into each other and start all over again.

CHAPTER 8

Anne waited in the Officers' Club lounge as specified. The OSC had sent a flyer indicating the various meeting times and places of the year's committees. She looked around the deserted room. Maybe there wasn't anyone else on the food committee. Hers had been the only name when she'd signed up. But as she was worrying about it, another person joined her.

Anne rose and stuck out a hand to greet the new arrival. "Hi, I'm Anne Hopkins...oops! Bradley." Anne laughed at herself. "I've only been married for a month and a half."

"Well, congratulations! I'm Beth Bennett," the other woman said, shaking Anne's hand.

"I'm hoping we're not the only two." Anne sent a glance around the room.

Beth shrugged. "We'll see. I've left my kids at day care. I only signed up for two hours, so I'll have to leave by noon."

"I've got an interview at one, so I won't be much behind you."

"It looks like there might be someone else." Beth nodded toward the door.

A girl was standing there, hesitating.

Anne raised an arm and waved her over.

The girl smiled and wound her way through the tables.

"I'm Anne Bradley and this is Beth Bennett," Anne said as the girl reached the table.

"Hi. I'm Karen Bannister."

"Have a seat, Karen," Beth offered. "Anne's been married a month and a half. How about you?"

"Seven years. We got married our freshman year," she said, answering the inevitable question before it was asked. She knew she still only looked about 17. "And you?"

"Six years."

Suddenly, there was another person at the table.

"I'm Rachel," she announced. "Mind if I smoke?"

Rachel was wearing a thigh-length A-line skirt in black with a white sleeveless shirt. Her lips were bright red. Anne thought they were a good match for her black hair. As she opened her purse, she kicked off the sandals she'd been wearing. Her painted toenails matched her lipstick.

"I'm Anne," the one with the long braided hair said. She was wearing something loose and silky, but not because she was fat. She looked as if she could run to the moon and back. "And, actually, you're not allowed to smoke in here."

"I'm Beth," said the woman with the square face and short blond hair. She was wearing shorts and a polo shirt.

"And I'm Karen."

Rachel immediately felt sorry for Karen. Her limp auburn hair didn't do a thing for her pasty white skin. The yellow jumper Karen was wearing just made everything worse.

Rachel smiled and put her cigarette case back into her purse. "Whew!" she exclaimed, unbuttoning another button on her shirt. "And I thought Italy was hot."

Beth and Anne exchanged a glance.

Beth pulled her information packet from her lap and placed it on the table. "Should we get started?"

Everyone except Rachel shuffled through their papers and pulled out the information that pertained to the food committee.

Rachel swiftly flipped through her cordovan leather three-ring binder until she found it.

"The food committee is responsible for four events," Beth explained. "The first is a Haunted House for Halloween; the second is refreshments for the Christmas bazaar. The third is an Easter egg hunt at General Pritchard's, and the fourth is a silent auction. Funds made from the events are applied to the OSC Scholarship Fund to provide scholarships to the local community college."

"So, the first event looks like Halloween. Does anyone know if we're limited to what's been done in the past?" Anne asked.

"No, but tradition is not easily bucked, if you know what I mean," Beth warned.

"So we're stuck with the Haunted House idea?" Anne asked.

"Basically. And the events committee actually works on putting it together. It's gotten pretty elaborate. Lots of moving parts. The guys would be disappointed if there wasn't one."

"Who exactly is it for?" Karen asked. She hadn't meant to be funny, but everyone burst into laughter.

"The children of all the military who are attached to the base. Officers and enlisted."

"Is that the same as for the Easter egg hunt?"

"Yes."

Rachel spoke into the general discussion. "Someone should take notes of the meeting."

"I can do it. I have my planner with me." Beth pulled her tote bag onto her lap and fished out a small notebook and pen.

"For the Haunted House, what sort of food is expected?" Karen asked.

"The usual. Orange and black cupcakes. That sort of thing."

Karen took a deep breath. This would be more cooking than she had imagined.

"The Officers' Club restaurant catered last year. It was fine. They served orange punch and cupcakes and each child was given a little treat bag."

"Do they have a place for the kids to sit down?"

"There were several tables set up at the end of the room."

"I think we should at least put dry ice in the punch to make it look spooky," Anne suggested.

"Can we give the kitchen ideas?" Karen ventured.

Beth shrugged. "Probably."

"Maybe they could make flat sheet cakes and then cover the icing with chocolate cookie crumbs and those gummy worms mixed in?" Karen said, feeling her face grow warm. She always blushed when she talked in front of people she didn't know. She hated herself for it.

"That sounds great!" Anne agreed. "And if they put enough food coloring in the cake, they could make it blood red."

"And the icing could be flesh-colored," Beth added. "That would be creepy. Perfect. I like it. Okay, punch with dry ice and the cake. Do we want treat bags?"

Karen was hit with an inspiration. "Will there be trick-or-treating on base?"

"From 6:00 to 8:00 the night of Halloween," Beth said, and then she sighed inwardly. She still had to figure out costumes for the twins.

"Then they don't need more candy. Maybe we could give them spider rings or something else that's inexpensive."

"And put them all together in a huge glass fish bowl so they have to stick their hand in to pick one out," Anne added.

Beth grimaced. "We could do that. It would probably be cheaper than buying candy."

Rachel was reading through the committee instructions. "We're supposed to report back to the OSC board with price estimates so they can approve the ideas. Do we know when the next board meeting is?"

"They meet the third Thursday of every month, so that would be this Thursday."

"So we need to get approval this week, or there's no food budget. Is that right?" Rachel verified.

"Guess so," Beth said. She thought for a moment. "We need an estimate from the kitchen and an estimate for spider rings and a fish bowl. Let's count on the same number of kids as last year."

"I can do the rings and fish bowl," Karen volunteered. "I'm going to the craft store tomorrow anyway."

"I'll talk to the kitchen," Beth said. "I know the catering people from CGOC. And if you'll call me with your estimate, Karen, I'll do it up into a memo and then fax it to one of the board members."

Anne looked at Beth quizzically. "CGOC? What's that?"

"The Company Grade Officers' Council. It's the association of lieutenants and captains. FGOs are field grade officers: majors, lieutenant colonels, and colonels."

"You were in the CGOC?"

"I just got out of the Air Force last spring. I was a captain, but now we have twins."

"How nice," Karen breathed.

"You can have them. I'll give you a two-for-one deal and throw in the dog for free."

Anne laughed. "How old are they?"

"Two. Old enough to get into trouble, but young enough not to be able to run away before I find them."

"Do you have pictures?" Karen asked.

Beth drew her wallet out of her purse and flipped it open, revealing three pictures.

Anne studied the most recent. "What are their names?"

"Andy's on the left and Josh is on the right."

"They're so cute." Karen's eyes softened, thinking of her own brothers.

"They are. But looks can be deceiving. How about you guys? Any of you have kids?"

"No," Anne said. "Just married."

Karen shook her head with regret. "Not yet."

"Not planning on it," Rachel said.

"Why not?" Karen was shocked.

"I'm the independent type. I think they would bother me. Anyway, when should we meet next?"

"Two weeks from now, same place, same time," Beth advised. "We should know by then whether the ideas are approved. Then maybe meet once more before the Haunted House."

Everyone nodded.

Rachel took her purse and rose. "Until then."

Beth gazed at her with envy as she walked out the door.

Karen dropped Kevin off at work on Tuesday.

"See you around 4:45?" He kissed her on the cheek. "Have fun."

Her eyes sparkled. "I will."

She drove into town, humming songs from church. Now and then, her voice broke into words before descending back into wordless joy. The only thing she liked more than going to the library was going to a craft and fabric store. And Liffsbury had a huge one. They always had a craft project on display, along with free instruction sheets on how to make them. She had to get started on Christmas crafts, especially if she wanted to sell things at church and at the OSC Christmas bazaar.

She turned the car into the parking lot of a donut shop. It was just eight o'clock. The craft store wouldn't open until nine. She'd decided to get a snack and eat it at the waterfront. She'd heard that people from church owned this particular shop.

A large woman smiled at her. She was wiping the counter, the flesh underneath her upper arm flopping back and forth from the exertion. "Morning, sugar."

"Hi."

"What can I get for you?"

"Do you have any day olds?"

"Sure. Right in that basket over there. Help yourself." She went back to wiping the countertop.

Karen selected an assortment of six yeast donuts that still had their frosting and weren't too squashed.

"Coffee with that?"

"No, thank you."

"That's ninety-nine cent."

Karen passed the woman exact change. "Can I take some napkins?"

"You go ahead. Take what you need. Come back now."

The day was warming quickly. Already the contrast between air-conditioning and the outside temperature was uncomfortable. On days like this one, Karen wished she could wear shorts, but her temple garments would have been visible. Unless she wore knee-length Bermudas—and it would be years before those came back into style. For the Southern summer, she had to make due with capris, like those she'd put on that morning, or long-skirted jumpers.

Karen parked the car under the stingy shade of a spindly pine tree. She jumped the railroad ties that tried to separate the parking lot from the sand dunes and landed on the boardwalk. Breathing deeply, she savored the smell of creosote that emanated from the boards. Everyone always teased her about it, but she loved the scent. Probably because she associated it with the sea.

She mounted the steps that crawled up the back of the dune. As she reached the top, a gust of wind tore the napkins from her hand and flung them across the beach. Another gust whipped her hair across her face. She tossed her head into the wind, trying to bring her hair back around. It was useless. She put up with it until she reached the beach and decided on a place to sit. She headed toward a free space the sea oats had left in the dune until she remembered hearing about the abundance of snakes in the state. Were there snakes in the dunes? Why wouldn't there be? A dry spot in the sand on the beach would have to do. Glancing at the sun, she remembered she hadn't put on any suntan lotion.

Half an hour at 8:30 in the morning can't kill me.

She plopped down into the sand, drew up her knees, and slipped the bag of donuts underneath them. Then she reached back her hands to twist her hair into a long rope, tying it into a giant knot on top of her head.

Karen selected a plain sugar-glazed donut from the bag and tore off a piece with her fingers.

This is too greasy. I knew I shouldn't have gotten these. I just won't put cheese in the casserole we're having for dinner.

Why not? I can eat this. It's just sugar on top. No filling. It's fine. No, it's fried.

She tore off another tiny shred and put it into her mouth.

I'll just let Kevin have the rest. He can have a couple for breakfast today and tomorrow. Then they'll be gone.

She looked at the remainder of the donut. Looking beyond it, she saw a seagull pattering along the mush between the beach and the ocean.

You have it.

She tossed it to the bird. He snatched it up and flew away, escaping the friends who had appeared out of nowhere.

Karen walked back to the car. Sticky fingers reached into her pocket for keys before she realized it.

Darn it! I knew I shouldn't have gotten those.

She wiped them on the inside of her pant leg. Leaving the door open for a minute to let some of the heat out, she unknotted her hair and let it wrap around her like a scarf. Then she got in and turned off the air conditioner so it wouldn't blast her with hot air. Catching a glance of herself in the mirror, she stared, stricken. Her hair looked as if it hadn't been washed in years. It was matted and tangled.

Shoot, shoot, shoot. I should have remembered to braid it. This is going to take days to untangle.

She looked at her watch.

Already 9:00!

There was nothing she could do but try to tie it back into a knot.

The spider rings were easy to find and price. Fish bowls were more difficult to locate, but she finally found them, covered in dust and stacked haphazardly on the floor. The rest of the time she split between feeling self-conscious for looking like a bag lady and losing herself in pattern books. The store's featured craft was pretty, but it was made mostly of silk flowers, and they were much too expensive.

Flipping through clothes patterns, Karen couldn't believe how many yards of material the new dress styles required. It was ridiculous. At seven dollars a yard for material and with the expense of the patterns, buttons, and thread, the cost could quickly climb to $50! It was cheaper to buy ready-made on sale.

She flipped to the backs of the books. Ideas for Christmas crafts were basic. Potholders. Stuffed snowmen and Santas. Placemats. There had to be something she could do.

Her stomach began its familiar twist and churn.

I knew that donut was too greasy.

She shut the pattern book and fled the store before her stomach cramps could get much worse. It was only 15 minutes back to base. Christmas could wait.

Karen called Beth later that morning. "I wanted to give you the estimate on the rings and fishbowl."

"Great. Just hold on a second. I need to put the phone down to grab a pen and a piece of paper."

"Okay."

The cord of the phone on Beth's end unwound and spun the phone to the floor. Shelby, who considered anything on the floor to be hers, looked at it with interest.

Karen heard a deep sniffing noise. Several slurps. Then Beth was back.

"Karen, I'm sorry. The phone dropped and our dog started playing with it. Anyway, what were the prices you found?"

"The rings come in bags of fifty and cost two dollars a bag. They had two kinds of fishbowls. Completely round was six dollars. The kind that has a round silhouette but flat sides was five dollars."

"That's great! A lot cheaper than buying candy. The kitchen at the O Club gave me some good quotes too. I'll get them to the board. Thanks for your help. With the twins, I would never have been able to get into town to do that." *Or anything else.*

"It wasn't a problem. I'll see you next week."

As Beth wrote the next food committee meeting onto her calendar she realized just how close Halloween was. She had to think of costumes for the twins—and quickly! Nothing too complicated. She didn't have the time, and they weren't old enough to really appreciate it. Something simple. Maybe there were some good ideas floating around in their two-year-old heads. She decided to ask them.

"All right, boys." Beth had walked into the boys' room to see them each crouched beneath their cribs, sucking on their fingers.

"Halloween is next month. I know you don't remember last year, but it's like pretending."

Andy and Josh took their fingers from their mouths and looked at her with interest.

Beth sat down on the floor between their cribs. "If you could pretend to be anything in the world, what would it be?"

"Garbageman," Josh said.

"Train," Andy yelled. "Choo-choo-whoo-whoo."

"I was thinking more like skeletons or dinosaurs," Beth said. She smiled hopefully.

"Garbageman."

"Train."

Lesson number 357. Provide appropriate choices. Do not let them choose for themselves.

CHAPTER 9

*O*n Wednesday night, R.J. came home from work with a great idea. "We should have a party."

Rachel's eyes lit up. "A party! That's a wonderful idea. When?"

"I don't know. I'll ask around and see when everyone's free. This weekend or next."

"But it would be impossible to have invitations printed so quickly!"

"Invitations? We'll just send an e-mail. No big deal, okay?"

"How many people do you think there'd be?"

"I don't know. Maybe thirty?"

Rachel's eyebrows lifted in surprise. "Thirty! There's no way we could do thirty in a week. Maybe in two. I suppose I should get in touch with a caterer right away, then." She flipped through the leather binder she always carried with her and then frowned. "Not formal, right?"

"No. No way. I was thinking we'd buy the beer and people could bring what they wanted to throw on the grill."

"Beer! What about sangria? It's so refreshing in the summer. Or there's always champagne." Her face brightened. "We could grill swordfish. And maybe some lobsters."

"Simple, Rach. Keep it simple. I don't want to spend a thousand bucks on this." R.J. was searching through some blueprints on the table, riffling through them and then letting them coil in on themselves. "Have you seen my sunglasses anywhere?" He stopped and smoothed out an elevation sketch. "Nice house. Someone's you know?"

"It's just an idea."

"How many square feet?"

"A little over five thousand."

"Five thousand? Geez! What do people need with all that room? What would you do with it?" He turned his wrist over to look at his watch. "I'll be late if I don't go. Sunglasses?"

"On the patio?"

"Right. Love you," he said as he bent down to kiss her.

"Love you too."

I could have told him. Should have told him.

Beth looked around the room one more time. It seemed as if she were forgetting something. "I left the phone number of the O Club by the phone."

"Okay, Mrs. Bennett." The teenager's braces flashed as she talked. She snapped her gum and reached a hand up to adjust her glasses.

"Thanks, Janine."

"No problem." The babysitter bent to pick up Joshua. "Say goodbye to your mommy."

"Bye."

"Goodbye, sweetie." Beth leaned over and kissed him on the cheek. "Where's your brother?"

Joshua took his finger out of his mouth and pointed toward the living room. A telltale movement from the beanbag chair betrayed Andy's hiding place.

Janine laughed. "They're so cute. I hope when I have kids they're just like Joshy and Andy." She jiggled the little boy on her hip.

Be careful what you ask for. "We'll be back by 7:30 or 8:00."

Beth adjusted her sunglasses and started the car. She turned to check for fastened car seats before she realized she didn't have to. Laughing, she backed out of the garage and turned the radio on. The drive to base was against the flow of Friday afternoon's traffic. She turned off the air-conditioning and rolled down her windows. Checked her watch. Almost 5:00. The Company Grade Officer's meeting should just about be finishing up. With the customary keg of beer. It was an important meeting. Responsibilities would have been assigned for the year's Christmas charity drive. And as vice president of the CGOC, Marc was assured a good portion of them.

She finally found a parking space in an unpaved area under a stand of pine trees to the left of the club. The Bullard workday started at 7:30. And on Friday, at least, no one worked past 4:30. The monthly CGOC meeting only made the parking situation worse.

She found Marc in the group of people talking around the keg. He slipped an arm around her shoulders and offered her his beer.

"Thanks." Beth took a sip and handed it back. She kicked at the foot of the captain standing beside her. "Hey, Skeech. How's it going?"

"Going. Going. Almost gone." The sturdy blond lieutenant winked at her.

"You're PCSing?"

"Yep. Two weeks."

"Where are you going?"

"California. Edwards. Test Pilot School."

"TPS? That's terrific. Congratulations!"

"Thanks."

"When did you find out?"

"Couple months ago."

"Oh. So you're a short-timer then."

"He's had his orders for quite a while," Marc said. He raised his beer mug.

Skeech took him up on the toast and crashed his mug into Marc's, sloshing beer onto the floor.

Beth shook her head at them. "You guys are worse than Andy and Josh. Best of luck to you." She tugged at Marc's shirtsleeve. "Let's go get something to eat."

"Go ahead. I'll join you there."

Beth relieved Marc of his mug and made her way out of the room. She stopped beside a first lieutenant she recognized from her working days.

"Shannon. How are you?"

"Beth! Great to see you."

"How's the test range?"

"I switched jobs in May. I'm in the SPO now."

Beth blinked in surprise. "I guess I'm out of it. Sorry. Are you happy you made a change?"

"It's not bad. I'm starting to look ahead to next year. Have to figure out where to go."

"What are you thinking? Ohio?"

"No. I don't really want to go to Wright-Patt. Dave's at LA Air Station, so I'd like to get over there if I can."

Beth stole a look at her friend's left hand. "Marc told me you got engaged!" she lied. "Congratulations."

"Thanks. The wedding's set for June."

"Here?"

"No. At my parents' near Philadelphia."

"That's exciting. Have fun with the planning. You going to have a military wedding?"

"Not if they put the new uniform changes through."

"Uniform changes?"

"You haven't seen the mock-ups? They're terrible."

"When did they decide?"

"They haven't officially, but they've been talking about it since last month. They probably figure people are too busy PCSing to hear or care."

Beth smiled. "Moving can keep you out of the pipeline." *And so can getting out.* "I'm heading toward the bar. See you later."

Beth found a large table and claimed it for the group of CGOs that would eventually move to the bar when they became hungry enough. She finished the last of the beer and set the empty mug on the table. She looked around the room, noting the raucous groups of pilots. Tight clusters of more dignified lieutenant colonels and full birds with their immaculate wives. And the group of retirees hovering over the free happy hour food at the buffet table.

At least some things never change.

"Ready?"

"I guess. You have the Bible?"

"Got it."

They arrived five minutes early.

"There's quite a crowd here!" *That's a good sign.* Anne's spirits lifted. *Maybe this is it. Maybe we can stop being church gypsies. Stop trying something new every week.*

"Madam?" Will requested as he opened Anne's door and gave her a hand out of the car.

"Do you take tips, doorman?"

"But of course."

Anne kissed him on the cheek. "Then you'll have to come up to my room sometime." She pinched his butt. "You're kind of cute."

"Watch it, lady. I could be fired for this."

They walked together into the church.

Anne nodded with satisfaction as they sat down. "This looks more like heaven."

"Every tribe, tongue, and nation."

"Let's just hope the preaching's good."

"Amen."

Will turned to her after the benediction. "So?"

"It was okay."

"Want to try something else next week?"

Anne sighed. She was so tired of this. "No, I don't. Let's just stick with this one and see if it gets better or worse. The sermon wasn't bad. I just had trouble paying attention. I must be tired."

"Me too."

"I just want a church where I feel like I can be me. Where I don't worry how they think about me. Or you. And I want to go somewhere people really sing. I don't want music that sounds like it's coming from a roller-skating rink. And I don't want to sing 'Amazing Grace' like I'm at a funeral. Or keep singing the same three-word chorus over and over again. Is that too much to ask?"

"No. But sometimes I think God puts you in a church so you can give instead of receive."

Anne and Will walked out of the church in silence as she thought about his statement. "Maybe you're right."

One evening later that week, Will opened the condo door. Heard the sound of chopping.

"Anne?"

There was no answer.

"Anne?"

"What!"

He put his briefcase on the floor and joined her in the kitchen.

"What are you doing?"

"The recipe says these have to be julienne," she said in a small, controlled voice, referring to the carrots on the cutting board.

"Those are *toothpicks*, Anne. They're way, way beyond julienne."

She continued chopping in silence.

"You're crying."

"Of course I'm crying."

"Why are you crying?"

"Because." Chop. "I can't." Chop. "Do anything." Chop. "I'm good at here." Chop. Chop.

"You can kiss me."

"*Don't* make me feel better," she said, threatening. "What time did you leave for work this morning?"

"Six."

"And not two minutes later I left to go running. And it was *too hot*. At six o'clock in the morning! I'm not waking up at five to do it! But I wasn't upset. I said to myself, 'Okay, it still feels like summer. I can handle this. I'll just not run outside for *six months!'* So I came back here. I couldn't run, so I decided to swim. That's good exercise."

She had been trying hard to look on the bright side.

How could she explain how much she missed running? She needed to run like she needed to breathe. It kept her sane; it kept her alive. And it was true what they said about the best runners. They never played games with themselves to keep on running. They just ran. She never coaxed herself, saying, "That's it. One more hill, and then you can decide whether to keep going or not. One more mile, and you can have ice cream when you get home." She didn't need motivation. She ran for the pure appreciation of motion. She ran because it was fluid joy. Because the harder she pushed herself, the more she found to give. She'd tested her body and trusted it like she trusted a best friend. Running gave her strength and fed her soul.

Will nodded.

"So I put on my bathing suit, went back to the beach, and dove in. I swam for two minutes before my goggles were so clouded I couldn't see anymore. Slimy green stuff. So I said, 'Fine, I'll just swim without them.' And I did. And then I came home and found out the slimy stuff was all over me. Everywhere. And I mean everywhere."

Will nodded again.

"And no one here will hire me to do anything even semi-intelligent. I could work at Billy's Burgers. I could even pump gas. But can I use my education? Is anyone interested in my brain?"

"I am."

"So, after lunch I decided not to be such a whiner; I drove into town for coffee. And you know what? There aren't any coffee shops in town. Not like in Seattle. I found a gourmet coffee shop at the mall, but do you know what gourmet is? Caramel-colored coffee beans coated with flavored oils. And no one says cents. They all say cent!" she said, railing against that final indignity.

"Sense?" Will was sure that his wife had flipped out.

"Cent. Like, 'That will be two dollars and twenty cent.' It's cents.

With an *s!* Cents! I'm so *mad* I could…" she groped for words, and finding none, ended up pulling a terrible face.

"Will these help?" asked Will, revealing the two yellow roses he'd kept hidden behind his back. "Happy two months."

She didn't know whether to laugh or cry.

Anne and Will ate pureed carrots that night. They decided, all things considered, that it would be the best thing to do with the mutilated vegetables.

"Why don't you meet someone for lunch tomorrow?" Will suggested.

"Who do I know?"

"How about one of those people from the OSC committee you're on?"

"I don't know…one of them has kids; she's probably busy."

"Aren't there others?"

"Yeah, but one of them's…different."

"How?"

"I don't know. Like someone from Mercer Island."

"Stuck-up?"

"Sort of. It's hard to explain. I'll point her out sometime. I guess I could call Karen. She seemed nice."

"Why don't you? I'll take care of the dishes while you call."

Anne found Karen's phone number in the OSC directory and made the call. "Hi, Karen. This is Anne Bradley. From the OSC committee? I was wondering, if you weren't busy tomorrow, would you like to meet for lunch somewhere?"

There was a pause. Karen *would* love to meet someone for lunch, but the money it would cost… "Maybe we could have a picnic somewhere. There's a park on the north side of base along the ocean. Would you want to do that?"

"Sure. Sounds like fun. You just want to meet there?"

"About noon?"

"I'll see you then."

Karen had dropped Kevin off at work that morning so she could have the car. She did their grocery shopping at the commissary before packing a lunch and heading to the park. Before she knew it, the speedometer had edged up over 35 mph. She lifted her foot off the gas pedal and let the car slow to 25 mph, the base speed limit. She'd never gotten a speeding ticket in her life and had no intention of doing so now. Especially not through inattention. Once he'd gone through OTS and been assigned to Hill, Kevin had explained to her that any ticket *she* received on base would automatically be brought to the attention of *his* commander. And since the base was federal property, it would be processed through the federal court system.

She shook her head. Just one of many things to get used to. The week before, she'd been driving home from the library and, all of a sudden, cars had pulled off to the side of the road, people in uniform had stopped on the sidewalks, and all of them, whether coming or going, pivoted in the same direction and stood at attention. She'd looked in her rearview mirror for flashing lights. Leaned forward over the steering wheel to see if there was a helicopter or plane coming in for an emergency landing. It was as if she were in a different dimension—one in which everyone but her had ceased to exist.

It was only when she turned the radio off that she heard the "Star-Spangled Banner" playing over the base loudspeaker. She glanced at her watch and then blushed as she realized what she'd done: She'd been driving straight through retreat. Every evening at 5:00, the flag was lowered. And at the first note of retreat, those outside in uniform were to remain at attention until the ceremony was finished. Civilians were to stand with a hand over their heart. Customarily, drivers pulled their cars to the side of the road…which is exactly what she'd done. Another blush crept over her face as she recalled the incident.

Now, she watched from her spot under the park's pavilion as Anne drove up.

"Hey!" greeted Anne. She had a bulging tote bag over one arm, a beach umbrella slung over the other, and a picnic basket in her hand. "I brought a beach umbrella and towels. Do you want to sit on the beach?"

"Sure." Karen was armed for anything; she'd nearly taken a bath in SPF 30 sunscreen. "Did you say that you live on the beach?"

"Yeah."

"Do you like it?"

"I like the location. We bought our condo furnished, so it still feels like someone else's place. I'm sure I'll get used to it."

"What did it come with?"

"Everything from sheets to wineglasses. It was perfect. The people who owned it divorced. Because it was a vacation home, they didn't need anything from it, so they sold it all. Diet Coke?" Anne offered from her cooler.

"No, thanks. I don't drink it."

"Don't like the taste?"

"It's the caffeine."

"Allergy?"

"No. LDS. We never drank it when I was little and I never acquired the taste."

"Oh." Anne couldn't think of what to say. She wished she'd paid more attention in Sunday school classes when they'd talked about other religions. "I don't know the first thing about your religion. Past Joseph Smith, anyway. I'm a Christian."

"I am too."

"But I thought…isn't LDS the same as being a Mormon?"

"Yes. But we're still Christians. Salvation comes through Jesus Christ, right? Why else would we call ourselves The Church of Jesus Christ of Latter-day Saints?" Karen unwrapped her sandwich and took a bite.

"And so Joseph Smith was…?"

"The Prophet. Just like Moses or Elijah."

Anne didn't know what to say, so she changed the subject. "Where did you go to school?"

"BYU," Karen said, after a swallow. Then she supplied an answer for Anne's blank stare. "Brigham Young."

"Is that where you met your husband?"

"Kevin? Yes."

They got married the spring of their freshman year and moved into married student housing. The plan was that Karen would go to school until she got pregnant. After that, she'd drop out and Kevin would continue to finish his degree.

She'd balked at the idea the first time they'd discussed her leaving school. Even thought about praying she wouldn't become pregnant because she'd always wanted to be a nurse. Ever since she spent her tenth summer reading a box full of her grandmother's *Sue Barton* nurse books.

"But you don't even have to have a degree. You could probably find work as an LPN right now."

"I want to be an RN."

"I'm not saying that you can't be. I'm just saying that you don't have to have a four-year degree in order to be a nurse."

"That's like saying you don't have to have a civil engineering degree in order to build roads in a sandbox!"

He took her in his arms and kissed her cheek. "The important thing is to have children."

She wrapped her arms around his waist. "I know, Kevin. It's not like I don't want to. I just wanted to do something else first. But you're right. I can always go back and finish up the credits somewhere." She nestled her head into his shoulder. Sighed, imagining the future that might have been. It would have been so perfect; she could have worked wherever Kevin was moved by the Air Force. Nurses could always find jobs. And with two salaries? Even if she only worked three or four years, if they invested the money she made, they could afford to have ten or twelve kids.

"Penny for your thoughts?"

Her thoughts about her soon-to-be abandoned career weren't worth mentioning. And the one thought she wanted to share was the one she never would. *Did you truly want to marry me?* But she didn't want to hear an honest answer. The only answer she wouldn't suspect would be, "Not really," and she prayed she'd never hear it.

But the answer didn't matter anymore. They were married.

"Penny for your thoughts?"

"Just staring off into space."

"So you met Kevin at BYU?" verified Anne, breaking Karen's reverie.

Karen nodded. "How about you?" She was anxious to turn from painful thoughts.

"I met Will at school too. The University of Washington. He was in ROTC. We met in the spring of his senior year. I was a junior. It happened pretty fast once we found out we both liked each other. But that's too long a story. Anyway, he moved here to Bullard in August last year. We only had a couple months together before he left."

Anne and Will enjoyed their summer as a couple while Will waited for his position in the Air Force to come open. They took full advantage of Seattle's Seafair celebration in July. On one of the Saturdays, they ran down to Green Lake to watch the Milk Carton Derby. "Is that a pirate ship?" Anne asked. "It's huge! You'd never think you could make something like that with *milk cartons*."

"First time you've been?"

"Yes. I wish I'd come before. This is amazing."

The lake was afloat with all types of boats. And all of them had been constructed with milk cartons. There were kayaks, canoes, skiffs, rowboats, and huge three-masted sailing ships, like the pirate ship she'd just mentioned. There was even an old-fashioned paddleboat built by some guys that Will knew. They were engineering majors.

Will and Anne moved out of the path of a small parade. Bringing up the rear was a pirate boat float. There were pirates on it throwing chocolate coins to the children in the crowd.

"Hello, lady. How about a kiss for a poor old scoundrel?" a man in full pirate regalia asked Anne. He must have been at least 70, and he looked so cute that Anne kissed his offered cheek.

"Har, har," he laughed as he slapped her shoulder. "You've been had!" he announced in his scratchiest pirate voice.

Anne looked down at her T-shirt as the would-be pirate pushed through the crowd back to his float. Sure enough, there was a sticker there that confirmed what he'd said.

"You've been had! Seafair Celebration," Will read. "Shall I fight for your honor?"

Anne had trouble speaking through her laughter. "Not necessary."

They ran together several weeks later in the Torchlight Run that wound its way through the city one evening. And then they watched the parade afterward; a friend saved them a piece of curb along Denny Avenue so they could have an unobstructed view. Periodically Will would stand up as the floats passed. It stopped bothering Anne after the third time. *Must be wanting a better look.*

Not everyone took it quite as well.

"Hey! Would you mind sitting down?" a woman behind them finally asked.

Will turned around to look at her. "I'm sorry, ma'am," he said without remorse. "I'm a member of the armed forces, and I stand when the flag passes."

After that, Anne stood along with him.

So did their friend.

And the family sitting behind them.

Will was scheduled to leave for Bullard Air Force Base in August after receiving his commission. They'd made one final run his last Saturday in town for old time's sake. He weaved her fingers through his as they sat watching the crowds of people make their way around Green Lake. "It's not like it's the other side of the world. We can e-mail."

She nodded, looking out at the lake. She really wanted to ask him if he planned to marry her, but she didn't want to force him into any corners. *Play it cool.*

"I'll be coming back for Christmas."

"Some of the girls in the house talked about skiing in Vale during the break." It was mean, but she couldn't help herself. Besides, she'd never go; she couldn't risk the injury just before track season.

"It's your senior year. Enjoy it."

She pulled her hand from his and bent over at the waist to stretch out her legs. She felt his hand on her back.

"I love you, Anne."

She stayed in her stretch long enough for the tears to go away, and then she straightened up and smiled at him. "I love you too."

Fall quarter didn't go fast enough. Anne didn't have Will to run with. They e-mailed every day, but it wasn't the same.

She checked her e-mail at the computer lab in the business school one afternoon between classes. The typing coming from the other students around her was almost deafening. She leaned an elbow on the tabletop beside the machine, and opened Will's latest e-mail: He'd found a condo for sale on the beach.

"It's a two-story place. Pretty new. The people who are selling it are getting divorced. Apparently, neither of them wants anything because it's being sold with everything in it."

"Sounds nice," she responded. "You really want to buy something?"

She read his reply the next day: "The housing market's depressed here. I can get a monthly mortgage for what I'd pay to rent somewhere else. Plus the advantage on taxes. Might as well, I guess."

"Might as well," she e-mailed back. It's all she could think of to say. It looked as though he was going on ahead with life. Without her.

No. There was one more thing she could say. "You'll probably meet lots of girls on the beach with a condo like that." She clicked "send" before she could change her mind. The message disappeared into the internet.

She left for class.

She avoided the computer room at the business school the next day. The day after, she checked her e-mails. There were *nine* messages from Will.

She opened the first one.

"I" was all it said. She scrolled down until she couldn't scroll anymore. That was it.

She opened the second and read "love." *Strange.*

The third one said "YOU." She smiled. Just a little bit.

She read "Anne" in the fourth one.

"Hopkins!" was the next one.

She didn't even bother closing the screens anymore.

"Will" was the sixth one.

"You" she mouthed as she read the seventh.

"Marry" she read, disbelieving.

"Me?" asked the last. She started to cry.

She hit reply, typed out "YES!" over and over in a row. Copied it and then pasted it 20 times before she pressed "send." She left the computer room sniffling.

Anne walked around in a daze all day. Was she engaged or not? Did it really count if you were asked by e-mail? Should she tell someone?

She walked back to the sorority wondering what, exactly, her relationship with Will had become.

She greeted the girls in the living room. It was almost time for dinner, and the crowd waiting for the dining room to open was growing every minute.

Someone hurried from the phone room. "Is Anne here yet?"

"I'm here."

"You have flowers on the piano."

"Me?"

"Who're they from?" someone asked.

Anne set her backpack down by the stairs and walked over toward the white grand piano. There were a dozen red long-stem roses sitting in a vase. She plucked an envelope from the bouquet and opened it.

"I mean it. Love, Will," she read.

"Who are they from?" asked someone else.

"They're from Will," she said calmly. Then she added, "And we're getting married!"

"That's so romantic," Karen said, sighing. She was envious. "Did you have the full military wedding?"

"Yes. A saber arch, an obligatory kiss, a whack on the butt."

"Do you come from a military family?"

"No. And that's one of the things that got to me. Everyone looked at me as though I'd decided to join a monastery or something equally radical after I told them Will and I were getting married."

"You guys, guess what?" Anne had asked her FCA small group the next evening, face lit with a smile.

Everyone shrugged their ignorance.

"I'm getting married!" she exclaimed.

"Anne!" screamed Suzy, hands flying to her mouth. "Hey, congratulations."

"Thanks."

"To Will? He graduated last year, right?"

"Yeah."

"But he's in the military, isn't he?"

That's when her friends had started acting weird.

"Are you *sure* you want to be a military wife?" Suzy asked her.

"I'm sure I want to be *Will's* wife. It's not a career choice; it's a marriage."

"But it's just so…military."

"What's wrong with the military? Somebody has to defend the country. Besides, he's in public affairs."

She looked around at her circle of friends. "Ryan, Bobby? Wouldn't you guys fight if there was a war?"

They looked at each other uncomfortably.

"If you were married. And had kids…?"

"Honestly, Anne, I always planned on heading to Canada if anything like that ever happened."

"Like they'd want you! Are you serious? You wouldn't stay and fight for your country?" she asked, voice rising.

They wouldn't meet her eyes.

That's when she knew she wouldn't have a problem being a military wife.

"I know," Karen agreed. "It's strange. People think that being a military wife is substandard. As if I've given up any chance at a normal life."

"I haven't been married that long. I'll have to reserve judgment for a couple months."

"Fresh from the honeymoon."

"Yep. Still a new bride."

They'd planned a luxurious two-and-a-half-week honeymoon, driving Anne's car across the country to Bullard Air Force Base. The first night was spent in Coeur d'Alene.

"I'll warn you, the other hotels I've booked aren't as nice as this one," Will said as he closed the door behind the bellhop.

"I hope not. I'd be spoiled."

"I just figured, for the first night..."

Anne walked over to the wall of windows that framed a gorgeous view of the lake. Sunset had lit the surface of the water with a golden glow. She stared at the scenery but failed to enjoy it. She didn't know what she was supposed to say or do. The ceremony had been easy; everything had been choreographed and mapped out in the smallest detail.

This was different.

Will came to stand behind her. He rested his chin on top of Anne's head and circled her waist with his arms.

She played with the arm hairs that peeked out from under his watch.

"I know we haven't done this before, but millions of other people in the world have. I'm sure we'll figure it out."

Anne smiled and turned around, putting her arms around his neck. "You think so?"

"Yeah. I do. Are you nervous?"

She kissed him. "Maybe."

"There's no big hurry. We have all the time in the world..."

She was shaking her head. Unbuttoning his shirt. "I've already waited a year and a half. I'm not waiting one minute more than I have to." She'd reached his belt buckle. Paused. Stepped away. "Unless, of course, you want to. I wouldn't want to rush you into anything." She stepped back toward him and began buttoning his shirt back up. "Just say the word."

His hands closed around hers and brought them to his lips. He kissed the knuckles of one hand and then the other. "Anne."

CHAPTER 10

*M*usic." Rachel opened the cabinet and ran a finger along her CD collection. "Latin? Cuban!" She always preferred to have music that fit her climate. And tonight was hot and sultry.

She flitted around the apartment, lighting candles and straightening the drapes. Then she stood in the middle of the living room and sighed. *Just two more months. Two more months, and the house will be done. If I ever have to put up with green carpet again, I'll scream!*

R.J. had insisted on doing the grilling and mixing the drinks, so Paolo—her chef—had only marinated the fish and lobster and prepared the salads and the desserts.

People started arriving at seven that evening, and by nine the apartment was crammed. Rachel had given up trying to greet everyone who walked in the door. At the moment, she probably couldn't have pushed her way through to open the door even if she'd been a bulldozer.

A sudden change in the temperament of the crowd caused her to pause on the stairs. To turn and look back down into the living room. Her eyes grew wide. R.J.'s friends were taking turns leaping from the coffee table to stop the ceiling fan with their foreheads.

"Go, Skeech! Go, Skeech!" they chanted as a big-boned blond with a misshapen nose took a jump and then crashed to the floor. An angry welt from the fan blade made a slash across his head as he scrambled to his feet and lifted his arms in triumph.

Rachel heard shouts from outside and bent down so she could see out the screen door and onto the patio. Naked bodies hurtled past her field of vision and splashed into the pool. They could only have come from her bedroom window. She turned around and took the stairs at a run. But by the time she'd reached the bedroom, the guests had finished jumping.

She spun on a heel and marched downstairs. The first thing she did was switch off the fan. The second thing she did was find R.J. He was out by the pool with a beer in hand, laughing at the antics of the people in the water.

"R.J.!"

He turned to her, laughing. "Can you believe those guys?"

"R.J.! It's midnight. If your friends don't shut up and quit jumping from our windows, someone is going to call the police!"

"Ah, come on, Rach. They're just having a good time!"

"Having a good time does not include stopping a ceiling fan with your forehead or leaping from our bedroom window. It's idiotic! And if you can't get them to stop, *I'll* call the police! This is out of control."

"Hey!" R.J. shouted at the pool people. "Hey, fellas! Let's put the clothes back on, okay? My wife's only got eyes for me. Come on, outta the pool. Let's go, let's go."

The six miscreants flopped out of the pool. Tried to high-five each other. They were so drunk, they missed.

"Rach, got any towels?"

She pivoted on her heel, grabbed a stack from a lawn chair, and dropped them at R.J.'s feet. Then she stalked inside.

She was back moments later with the pile of clothes and shoes the deviants had shed in her bedroom before jumping into the pool. "I want everyone out in the next ten minutes."

To his credit, R.J. was able to clear the apartment in just under 15. Then he and Rachel stood silent in the wreckage of their living room. The Cuban CD skipped from the collapsed stereo console.

"I don't think it's as bad as it looks."

"R.J., this is worse than anything I've ever seen."

"It's mostly just beer cans."

"Is this what your life was like before we met?"

R.J. began to shake his head, but then he let it drop into a slow nod. "I'm a pilot, Rach. Fly hard, play hard."

"Like you've got some sort of reputation to uphold?"

"Well...yeah."

"Do you miss it?"

"No."

"Good." Rachel took a deep breath. *It's now or it will be too late.* "I have something you need to see." She grabbed a key from a kitchen drawer, took him by the hand, and led him to the car.

"It's kind of late, Rach. It's nearly 1:00."

"Are you tired?"

"No."

She started the engine and whipped the car out of the parking space. They sped past the beach and up into the hills that lined the shore. She threaded her way through increasingly smaller roads until, finally, she turned off onto a dirt trail.

"I don't think the Alpha's going to like this," R.J. said.

Rachel stopped the engine and pulled the parking break. "We can walk from here."

"But, what if someone wants to get out?"

"No one lives on this road, R.J." *Yet.*

"Rach, I don't like this. It's not our property."

"Just come with me for a minute."

R.J. looked up as a cloud passed over the moon. "Fine." He took her hand and let her lead him down the trail. They walked in silence. After 200 yards, it bent toward the left. They followed for a few seconds, and then suddenly R.J. refused to go any farther. The moon pushed past the clouds and the landscape before them was illuminated.

"Holy—" R.J. gaped. "Whose castle is this?" There before them on top of the slope was a castle. There could be no other term for it. A four-story stone structure with a tower that rose from the center.

Here it was. Time to answer the question. "It's ours."

"Ours!" R.J. yelped. "I swear I never signed anything to buy this place."

"You didn't. I did."

"*You* did? With what?" he was yelling now.

"I did it with my own money."

"But, Rach, this had to cost at least a couple hundred thousand!"

At least.

R.J. shook his head. "Listen. I wanted you to hang onto your grandparents' money so that you could use it if you ever needed it. I wanted you to keep it for you. I earn enough to take care of us."

"R.J.?"

"You shouldn't have done this. You can't have anything left for yourself. Do you? Did you save any of it?" He stood there looking at the castle in silence. It was pretty cool. But it was way, way too big.

"Some." *Okay, this was it. This was the time to tell him. One for the money. Two for the show. Three to get ready, and four to—*

"Rachel, why did you do this?"

She couldn't say it. The house was enough for one night. Besides, it didn't count, she hadn't gotten through four. She dangled the key in front of him. "Don't you want to take a look inside?"

"No." He glowered at her.

She grinned at him.

He threw up his hands. "It's already bought?"

"Already bought."

"How'd you know it was here?"

"It wasn't. I had it built."

"Geez."

Rachel shivered. It was chilly at night.

R.J. wrapped his arms around her. "You're freezing!"

"It's cold out here."

"You know we're only going to be here a couple more years."

"I know."

"You'll never find anyone who's going to want to buy it. What will we do with it?"

"I'll take care of everything. Don't worry."

He just couldn't believe it. What was he going to tell all his friends? "I guess we could take a look inside."

R.J. tiptoed through the house in awe. It was like somebody's private mansion. In fact, it was somebody's private mansion: his.

The food committee met again the next week.

Beth was the first to break away from small talk to focus on the business at hand. It wasn't because she was a type A personality. She was thinking of all the cleaning she needed to get done at home. "Let's talk about the Halloween Party. Does anyone know whether Rachel was planning on being here?"

Anne shrugged. "I didn't talk to her last week."

"I didn't either," Karen said, "although it sounded last time like she'd be here."

The clicking of heels became audible in the distance.

"Maybe that's her. We'll wait for a minute." Beth was hopeful.

The footsteps broke off for a few seconds. Began again.

And then Rachel appeared. "Sorry I'm late. It's the rudest thing in the world. My plane was delayed."

"Where did you go?" Beth wondered.

"New York."

"We could have met later this afternoon." Anne watched Rachel as she sat down and crossed one thin ankle over the other.

"No. This would have been fine if the plane hadn't been late."

Beth dealt a memo to everyone. "I thought we could start with this as a proposed timeline. Our ideas were approved, so we'll go with what we'd planned."

Rachel scanned the sheet quickly. "At least one of us has to be at the Haunted House at all times?"

"I thought it would be best. To make sure food doesn't run out." Beth noted that the others were agreeing.

"And to make sure no one takes too much cake," Karen added.

"Sounds fine." Rachel flipped through her leather portfolio. "I'd rather be here later if that works for everyone."

"That works for me." Anne was hoping to get her stint over early in the day.

"I already volunteered to help out around lunch time with something my church is doing." Karen crossed her fingers, hoping she could work it out with Beth.

"That's okay. Marc's home on weekends, so he can look after the twins during lunch. I can be here. So, Anne's on from 10:00 until 12:00. I'm from 12:00 until 2:00. Karen, 2:00 until 4:00, and Rachel is 4:00 until 6:00. Great. I thought we should tour the reception room and also meet the catering people who will be helping us."

"Good idea," said Anne. "Since I'm first up, I guess I should know what to do."

"It's no big deal." Beth scooted away from the table and grabbed the canvas tote bag that substituted as a purse. "Let's take a look at the room first."

They all followed Beth down the hall to the room where the first OSC meeting was held.

"All of this," Beth said, waving toward the right side of the large room, "will be taken up by the Haunted House. What we'll have left is about a quarter of the room. Four circular tables will be set up for the kids to sit at while they eat. And we'll have one long rectangular table to serve the cake and punch from."

"So, all I have to do is…?" Anne was anxious to know exactly what would be expected of her.

"The cake will already be cut by the kitchen. All we have to do is serve it onto plates and ladle out the punch." Beth thanked heaven that she'd chosen the food committee. There was really nothing to it.

"And make sure they each take a ring." Karen didn't want the kids to leave empty-handed.

"Where's the kitchen?" Rachel tried to speed the meeting up. She wanted to be home before R.J. arrived. There were a few things she needed to finish up.

"The kitchen is down this main hall."

They all turned, once more, to follow Beth, who was moving in the direction of clanking pots and running water. They stopped just short of it.

Beth knocked on the catering office door. A tall slender woman with short black hair answered it.

"I'm Beth Bennett with the OSC Food Committee. We wanted to go over the food for the Haunted House with you."

"Of course. Seat yourselves around my desk and we'll take a look."

She pulled a file out of her desk drawer and consulted it. "Just cake and punch. Four circular tables, food on a rectangular table."

They nodded.

"All I need to know is what you want on the tables."

Rachel's eyes narrowed. "What's usually on them?" Standard business practice was to make someone ask for more than the minimum, simply because they didn't know what the minimum was.

"We'll have tablecloths and candles unless you don't want them, and we can add anything you'd like."

"What color tablecloths?" Karen knew they wouldn't have orange, but she was hoping for black.

The caterer picked up a basket that was sitting beside her desk. It was filled with different-colored napkins. "You can choose the colors from these."

They decided on black tablecloths for all the tables, and orange paper napkins to go with the refreshments.

"I'll be working your event, so I'll check with you from time to time to see if you need more of anything or if I can help in any way."

"I'll be the first one here. Do I need to come here to the office to check in with you? Or will you be in the room?" Anne still couldn't believe that all that was expected of her was to be present.

"If you don't see me by your refreshments table, then just stop by here. I think we're all set. Unless any of you have questions?"

Beth answered for all of them. "I don't think so. And you have my phone number, so if anything changes, just call."

As they left the office and walked toward the parking lot together, Karen asked a favor. "Is anyone leaving by the back gate?"

Anne was. "I go home that way. You need a lift?"

"Just to the housing area that side of base."

"It's not a problem. I have to stop by the BX, if you don't mind waiting a couple minutes."

A moment later Anne and Karen waved from Anne's car as Beth and Rachel drove out of the parking lot.

"Do you like living on base?"

"It's nice to have everything so close. Kevin and I only have one car. It's easier to share it when we live near to where he works."

"Will and I weren't married when he moved here, so he didn't have the option of base housing. We'll probably consider it next time, though."

"I'd do it again. All we have to pay are the phone and cable bills. Of course, we had to buy a washer and dryer, but we found them secondhand."

"Do you go to church at the chapel?"

"No. Ours is in Liffsbury."

"I'm sorry, Karen. I forgot that you told me you were a Mormon."

To Karen's sensitive ears, it sounded as if it were said as a slur. "LDS are Christians too."

"That's what you told me before, but that's not what I've heard."

"Most every sermon I hear and every song we sing talk about Jesus."

"Really?"

"Of course. I mean, the definition of being a Christian is believing in Jesus Christ, right?"

"Yes." Anne wasn't so sure. This didn't sound like what she'd heard about Mormons. "But what exactly is it that you believe about Jesus?"

"The same things you do." Karen couldn't help being surprised. Everyone knew that LDS were real Christians. "That he was resurrected from the dead. That he visited the Americas after his resurrection. That he's a spirit-brother of Lucifer. All that stuff."

"That doesn't sound right. The only place he went after his resurrection was to Israel, for forty days—"

"Doesn't that seem unfair? In the Book of Mormon, it explains how God loved the Gentiles so much that Jesus visited the Americas too before he was taken back up to heaven. Doesn't it seem strange that he would only care about the people in Israel?"

"But Lucifer and Jesus are unrelated. Jesus is God's Son. Lucifer is a fallen angel, a created being. Definitely not on the same level as God and Jesus. What do you believe about God?"

"That he was the offspring of another god, a moral man who attained godhood. Just like we can."

"The God I worship has always been God. And we can never hope to be like him."

"But God is our Father, right? And wouldn't a father want to give the best of everything to his children? Why wouldn't he want to help us be like him?"

"He tries to perfect us, but only through the salvation of Jesus. We can never be gods like he is. Anyway, Christians only believe in one God."

"We do too. One God."

"But you just said you believed that God was the child of another god."

"Oh. Well, LDS do believe in one God. The God I'm talking about is the god of this planet, the only god of this planet."

"So…other planets have other gods?"

"Right."

"None of this is in the Bible anywhere."

Karen was unconcerned. Anne might claim to be a Christian, but LDS was the only true Christian church. The only keeper of the restored Christian message. "That's because the Bible is correct only as far as it's been translated correctly. Joseph Smith, the founder of our religion, had to restore the Christian gospel."

"Why?"

"Because it had been corrupted after the twelve disciples died."

"How so?"

"There was no priest or prophet to keep it safe. And those priests and monks who transcribed the Bible did it so carelessly that it's full of errors. So, God restored his gospel and Christianity through Joseph Smith."

"It seems like if God were really all-powerful he would have been able to make sure the Bible was correctly translated."

"Think of all the opportunities there were to introduce errors. How could there not be some after two thousand years?"

"If there were, and if they were that critical, why would God have waited two thousand years to correct them? That doesn't make any sense. But what were you saying about being a Christian? Can't I claim to be a Mormon?"

"Oh, no!"

"Why not?"

"Do you believe Joseph Smith was a prophet or that people can become gods or that the LDS Church is the true church?"

"Well…no. How does heaven work for you guys, Karen?"

"What do you mean?"

"How do you get there and what is it like?"

"There are three levels of heaven: celestial, terrestrial, and telestial. And in the celestial, there are three levels. To reach the highest of the highest heavens, you have to be married or sealed in the temple for eternity and you have to keep all the commandments."

"And what is it that people do in this highest heaven?"

"They rule with their children. And they have children. Like God and his heavenly wives do on this earth. That's why it's so important to have a temple marriage. If you aren't married in a temple, then your marriage doesn't last forever and you don't get to spend eternity with your children."

"So, basically, when you get to heaven, you become like God?"

"You become a god. Like God is god of this earth, we'll be gods of our own planets."

"But you only worship one God?"

"We worship God. He's the god of this planet."

"So you're not saying there aren't other gods; you're saying that you only worship one of possibly thousands of gods."

"Yes."

"At one time God was like us?"

"Yes. He was like us, so we can be like him."

"So, basically our planet, Earth, is our God's heaven?"

"Yes."

"This is his reward for a good life?"

"Yes."

"But how can this be heaven, Karen? If you were God, wouldn't you intervene to stop things like the holocaust? This isn't paradise."

Karen hadn't thought of that before.

"And what if you have children and they either don't get married, don't get married in a temple, or don't keep all the commandments? What's the rule? Are they okay because you were married in a temple and kept the commandments?"

"I'm not an elder or a bishop. I'm sure you could ask one, though, and they would have an answer."

"Or what if you had a daughter? And she was married in a temple and she kept all the commandments. Does she live with you in your heaven, or does she live with her husband in his? And what if you have a kid, but he dies at age six. It's not like he would ever even have a chance to be married. Is it just his tough luck? I don't understand how it works."

"Well, how does your heaven work?"

"There's one heaven. And there's only one way to get there: through Jesus. It doesn't matter if you're married or single. And whether or how much you sin. As long as you take Jesus at his word, you're in."

"But what about Will?"

"Same thing for him."

"But how do you stay married when you're there?"

"There aren't any marriages in heaven. I won't be up there to hang around Will all day. I'll be up there to get to know God. To worship him. For an eternity. We're God's children, and we never have a hope of being a god like Him. Our hope in dying is that we'll finally be able to be with him." Anne stopped talking as she turned into the BX parking lot and looked for a place to park.

Karen waited for Kevin to come home that night with a question on her mind. She asked it just after they were finished with dinner.

"Kevin, I was talking to Anne this afternoon about LDS and Christianity. She was saying that we aren't Christians."

"Of course we are. LDS is the true restored church." He felt as though he were back in Canada doing his mission. It seemed as though all the conversations he had back then started like this.

"But we were comparing what we thought about God and Jesus, and they weren't the same."

"Of course they weren't the same. What she believes, or has been told to believe, was corrupted. You know that." It was amazing how such a little thing could shake some people's faith.

"I know, but...are you saying that Christians aren't Christians? Because they say that LDS aren't Christians."

"I know that's what they say, but how would they know? They don't know the truth."

"So, they're wrong and we're right."

"Right."

"She asked some interesting questions about heaven. Like, if we have a son, and his marriage is sealed and he obeys all the commandments, he gets to the highest heaven, right?"

"Right."

"So he becomes a god, right?"

"Right."

"But then does he live on our planet or on his own? And what about his wife? He's supposed to be with us because we've been sealed. But she wouldn't have been sealed to us, but she would have been sealed to him."

"Don't let an unbeliever shake your faith. That's what they try to do. Ask tricky questions about things that don't really matter. All we have to do is to make sure we live our lives the right way, and we trust Heavenly Father to do the rest. Right?"

"Right." *Things that don't really matter?*

Temple marriages were a basic tenet of the LDS faith. It was what she lived her life for. Because if she didn't live right in this life, she sure wasn't going to get anywhere in the next. It was essential for salvation.

It mattered.

CHAPTER 11

ill came into the house grinning. He couldn't wait to surprise Anne. He found her in the laundry closet and kissed her breathless. "I found the perfect sport for you."

Anne pushed away from his chest. "I'm not interested. This climate makes it impossible to play sports."

"Oh, come on. I even brought a surprise home for you."

Anne rolled her eyes. "Okay. But I'm *not* going to like it."

Will took her by the hand and led her to the back of his car. Then he opened her palm and put the car keys into it.

Anne unlocked the hatch door and then started to laugh. "Golf?"

"It's the perfect sport," Will insisted.

"For an old white guy, maybe! If you didn't know it before, let me fill you in on something: Golf clubs are notoriously insular bastions of wealth and snobbery. I don't think the members are going to appreciate this black girl playing on their course."

"Just give it a try. I bought ten lessons for you at the city golf course, okay? Everyone in the military plays. I think you'll like it."

"Really?"

"Really. Just give it shot this Saturday and see what you think. If you don't want the lessons after that, I'll use the rest for you."

"All right, all right." Maybe golf would be fun. She'd tried worse things. Like boiled peanuts. And grits. In any case, it would be something to look forward to; something to get her past the week's job interviews.

"The squadron's having a thing on Wednesday night," R.J. announced when he came home.

"This Wednesday?"

"Yeah. They're going to hear some financial planner person."

"I already have advisors."

"But it's a squadron thing, and it's better to think about the financial future sooner than later." He'd read that from the flyer that had been passed around at work.

"What time on Wednesday?"

"It's for dinner. And it's free."

"R.J., nothing is free."

Nevertheless, they showed up at Tom's Beach House on Wednesday night at 6:00. The financial advisement company had reserved the party room. The spiel began as soon as dinner was over.

The usual charts were shown explaining how $500 per month invested at 12 percent over 20 years can multiply into $100,000 dollars. The two men talked about the importance of becoming debt free. They mentioned how no retirement plan is guaranteed, and then, finally, they introduced their plan.

"This fund, AAAStocks, is a low-risk, high-return combination. If you can commit to a monthly investment, you can maximize your investment dollars by dollar-cost averaging. Sometimes you'll buy high, sometimes low, but over time, the average makes it the best investment strategy available."

R.J. was listening with some interest. Originally, he hadn't trusted the speakers. They'd seemed just a little too slick. But what he'd heard so far had made sense.

Rachel raised her hand.

"Yes, ma'am?"

"There is no such thing as a low-risk, high-return stock market investment. The market intrinsically rewards risk."

"What's your name, honey?"

"Rachel Hawthorne."

"Well, Miss Rachel, sometimes those big-city folks will tell you that, but it's simply not true. You *can* find an investment that beats the odds, and that investment is AAAStock Mutual Fund."

"It has an up-front load fee."

"I'm sorry?"

"I said, AAAStock Mutual Fund has an up-front load fee. Is that not correct?"

"Well, yes, ma'am, but there are good reasons for that."

"Maybe for you, but there are no statistics that say load funds perform any better than no-load funds. At this stage in these people's lives, don't you think you'd be doing them a favor by recommending a no-load fund?"

"The fee guarantees that only serious people invest in that fund. It remains more stable that way."

"Serious people make their own investment decisions about their money. How much commission do you make by selling this fund?"

"Pardon me?"

"I said, how much do you make for each share that you sell?"

"Why don't we leave the question period for people who have money to invest."

"Let's say you take a ten percent commission on what you sell. If I gave you all of my money to invest and you earned ten percent on the money you invested for me, you'd have so much money you'd be afraid to invest it for yourself. And if you did work up the nerve to do something with it, you sure wouldn't put it in that fund."

She rose from her chair and left the party room. R.J. followed on her heels.

"If you ever want to invest your money, R.J., talk to me first. Don't talk to people like that," she said as he backed the car out of the restaurant parking lot.

Speculation about how much Rachel was worth flew around Bullard the following week. Estimates topped out at 15 million.

They didn't even come close.

Opinion was unanimous about one thing: R.J. was one lucky guy. His own estimate was one of the lower ones. In fact, he didn't really want to know how much money his wife had, and he still thought she was exaggerating when she implied that she was rich. But he didn't care.

He loved her anyway.

Anne found herself in the middle of what experience told her was a typical Liffsbury interview.

"I see from your résumé that you graduated from the University of Washington last spring." The hiring manager of Entim Corporation looked at her over the frames of her bifocals.

"I did," said Anne, squeezing her clasped hands. "With a major in business. Human resources." *Here comes the question.*

"And what brings you here?"

"I got married."

"And what does your husband do?"

"He's in public relations."

"I see. And where does he work?"

There was nothing else she could say. "Bullard."

"Well, thank you for coming in for the interview. After we've interviewed all the applicants, we'll make our decision."

Anne made sure she was in the car before she exploded. With all the windows rolled up, she screamed out all the rage and frustration of her three-month job-hunting process. Then she started to cry tears of anger. Seeing them drop onto her lap just made her angrier.

She'd learned after her first two interviews not to admit that Will was in the military. She tried to stay away from the topic of his work altogether. But when she was asked point-blank, she couldn't lie. She couldn't bring herself to swear, either, so she said the words to herself inside her head.

It made her feel better.

She hit the steering wheel with the heel of her hand. *It's just not fair. What kind of backward place is this that won't hire a person because of what her husband does for a living!*

Several series of deep breaths calmed her emotions, but she placed her hand heavily on the car's horn for a long minute before she pulled out of the parking lot.

Anne Bradley was here.

She went through Billy's Burgers' drive-through for a milkshake before heading home.

I deserve this.

"What are your other options?" asked Will after Anne had recounted the day's events.

"Let's see. If no one will hire me, I guess that means…I won't be able to work!" said Anne, kicking at the sand. They were taking their sunset walk on the beach.

"No one's made you an offer in personnel, but that doesn't mean you can't apply to work in some other area."

"Like what?"

"I don't know. This is a tourist area. Something touristy?"

"I went to school for four years for my degree. I'd kind of like to have the chance to use my brain!"

"This town is full of retired military people and spouses, like you, who want to work, not because they have to, but to pass the time.

There are too many people looking for work. It's keeping wages down…
and it's giving companies the chance to choose a person who lives
here permanently over a person living here temporarily. It's a business
decision. You can't fault a company for that."

"Whose side are you on?"

"I'm just trying to help explain."

"And I just want a job!"

"What about temporary work?"

"What about it?"

"Why don't you sign up with a temporary agency? Then you could
work when you want. No commitment. We could take vacations
whenever we wanted to. I have thirty days a year. We'll never be able to
use them otherwise."

"I don't know."

"Think about it?"

Anne shrugged.

They found a dune where they could watch the sun kiss the ocean
and then dissolve in ecstasy.

"Thanks for talking to me. I feel better." Anne put her hands behind
her head and leaned back into the sand.

Will settled next to her, propping himself up on an elbow. "The
beach is pretty romantic at night, huh?" he asked, leaning over to kiss
her.

She kissed him back.

"Ever wonder what it would be like to make love on the beach?"

Saturday dawned bright and cool. It was invigorating. And
encouraging to think that even in Liffsbury she could still enjoy her
favorite season: fall.

Will threw his clubs in the car along with the clubs he'd bought for
Anne.

She jumped in beside him, and they set out for the golf course. They
parked their humble Mazda hatchback next to a sleek Jaguar, and Will
took the clubs out of the back and threw each bag over a shoulder. Then
they walked into the clubhouse and were met at the reception desk by a
man Anne judged to be in his sixties. His kind blue eyes twinkled. He
looked dapper in a baseball cap and a polo shirt.

"Are you Anne Bradley?"

"I am."

"I'm Ben." He reached out to shake her hand.

"Hi, Ben."

"Have you ever played golf before?"

Are you kidding? "No. I've never even picked up a club."

"Well, your husband Pete here told me he's afraid that if you learn how to play, you'll be able to beat him soon. How does that sound?"

Anne looked at Will and mouthed *Pete?*

Will shrugged.

"Sounds good to me."

Ben picked up a bucket of balls. Then they walked together to the practice range down a path cut through a dew-drenched hill.

"How long have you been teaching golf?" Anne asked.

Ben sucked in a mouthful of air and let it out slowly. "About 30 years now, I'd say. I was on the tour for about 15 years. Never won anything big, but I sure did get to play a lot of pretty courses. There's quite a few people who play golf and end up hating it. It takes a lot of time: four hours to play eighteen holes. Before we start with lessons, you have to understand that you will probably never play a perfect game. Very few people ever do. But the longer you play, the less poorly you'll play. It's kind of like life. The longer you live, the more you figure it out. And those few who live life well are the ones who enjoy the journey along the way. If you can appreciate a golf course, if you can listen to birds singing and frogs croaking, if you can savor that rare perfect swing, then you'll find golf refreshing. If you concentrate on how many strokes you are over par, and how many times you end up in the sand, you'll find golf frustrating. The other thing to realize is that you never play golf against anyone but yourself. That's why scorekeeping is so important. The only person you hurt when you cheat is you."

They arrived at the range. Ben rummaged through her golf bag and pulled out a club. He handed it shaft first to her. "The first thing to learn in golf is the grip. If your grip isn't right, your swing doesn't have a chance of ever being right."

Anne closed one hand around the shaft.

"You're right-handed."

"Yes."

"Okay, then. We want a grip that's not too loose or too tight. Too loose, and it'll fly from your hands midswing. Too tight, and you'll block the power in your swing. Open up your left hand." Ben turned her hand over so the palm was facing up, and then he placed her hand on the shaft of the club. "Always grip the club the same way every time. Always do these things in the same order."

Ben was molding her hands around the club as he said this, moving her fingers until he was satisfied, and then he closed his hands over hers.

"This is the grip. Your right pinky finger nestled between your left pointer and second finger. Your thumbs are headed the same direction." He squeezed her hands. "How does that feel?"

Ben took his hands away and Anne moved the club up and down, back and forth. "It feels okay."

"All right, then," Ben extended his hand. "Let me have the club and we'll try it again." He took it. Gave it back to her.

Anne practiced the grip until it was cemented in her brain.

"Okay. Now I want you to take your grip again and swing."

"You want me to hit the ball?"

"Sure. Go right ahead."

Anne tried to remember what a golf swing looked like, wound up, and then swung with all her might. She missed the ball, but almost succeeded in wrapping the club around her neck.

"You ever play softball?" Ben asked.

"Every summer until I was 16."

"And what's the first thing to remember in softball?"

"Keep your eye on the ball."

"That's right. Did you do well at softball?"

"My team almost always won the district championships."

Ben nodded. "A softball swing is horizontal. A golf swing is more vertical. They have a similar arc and axis; it's just that the plane is different. Does that make sense?"

Anne nodded.

"A softball swing is usually made with bended knees, right?"

"Right."

"So is golf, but golf is a gentleman's sport. A golf swing is about elegance, where a softball swing is about power."

Anne nodded.

"The first thing to do is to address the ball. This is another thing we're going to do the same way every time. Place the club right behind the ball. Stand so that you're not bending over the club; that would be too close. Or reaching for the club; that would be too far away. Place your feet together and then take your grip."

Anne carefully placed her hands around the shaft.

"You want your feet to be about shoulder distance apart. And for a seven iron, like you're holding, the ball should be in the middle of your stance. So go ahead and move that left foot out a little bit and then move your right foot out. Do this the same exact way every time."

Anne placed her feet farther apart.

"Your ball should be in the middle of your stance. Now's the time to check it."

Anne looked at the ball and then adjusted her feet slightly.

"Now bend those knees just a little, like you're about to sit down."

Anne did a knee bend.

"Too much. Just a little bit."

Anne straightened slightly.

"Good. Now keep your eye on the ball and hit it."

The ball flew up into the air and soared thirty feet before landing almost squarely right of where Anne was standing.

The golfer on the practice mat where the ball landed turned to glare at her.

"Sorry!"

"That's exactly what I wanted to see. Well done!"

Anne looked Ben straight in the eye. "I'd better get a lot better than that before these lessons are over."

"You will. I guarantee it. One thing at a time. You going to stick with me?"

"I'll stick it out."

"Good girl." Ben gave her a smile. She felt as though she'd just been given a gold medal. "Women have some definite strengths when it comes to golf. Are you listening there, Pete?"

Will smiled. "Yes, sir." Maybe Ben had known a Pete Bradley way back when.

"Women are easier to teach because they do almost exactly what you tell them to every time. And once they learn the swing, they usually hit straighter. And most of the time I'd take straight over long."

Anne laughed.

"But women do have some things to be careful of, and one of them is a floppy wrist. Push the club back straight and keep it straight."

Ben demonstrated with a club as he talked, drawing it back and up toward his head.

"Up here, at the height of your swing, what happens if your wrist goes from being straight to being floppy?"

He let his wrist flop. "Did you see what happens to the club face? Here, watch it again." He cocked his wrist and then swung in slow motion at the ball on the ground, stopping the club just before impact.

"If my club hits the ball like this, which direction is the ball going to go?"

"Left."

"Left," he agreed. "So this is what I want you to work on this next week. We're going to strengthen those wrists."

He took Anne's club from her and stood beside her. "Practice your grip and taking your stance the same way every time." Ben demonstrated. "Then I want you to do a quarter swing. Push the club away from the ball in a straight line, but don't bend those wrists or elbows. You'll only be able to get to about here." He indicated a point about three feet from the ground. "Then I want you to come through and hit the the ball, but remember, without bending those wrists. That means no follow-through. Just stand across from me and watch for a couple shots."

Ben demonstrated several swings and then handed the club to her. "Your balls won't go more than ten, twenty feet, but that's just fine." He gave Anne a squeeze on the arm and said, "Next week we should be able to get a real swing going. Just hit the rest of those practice balls out like I showed you."

After he had ambled away, Anne hit a few balls. She straightened up and stretched her back. "Hey, *Pete*, why don't you come over here and try this for a while."

"He's such a nice guy. I just hated to tell him that I wasn't Pete." He took a club from his bag and stepped up to the practice mat as Anne stepped away from it.

She put her club down on the ground, rested a heel on the club face, and leaned an elbow on the shaft as she watched him.

"Maybe this will help my game too." He put a ball on the mat, hit it, and watched it drop to the ground. "So, what did you think?" He fished another ball out of the wire basket with his club.

She shrugged. "I think I just might like this game. By this time next year, after I tee off, all you'll see of me is my backside."

"I hope so. It's almost better than your front side."

CHAPTER 12

⟨⟩

*A*nne took pleasure that week in going to the driving range in the mornings. When she arrived, zipped into a windbreaker, she could still see the sweeping arms of the sprinklers shick-shick-shicking across the driving range. By the time she left, her jacket had been shed. The sprinklers had stopped. The mowers had started. Her balls didn't do anything special those mornings, but she was concentrating on her wrists.

And every morning after hitting a bucket of balls, she stopped to buy a paper and then searched the want ads over coffee at McDonald's. It wasn't good, but at least it was cheap.

She read again an ad for an office assistant at the city manager's office. It had been in the paper for the last three weeks, but she hadn't responded. Of all the places where the hiring manager would be biased against outsiders, the city government would be the one.

She reread the ad. It was nothing she couldn't do: answer phones, type correspondence, file. Like Will had said, it wasn't as though she had to find a job in the personnel field. And this job was definitely one she had the skills for.

When was the closing date?

She consulted the ad.

Friday.

She found a pen and circled the advertisement. She'd download the application from the city's website and send it out with a résumé and cover letter that afternoon…along with ten more thank-you notes from the wedding. She wrinkled her nose. She'd be writing thank-you notes for Christmas gifts before she finished those from their wedding gifts.

She drained her coffee, grimaced at the dregs she encountered, folded the paper, and consulted her watch. Eleven. She'd agreed to have lunch at Karen's. At this point, she just wanted to get the day's thank-you notes written and in the mail, but she couldn't cancel this late. Besides, she had a question she wanted an answer for.

She stopped by a flower shop to pick up a small bouquet for her friend. But after looking over the assorted arrangements of chrysanthemums and straw flowers, she decided on a shiny-leafed ivy that had been trained into the shape of a heart. She asked the cashier if she would put a bright fluffy bow on it and then picked out a mini-card that had to do with friendship and signed it.

Thus armed, she got back into the car and drove onto the base and into the housing area.

Luckily, Karen was standing on her porch, watering a hanging plant. She waved as she saw Anne pull up next to the curb.

"I'm glad you were outside! I forgot to write down your address and couldn't quite remember where I dropped you off last time."

Karen smiled. "Looks like you did fine." She hugged her arms to her body. "It's a little cool today!"

It had been earlier, but now Anne was in shorts, Birkenstocks, and a long-sleeve shirt. She'd rolled the sleeves up just before getting out of the car. It wasn't hot like it had been that summer, but she definitely wouldn't say it was cold. "Looks like you're prepared to winter up in Canada!"

Karen looked down at her jeans, turtleneck and sweatshirt. She shrugged. "It just seems like I'm always cold."

"It's got to be at least seventy-five today! This weather is perfect." She presented the ivy to Karen. "For you."

"Thanks!" Karen held the screen door open for Anne to pass through. Then she led her into the living room. It was decorated in country blue and peach.

"Would you like something to drink?"

"Water?"

Karen went to the kitchen to get some glasses.

Anne made herself at home on the couch. It was slipcovered in a blue-and-white plaid and skirted in a matching floral print that had blue and peach flowers.

"Comfy couch," she called to Karen.

"Thanks. It's one of those old '70s beige-and-brown couches, but I covered it a couple weeks ago. It looks a lot better." She returned from the kitchen with two glasses of water and handed one to Anne.

"I'm impressed. Must have taken a lot of time."

Karen shook her head. "Not really. They're just sheets. It was pretty easy."

"I'm still impressed."

"I just wish I could do something with that old chair." She nodded toward a huge armchair that lurked in the corner of the room. It was striped with brown and orange. "It doesn't look nice, but it's comfortable, and if we didn't keep it, we'd only have the couch to sit on. Mostly, I pretend it's not there."

Anne imagined that she'd have a hard time doing that.

"Anyway, how about some lunch?"

Karen pushed a bowl of peach-scented potpourri out of the way and set the table with rustic woven placements and blue napkins to match.

They ate one of Karen's favorites: chicken salad with mandarin oranges and almonds. "The nuts are high-fat—I didn't put many in— but everything else is nonfat. From the mayonnaise to the turkey-bacon. Eat as much as you want."

She did but noticed that Karen took only a small portion.

Anne took a sip of water and then wiped her mouth. "After talking to you about Mormonism the other day, I did some reading. Please don't take me wrong. I don't mean to be confrontational, but have you ever heard about the Curse of Cain?"

Karen flushed. Of course she'd heard of the Curse of Cain. She really liked Anne and hoped she wouldn't take the explanation wrong. "What did you read about it?"

"That all black people are cursed of God because of the sin of Cain, which was committed thousands of years ago. And that we can't hope to receive your Mormon priesthood because one drop of our blood in a white person condemns that person to the eternal curse and the hottest fires of hell. It's kind of hard not to take that personally. In fact, it made me really angry when I read it."

"It used to be that way, but the prophet gave a different message in 1978. So it's fine now."

"Does it make sense to you that God would curse black people for centuries and then, suddenly, on the coattails of the civil rights movement, change his mind? Especially when people like me are cursed in the...what is it called? The Journal of Discourses and in Mormon Doctrine?"

"The current prophet always takes precedence over earlier prophets or the Book of Mormon or anything else."

"But God never lies and never changes his mind. He shouldn't have to. God knows everything, past and future. So if God has all the necessary information to make a policy decision, there would be no need for him to change it. Ever."

"But you know how people were. They were prejudiced."

"But your religion and its prophets are inspired directly from God, right? I mean, they only say what God wants them to say."

"Right."

"So then your God must be a racist. You know, people have misinterpreted the Bible to support racial discrimination for centuries. For Jews, blacks, Native Americans. But at least when a person actually reads the words, they can see it doesn't really support those prejudices. The Journal is different. It really does."

"But, like I said, the current prophet takes precedence."

"Then that makes God contradict himself. It just doesn't make a whole lot of sense to me, Karen. What about East Indians? Asians? South Americans?"

"I don't know. I never thought about it before."

"It's not logical."

"But the message in 1978 said that black people can receive the priesthood."

"The phrase was 'worthy black people,' Karen. As if most of us just aren't up to standard. Are there many black people in your church?"

"Here? No."

"Haven't you ever wondered why?"

"There comes a point where you just have to believe. It's called faith."

"Listen, I'm not questioning that you're sincere in your faith. I'm just asking you, as a friend, if this policy embarrasses you. It's redneck theology straight from Hicksville. Think about it, Karen. You're a smart person. I brought it up because I was interested in how it fit with what you believed."

Karen didn't know how to reply.

Thankfully, Anne began to eat and switched to a different topic of conversation. "So, what are you going to dress up as for the CGO Halloween Party?"

After Anne left, Karen washed the dishes, dried them, and put them away. She rubbed moisturizer into her hands as she thought about the Curse of Cain. Anne was right. It did sound like redneck nonsense. And she *was* embarrassed by the policy. She'd have to do some reading on it.

How can the LDS Church have really believed in that sort of thing? And if it did, how can I believe in them? Karen asked herself later that evening. *Apostate,* she chided herself. *Don't doubt. Just believe.*

The next Saturday, Ben was pleased with Anne's progress.

"That's great." He was beaming after she had finished hitting five balls. "Look's like we're ready for the whole swing. We'll switch places. Just watch me."

Ben gripped the club and then took his stance. "The golf swing is powerful but contained. There's a lot of twisting going on, but not much horizontal movement. You want to push the club back, keeping it in a straight line, and then you want to twist your torso until your shoulder is below your chin. Of course, it goes without saying…"

"Keep your eye on the ball."

"That's right. At this point, your left arm should be straight. This is the highest point in your swing, and it has served to wind you up. That's all. Speed in the backswing holds no good purpose. You might as well do this in slow motion. The power comes in your downswing. This is where energy is released. You've wound yourself up. Now, let yourself go. Let the club follow gravity. Keep it in a straight line. And follow through."

Ben's ball soared for a hundred yards before dropping to the ground and rolling for another ten. He hit another after pushing the club back in minute increments.

"It's all yours."

Anne took the club from Ben. She took her grip and then addressed the ball.

"Let's see you push the club back and up. Just that much. Stop at the very top."

Anne pushed the club along the ground, her eye never straying from the ball.

"That's right. Now take a look at those wrists. That's the result of working hard in practice this week. Well done. Now take a swing."

Anne let the club drop and swing through the ball, finishing in a classic golfer's pose.

Ben whistled. "Nice swing, Champ. I'd say that's seventy yards."

Will was clapping in the background.

Anne frowned. "But I wasn't aiming that far right. I was aiming for the 100-yard flag." This flag, flapping in the breeze, mocked her.

"Patience. One small adjustment to your swing will make a big difference. Just stick with me." Ben placed a hand on her club and shook it slightly. "How tight are you holding onto that?"

Anne squeezed her hands and then relaxed them. "Pretty tight."

"So we add one small thing when you address the ball. Right before you bend your knees, I want you to squeeze your hands and then relax them, okay?"

Anne tried his advice and found that it worked. Her shots straightened out.

They spent the rest of the lesson hitting balls. Ben explained the significance of the angle of the clubface. "The flatter the face is vertically, the flatter the ball will fly. The more angled it is, the steeper the arc it will have." He demonstrated by first hitting a ball with her three iron and then hitting it with her nine iron.

He also showed her how to position her feet in regard to the ball. "The higher the number of the club, the more you want the ball toward your right foot. The lower the number, the closer you need it to your left foot. It's so the club catches the ball in the correct position to pitch it up."

He squeezed her hand when the hour was over. "See you next week, Champ. Just practice hitting balls at the range here. Use all your irons and get a feel for the different lengths of the shafts. Next week, we'll work on your woods."

He turned to shake Will's hand. "See you, Pete."

"Bye, Ben."

On Monday, the city personnel office called Anne.

"Ms. Bradley? This is Pam from the city personnel office. We received your application for the office assistant job in the city manager's office and wanted to know if you'd like to interview."

"Yes."

"We have an opening tomorrow at 2:00."

"That would be fine."

"Do you know where the city manager's office is?"

Anne reviewed her knowledge of Liffsbury's downtown area. "I'm afraid I don't."

"It's the tall four-story building with three flag poles in front of it."

Anne thought she knew what the woman was referring to. Liffsbury didn't have many building over two stories, so a four-story building stuck out. "What floor is it on?"

"On the top floor. Room 403."

"Okay. Tomorrow at 2:00?"

"Tomorrow at 2:00.

Mr. Trumble, the city manager, was a tall, florid man who looked to be in his forties. From his dark green sport jacket and orange tie to his polished loafers, he created an impression of motion. If he wasn't twiddling a pen between his fingers, he was crossing or uncrossing his legs.

He invited her to take a seat and then folded himself into the leather chair behind his huge oak desk.

"Ms. Bradley—"

"Please, call me Anne."

"Anne. Why do you want this job?" He clasped his hands and placed them on the desk in front of him.

Why indeed. "In actual fact, Mr. Trumble. I really don't. I just graduated from college. Just got married."

"Congratulations."

"Thank you. In any case, what I would love to do is be the personnel manager for a Fortune 500 company. Unfortunately, I don't have any experience in the field. I have to start somewhere, and this job would give me experience with municipal government. You study state and federal government in school but are never told a thing about local government. And local government is what affects people most. What is it they say: All politics are local?" Anne smiled her very best smile, praying that Mr. Trumble wouldn't see through her smoke.

"Have you ever been a secretary before?"

"I was my very own secretary in college."

"How so?" He leaned back into his chair and swung his legs around to the side.

"I typed all my own papers, drafted my own correspondence, kept my own appointment calendar. I even answered phones and took messages on a multiline system for other people that I lived with." Anne decided to come clean. "I have to be honest with you. My husband's in the Air Force. We just moved here, and they've told us we'll be here for three years."

Mr. Trumble didn't seem surprised.

"And there's one more thing I should mention."

Mr. Trumble leaned forward. "Go for it."

"I will not be referred to as 'your girl' or anyone else's except my parents'. And my name is not sugar, sweetie, or honey."

Mr. Trumble nodded.

"And I would not be your secretary. The title is office assistant. I prefer to think that we would work together. And that I would assist you."

"So, what are your most positive qualities?"

"Efficiency. I did track in college. You don't win if you don't run straight and if you don't channel your energy into using resources efficiently."

Mr. Trumble looked at her with the most interest he had during the entire interview. "Were you any good?"

"How'd it go?" Will asked later that evening.

"Not good. I told him my dark secret about your being in the military. And how I resented being talked down to. And how I absolutely didn't want to be a secretary."

"So basically, he's not going to hire you."

"No."

"Hey, better luck next time."

"Next time I need to keep my mouth shut."

Anne received the biggest surprise of her life the next day when she picked up the phone.

"Anne Bradley?"

"Yes?"

"This is the city personnel office."

"Yes?"

"We're calling to ask if you would still like the job as Mr. Trumble's office assistant."

"I would. But why does he want me?"

CHAPTER 13

⟋

*A*re you sure we were supposed to turn back there?" Will asked for the third time.

Anne consulted the map Rachel had given her. "I'm positive. Pull over if you want and take a look for yourself." She held out the map toward him.

He searched the road ahead for signs of civilization. "Wait…it looks like there's a break in the trees up ahead. Maybe that's them."

Anne and Will both looked at the widening gap in the trees before them, but they weren't prepared for what they saw as the car followed the road as it curved left.

A stone mansion sat on a small rise before them. The road they'd been driving on ran ahead to meet an elegant stone staircase, and then looped around to rejoin itself. The mansion looked exactly like a castle. It even had a tower projecting from the middle.

"Wow," Anne breathed. "I wouldn't even have known how to dream of something like this."

Beth and Marc pulled into the driveway and found Anne and Will standing in front of the house in amazement. Beth couldn't blame them. Rachel's new house looked more like a small castle.

Marc parked the car along the edge of the circular drive, and then he and Beth joined the Bradleys.

"Will swears to me that there's something strange about this front door, but I just can't see it. How about you guys?"

Beth and Marc looked at the door, tipping their heads from side to side. Suddenly, they both began to laugh.

"So I'm the only one who doesn't get it?" Anne looked at the rest of them in exasperation.

Will took her by the shoulders and walked her away from the house a few steps. "Now try. Look at the top of the door frame."

Anne obeyed, and suddenly she saw what everyone else had been seeing. The front door was framed by a giant's open mouth. Above the doorway could be seen his angry eyes and gnarled nose. Stepping through the door was like stepping into his mighty roar of rage.

"This would be a great place for a Halloween party!"

They all turned as they heard Karen and Kevin pull up and waited for them to join the group.

They both saw the giant right away.

"So, I guess I'm the slow-brained person of the evening." Anne shrugged and then marched up the horseshoe staircase to the front door and rang the bell.

From far away inside the house, they heard the clicking of heels, and then Rachel was opening the door, cigarette in hand. "Welcome."

"Rachel, this place is terrific!"

"Be sure to tell R.J. He thinks it was an extravagant waste of money." She threw a glance behind her shoulder and then posted a silent appeal to her friends as R.J. joined her.

Marc stepped forward to shake R.J.'s hand. "I'm Marc. This house is great. Beth said you'd moved to a new place, but she didn't say it was a castle!"

Rachel winced. Not exactly what she'd been hoping they'd say.

R.J. sent her a "what did I tell you" look before clasping Marc's hand and pulling him into the house. "Don't tell me. I just live here. Come to think about it, don't tell the base commander, either. He'll report to DC that our housing allowance is too high!"

Rachel jabbed him with her elbow before he disappeared into the house with the guys. Then she smiled at her friends and ushered them through the door.

Anne, Beth, and Karen hardly had words to describe what they saw as they were led down a long hallway through the house to the patio behind. The first set of rooms off the hallway were a contrast in color and style. To the left, a white room with gilded moldings was filled with delicate canary yellow furniture. To the right, a smaller sage green room was lined with bookshelves and housed a sturdy pair of plum-colored velvet armchairs. Next they passed by an orange room spiked with modern African art and a blond wood-paneled dining room with red-and-yellow brocade-upholstered chairs and a table that was at least 20 feet long. The hallway ended in a circular room that was ringed with columns and topped with a glass cupola. In the center was a blue circular piece of furniture that sprouted a huge palmetto tree from its center and sat six people in an outward facing ring. Scattered around the room were several couches that had special curved frames which allowed three people to sit—the two on each end facing one direction, and the third in the middle, the other—and carry on a conversation.

They followed Rachel through a door in the wall, hidden between two columns, and walked into a jungle. The air was thick with humidity and laced with the primitive smell of earth. This last room of the bottom floor housed Rachel's prized exotic plant collection, as well as several birds.

The whole tour had been like walking through a museum. Rachel gradually became aware that no one was talking. She pushed aside the broad leaves of a large banana tree. "Just come through here and we'll join the men by the pool."

Anne, Beth, and Karen followed meekly behind her.

The guys were already deeply involved in conversation and firmly ensconced around a turned-iron-and-glass patio table. Rachel dragged over heavy cushioned iron chairs so the women could join them. They were talking about a favorite military topic: promotion boards.

"So, R.J.," Marc was saying, "what do you think about the new major's boards policy?"

"No below the zone promotions? I think it sucks."

"Below the zone, above the area, I can never understand what you're talking about!" Rachel stamped a foot as she broke into the conversation.

R.J. pulled her onto his lap as he explained. "There are official periods in every career when you are looked at for promotion. First promotion is from second lieutenant to first lieutenant, and it happens when you've been in the Air Force two years. The second promotion is from first lieutenant to captain, and it happens at four years. The third promotion is from captain to major, and that happens at about the II-year point. That year, you are in the zone for promotion, so that year is the year you should be promoted. Used to be you could be looked at starting your tenth year. If you were promoted in your tenth or eleventh year, you were promoted below the zone, or ahead of what is expected. If you don't make your promotion in your twelfth year, you're still looked at for the next two years. If you get promoted in your thirteenth or fourteenth year—"

"Then it's above the zone."

"Exactly. Except they don't do below the zone to major anymore. Just to lieutenant colonel and above."

Rachel spread her hands in front of her, palms out. "Time for a commercial break. No one talks any more until they tell me what they want to drink. I have Lillet, Pinneau, Porto…?"

"We also have beer, colas, and all that other stuff," R.J. added.

"Sprite?" Kevin asked.

"That too."

Rachel took the drink orders and disappeared into her jungle to fill them. The others returned to the conversation.

"So was this change a big deal?" Anne asked. "How many people ever got promoted like that?"

"About two a year," Marc said.

"No, maybe six," Will said. "It was never very many, but if you were one of them, then your career was set. You were golden."

"How do you get promoted below the zone?" Karen was curious.

"Be a pilot, for one thing," Kevin said.

Everyone turned to look at R.J.

He shrugged. What could he say? It was the truth.

"In fairness, the Air Force is about flying," Will conceded. "If you're not a pilot, you're not making general. That's a given."

"Not completely true," Marc argued.

Give me a break, Will seemed to say with his eyes. "Mostly true."

"Mostly." Marc could agree with that.

"So how do you get promoted?" asked Anne.

"That, my dear, is the twenty-four-thousand-dollar question," Will told her.

"Talk to ten colonels, and you'll get ten different answers." Kevin slumped back into his chair.

"Well, you have to go to SOS," R.J. began.

"Squadron officer school," Kevin whispered into Karen's ear. "It's a five-week leadership training course in Montgomery. Two weeks of school stretched into a five-week course."

"Well, sure. You're supposed to go, but has your organization sent anyone recently? It's not like you can send yourself," Will pointed out.

"You can always do it by correspondence." Marc himself had done it that very way.

"But you don't have a chance at distinguished graduate then," R.J. added.

"If you graduate at the top of the class, it shows on your record," Kevin whispered again into Karen's ear.

"Okay, so everyone agrees that you have to go, but they don't send everyone?" This sort of policy sounded a little screwy to Anne.

"It's hard for some people to fit it in between assignments. And if your organization has limited slots, then they can't send everyone. So they usually send the person who's been around the longest but hasn't gone. If your luck is wrong…" Will let his voice trail as he shrugged.

"Okay. So even SOS is open for discussion," said Anne. "Does it matter if you go in residence?"

"Yes," said R.J., nodding.

"But have people been promoted who do it by correspondence?" Anne clarified.

"Yes."

"So…?"

"Well, here's something. Operational experience. I was talking with a general once, and he said that to make colonel, I'd need operational experience." Will took a long look at everyone. "How am I going to get operational experience working with an airplane as a public affairs specialist?" He threw his hands up in the air and shook his head. "And the scary thing was that this general had just sat on a promotion board."

"Sign me up for that complaint," Marc said. As an aero engineer, he didn't have any chance at operational experience either. "How about this? One of the recent Secretaries of the Air Force decided that basic research and development functions should be performed by private sources like universities or other laboratories. No more military doing R and D. Do you know how many developmental engineers there are in the Air Force? If his policy takes precedence, what promotion board would even want to promote engineers?"

Rachel returned with Paolo and handed around the drinks. "Why is promotion such a big deal, anyway? That's all it seems you guys ever talk about."

"Because it's up or out," Marc responded. "If you don't get promoted, they boot you. And you don't get any of your retirement. So your only hope of touching retirement is putting in all 20 years. People think the military has it easy. You get in when you're 21 and retire at 41 to start a second career. But it's 20 years or nothing. And it's not us who decide if we stay in. It's the promotion boards."

"I didn't realize that." Rachel's eyebrows knit together. That was a rather odd policy.

"And this is officers complaining," Marc added. "Some of the enlisted can spend entire careers on food stamps."

Anne thought Will must be exaggerating. "But they're working for the government!"

"They're working for the military," he corrected.

"That just doesn't seem right."

"So there must be *some* kind of ideal career." Anne still couldn't get a handle on the Air Force's promotion practices.

"Pilot," all the guys said at the same time.

Anne rolled her eyes. "I mean besides the rated people. The ones who fly. There must be some solid advice on getting promoted."

"That's the thing, there isn't. I guess the closest would be that you shouldn't spend your career in one location doing the exact same thing. Like in the Air Force Research Lab. There are branches in Florida, Ohio, New Mexico, and Massachusetts. You could move locations every three years, and it would still look bad because you're still working for AFRL," Marc warned.

"But what else can you do?" Anne asked.

"Career broadening. It gets you out of your field and into something else. Like the Engineer and Scientist Exchange Program in Europe. Or attending some other country's professional military education program," Marc said.

"If you can do something different than the norm, then it makes you stand out." R.J. added. He could agree with that.

"But you just said there was no norm." Anne was really getting frustrated now.

"Well—"

"Listen, I've heard the Army does it better," Kevin was saying.

"The Army?" Marc found that hard to believe.

"The Air Force compares all of us to each other: pilot, PR, civil engineer, aero engineer. There are a predetermined number of slots for promotion, and we all compete for them."

"Sounds about right," Marc said.

"In the Army you only compete against other people in your field."

"That makes more sense. So none of the rest of us would be competing against R.J.?" Will liked that idea.

"Nope."

"How'd the Army get so smart?" Will asked.

Kevin shrugged.

"Bottom line is that there is no clear way to get promoted." Anne had finally figured it out.

"Nope."

"Well, then here's what I think," she continued. "Take the jobs you want to take, the jobs that sound like fun. That way, you'll like the jobs you do, and if at any point you're made to get out, at least you won't have regretted what you did during your career. Sound good?"

The guys all shrugged.

"Good. Because you are forbidden from talking about promotion boards for the rest of the night." Anne had grown tired of talking around a subject that for all intents and purposes appeared to be imcomprehensible.

Karen took the opportunity of a break in the conversation to let her gaze wander over the backyard. Her breath caught as she saw the pool. There were columns standing sentry over it on the opposite side. Ivy spilled onto the glazed terra cotta tiles that surrounded the pool area, and palmettos were everywhere. There was a huge ceramic jug, as tall as she was, tipped on its side. Water spilled from its mouth into the pool.

She caught Rachel's eye. "I love your pool."

"Thanks. I don't swim in it very often, but I like the sound of it. Looks Italian, don't you think?"

Karen nodded. She'd never been to Italy, but she could easily imagine it looking like this.

They chatted amiably for another hour. Rachel eventually lit some citronella candles to keep the mosquitoes away. Beth began to wonder when they'd eat. It was already eight o'clock. She'd told the babysitter to expect them home around ten.

Anne began to stir in her chair. She didn't like being cooped up in one place for so long.

Half an hour later, a buzzer sounded.

Rachel got up and pushed a button that no one had noticed on the outside wall. She spoke for several seconds before releasing it and turning to call everyone in to dinner.

Kevin smiled a huge smile of relief. He was practically dying of starvation.

Everyone followed Rachel and R.J. back through the plant maze and into the house. They sat in the red-and-yellow dining room they'd had a glimpse of on their way to the patio.

Anne was impressed by the salad. It was heated chèvre cheese on toast served on a bed of foreign-looking greens. She took a bite. It was wonderful. The vinaigrette was tangy without being too powerful. The greens were crisp and flavorful without being bitter. And the cheese! She had never known how creamy goat cheese could be.

Karen couldn't believe what they were being served. "Surf 'n' Turf" R.J. had called it. Karen called it expensive. Outrageously expensive! T-bone steaks and huge lobsters. Accompanied by something Rachel had called Potatoes Dauphinoise. They looked like tator tots without appearing to have been shredded.

Beth could hardly finish dessert. And that was saying a lot, because she loved chocolate. But this was beyond even a death-by-chocolate experience. She couldn't think of the words to describe it. It wasn't a cake or a brownie or a pie, but it was cut in a wedge and it was heavenly.

Marc heaved a sigh and pushed himself slightly away from the table. "That was absolutely wonderful!"

Karen agreed, but she wished it hadn't been so rich. She could already feel her stomach roiling in rebellion.

Beth took a surreptitious glance at her watch. Her eyes widened. It was eleven o'clock. They'd been eating for almost three hours! "I didn't realize how late it was! Our poor babysitter."

"You can't go until you've had coffee."

"It would keep me awake for hours at this time of night," Anne said.

"Not to mention me," Marc chimed in.

Everyone laughed.

"Coffee for anyone?" Rachel asked.

No one took her up on the offer.

Karen hated to be the first one to leave the table, but she was going to explode. "Could I use your bathroom?" she asked Rachel.

"Sure. Second door on the left. It blends in with wall, so you'll have to look for it."

She was right. It took Karen five minutes to locate it and another couple to figure out how to operate the latch. By that time her stomach cramps had made her break out in a cold sweat. She reached the toilet not a moment too soon.

When she reappeared to join the crowd, they were all standing in the hall near the front door. Rachel was thanking them for coming.

"Anytime you need a housesitter, ask me!" Anne said. "I'm serious. Thanks so much. It was a fabulous meal in a fabulous house."

All the others echoed her sentiments.

"Is everyone going to the CGO Halloween Party?" Marc asked, pumping the event for his organization.

They all nodded.

"In costume," he added. "You have to go in costume. It's Halloween. It doesn't have to be something extravagant. Just simple. Any kind of costume."

"Yeah, yeah," Anne muttered. "That's what the guys always say. It's the girls who always have to figure those things out."

Karen and Beth agreed as they walked out the door and to their cars.

Beth still hadn't figured out the garbageman costume for Josh, let alone something for her and Marc.

Rachel and R.J. stood silhouetted in the doorway until the last of the cars disappeared around the bend.

"That was nice, huh?" Rachel asked R.J. as she leaned against him.

"It was nice." He wrapped his arms around her and gave a squeeze. "But I still think this place is way too big."

"I wonder how they can afford that place." Anne said to Will as they made their way slowly through the forest. Their headlights panned up and down through the trees as the car grappled with the road.

"R.J. can't, even with his flight pay. That I know for sure."

"It must be Rachel's money, then."

"I guess."

"Must be nice to be rich."

CHAPTER 14

*T*he evening of the CGO Halloween Party came as if it were specially ordered for the occasion: crisp and clear with a full moon.

Anne and Will arrived half an hour late. The party was already raucous.

They found Rachel and R.J. at a table just off the dance floor.

"King Arthur and Guinevere," Rachel said, eliminating their need to guess.

R.J. wore his crooked crown and colored tights well. And the circlet on Rachel's head might always have been there.

"Man in a windstorm," explained Will, holding up his inside-out umbrella and leaning as if he were walking against the wind.

"And highway with roadkill," said Anne, holding up her arms. Her black cat suit had yellow felt rectangles pasted up the center and a small squashed stuffed animal stapled to her side.

R.J. lurched to his feet. "Roadkill? I'm going to be sick." He held out an unsteady hand toward Rachel. "Want to dance?"

Beth and her husband waved at Anne and Will from the back of the room.

"Pair of dice?" Will guessed.

"Looks like it," Anne responded. "Look! There's Karen and Kevin. Let's go say hi."

They weaved their way through the crowd.

"Hey, Karen!"

"Hi, Anne. We're Napoleon and Josephine."

"Great costumes," said Will, shaking Kevin's hand.

"You look like a ghost, Karen. Are you in there anywhere?" Anne asked. Karen looked so thin that Anne feared she'd float off into the netherworld at any moment. And the light blue gauze of the dress made her skin look even more pale.

Kevin squeezed Karen's hand. "She's even thinner than when we got married. And people say they get worse with age! Not my Karen."

"Why don't you sit with us?" Karen suggested.

Anne looked at Will and shrugged. What she really wanted to do was dance, but she guessed that could wait. Will pulled out a chair for her and she sat down.

"Now there's a costume!" Will said with a low whistle as a would-be Elvira slunk by.

Anne looked at Karen and rolled her eyes. She punched Will's arm. "What am I? Roadkill? Don't you love me anymore?" She laughed at her own joke.

Karen felt the sharp barb of envy. She wished she were so convinced of Kevin's love that she could joke about it.

Rachel and R.J. danced by.

"How come they always look so perfect together? Even when they're falling-down drunk?" Kevin asked rhetorically.

"How's your job going?" Karen asked Anne.

"What job?" Anne snorted. "Answering phones and typing letters? I could do it with my eyes closed."

"All right," said Will, slapping the table. "It's time for my wife to dance with me, unless she's afraid she'll be blown away...?"

"Ha-ha," said Anne, rising to her feet. "Not a chance. You guys dance?"

Karen shook her head. She didn't like dancing. She never knew what to do with her hands. Or her feet.

Rachel and R.J. fell into the seats Anne and Will had left empty.

"Hi," said Rachel, adjusting R.J.'s slipping crown.

"Hi. I like your costumes," said Karen.

"Really?" said Rachel, frowning down at hers. "I like yours."

"Thanks."

Rachel grabbed R.J.'s hand. "Hey, lover, light my fire."

He smiled and then bent down to kiss her. After that, his fingers drummed the table, keeping time with the music. "Halloween's my favorite holiday."

"Better than Christmas?" Kevin asked.

"Much better. On Halloween you can be anything you want. On Christmas you have to be what everyone else expects you to be. You have to listen to everyone tell stories about the things you did when you were little, and you realize that they all think you're still twelve." He paused to re-create the drum solo on the table. "No thanks. Halloween is fun without the expectations. And you don't have to spend it with family; you get to spend it with your friends. It's the perfect holiday. You actually get to do what *you* want to do."

Work had settled into a routine for Anne. The city manager was never anything but pleasant to her. His only two requirements were that she take a phone number for every phone message she gave him and that she try to keep his plants alive. The latter was a bit unfair; Anne suspected that his scraggly ferns were planted in soil he dug up from his own yard. But she was giving it her best effort.

The work was easy. She answered phones and made copies. She was the gatekeeper of the filing system and did any other work she could dredge up. Mr. Trumble had an executive secretary, Nita, who took dictation, managed his calendar, and drafted his correspondence. Nita had worked for 20 years in the city manager's office, a fact that gave her even more authority than the city council members.

The job was a crash course in local government. Anne had known that states were divided into counties, and counties were populated by cities, but she had no concept of what city business was or how it was accomplished. Liffsbury, at least, had seven city council members who were the symbolic heads of the city. They appointed a city manager who oversaw the daily operations of city departments like public works, with its responsibilities for the cemeteries, recycling, and water and sewer operations. He was also the head of the fire department, parks and recreation, human resources, and purchasing. Mr. Trumble was responsible for implementing the desires of the city council. He was also the liaison between the city council and the agencies they contracted with, such as animal control and waste removal services. The council members were elected; the city manager was appointed.

Anne came into contact with the council members frequently. They were an interesting bunch. Among them were one career politician, one retired colonel, one retired master sergeant, one libertarian, and one self-made millionaire. And theirs was a tense relationship with Mr. Trumble. None of them wanted to be accused of passing their job over to the city manager, but none of them had the technical expertise to be able to oversee the departments the way Mr. Trumble did. They wanted the city manager to do his job well, but they didn't want him to do it too loudly or obviously enough that they were shown up. The city manager was constantly on the phone building consensus with the council members, keeping them informed of everything he did. And somehow, he found enough time to meet with his department heads and take phone calls from city citizens.

From answering phone calls and taking complaints, Anne found out lots of things she'd never known before, such as who was responsible for filling potholes and changing traffic lights. Who cleaned the beaches, who enforced jet ski regulations, and who assigned street addresses. Every time someone called, she had to put them on hold and ask Nita for the answer.

She propped her head up on an elbow and watched the second hand on the clock spin around again.

"Shall we go?" Anne called across the hall and into Nita's office. The city manager had left at 4:30 and told them they could leave when they were done.

"Nope. Can't leave yet."

"Why not?"

"Because Ethel always calls at 5:00 on Fridays."

"Who's Ethel?"

"One of my favorite citizens," Nita said, although it was clear that she was lying.

"What does she call about?"

"She wants to make sure someone's here on Fridays until 5:00."

"What if you're not?"

"It's a matter of honor at this point."

Anne hated to ask, but she did it anyway. "Can I go?"

"Of course." Nita waved her away from across the hall. "Go. Have a nice weekend."

"The chili smells great!"

"I read an article the other day that said you could use yogurt instead of sour cream. It has less fat."

Kevin dumped a dollop of yogurt onto his chili and then took a big bite. He had finished his bowl before he realized Karen was just picking at hers. "Aren't you hungry?"

"Not really. I was when I started cooking, but I'm not anymore."

"Too much taste-testing."

Karen smiled. "Something like that."

He came around the table and pulled her to her feet. "I got a present for you today."

"What is it?"

"Something I think you'll like." Kevin walked to his briefcase and pulled a paper sleeve from it, and then he came back to Karen and placed it in her hands. It was from a travel agency.

Karen tore it open. "Plane tickets? To Salt Lake City! We're going home?"

"For Christmas."

"We're going home!"

The food committee met on November 2 to plan for the Christmas bazaar.

"So how'd your shift at the Haunted House go?" Beth asked Anne. So far they were the only two there on time.

"It was great! Those kids were so cute. There was even one dressed as Big Bird. People are so creative. What did the twins dress up as?"

"I made the mistake of asking them what they wanted to be. So Josh was a garbageman aka construction worker, and Andy was a train. Hard hat and overalls for Josh; that wasn't really too hard. But Andy was a little difficult. We finally painted a cardboard box and strapped it onto him with suspenders. And we were able to find an engineer's cap and striped overalls. They both looked pretty cute."

"How was your shift? It had just gotten busy when we switched off."

Beth agreed. "You had it easy compared to the hoards I had. Plus the fact that all the kids were hungry. I felt like a monster, but I didn't let anyone have seconds. Or I tried not to, anyway."

Rachel slipped into a seat beside them.

"How was your shift?" Beth asked.

"Fine. Slow. I even had some cake." She smiled.

"Anyone hear from Karen?"

"She should be here soon."

Beth took a file folder from her canvas bag instead of the usual fistful of papers. "I'm trying to get myself organized before Christmas." She took a sheaf of papers from it.

Karen appeared in the doorway and walked over to join them. "Sorry I'm late. I had to wait for a ride from Kevin, and he got tied up."

"I could've picked you up. Just give me a call next time," Anne said.

"I hate to be a bother."

"It's no bother. Really. I drive past you on my way here."

Beth tried to get them all to focus. "The bazaar is going to be held the first Saturday in December. We're responsible for the OSC food booth."

"So cookies and spice breads? Things like that?" Karen guessed.

Beth read further down last year's report. "No. They did that last year, and some of the vendors complained because it took business away from them. But we need to sell something to raise scholarship money."

"What time does it run?" Anne asked.

"From 10:00 until 5:00," Beth replied.

"Is anyone else selling food for lunch and dinner?" Rachel asked.

"No. At least they didn't last year."

"That's what we should focus on then. What about a nice *Carbonnade* or *Cassoulet?*"

"What are those?"

"Thick soups. Substantial. Good in the cold weather."

Karen hated to disagree, but... "That might be a bit messy. We should sell something that people can eat standing up while they walk around."

"Nothing hot, then."

"No."

"We could always do hot dogs. Those are easy," Beth suggested.

Anne and Rachel wrinkled their noses.

"Not at a Christmas bazaar. Hot dogs are good at baseball games. Christmas needs something special," Anne said.

"Baguette sandwiches are easy. Brie or camembert, *rillettes, paté,*" Rachel suggested.

"What about turkey?" Karen asked. Turkey had much less fat in it than cheese.

Rachel frowned, but everyone else nodded approval.

"*Paté* won't go over well. I can tell you that right now. But Brie would be a nice touch. What about Brie and then turkey with cranberries and cream cheese?" Beth was already making notes.

"Cranberries, but without cream cheese, because if someone is allergic to milk, then at least they'll be able to eat something." Karen was planning to have a crafts table, and she didn't want to have to starve that Saturday. And she definitely wouldn't eat cream cheese. Just the word cream made her stomach quiver.

"Sounds good. Brie and turkey baguette sandwiches." Beth noted it on the worksheet. "That takes care of lunch. We can sell cans of soda. What about if people just want a snack?"

Anne gave the question some thought. "Maybe hot drinks, like hot chocolate."

"And mulled wine," Rachel added, her mouth watering for the *glugwein* she'd had last year at a Christmas market in Germany.

"Can't. We don't have a liquor license." Beth shook her head. "Too bad, though, because it's a good idea."

"Spiced cider?" That was always Karen's favorite at Christmas.

"That sounds good!" Anne was pleased with the idea. "Hot chocolate—maybe we can even squirt some whipped cream on it—and spiced cider."

"We could serve them in red and green cups."

"Good idea." Beth noted all the suggestions on the worksheet. "That's it then. We'll need napkins, of course. Anyone think of anything else?"

"Coffee, maybe?" Anne asked.

"Tea then too. Regular and herbal." Karen knew there would be other people besides herself who wouldn't drink caffeine.

"The bazaar is from 10:00 until 5:00. Is there really a need for coffee? For coffee and tea, we'll need at least two machines and two pots for each. Then we'd have to have cream and sugar and stirrers. With the cider and hot chocolate, we'll only need thermal pots."

"No coffee." Anne could see her reasoning.

"That looks like about it." Beth glanced at her watch. They'd only been there half an hour. "We're getting more efficient! Congratulations, you guys. I'll talk with the kitchen and ask them to cost everything, and then I'll submit our ideas to the OSC board. When I hear back, I'll let you know. We can plan our shifts closer to December."

Karen hated to bring it up, but she had to. "I'm sorry, but I won't be able to staff the counter because I'll be selling some crafts at the bazaar."

"What do you make?"

"I tat."

"I'm not sure whether to congratulate you or incarcerate you," Anne joked.

"It's a type of lace made using a shuttle. A lost art. My grandmother taught me," she said, flushing with the attention they were all giving her. "Anyway, you can make snowflakes for Christmas tree ornaments…and that's what I'll be selling."

"They sound beautiful." Karen looked so uncomfortable that Anne regretted cracking the joke.

They talked about plans for Thanksgiving for a few minutes. Beth was having dinner with some friends. Karen had already agreed to cook a turkey for a church event. Anne hadn't even thought ahead that far yet.

"How about you, Rachel?"

"We're going to R.J.'s parents'."

"That's nice. Do you get along with them?" Beth asked.

"I don't know. I've never met them."

CHAPTER 15

*O*kay, are you ready?" R.J. asked, fiddling with the car radio. He'd been adjusting knobs and buttons on the rental car's dashboard since they'd left the airport. The country they were driving through was half sky. Rachel had never seen anything like it. She'd never felt so dwarfed by a landscape. When she'd mentioned it to R.J., he had grinned and said that Montana was known as Big Sky Country. At the time, he'd been relaxed. Now, two hours later, he was getting tenser by the minute.

"R.J., relax. I'm fine, except that you're making me nervous."

"I'm sorry. I just want everything to work out."

"It will." Rachel paused a moment in thought. "Are you worried that I won't like them or that they won't like me?"

"I don't know." He switched radio stations again.

"Of course you do. Which is it?"

R.J. positioned and then repositioned his hands around the steering wheel. "I'm just afraid that you won't understand each other."

"What's that supposed to mean?"

"My parents are deaf."

"Deaf?"

"Deaf."

"Like in they can't hear anything?"

"No."

"Then what do you do when you visit?"

"What do you mean?"

"I mean, literally, what do you do?"

"We visit; we fish. We take walks." R.J. took a deep breath. "The reason I never told you before was that I didn't want you to worry."

"About what?"

"About me going deaf or our kids being born deaf. You know, stuff like that."

That thought had never crossed my mind. Let alone the thought of having kids. "So it's not hereditary?"

"No. My mom got meningitis when she was little. They thought she was going to die. She didn't, but when she recovered, they found that she'd lost her hearing."

"What about your dad?"

"Dad was born deaf, but it's not genetic."

"What was it like when you were growing up?"

"Normal. For me, anyway. It had its advantages. Mom and Dad never yelled at me."

She smiled and put a hand up to massage his neck.

"That feels great." He leaned forward toward the steering wheel. "Would you mind? My left shoulder, just underneath the shoulder blade."

She began to massage his back.

"You have the best hands, Rach. If I were a dog, my foot would be going a mile a minute."

"So, do you know sign language?"

"Like a native."

Rachel mulled over the new discovery for a few minutes. "That must have been hard growing up. You probably felt like you had to be extra good. That it wasn't fair to them if you did some of the things teenagers usually do."

R.J. gave her an appraising glance. "You're right. I didn't want to give them any more trouble than they already had."

"You said you played football in high school?"

"Star quarterback." He struck a pose and looked at himself in the rearview mirror.

"Did they watch you play?"

"Every game."

"How did they cheer?"

"Between you and me, in junior high there wasn't much to cheer for."

Rachel laughed.

"But in high school, they mostly cheered with their eyes."

"Their eyes?"

"You'll see." R.J. made a wide left turn off the highway and swung onto a small dirt road. "Rach?"

"Yes?"

"I'm sorry I didn't tell you before."

Rachel plastered on her society smile as she saw R.J.'s mother and father step out onto the porch. Large jumping dogs surrounded them. *Great. It's only for a week. Smiles, everyone.*

It was a strange experience to be part of a family reunion and hear no words being exchanged. But R.J. was right, his parents did communicate with their eyes.

His father was as tall as R.J. He might have been taller at one time, but he now stood with a slight hunch.

Better keep an eye on R.J. to make sure he doesn't start slouching around.

His father's hair was still black, except at the temples, where it was beginning to gray. He looked exactly like what he was: a rancher. A ruddy complexion spoke of many hours spent outdoors. And he had a straightforward manner she'd always associated with people who worked for themselves.

R.J.'s mother was tall and slender. Her hair, too, was just beginning to show her age. It was sandy blond, cut short and swept away from her face. Wearing jeans and a thick turtleneck sweater, she looked as uncomplicated as her husband.

In fact, they looked just like a normal family, except that they were all talking in sign language. R.J. accompanied his sign language with speech. Rachel had no doubt that it was for her benefit.

"The flight was fine. No turbulence. I could have done a better landing, but, then again, this is vacation."

His father smiled and clapped him on the back. Then he made a series of signs.

"It's good to *be* back."

Rachel was known for confidence in social situations, but this was not like anything she'd ever experienced. She was out of her element. And she was trying to keep the dogs from sniffing around her.

R.J. saw that they were bothering her and snapped his fingers. Immediately they sat down, watching him with expectant eyes. He put an arm around her and drew her forward.

"And this is Rachel," he simultaneously said and signed.

R.J.'s mother smiled and then opened her arms to her.

Rachel stepped forward and was engulfed in a hug. It was strange to be accepted without reservation by someone she'd never met.

"Dad's saying he understands now why I waited so long to get married. There really were better fish in the sea."

"You can tell him that the best fish of all is his son."

R.J.'s dad smiled at her.

She responded by kissing him on the cheek.

Rachel soon found that the visit wasn't as bad as she had feared. Both of his parents read lips.

"It helped to have me around," R.J. explained as they were unpacking and getting settled in his old room. "That's why I got in the habit of speaking while I sign. It helped them practice."

"But how did you learn to speak?"

"They had me play with the ranch hands, and I liked to hang out in the kitchen with the cook."

"They have a cook?"

"Sure. They have about ten people who work the ranch. Mom doesn't mind cooking, but she doesn't really enjoy it. And she has her own work to do."

"What's she do?"

"She's a sculptor. I'm sure she'll show you her studio if you ask."

"Maybe you can ask for me."

"Maybe you can talk slow enough and enunciate clearly enough so that she can read your lips."

Rachel blushed. "I forgot."

"It's okay. Just one thing to remember."

"What's that?"

"Talking louder isn't going to make it any easier for her to understand." He managed to duck the pillow Rachel threw at him.

Later that afternoon they drove into town.

R.J. had warned her that it was small, but Rachel couldn't comprehend how anyone could spend a childhood in a place so tiny. There were two main parallel streets, and after that, the town surrendered to vast open fields. The only visual stimulation she found were the clouds that ran laps between the horizons. They walked the two main streets in 20 minutes, R.J. popping in and out of stores to greet the owners. He knew them all. And it was plain to see that he took pleasure in introducing Rachel to each of them.

He insisted that they eat lunch at his old high school hangout: T's Burgers.

"They have the best shakes!" he exclaimed as they slid into a booth and sat on red vinyl-covered benches.

Rachel looked over the greasy plastic-covered menu without enthusiasm. "What do you recommend?"

"I always have the T-Rex burger, but it's a triple decker." He consulted the menu. "Get a Baby T with curly fries."

Rachel shook her head. She only had fries in Belgium, their birthplace, where the crispy outsides hid melt-in-your-mouth insides. She ordered a Baby T without fries and a vanilla milkshake. Vanilla was her quality index for milkshakes. Only if she could see black flecks of vanilla beans and taste the richness of real cream was a milkshake worthy of the title.

The hamburgers hadn't changed at all in R.J.'s opinion, which was too bad as far as Rachel was concerned. They could have done with a makeover.

The milkshake, however, was fantastic.

"What did you do here?" Rachel asked as they drove back home.

"What do you mean?"

"For fun. What did you do?"

R.J. looked out the window at the expanse of open fields. "I don't know."

"For instance, what would you do after a football game?"

He couldn't suppress his smile. "We'd go to T's Burgers after every game. But they close at midnight. So after that, sometimes, we'd go to my friend Al's."

"And do what?"

He began to turn red around his collar. "Umm...we'd go with whoever we were dating, and...you know...his parents traveled a lot."

"No. I don't know. Tell me." She couldn't keep the edge out of her voice.

"Gosh, Rach. We were just kids."

Why did this revelation about her husband's sexual history bother her?

R.J. shot her a sideways look, and then he guided the car over to the shoulder and pulled the emergency brake. He turned to her and took her hand. "Rachel, if I had known there was you, believe me, I would never have done any of those things."

She looked at him a long time, and then she took his face between her hands, drew it forward, and kissed him on the forehead. "I know."

For dinner, the four Hawthornes ate at one end of a long sturdy table in the dining room.

"At lunch, all the ranch hands eat here," R.J. said as they took their seats. "It's easier than going home and warmer than packing a lunch and eating it outside."

Rachel nodded. It made sense.

It was a new experience to have a meal in which only one person talked. But R.J. pulled her into their conversations, and by the end of the meal it seemed less strange.

"How about fishing tomorrow?" he asked her as he began to help his mother scrape and stack dishes.

"It's kind of cold out, isn't it?"

"We have lots of things you can wear."

The idea didn't sound very appealing, but she could tell R.J. wanted her to go. "Okay."

His mother made a flurry of signs from across the table.

"Mom has boots and a down coat you can borrow."

"Thanks."

The next day R.J. woke her way too early.

"It's time to get up." He poked her in the ribs with an elbow before jumping out of bed.

Rachel rolled onto her stomach and pulled the pillow over her head. "Why?"

"Because," R.J. said as if she were obtuse, "we're going fishing, remember?"

"The fish are still sleeping."

"They're biting. They've been up all night swimming, and now they're hungry."

"Then tell them to swim on down to T's Burgers."

"Come on!" he pulled the wool blanket off the bed. "You'll miss breakfast if you don't get going."

"What time is it? Just out of curiosity."

"Just before 5:00."

"I thought this was supposed to be vacation."

"It is." He stripped the sheet from Rachel, causing her to curl into herself like a sea anemone.

"I need something to wear."

"Right here." R.J. dumped a pile of clothes onto the bed.

Rachel gave in to the inevitable, uncurling her legs and then swinging them over the side of the bed. She dressed in a daze, and it was only when she passed a mirror in the hall that she realized what she looked like. She never would have recognized herself. She no longer had a shape. She was a series of bumps lumped one on top of another. Three pairs of socks, thermal underwear, black turtleneck, navy wool sweater, moss green wool pants, and flaming orange flannel-lined overalls. She carried a school-bus-yellow down jacket and a red stocking cap in her arms. She could no longer walk, so she shuffled along the hardwood floors until she came to the dining room, and then she could hardly sit down.

"Is all of this really necessary?" she mumbled to R.J. She took a sip of strong black coffee and nibbled at a piece of toast.

"We're going to be out all morning. And once we start fishing, we won't be moving around much." At least he looked as awful as she did. They could have been twins.

She smiled a perfunctory smile and reminded herself that it was just four hours. She could do anything for four hours.

R.J., his dad, and Rachel piled into a stripped-down pick-up truck. The heater wasn't on, so Rachel leaned forward to adjust it.

"Don't," R.J. said.

"Why not? It's below freezing out here."

"I know, but if you heat up the cab now, you're going to be even colder when we get out again."

Rachel closed her eyes and wished herself in Tahiti. Why did people choose to be cold when the world was always equally divided between summer and winter? If you followed the sun, you never had to look like a walking rag heap. The Riviera in the summer, Tahiti in the winter. She'd have to enlighten R.J.

She had to go to the bathroom, but she decided to wait until they got to where they were going. She'd use the one there.

After too short a time, just when she was warming up, the pickup jerked to a halt and they tumbled out. R.J. distributed the fishing rods and took the tackle box, and they started off through the woods. The leafless trees were a jumble of trunks and branches, and she could discern no path. After walking for under a minute, her rod tangled itself in a branch and refused to give.

R.J. spent several minutes unthreading it before giving it back to her. "Never carry your fishing rod facing forward." He said it as if he'd already told her that a hundred times before. "Tuck it close to your body and carry it tip *backward*. And how did the fly come unhooked anyway?" He secured it to one of the eyes on the pole.

Rachel didn't tell him that she'd unhooked it to let it dangle in front of her. She'd wanted to see what the fish saw. It was a useful exercise, seeing things from an opponent's perspective. Tears pricked her eyes. It was 5:30. She was glacially cold. And she hadn't wanted to come fishing anyway.

After ten minutes, she began to hear the sound of water, and in another five, she and R.J. followed his father down to the river.

R.J. unfastened the fly on Rachel's line and showed her how to cast. "You try," he said after a few moments.

Rachel did her best to imitate him, but the fly fell to the ground at her feet.

"You need to release the line," R.J. said.

Rachel tried again. It went further but still failed to reach the water.

"You have to release it midswing and leave the tip of the pole pointing toward the sky." R.J. took the pole from her and showed her again.

She tried once more, and it almost made it to the water.

"Let me cast it for you and you can fish from that." He was anxious to get his own line into the water.

The sound of the water was deafening. She couldn't even hear her own thoughts, and soon her mind was numbed as much from the sound as from the cold. She had to go to the bathroom, but she couldn't work up the energy to do anything about it. Her eyelids felt as though they were frozen to her eyeballs. She had no idea what she was supposed to be doing, but she knew she was getting more and more cold while she did it.

Suddenly, her fishing line snagged on something.

"R.J.!" she tried to yell above the river.

He didn't hear her.

"R.J.!"

He didn't turn.

She tried to walk away from the river, pulling the line with her, but it didn't give. She jerked the rod hard, and it suddenly broke free. But just seconds later, it stuck again. She tried reeling it in, and it worked for a few seconds, but then it wouldn't budge anymore. She decided to try to walk over to R.J. and see if he could do something. Rachel alternately jerked at the line and tried reeling it in. Over the course of 15 minutes, she finally came within yelling range.

"R.J.!"

He turned toward her voice.

She held up her rod. "Help!"

He reeled in his line quickly, came over, and took the rod from her hands. He felt the weight for a moment, gave it a tentative tug, and then let out a whoop.

"You've got a fish!"

"A fish? I thought it was stuck."

"No." He handed to pole back to her. "Bring it in."

"I don't know how."

"Just do what you've been doing."

"But I don't know how to do it."

"Just reel it in slowly."

R.J. helped her play in the fish, and in ten minutes it lay heaving on the rocks at their feet.

"It's at least a five-pounder!"

"I could tell." Her arm was beginning to hurt from the struggle.

In the distance, up river, R.J.'s dad fished, oblivious to their triumph. R.J. gave her a kiss and then picked up the fish by the gills to show his father.

Rachel walked along beside him, proud of her prize.

R.J.'s father gave her a hug and a thumbs-up. Then he returned to fishing.

Rachel watched him for several moments. "R.J.?"

"Yeah."

"Why does he like fishing?"

"What do mean?"

"You said people seem to like it because they can hear the sound of water and commune with nature. Your dad can't hear. So why does he like it?"

"Good question." R.J. caught his father's attention and signed for a moment.

His dad took a deep breath and looked out across the river. Then he looked up into the trees. Finally, he gave R.J. an answer.

"He says he likes it because he can see and feel the sound. He says that here, sound invades him. It's one of the only places he can imagine he knows what it's like to hear."

Rachel placed a hand on R.J.'s arm and squeezed.

R.J. took a camera from his pocket and made Rachel pose with her fish.

"What do you want a picture for?" she asked.

"To keep in my helmet bag. It's your first fish!"

And me looking like a street urchin. She smiled anyway.

R.J. snapped the photo, squatted down by the river, and put the fish into the water. Then he opened his hands and let it swim away.

"Hey!" Rachel yowled. "That's my fish!"

"I know. But it's a cutthroat, so it has to be released."

"Why?"

"Because there aren't enough of them around."

"But—" There was nothing Rachel could do but stare as it swam away. All that hard work, swept away by the river.

R.J. and Rachel walked back to their places. He cast the line for her again and then handed over the rod. The excitement of the big catch wore off and the cold seeped in through her clothes. Finally she couldn't stand it any longer. She worked her way over to R.J. "Where's the bathroom?" she yelled above the rumble of the water. It was so cold that her face had lost its flexibility; her mouth had trouble moving.

"What bathroom?"

"The bathroom where I can go to the bathroom."

"There isn't a bathroom. You'll have to squat somewhere."

Squat somewhere? "Where?"

R.J. shrugged and looked around. "Just go up the bank and pick a tree."

"Easy for you to say! How am I supposed to go to the bathroom in this?"

"Can't you just hold it?"

"I've been just holding it since we got here."

He reached out to take her fishing rod from her. "Go ahead and find someplace above the bank. I'll hang on to this for you."

She looked at him unbelievingly. There really was no bathroom. She wouldn't have had coffee at breakfast had she known. Forlorn, she turned away and stumbled up the riverbank. At the top she tried to look for a good place, but nothing materialized into a toilet seat. Finally, she found a fallen tree she thought she could climb up and sit on. The immediate problem was how to get her clothes off in order not to soil them. She started with the coat. That was easy. She hung it on a branch next to her.

She had overalls, wool pants, long johns, and her own underwear to figure out what to do with next. She unhooked the overalls underneath her sweater. They dropped to the ground. She tried to pull them off over her boots, but the leg openings were too small and she fell over trying to wrestle with them. So she took her boots off and then pulled off the overalls, the pants, and the long johns. It was even colder out than she had thought.

She began to shiver.

At least she still had her sweater and turtleneck and thermal shirt on. She climbed onto her perch and tried to relax. But it was hard to relax while she was trying not to fall off and shivering at the same time.

Rachel had been gone so long that R.J. had begun to worry. He left both of their poles with his father and went looking for her, rounding the top of the hill. He stomped through the trees.

He was expecting to see her sitting on the ground or maybe limping through the trees toward him with a twisted ankle. He was completely unprepared to see her sitting half-naked on a tree, crying her eyes out.

He ran toward her, careening off tree trunks. "What happened!" He gathered her clothes from the branches beside her and began to pull them on her.

"I can't go to the bathroom in the *woods*. How am I supposed to go to the bathroom?" She was indignant.

"You just squat. Why'd you climb up on this tree?"

"Because you have to sit down to go to the bathroom."

"Well, then why did you take your pants off?"

"So I wouldn't go to the bathroom on them," she wailed in between shivers. "And now, I can't even go."

He took her down from the tree and sheltered her with his body as he helped her finish putting her clothes on.

He enfolded her in his arms until she stopped shivering. "I'm sorry," he whispered into her ear.

Finally, at long last, she felt warm enough to open her eyes and talk.

"R.J.?"

He loosened his grip on her and tipped up her chin so he could see her eyes. "What?"

"I still have to go to the bathroom."

CHAPTER 16

⁓

With Mr. Trumble and Nita on vacation, it was slow at work. Anne daydreamed at her desk. In her world, she was the vice president of human resources for an international company. She had regular business trips to exotic places like Paris, London, and Rome. And, since she was daydreaming, Will always got to come with her. And really, there wasn't much business to be done on these business trips, so they got to visit all the famous things. The Eiffel Tower, the Tower of London, and the Colosseum. She sighed. *I like it in my own little world. Everyone knows me there.*

The telephone rang.

"City manager's office."

"Hello, ma'am. I'm a taxpayer, and I want to register a complaint."

Oh, no. Here we go. These people are the worst! Don't they realize everybody's a taxpayer? "Yes, ma'am."

"Do you have something to write with?"

"Yes. I'm armed and ready."

"Are you making light of my complaint?"

"Of course not. I don't even know what your complaint is yet."

"I think you're making fun of me. I want to register a complaint against you."

"Ma'am, I'm a taxpayer too."

"But, but…" the woman sputtered. "But that's insubordinate."

"No, ma'am. In order to be insubordinate, you'd have to be my employer."

"But I am. I'm a taxpayer! I pay your salary!"

"Then, by your definition, I'm self-employed. Ma'am, if you want to give me your address, I'll send you your 15 cents back. I've got no problem with that. I don't want to be employed by you anyway."

Rachel and R.J. survived the rest of their Montana holiday. Rachel still shuddered when she thought about fishing. She was glad to be back at Bullard, even if it meant doing things like taking her turn at the food committee's booth at the Christmas bazaar.

She was thinking about the possibility of a shopping trip to Paris after Christmas when she relieved Beth at the counter, so she was justifiably horrified when she saw the sandwiches. "These aren't baguette sandwiches!"

"Sure they are. They're on French bread."

"French bread is not a baguette." She pushed a finger into a Brie sandwich with disdain. "This is plastic foam. A baguette is long," she spread her arms apart, "and thin." She spread two fingers an inch and a half apart. "They are crunchy on the outside and moist on the inside. And baguette sandwiches are made from a third of a baguette cut horizontally in the middle."

The French bread sandwiches, protecting slices of turkey and Brie between vertical slices, received a withering look from Rachel.

"Hey, at least they're selling. I'll think we'll make a lot more than last year."

Beth decided to take a walk around the bazaar before picking up the twins. Maybe she'd even be able to cross a few Christmas presents off her list. Halfway around the periphery, she found Karen.

"Wow!" Beth was amazed at how delicate Karen's lacey snowflakes were. They ranged in size from the diameter of a half-dollar to that of a small hamburger. She even had some three-dimensional bells on display. Beth fingered several that hung from a miniature Christmas tree on the table. "These are beautiful."

"Thanks."

"How long does it take you to make them?"

"The smallest are easy. Maybe half an hour. The bells are the most difficult. They take about four or five hours."

Beth whistled softly. "How are sales?"

"Going well. I've sold more than I expected, and it's only half over!"

Beth selected several for gifts. "I'd love to see how you make these sometime."

"I'll bring my shuttle to the next food committee meeting." Karen greeted several women who had joined Beth in front of the table.

"I'll see you later," Beth whispered. "Good luck!"

That evening, Beth sighed as she put the dishes away. It had been at least a year since she'd used their nice wedding china. It was a shame because they had eight place settings. It had been ages since they'd had anyone over for dinner at all.

She brought the subject up as she and Marc were getting ready for bed.

"I was thinking that maybe we could invite some people over for dinner. We could do something kind of fancy."

Marc raised an eyebrow and continued to brush his teeth.

"Nothing like Rachel's of course, but we could have the same people over and do something nice."

"Sounds like fun."

"You don't have anything next Friday, do you?"

"No. Go ahead and set it up."

Beth called everyone the next morning. They all agreed to the date. Beth pulled out her cookbooks to decide what to make. Then she thought of the fact that she didn't have many serving dishes that matched her china. And that they didn't even have eight dining room chairs that matched. They'd always kept putting off that purchase, and now with the twins...

It doesn't matter. The point of a dinner is to get people together to eat, not to look at matching chairs or serving dishes. The point is to have fun.

Reassured by her own pep talk, she flipped through recipes before deciding on enchiladas with green sauce and a red pepper and rice salad; the colors would look nice for Christmas. Chocolate pie for dessert. It was Marc's favorite. But appetizers? She spent a half hour trying to decide on something before remembering a bean, corn, and salsa chip dip. Perfect.

The evening began flawlessly. Snowflakes started fluttering around five o'clock. Not enough snow to snarl traffic, but just enough to provide atmosphere.

Karen and Kevin arrived first.

"I love your sweatshirt!" Beth remarked as she took Karen's coat. The red sweatshirt had a big Santa face painted on it, along with "Ho-Ho-Ho."

"Thanks. It wasn't hard. I just followed the example."

"I have absolutely no talent for drawing. I don't believe you and am impressed beyond words."

Karen beamed. Beth looked cute herself in a green rolled neck sweater.

Kevin handed her a Christmas tin. "Merry Christmas."

"Thanks." Beth took a peek inside. "Toffee? You made it?"

Karen nodded.

"Fabulous. We'll serve it with dessert. Just go into the living room and make yourselves comfortable. Marc's putting the twins to bed. He'll join you in a few minutes."

Karen and Kevin were listening to festive Christmas music when one of Beth's kids ran into the living room. He was stark naked.

"Hi," he said, giving them a face-splitting grin.

"Hi," Kevin answered. "Aren't you kind of cold?"

"I'm Josh," the toddler said, oblivious to more practical concerns.

"So, where's your brother?" Kevin asked.

"With Daddy."

They heard Marc bellow the little boy's name.

"I think your daddy wants you." Kevin stooped to pick up Josh. "Why don't we go find him?"

"No bed," Josh informed them. "Want to play. You play?" He squirmed in the direction of the toy box in the corner.

"Let's go find your daddy." Kevin walked away down the hall with him.

Karen followed with her eyes until she couldn't anymore. Seeing Kevin with kids always made her wish they had some. He was so good with them. *If only…*

The doorbell rang and Beth opened it to find Rachel and R.J. She was wearing black leather pants and a low V-neck cherry red sweater. R.J. was sporting a Santa Claus hat. Shortly afterward Anne and Will joined them. Anne looked warm in a red turtleneck and forest green blazer. Will was wearing khaki pants and a heavy turtleneck sweater. By the time the new arrivals were seated, Kevin and Marc had returned from putting the twins to bed.

Beth scurried in from the kitchen, pausing just long enough to place a tray of chips and dip before them, and then she hurried back to work.

Marc took orders for drinks and then distributed them. He coaxed Beth from the kitchen for a little while to chat, but then a buzzer rang and she disappeared again.

"Bring people to the dining room in about ten minutes," she whispered to Marc on her way out.

"Aye, aye, Cap'n," he said, giving her a smart salute.

The enchiladas with green sauce and Mexican pepper and rice salad were a hit. Even Rachel liked them.

"Is there lime in this?" she asked, after tasting the enchiladas.

"Just a squeeze," Beth replied.

"Very nice."

"Your china is so pretty," Anne commented as they ate dinner.

"Thanks. I think we've used it maybe ten times since we were married. Things just get so busy. It takes too much time to wash by hand. You know how it is."

"Put them in the dishwasher," Anne said.

"With the gold edging?"

"Sure. Just make sure they've dried and cooled before you take them out."

"Who's going where for Christmas?" Kevin asked.

"We're staying in town," Will volunteered. "We want to see what a Southern Christmas is all about."

"There's a singing Christmas tree at our church on Christmas Eve," Anne added.

"What's that?" Rachel asked.

Anne looked at Will for help.

"It's a choir that sings on a stage made to look like a Christmas tree," he explained.

Rachel lifted an eyebrow but gave little other response.

"What are you doing?" Will asked.

"Going to the Big Apple," R.J. said. He didn't sound very enthusiastic. "Rachel's choice. Payback for Thanksgiving."

"It'll be fun."

"Sure. We'll celebrate with eight million of our closest friends."

Rachel ignored him. "How about you, Karen?"

"We're going home." Karen's eyes glowed with pleasure.

"Where's home?" Marc asked.

"Utah."

"Going skiing?" Rachel asked.

"Oh, no. Going to see family." Karen had never skied in her life.

"Hey, Kevin? Didn't I hear that the 919th is going to Iraq?" R.J. asked suddenly.

Karen looked at him with alarm. The 919th was Kevin's civil engineering squadron.

He sent R.J. a look under gathered eyebrows. "Yeah."

"When?" Karen asked. She felt as though she'd just been punched in the stomach.

"Second week in January," Kevin said, avoiding her eyes.

"The second week in January?" Karen echoed. That was right after they got back from vacation. "For how long? Why Iraq?"

R.J. was watching the interplay between the couple. "Hey, sorry, man. I thought you would have told her. First rule. Always tell your wife everything. Right, Rachel?"

"Right. Especially the things you don't want to tell her. Right, R.J.?"

"*Especially* those things."

Kevin cleared his throat. "For 120 days…although it might be…will probably be longer. It's our turn."

Marc deflected attention from Karen and Kevin by asking for thoughts on the Orange Bowl.

"Florida State," R.J. said without hesitation.

"They're not in this year," Marc replied.

"I know, but the way the papers report on the Seminoles, they make it sound as if they'll win the national championship anyway."

They soon finished the chocolate pie and then stayed at the table chatting until Beth's folding chair became too uncomfortable. "Let's move to the family room. Coffee or tea for anyone?"

Conversation in the family room shifted from sports to holiday traditions to what Beth and Marc were getting the twins for Christmas.

Beth looked guilty. "They're both getting Jungle Joes."

"I heard those are already sold out," Karen said.

"They are, but I stood in line last month at Toys Unlimited to get them."

"You didn't!" Marc looked at her in astonishment. "I thought we'd decided no trendy toys for the boys."

"Well—they watch Jungle Joe videos. I thought they would like them."

"But—how long did you wait?"

"Only two hours."

"Two hours!"

She placed a hand over his mouth. "Shhh. It's already done. They're already bought. There's nothing that can be done about it. Santa can give me coal in my stocking this year if he wants. Next year, I'll be good. I promise."

The evening ended in a flurry of hugs and wishes for merry Christmases.

As Karen and Kevin put their coats on to leave, Beth placed a hand on Karen's arm and whispered into her ear, "If you need anything at all while Kevin's gone, just ask, okay? I mean it."

Tears sprung to Karen's eyes. She'd been trying to put off even thinking about it. The kindness in Beth's words was almost too much to bear.

Later that night, Rachel ambushed R.J. just after he'd brushed his teeth and right before he'd climbed into bed.

"I want you to try this on. I need to know how it fits." Rachel pulled something from his closet and brought it over to him.

"What is it?"

"It's a suit. I noticed that you only have one."

"It's not like it's threadbare or anything. I've hardly ever worn it."

"Just try this. For me," Rachel wheedled.

R.J. obliged, but not before doing a striptease with the shorts and T-shirt he was wearing.

Rachel fussed at the shoulders and the sleeves of the suit jacket while R.J. looked at himself in the mirror. "This material's kind of shiny. Don't you think it's too Las Vegas? Maybe I could be the godfather."

He struck a pose with an arm crossed in front of him and his chin resting on the hand. He glowered.

"Or how about this?"

He turned his head, stuck out an arm and grabbed the cuff of the suit jacket with his hand. "It's my catalog pose."

"How about in here?" asked Rachel, feeling for room in the crotch. "Are the pants too tight?"

"Geez! Careful," R.J. yelped. "You're worse than my mom! I know how tight too tight is. I've been wearing pants for years."

"Just checking. How about the waist? Too tight in the waist?"

"They're fine."

Rachel hurried to his closet and came back with a pair of loafers. "Try these on with it."

"Honestly, Rach. I am never going to wear this. Can't we go to bed? I'm tired."

"I couldn't find any other shoes. Don't you have any nice ones?"

"These cost me eighty dollars. How much nicer can you get?" He squirmed for a minute inside the suit. "This feels nice. I like it."

"It should feel nice. It's lined in silk."

"This is silk?"

"Six months?" Karen reproached her husband at home later that night.

"It's our unit's turn. They're moving people in and out. Six-month rotations," he said, as he rummaged through the refrigerator. No matter what, Kevin always had a bedtime snack.

"When were you thinking of telling me this?" she asked, leaning against the kitchen counter and crossing her arms over her chest. "Just before you got on the plane?"

"Karen, it's not like I *wasn't* going to tell you. It's just that I didn't know *how* to tell you. 'By the way, I'm going to Iraq for six months.'" He gave the refrigerator door a shove. "I didn't want it to spoil Christmas for you."

"And now it has," she said, twisting her wedding ring.

"Hey," he said grabbing her hands. "I love you. I hate to see you upset. I knew you wouldn't like it, that's all. I didn't want to…"

"I know. You didn't want to upset me. Do you ever think of me in any other way than as the future mother of your children?"

"Karen—"

"Is that the only reason we're married? To have children? Because it might not happen. And maybe I don't want it to happen. Is there anything so terrible about not wanting children?" Even as she said the words, she knew she didn't mean them. She wished she could take them back.

"Karen—"

"And is there anything so terrible about wanting your husband to love you for you? Do you really love me? Did you mean to marry me before it turned out that you had to? Or was I just someone to fill in until you found the person you were looking for?"

"Karen—"

"I'm not stupid, Kevin. I know I'm not beautiful. I'm not even really pretty. I'm smart, but I'm not witty. I don't have a sparkling personality. Why *did* you marry me?" she whispered, daring him to tell her.

"Karen? I *didn't* have to marry you. You know that. I married you because I wanted to. *I* asked *you*, remember? And you've been a good wife to me."

"I don't want to be a good wife," she spat. "I want to be me. I want to be *Karen*. And I want you to love me."

"I do love you," he shouted. "What more can I say? What do you want me to do? Have someone write it in the sky for you? Take out a billboard?"

"If you could have just kept your pants zipped."

"That was seven years ago! And I never heard you complaining. If you'd have said no, I would have stopped."

"I *did* say no. I said 'no more' after every time we did it. Don't you remember? But then you'd start kissing me and it would happen all over again. I loved you, but I *hated* myself for not having the strength to back up my words." She began to sob her heartache.

"If it was such a nightmare experience, then why did you keep going out with me? It's not like I was holding a gun to your head!" he said, clutching her arm.

"Because I thought eventually you'd love me enough to stop."

CHAPTER 17

Karen slowly reconciled herself to the fact that Kevin was leaving. It happened in direct proportion to the increase in her excitement about going home for Christmas. She had her clothes packed and presents for everyone wrapped a week before they left. The plane trip felt as though it took forever, but then before she knew it, she was walking up the concourse and flying into the arms of her father and mother.

It felt as if she'd been away for a thousand years. Everything was exactly the same, but it seemed so different. The kitchen she'd remembered as cozy, crammed with plants and framed by frilly curtains, now seemed a cluttered, claustrophobic jungle. The familiar sounds of brothers and sisters living in close proximity now more resembled the incessant noise of a busy freeway. Shrieks and the clatter of feet up and down the stairs punctuated the underlying rhythm of ever-present music.

"It's so great to have you both here," her mother said for the hundredth time.

Karen tried to smile in response. After a week back at home, all she really wanted was quiet. She wanted peace. Her hand groped for Kevin's and found it. An oasis of stability in a storm of family togetherness.

But this is what I've always dreamed of. This is what I've always wanted, a house full of kids. Before, she'd always assumed the dream to be a happy one. Now it began to seem rather depressing. Her mother had been a mother with children at home for 27 years. And she still had eight more to go until Karen's youngest brother went to college. The burden of that responsibility now seemed oppressive to Karen.

That night on the sofa bed, under cover of darkness, Kevin turned to her and gathered her to his chest. He kissed her forehead and then nestled her head into his shoulder. "Your family is so wonderful. This is my dream. To have a happy house full of children. We'll have this Karen. I promise. We just have to keep trying."

Karen couldn't help herself. She shuddered.

Kevin wrapped her even tighter in his arms.

R.J. would have sympathized with Karen. He stared out the apartment window. He needed space. Lots of space. He'd been in New York City for only 24 hours, and already he had an overwhelming desire to go home. There were too many buildings, too many cars, and too many people trying to go to the same place at the same time. He felt trapped. What he really needed was a plane and the open sky.

"Where's your suit?" Rachel called from the bedroom.

"What suit?"

"The one I bought for you."

"It's at home."

Rachel came out from the bedroom looking as though she was going to cry. "How can it be at home? I put it in your bag."

"And I took it out. I didn't know we'd be doing anything here that would require a suit."

"Why do you take such perverse pleasure in refusing to dress up?"

"Calm down. It's okay. So I didn't bring a suit. Big deal." He turned back to the window wondering how people could survive in such a huge depressing place.

Rachel was already dialing the phone. She spoke rapidly in Italian and eventually hung up with a satisfied look on her face. "He'll send another right over."

R.J. slouched into a chair. "Well, what about shoes? I only have tennis shoes."

"He's sending those over too."

"I don't know what to think about this guy. He knows my suit size and my shoe size." R.J. knew he was sulking, but he didn't care. He didn't like it here.

Rachel knelt in front of him. "R.J., I need to talk to you."

"Why do I always feel like I'm being called in to see the big boss when you talk that way?"

"Well, that's part of it. I need to be completely honest with you." Her dusky eyes were serious.

A corner of his mouth turned up. "You had a sex-change operation, didn't you?"

"No."

"You're really my first cousin and our marriage isn't legal."

"No."

"You can't have AIDS."

"No."

"Okay. Lay it on me. I can take it." He pulled her up from the floor and onto his lap.

"R.J., I never really told you who I am."

"Sure you did. Rachel Porter-Smith."

"And it didn't mean anything to you."

"Of course it did. You mean the world to me." *Can we go home now?*

"That's not what I meant. What I want to say is that the name didn't hold any significance to you."

"Significance? You're the most significant thing in my life."

"R.J., remember when that financial investment advisor came to speak to the squadron and I told him I was rich?"

"Yeah."

"Well, I am. I'm rich."

He waved a hand. "I already know that."

"Yes, but I want to tell you how rich."

"It's not important. I don't need to know."

"I think you do. Who is the richest person you can think of?"

"Bill Gates."

Rachel rolled her eyes. "Think a lot smaller."

"Michael Jordan."

"Think a lot bigger."

"I have no idea."

"I have five times as much as Michael Jordan."

"Rachel, nobody has that kind of money."

"I do."

"Okay, so how much do you have? A couple hundred thousand?"

"Multiply that by ten thousand."

"That's billions."

"Yes, it is."

"You're joking, aren't you?"

"No, R.J., I'm not."

"Did you win the lottery or something?"

"No. It's family money."

"You mean you're one of *those* people?"

"Yes, I am."

R.J. looked at her as if he were seeing her for the first time. She had a hard time looking him the eye. She bit her lip and looked away. Then she stood up in front of him. "I'm sorry."

"So what is it that you do in that office of yours at home?"

"I oversee the company."

"Everything?"

"Not everything, exactly, but I am chairman of the board."

There was a long silence between them.

"Quit sulking," she finally said.

"I'm not."

"You are."

"I'm not!"

"Then why are your lips all pouty?"

He stood up and crossed his arms in front of him. "Well, if you're rich, then where's the private mansion and the apartment in New York and the beach house in Miami and the vacation house in the Riviera..." His eyes widened with the dawn of realization.

Rachel winced. "Monte Carlo, actually. The vacation house is in Monte Carlo."

"Boy, am I ever dumb. Why didn't you—?"

"I tried. But you would never let me talk about it."

R.J. looked as though someone had just poked him with a pin. His ego had just been deflated. "Rachel, why did you marry me?"

She took his head between her hands and looked straight into his eyes. "Because I love you."

"Yeah, but I don't play tennis and I hate caviar and I don't wear monkey suits. How much did that suit cost, anyway?"

"Fifteen thousand dollars."

R.J.'s face blanched. "Fifteen thousand! There's no way I'm wearing that. What if I wore it and spilled ketchup on it? Ketchup is the worst kind of stain. It never comes out. Fifteen thousand dollars..."

"R.J., look at it this way. The good thing about being rich is that money is no longer a reason not to do something."

"It's like lady and the tramp. Were you laughing at me all this time?"

"No."

He took her hand and looked at the wedding ring on her finger. "This was the biggest diamond I could afford."

"It's a beautiful diamond."

"You probably have lots that are much bigger. This is probably the smallest one you have."

"R.J., there's no comparison. This is the one that means the most to me."

R.J. dropped Rachel's hand and then stood up, avoiding her eyes. "I need to go for a walk."

Rachel waited until 7:30 before becoming worried.

By 8:00, she was furious. She strode to the phone and violently punched in a number.

"I told him and he left."

"Darling, I'll be seeing you at dinner in just half an hour."

"Conrad, that's just it. He isn't here."

"What happened?"

"I finally sat him down and explained to him about the money."

"Wonderful. What did he say?"

"He went from being a cocky pilot to being a disillusioned little boy."

"Tsk, tsk. Most people love money. The only bad thing they have to say about it is that they don't have enough."

"I know. He thinks that I deceived him."

"Did you?"

"No...well, maybe. He's the one who never wanted to talk about it."

"What would he say when you'd bring it up."

"Save it for a rainy day. We can live comfortably on what I make."

"Mystery solved. He liked to feel like he was taking care of you. Now he feels like a kept man."

"That's ridiculous."

"Is it? Do you still want to have dinner?"

"Come over. You can wait with me."

"A toute à l'heure."

"Bisous."

R.J. was walking the streets of New York City with a vengeance. He made death-defying street crossings, bringing taxis to screeching halts. He forced others onto the street to make way for him. He even practically ran over a man trying to sell papers on a street corner.

"Hey! What's with you?"

R.J. started to speak but then closed his mouth. What could he say? *Life sucks. I just found out my wife's a billionaire?*

R.J. burst into the room. "I'm going home. I don't belong here."

Now it was Rachel's turn to blanche. "What are you saying, R.J.? You don't know if you can live with me because I'm too rich?"

His confused eyes swept the room and settled on an elegant silver-haired man that he didn't know. "Who are you?"

"Conrad."

R.J. looked at Rachel.

"He's my business manager. And longtime family friend."

"And how would you feel, Conrad, if your wife just told you she were as rich as Bill Gates?"

A corner of Conrad's mouth lifted in a smile. "Hardly that rich."

"What is it with you people? Why do you draw such big distinctions between tens of billions of dollars and a few billion dollars? What would you do with 20 billion dollars that you can't do with one billion?"

"I think," Conrad said carefully, "that I'd bless my stars that my wife is not only beautiful, but that she also comes with a substantial dowry."

"I don't want her money."

"Would you like to sign a postnuptial agreement? Would that make you feel better?"

"No." He walked over to his wife, staring at her as if he'd never seen her before. "Rachel, you're not the person I thought you were. I feel like I've been violated."

Rachel took up his hand. She interlaced his fingers with hers. "R.J., I'm just like you."

"No, Rachel. You're not. What are you doing with me anyway? Slumming? Am I just a fling?"

Rachel slapped him across the face. "You are my husband. When I said my vows it meant something. Most people have a problem with the 'for worse' part. I can't believe your problem is with 'for better.'" She was trembling with rage.

He suddenly melted and enfolded her in a sheltering hug. "I deserved that. But, geez, Rach, why didn't you just tell me?"

She slumped against him. "Because I was afraid of what you'd say. And I didn't know how to say it." She was weak with relief. Months of trying to find a way to tell him had taken their toll.

"How come I love you so much?"

From his corner, Conrad had looked on with watchful eyes. At this he got to his feet and clapped his hands. "*Ça va, les enfants?* We can eat now?"

The day she'd come back from Utah, Karen telephoned Anne to arrange a lunch meeting for the following day. She'd even agreed to meet at Bozo's Café. She didn't care about cost or grease; she just needed to talk to someone. And she had to talk with someone objective. Her thoughts were so foreign that she felt as though she'd invaded someone else's body or borrowed someone else's brain.

Karen looked again at her watch. Anne was ten minutes late. She fiddled with the ketchup bottle and then gave it up, closed her eyes, and stretched her neck to release some of her tension.

Anne nearly scared Karen out of her skin when she slid into the booth and parked her purse next to the wall.

"Sorry I'm late. My favorite city citizen called on the phone just before I walked out the door. And, stupid me, I answered instead of letting the answering machine pick it up. I have to remind myself that I don't need to answer the phone every time it rings. Technology has its uses. Did you order yet?"

"No."

They took a couple minutes to look at the menu. Karen decided on a chicken breast sandwich. Anne ordered homemade macaroni-and-cheese. "It's been a long time." Her tone was apologetic for choosing something so boring. "So how was your trip? Isn't it great to go home?"

"It wasn't at all like I remembered it, Anne. I went home expecting to find myself. Things have been kind of tough lately, so I'd been looking forward to it. But I felt like a stranger. It seemed like the Twilight Zone."

Anne smiled in sympathy. "Things change."

"But that's just it, Anne. The thing was, nothing had changed. Everything was absolutely the same. From the clothes my mother was wearing to the living room furniture. Identical."

"And that bothered you? When I went away to college, my mother rearranged my room and I had a fit."

"Yes. No." Karen took a gulp of air and decided to start again. "I used to think my childhood was a fairyland. I always wanted to duplicate it. That's how I wanted my life to be. Seven children. Or more. A big family. A big enough house. A huge van so that we could always go places together. I thought a week's vacation would be too short, but it was almost too long. I couldn't have stood it any longer. I love my parents, and I love my brothers and sisters, but I couldn't wait to get away."

"Maybe you've changed, Karen. It's okay to modify your dreams. It's all right to change your mind about what you want."

"It's not like I don't want kids. I do. I just don't want seven of them."

Anne snorted. "Seven kids are quite a few. Can you imagine cooking for seven kids and you and Kevin every night of the week?"

"Yes! Because I've watched my mother do it for years."

"So what's the big deal? Wanting two kids or even three is normal, Karen. But seven? Only very special people have that goal."

"But what if I only want one?"

"Fine. Have one. I still don't see what the problem is."

"Besides the fact that we've been trying for seven years and it hasn't happened? There's our religion. I'm supposed to want as many kids as I can have."

"And right now that's zero."

Tears sprung into Karen's eyes. "I *have* to have kids."

"Why is it so important? What's the worst-case scenario? What would happen if you didn't ever have kids?"

"We won't have anyone on our planet if we don't have kids."

"What are you talking about?"

Karen took a deep breath. At this point, she really didn't feel like talking about the tenets of her faith, but she supposed it was the only way to make Anne understand. "LDS believe that Heavenly Father has millions of spirit children waiting for bodies. That's why LDS believe in having as many children as they can; to give birth to the spirits who are waiting to have bodies."

"And give them good Mormon homes, huh?"

Karen scowled. She wasn't in the mood to be ridiculed.

Anne caught her look and was immediately penitent. She took Karen's hand. "Hey. I'm sorry. I'm here to listen. You talk."

"And families are important because if your marriage is sealed, like mine and Kevin's, then your family is eternal."

"You were telling me about this before."

"You get to have your family with you in heaven."

"If you've been good enough and if you reach the right heaven."

Karen nodded. "I'm supposed to want to have as many children as I can. I'm not thinking like myself lately. I don't know what to think anymore."

"Karen, you're the woman. You're the one who would have primary responsibility for the children. You're the one who has to give birth.

Kevin's not the only person in the marriage, and the Mormon Church has no right to impose its demands on you. If you only want one child, that's your personal decision. Talk to Kevin about it."

They paused in their conversation and leaned away from the table as their food was delivered.

"We *have* talked," Karen continued as soon as the waitress had gone. "He wants a large family, Anne. He wants a huge family. And when we married, that's what I wanted too. How can I change my mind now?"

"Karen, it's not like you've committed a crime. You've just reexamined yourself and decided to adjust your dreams. Marriage isn't static. It has to adjust because everybody's human. Everybody changes. Talk to Kevin about it. You know you'll have to at some point."

Karen looked at Anne with hunted eyes. "I can't. It's my job, Anne. It's my destiny. My purpose in life is to have children. I don't have a choice."

"Then make one up. There's always a choice."

Time with Kevin was becoming short. He would be leaving in three days. They'd finally gotten over the argument they had the night of Beth's dinner. Karen didn't want to make waves again, but she had to talk to him before he left. Her thoughts were too loud and too overwhelming to keep to herself. She brought it up that night in bed. They had just turned out the light.

"Kevin, could we just start with just one baby?"

He kissed her on the forehead and laughed. "That's how it usually does start. With the first one."

"No. I mean," she paused and searched for words. "I mean, could we have the first baby with the idea that maybe it might be the only baby?"

"I thought you wanted a big family like I did."

"I did. But I've been thinking about it, and I don't know if I do anymore. Maybe I've changed my mind."

"You can't just change your mind, Karen."

She flipped over on her stomach and propped herself up on her elbows. "When we were at home, I watched my mom for seven days. Do you know what she did while we were there?"

"No."

"She cooked. And when she wasn't cooking, she was cleaning up from cooking. And in those rare moments when she wasn't doing either of those two things, she sat down for a quick cup of tea. But only in between doing laundry and tidying up the house." Tears filled Karen's eyes, but she blinked them away. "The thought of spending every day of thirty long years like that scares me, Kevin. I don't want to live my life that way."

"Thirty years." Kevin scoffed at the figure.

"Thirty-*five* in my mother's case. Irene is twenty-seven. Cody is ten. It will be *thirty-five* years by the time Cody goes to college."

"But children are fulfilling."

"Of course they are. They also take a lot of energy, Kevin. I'm only 25, but the thought of even two children makes me bone weary. I'm not saying I don't want children. I'm just saying that I'm sure I don't want seven. Or even five."

"Four." Kevin leaped at the number as if he were at an auction.

"I'd like to start with one and see how it goes from there. Besides, at this point, this discussion is only hypothetical anyway." Karen flipped her hair over her shoulder and looked at her husband with bruised eyes. She felt like adding, "And that's my final offer."

"Okay, Nita, you have to tell me. Why don't people expect me to be Anne Bradley? Is there another Anne Bradley in town?" Anne decided to solve the mystery that had haunted her since her move to Bullard.

Nita looked at her with a pained expression. "You have to promise not to get mad."

"I'm not going to get mad. I want to know."

"Now, you know you don't have a Southern accent."

"No, I don't."

"And you know you really don't have *any* accent."

"What do you mean?"

"I mean, you sound like anybody. You could *be* anybody."

"Okay."

"And over the phone, you sound like…"

"Like what?"

"Like a white person. And when someone's looking for an Anne Bradley in the South, they *expect* a white person. Anyway, you promised you wouldn't get mad."

"I'm a *person*, Nita. In Seattle I was just Anne. Why do people have to label things black or white?"

"I don't know, Anne. I'm only telling you because you asked."

"Well, thanks. I think."

"Honey, this is the South. Whether you like it or not, there's a different reality here. It's not like it used to be, and most people here have hearts of gold…but the expectations…" she sighed, *"Anne* Bradley, they're just hard to change."

Chapter 18

‿

$\mathcal{B}$eth had already dried and put away the dishes by the time Marc had gotten the twins cleaned up from dinner. Then he'd started to play with them in the living room. They liked to "work out" with their daddy. It was while they were straddling his back, squealing with delight as he counted out push-ups, that Marc told her.

"You should have stayed in," he said, not looking at her.

"What?" she asked, looking up blankly from the newest issue of her magazine.

"If you'd stayed in, then at least one of us would have had the chance to be promoted to major."

He didn't see her face drain of color and then flush an angry red. He did hear her say, "Oh, honey." It was more than he could bear. He stopped counting and pushed his chin farther into his chest as his elbows snapped the push-ups out of his body.

She stared at the article titled "10 Ways to Make Your Kids Eat Spinach" until he finished. Then she hugged the twins close as he left the room.

She brought it up in bed. She couldn't stand not to. "Honey?"

"What."

"What happened?"

"The lab commander refused to sign my evaluation."

"Why?"

"Because I refused to let him edit it."

"Why?" Beth was mystified. Evaluations were important. If the lab commander wanted to have some input on Marc's evaluation, all the better.

"Because the regulations state that the primary rater has to write the evaluation."

"Yeah." That was standard. According to the regs, Marc's boss was the one responsible for rating him. But that was in theory. In practice, usually the primary rater asked the ratee to write their own evaluation and then the rater tweaked it. The ratee ended up doing most of the work, but he also got to influence the write-up.

"Well, I made Singh do it. And when he asked me for inputs, I refused to give him any."

Beth didn't understand what she was hearing. "But Singh hardly speaks English." He was a good engineer, but English wasn't his native language, so that was the last thing Beth could have imagined Marc would want. Evaluations were pored over by everyone involved. Minute nuances between words like "excellent" and "star performer" were debated for days.

"The Air Force hired him. They must have faith in his expertise."

"Okay, fine. But why not help him along a little bit?"

"Beth, I am so tired of writing my own evaluations. I always get a 'definitely promote' evaluation anyway. But what does it matter? Everyone gets a DP. It doesn't mean anything."

Beth sighed. Air Force evaluations were notoriously inflated. But if everyone else's evaluations were inflated, then yours had to be, too, just to compete.

Beth tried to calm herself. Worst-case scenario, he wouldn't get promoted. Although, realistically, almost everyone was being promoted to major these days. Major shouldn't be a problem, and it was still four years away. It was lieutenant colonel that could be tricky with an evaluation like the one Marc had been given. Correction: the evaluation he let himself be given. It was bad enough that Marc had let Singh write the evaluation, but it was even worse that the lab commander wouldn't sign it. Beth didn't know how Marc would overcome that one.

She wanted to touch him. To just reach out a hand and put it on his shoulder. Let him know that she understood. Because she did, even if she didn't agree with him. But if she put a hand on his shoulder, then he would roll over and hug her close. And if he did that, then they would start kissing. And kissing would lead to sex, and when was the last time that had happened?

She punched her pillow and rolled away from her husband.

Hadn't he learned anything at USAFA? The academy was mostly a place where cadets learned how to obey authority and work together as a team toward a common goal. But they also expected integrity. And once in a while, integrity demanded going against the established order. And once in a while, going against the establishment took courage because you were never sure what they'd do to you. Cadets called it "falling on your sword."

At some point in life, everyone falls on their sword. At the academy they tried to teach you how to choose those issues wisely, because sometimes, they really did leave you to die. And you wanted to make sure it was worth it.

Of all the stupid, stupid things to fall on your sword for. I'm here at home knocking myself out, trying to raise twin monsters, and he's piddling away his career.

She lay in the darkness, listening to his breathing slow and slacken. When he was asleep, she got up. She looked in on the twins. Pulled their blankets back over them. She wandered into the kitchen, opened the freezer, and took out a carton of ice cream. Found a spoon. She opened the blinds to let the moonlight splash onto the table and spill onto the floor.

She stared out into the moonlit darkness. Out beyond the neighbor's clipped hedges. She stared up at the fathomless night sky, remembering a time when life wasn't so hard. Or so endless. A time when she believed there was something beyond that sky.

She didn't get it. Motherhood was supposed to be a pleasure. A joy. She was supposed to feel fulfilled. As if her life had purpose. And it did: getting through one more day. And one more day. Until that day turned into the first day of kindergarten.

Just three more years.

After the academy, she'd thought she could survive anything, but now she wasn't so sure. Was she the only mother in the world who felt this way? She must be. She'd never heard anyone talk about feeling like this. Because if she had, she would have reconsidered. If someone had told her she would have to give up all the things she loved—work, racquetball, cooking, sex—she would have said no. And what kind of person did that make her?

She cried silent tears as she stared out at that cold, hard sky.

Karen woke to silence. No one was in the shower singing. No one was shaving. No one was jingling coins into his pockets. She lay in bed with her eyes closed and listened. Then she imagined what it would be like to own herself. To have complete control over what happened in a day with no need to report to anyone or be responsible to anyone. As she thought about it, a smile spread across her face. For the first time in her life, she *was* on her own. For six whole months. The thought propelled her out of bed. There was no way she was going to miss one second of it.

That is when the phone began to ring.

It was as if everyone in the ward knew Kevin was gone. And they all had a job for her to do, wondering if she would accept these as callings from God. By 5:00 that evening, the next six months were scheduled on a calendar. Assisting the ward Sunday school presidency as the Sunday school secretary. Visiting church members in nursing homes and along with that, helping out with their Mutual activities with the church's Young Men's. Addressing church mailings on Thursday. Helping with Young Women's. Baking for the Relief Society meetings on Sundays. She couldn't, of course, say no. She wouldn't. How could she when God had so clearly called her?

How do you say no to God?

"Nita?" Anne had wandered into her coworker's office. She was there mostly to look out the window and see if it was raining, but she also had a question about her job. "What's the difference between my job and yours?"

Nita looked up from Mr. Trumble's agenda book and queried her with her eyes.

"I know that we do different things, but as far as job requirements, what's the difference between an executive secretary and an office assistant? Besides the pay?" Which was substantial.

Nita tapped her pencil on her desk as she thought about it. Then her face brightened. "Dictation. It's a requirement to know shorthand for this position."

"That's sort of old-fashioned, isn't it?"

Nita shrugged. "Maybe. But Mr. Trumble won't use a Dictaphone or a handheld tape recorder. He doesn't like them. He's always afraid of running out of tape. That's the main difference. The other difference is that I draft correspondence for his signature. And I keep his calendar. Those put me another notch up."

Anne was glad she could ask Nita these sorts of questions without the secretary feeling threatened. Nita was old enough to be her mother, but she felt more like a big sister.

The phone rang, and Anne returned to her desk to answer it. She hated letting it ring more than three times.

"City manager's office."

"Is he in?"

"No, sir. May I help you?"

"Where is he?"

"He's meeting with the city council."

"Why? He in trouble?"

"No. It's a planned weekly meeting."

"Oh. You just the secretary?"

"No, sir, I'm not even the secretary. I'm just an office assistant. I can try to take a message, but you'll have to speak very slowly because I don't take shorthand."

After she'd replaced the receiver, she thought of another reason Nita differed from her. Nita was proud to be a secretary; Anne was not.

The food committee met at the end of February to plan the annual Easter egg hunt.

"Is it on Easter morning? Who's invited?" Anne asked.

"It's the Saturday of Easter weekend," Beth replied. "And all the kids of military personnel under six years old are invited. Enlisted and officer. General and Mrs. Pritchard host it at their house every year."

"Where do they live?"

"You know that road just past the BX on the right? The one that says 'Private Drive, No Admittance'? Their place is on a bluff out there. The backyard has a great view of the bay."

"We don't have to dye eggs, do we?" Karen asked. She didn't think she could fit one more thing into her schedule.

"No," Beth replied. "And thank goodness! We'd have to dye at least two hundred. The OSC hides plastic eggs on the lawn…if you can really call it hiding. It looks like they just have an airplane fly over and drop them from the sky. But the good thing is, every kid finds at least one."

"So what is our part in this?" Rachel asked.

"It's a punch-and-cake sort of event," Beth responded. "Last year they had coconut cakes and served tropical punch."

"Why is it that people always associate coconut with Easter?" Anne pondered. "That's kind of strange, don't you think?"

"Maybe because it looks like rabbit fur, or grass, if you dye it green," Karen offered.

"Maybe." Anne still wasn't sure about the idea. She wasn't a big fan of coconut.

"I like the idea of coconut cakes. They were sheet cakes, right?" Karen asked.

Beth looked at the worksheet. "Yep."

"We could do the same, but have green coconut, like grass, and have foil covered eggs on top to decorate them."

The rest of the women nodded.

"Any problems with punch?"

They shook their heads.

"Good. So let's keep the punch idea." Beth made notations on the worksheet

"Is that it?" asked Anne.

"That's it," said Beth, putting her paper file back into her bag. "But don't worry. The silent auction will be much more work, I promise." She grinned, her eyes keeping secrets.

"Do we have to be around to serve for the egg hunt?" Anne asked.

"Nope. Kitchen catering staff does it since it's all off-site. Couldn't be easier."

The day before Easter didn't dawn. It was too gray and rainy for anyone to have noticed the sun come up. Across the Liffsbury area, military personnel looked up at the rain pouring from the sky and wished they had the choice to not go to the general's Easter egg hunt. But General Pritchard was, after all, the wing commander. What the general wanted, the general usually got. So little girls wore heavy tights and turtlenecks under their fancy Easter dresses, and little boys wore galoshes over their fancy trousers. Mothers and fathers thought wistfully about going to the egg hunt in sweats, but who in their right mind would show up at a general's house in jogging pants?

At nine o'clock, hoards of families suddenly appeared from the rain as if by magic. They huddled under umbrellas until the shooting of a pistol indicated the start of the hunt. Fathers who would not have been content the year before with a less than overflowing basket of eggs collected their children after finding just two. Families inhaled cake, trying to keep it from dissolving in the rain. The punch, hopelessly diluted by the downpour, soon overflowed its cups and became a pink fountain, cascading over the folding tables. Everyone was gone by 9:30.

It was the fastest Easter egg hunt in Bullard history.

Karen was over at Anne and Will's for her regular Friday night dinner. They'd adopted her since Kevin went TDY. Some weeks, it was awkward. She felt like their personal conversion project. Not that they were aggressive at trying to get her to leave the church, but they were very earnest. And religion always seemed to come up. Sure, it was always on her own mind; she was trying to decide for herself what she believed. But she didn't always want to talk about it.

They even gave her a Bible one week, in spite of her having told them she had a perfectly good King James Version on her bookshelf at home. They'd laughed when she said that and explained that theirs was so much easier to understand. She didn't bother to tell them that her version was the only correct translation. They had stopped listening.

But she had to admit that some weeks, like this one, she really looked forward to dinner with them. Today had been a tough end to a busy week.

"You look pretty beat. Hard time sleeping?" Anne asked as she passed around the rice.

"No. I had to do some counseling at church and it was rough. I just didn't know what to say. It was a sixteen-year-old girl. To see her you'd think her life was perfect, but she wants to commit suicide."

"Wow. What did your pastor say?" Will had no idea what he would have said in a similar situation.

"He wasn't there. It was just me."

"Have you had training in this sort of thing?" Will was impressed. It took special skills to do counseling.

"No. But I'm in charge of Young Women's, so if one of the girls has problems, I'm the one she'll look for. All I could think to do was to let her talk."

"Have you ever talked about it with her before?" Anne assumed the girl had built some sort of relationship with Karen.

"No. Not at all. Her mom just wanted her to talk to someone."

"Why was she so depressed?" Anne remembered high school as challenging, but certainly nothing to die for.

"She said she couldn't be perfect. She said it was too much pressure."

"What was? School?" Will thought that was taking life a little too seriously.

"School. Life." *Faith,* Karen thought, though she wouldn't say it. She'd never forget what the girl had said.

"Why should I devote my life to following the made-up religion of some lecherous old goat? Have you ever read anything about Joseph Smith?" The girl had leaned forward in her chair, her eyes earnest.

Karen nodded.

"I mean anything objective. Outside the church."

"You know you're only supposed to read faith-promoting material."

"Who would think that a biography of Joseph Smith wouldn't be?"

Karen had to agree with the reasoning.

"I can never be anything without a man as an LDS. Do you realize that?" The blond cheerleader crossed her arms over her chest and glared at Karen.

"Why do you say that?"

"Because the only way to get to celestial heaven is to be married. In a temple. What about me? How come I can't be good enough on my own? And what about babies who die? Do they get to go to heaven?"

"I'm sure God cares for them."

"But you don't know that, do you?" She pointed an accusing finger at Karen. "And how come God can't make up his mind and stick to it?"

"What are you talking about?"

"All the things we're not supposed to talk about: polygamy, racism. If something is eternal, it lasts forever. How come these eternal policies were suddenly changed?"

"A living prophet takes precedence over a dead prophet."

"And how come if Joseph Smith was such a great prophet, nothing he said ever came true?"

"I wouldn't say that nothing ever came true."

"I wouldn't say that he had such a stellar moral character, would you?" The sea-green eyes bored into hers, demanding truth.

"He was very sincere and passionate in his beliefs."

"So was Adolf Hitler, but no one ever held him up as someone to emulate."

"I'd hardly equate the two. Listen, I know you're questioning what you believe. Just don't do anything you'd regret later. Please."

"I don't have any really great choices, do I? Deny my faith and lose my family or embrace the faith and deny myself. I'm just asking you to give me a reason to believe. Because I can't think of one."

What gave this girl the right to so much self-confidence? How could she sit there in her perfectly coordinated outfit with matching shoes and question Karen's convictions? "Religion is about faith. All you have to do is believe."

"There are no reasons, are there?" Those captivating eyes, fevered and searching, just seconds before, now glazed over and became vacant. She picked up her backpack and swung it over her shoulder. She popped her gum as she stood up and plastered a smile on her face. "Well, thanks for talking to me."

"I can't believe what pressure kids are under these days," Anne was saying. "Seems like every parent wants them to get a free ride to the Ivy League."

Karen smiled weakly. "Yeah. Poor kid."

CHAPTER 19

I have the perfect idea for a vacation."

Rachel was startled when R.J. burst into the conservatory, but she was also pleased. She had been thinking of a vacation just that morning. She'd recovered from Montana and he'd recovered from New York City. It was time to try again. "So do I. I just thought of it today!"

"You first."

"No, you go ahead."

R.J. grinned and then blurted out, "Camping!"

Rachel grimaced. "Like in log houses on a lake?"

"No. Like outside, under the stars. It'll be great. We always went camping when I was little."

"And where did you want to do this?"

"I thought we could go to Great Smoky National. If we can do two hard days of driving, we can enjoy five days camping before we have to start back."

He looked so earnest, she had to say yes. Visions of exploring Tokyo underneath a canopy of cherry blossoms wilted in her head. "When do you want to leave?"

Beth called the food committee meeting to order. "Let's discuss the spring silent auction, and I don't want to hear any whining or complaining. I told you this would be a complicated one."

"Lay it on us," Anne said, sticking out her chin in a pose of fearless courage.

"Have you guys ever been to a silent auction?"

"Is it a requirement for planning?" Karen asked.

"No. It would just give you a better idea, that's all." Beth looked at a loss on where to start. "You know this is an event to raise money for the scholarship fund, right?"

"Of course," Rachel answered.

"The idea of an auction is to bid on things, right?"

"Right." This didn't sound very complicated to Anne.

"This auction is the most prestigious event the OSC puts on. It's as close to black tie as base ever gets."

"Is it a dinner?" Rachel asked.

"Yes. People pay thirty dollars for tickets. But that's only part of the problem."

Karen bit her lip. She didn't like the way this was sounding.

"The idea is to have businesses and individuals donate things, and then to auction them off. When attendees enter, they are assigned a number. Like, say I donate tickets to a Braves game. There will be a sheet of paper next to the tickets. If you want to bid, you write down the price you're willing to pay and then your number. The bidding is open for about an hour before dinner. You can bid on something as many times as you want, but only until the bidding period is done. At that point, dinner is served. After dinner, the highest bidder on each item is announced."

"That sounds like fun!" Anne exclaimed.

"Well, it is fun, but the idea is to make money by getting donations."

Everyone nodded. They all understood that.

"Including the food."

Karen's heart sank. She hated asking people for things. When she was a Girl Scout, she made herself so sick over selling cookies that her mother finally asked Karen's grandmother to buy them all.

"Is this easy to do? Are town merchants expecting people to come around asking?" Anne wanted to know how difficult this would be.

"Yes, but the idea is to provide a gala dinner. And sometimes that's been a little more difficult. Almost anyone is willing to give away cases of hot dogs, but what we'd really like is lobster."

They all fell silent, thinking of how best to tackle the project.

"What we should do is decide first what we want to serve." Always have a plan. That was Rachel's motto.

"But what if we can't get what we want?" Karen asked. This was impossible.

"There are always ways of getting what you want." Rachel said it with such confidence that they almost believed her. "So, what is your ideal menu?"

"Guys?" Beth looked at them for help.

"What did they serve last year?" Anne asked. Might as well not reinvent the wheel.

"Pretty standard. Green salad, baked potato, steak, and cheesecake for dessert."

Rachel was shaking her head by the time Beth had finished her recital. "That's boring. It's not even worth the effort to put on an evening gown for a meal like that."

"Well, then what would you serve?" Beth asked. Her voice was tinged with frustration. Rachel could really be a snob sometimes.

"Start with champagne." She said this as if it were an inviolable rule.

Anne and Beth nodded. Sure. If they were just dreaming, it sounded like a good start.

"*Foie gras* or *pâté* as a starter."

Anne and Beth exchanged glances. This wasn't part of their dream. Definitely not.

"I would have duck as the main course, although I'm sure others would disagree with me. You could have veal if you wanted. And *haricots verts* to go with. Small green beans."

Veal was a good idea. No one ever made it for themselves.

"And then cheese, of course. And you can only serve chocolate as dessert. No other choice."

They were all in agreement on that particular point.

"That's what I would serve." Rachel dared anyone to disagree with her.

"I don't think the *pâté* idea would go over very well, to be honest." Anne found the courage to contradict her. "Besides, I don't think anyone around here carries it."

"You're probably right." In fact, Rachel knew she was. "What about melon and prosciutto?"

"That sounds nice. Out of the ordinary, but not overly expensive," Anne agreed.

Beth flipped the worksheet over. "I'll write down our thoughts before we decide."

"I liked the veal idea for the main course," Anne added.

"Me too," said Beth.

"You could do *blanquette de veau*. It's fairly simple. Just chunks of veal and a sauce."

"Veal scallops would look better."

"But they'd also be more expensive."

"You could serve *blanquette de veau* with a timbale of rice and *haricots verts*."

"In English!" Beth ordered.

"Veal with a turned-over mold of rice and French green beans."

They all agreed it even sounded nice. In French.

"No cheese," argued Anne. "I don't think people would appreciate it."

"You're probably right." Karen for one knew she wouldn't touch it. "But what about chocolate mousse for dessert?" Might as well try to keep things on the lighter side.

"No. Every banquet serves chocolate mousse." Beth had attended enough of them to know.

"Chocolate tarte," Rachel decided.

Beth and Karen agreed with her.

Beth looked up from note-taking. "If, and I emphasize that word, we could serve exactly what we wanted for the auction, this is what we'd do: champagne, melon and ham, veal with rice and green beans, and chocolate tarte." She laid the paper on the table. "Is this possible?"

That was the question.

"I think it might be difficult to find someone willing to donate the champagne. How many bottles would we need?" Anne hated to burst Rachel's bubble, but she was trying to be realistic.

"You can serve six to eight people with one bottle," Rachel said.

"How many usually come to this auction?" Anne asked.

"Three to four hundred," Beth said. She continued, noticing everyone's expressions of disbelief, "Like I told you, it's *the* event on base. So, let's see, that would be..." she made a calculation on the back of the worksheet, but before she could finish, Rachel answered.

"We'd need between fifty and sixty-five bottles. That's only about ten cases. It's really not that much."

"But champagne!" Beth exclaimed. "That has to cost a fortune."

"I know a great chateau that sells it for twenty dollars a bottle."

"Twenty dollars! That's a little expensive, don't you think?" Anne couldn't even begin to imagine herself asking someone to donate 50 bottles of champagne at $20 a bottle.

"No. That's actually a very good quality price ratio. You can easily pay up to one hundred dollars. Frankly, I wouldn't pay less than twenty dollars a bottle."

"Well," Beth said, "if you're so sure of your facts, why don't you be in charge of the champagne donation?"

"Thank you." Rachel made a note in her portfolio. Everyone else sighed in relief.

"All right. Champagne taken care of." Beth crossed it off her list. "Cantalope and ham."

"You want to make sure it's prosciutto," Rachel reminded her.

"I'm an engineer. Help me out. How do you spell it?" Beth asked.

"P-r-o-s-c-i-u-t-t-o. Prosciutto."

"Anyone volunteer for this one?"

"Isn't there an easier way to do this? Maybe we could draft a letter and send it to grocery stores." Anne was feeling overwhelmed.

"That's an idea," Beth said.

"How's this going to work, though? Who's going to do all the cooking?" Karen asked.

"We'll have to pay someone for that part and for serving staff too. It's our choice, but if we're going to hold it here, then we might as well pay the O Club to do it." Beth knew for a fact that it had been done that way the previous year.

Rachel thought about it for a moment and then conceded the point. "You're right. They're used to doing high volume. But can we give them the recipes?"

Beth shrugged. She didn't see why not. "I'll ask the events manager."

"Actually, we should give the recipes to the kitchen before we write the letter so they can increase them for four hundred. That way we ask for donations of everything we need. It would probably work best to have one company sponsor an entire dish and take responsibility for providing all the ingredients for it."

The rest of them nodded.

"And what about corporate sponsorship?" Rachel wondered.

"What do you mean?" Beth asked.

"How are we going to recognize these companies for donating the food?"

"Last year there was a paragraph in the base paper that thanked all the donators."

Rachel was already shaking her head. "That wouldn't do it for me. I'd want my name associated at the event more closely with the items I provided. For everyone who buys a ticket, a menu should be included that would list the sponsors with the items they are sponsoring."

"We'd have to ask the OSC board because that's not really food committee-related. I mean, it is, but not directly." There would be enough for the food committee to do in Beth's mind without creating extra work for themselves.

"I think it would make it easier to ask for donations." What Rachel had said made sense to Anne.

"I'll put it in the preliminary report. Who wants to draft the letter?" Beth asked, hoping that someone else would take that responsibility.

"I'll do it," volunteered Anne. "I'll do a form letter with an attachment listing the courses. Does that sound good?"

"How do we know who to send it to?" Karen asked.

"We'll just send it to the big grocery stores, I guess," Beth said, shrugging. Shouldn't be too difficult to figure out.

"It would probably be better to ask the chamber of commerce for a list of food and food service companies. That way we wouldn't leave anyone out," Rachel advised.

"I can do that," Anne responded. It wouldn't be very difficult; the chamber of commerce was just across the street from the city government building. And she talked to the director of the chamber of commerce all the time.

"Yes. But, remember, we need to get quantities first so we know what to ask for," said Rachel.

"In that case, we need to limit tickets. If we ask for donations and we get them, I'm not going to be the one to call and say, 'By the way, we need just a little bit more.'" Anne was only going to do this once.

Rachel agreed. "What sounds good, Beth?"

"I'd say four hundred tickets."

Everyone agreed.

"And I think we should sell tables," Rachel added. "People should be able to buy a table and sit with the people they want to."

"We'll have to find out how they plan to set up the room." Beth made the note. One more question to ask the events manager.

"Will people get a discount then?" Karen thought it only fair.

"No, but it will sell more tickets. It's psychological. People will do their own recruiting for the dinner." Rachel was an expert at fundraisers.

Anne was filing one afternoon when she ran across a folder full of applications of the people who had applied for her position. She stuffed it into an envelope, marked it "Personnel," and almost sent it through interoffice mail. Applications contained private and possibly sensitive information. Best to let the personnel department deal with it.

But curiosity got the best of her, and she decided to see what kind of competition she'd been up against. Half an hour later, she discovered that she'd been the youngest person to apply with the least amount of experience. Her eyes narrowed. Something didn't seem quite right. She decided to have a chat with her coworker.

"Nita, lots of other people interviewed for my job, right?"

Nita paused at her typewriter, and then she turned around to face Anne. She had a puzzled expression on her face. "There were about 15, I think."

"Fifteen?"

"At least."

Anne nodded. There were 17 applications in the file. "But I'm sure there were others with more experience."

"Plenty."

"Then why'd they hire me?" Anne only wanted an honest answer.

Nita cast a glance toward the door. Motioned for Anne to close it. "You have to promise that your feelings won't be hurt."

"Come on. Tell."

"A couple years ago, the city was involved in a class action suit."

"For what?"

"Not hiring enough minorities."

"Are you serious?" Anne could feel her blood pressure rising. "So my color was more important than any skills I could or couldn't offer?"

Nita shrugged.

"Well, that sure makes a person feel good about herself." She slumped into the chair in front of Nita's desk.

"You're the one who asked. Besides, we love you."

"And I love you guys too," Anne mumbled back. "Most of the time."

Nita looked at Anne with gentle eyes. It was hard to see her so deflated, but she knew that Anne would have dealt with this sort of thing before. "What did your parents think about you marrying Will?"

"They were basically okay with it. They asked me if I was sure about it." She shrugged. "I told them he was a Christian. And honestly, which is worse? To marry a black person who's not a Christian or a white person who is? I can't believe I'm even thinking like this. Which is the greater evil? I married someone I love. What's the big deal?"

The first thing Anne did after she finally got Will to admit that he liked her was to invite him to Mercer Island to meet her parents. She tried to prepare them first.

"Is it okay if I invite someone to dinner tonight?" she asked them on Saturday morning over breakfast.

"Of course. You know we don't mind if you have friends over." Her mother got up from the table to pour herself another cup of coffee. She raised the pot, looking over the rims of her bifocals to see if anyone else wanted any. Anne and her father both shook their heads. "Will you be home tonight, Christopher?" she asked her husband.

"Tonight?"

"The fifteenth. Saturday."

"I didn't pull weekend duty." Anne's dad was a surgeon at Harbor View.

"One of the girls from the house?" her mother asked, as her father spread open the Sports section of the paper.

"No. Someone I've been running with."

"What's her name?"

"*His* name is Will Bradley."

"Oh," she said with a raised eyebrow.

"He writes for the the *Daily*. The campus paper. He interviewed me for an article a couple months ago."

"That's nice." Her father smiled beneath his salt-and-pepper mustache.

"I brought it so you could read it," she said, taking it from the pocket of her bathrobe.

Her parents took the article and bent over it. They spent more time looking at his picture than reading the column he'd written.

"Are you sure about this, honey?" her father finally asked. They seemed to know it was important to her that they say *something*.

"Daddy, he's a Christian."

"I'm sure he's a very nice boy," said her mother with a smile, patting her father's arm with her hand.

Anne called Will immediately and asked him to come.

"Your parents won't mind?"

"No."

"Are you sure?"

"Don't be silly."

He showed up right on time with a bouquet of flowers for Anne's mother.

"Thank you." Her smile was gracious. "White roses have always been my favorites."

Will's eyes sought Anne's. She gave him a smile of encouragement.

Dinner went well. Will complimented Anne's mother on the meal and engaged her father in a conversation about hockey. Anne steered the conversation now and then, making sure everyone was taking part.

After they'd finished eating, Anne's mother pushed her chair away from the table and began to collect the dishes.

Will stopped her. "Let Anne and me do that for you, Mrs. Hopkins."

Anne's mother shot a glance at her husband.

He shrugged.

"What do you think?" Anne's mother and father whispered to each in the living room.

They were silent a moment as they listened to the laughter in the kitchen.

"I think it doesn't matter what we think. I don't think he'll be going away anytime soon."

"I like him," Anne's mother said. She'd made her decision pretty early on about Will.

"I didn't say I didn't. I just said that his mind seems to be made up."

The wedding took place in Seattle at the church where The INN was held. Will's parents and relatives drove up from Tacoma and Anne's relatives flew in from Chicago.

In the minutes before the wedding began, Anne's mother took her by the hand. "Honey, your father and I have always wanted the best for you. We've given you every chance, every opportunity that we could. We sent you to the best schools. We would have sent you to Harvard if you hadn't insisted on the U."

Anne nodded. She knew all of this.

"We love Will. We think he's a man of integrity and, if I thought it possible, I'd say he loves you more than we do."

Anne blushed and smiled.

"Honey, just remember that no matter how much you love Will and he loves you, there are some things that people have to deal with and settle themselves. And sometimes those are things that the other person will never be able to understand."

"Mom, I know you and Daddy love me. This is who I want to spend my life with. Please, don't worry."

"I just want you to have the best of everything."

"I do. I have Will."

Her mother's words echoed in Anne's head that night as she drove home from work. This was one of those things. One of the things she had to deal with herself. Finding out why she'd gotten her job made her feel strange. Off-kilter.

Insecure. I feel insecure.

She almost told Will that night over dinner. In fact, she'd opened her mouth to say the words, but they just wouldn't come out.

"What?" Will asked, pausing midbite. "Is there something you wanted to say?"

Anne closed her mouth and thought about it for several seconds. "Yeah. I love you. Do you know that?"

He smiled and continued eating.

She felt like a big phony. She'd never said those words before without meaning them. Not that she hadn't meant them. She just hadn't been thinking them. She'd used them. She'd used the words "I love you."

And now she felt like a big insecure phony.

Chapter 20

⌒

Rachel wasn't looking forward to their impending vacation, but R.J. couldn't get the camping gear out soon enough. He set up the tent in the front yard just to make sure it was still in good condition. Then he barbecued a hot dog over the Bunsen burner to make sure it worked. Next, he took out a backpack and started stuffing things inside it.

And that was the first problem they encountered: packing. Rachel's packing.

R.J. frowned at the waist-high pyramid of perfectly matched French leather luggage she stacked behind the car.

"I think I did pretty well on packing light, don't you?"

"Rachel, how do you propose that we get all of this up into the mountains?"

"You said we were driving. And we're taking the pickup, right? It should have room enough unless…did I not leave enough room for your things?"

"No. I mean, yes. It's just that we drive to the mountains, and then we throw on the backpacks and we hike."

"I don't mind hiking."

"Rachel, we're going to park the car, and leave it *by itself* for five days while we go up into the mountains. There's no way you can carry all of that."

"R.J., this is the absolute minimum. What if we want to go out to a nice restaurant? Or what if we want to go dancing?"

"Rachel, what part of this don't you understand? We're going to be in the mountains, at least ten miles from another living soul for five days. No restaurants, no phones, no people."

"Why do you want to do that when there are perfectly acceptable resorts to stay at?"

"Because it's fun."

"Fun?"

"Please, Rach. If you do this for me, next vacation we'll do what you want."

"Whatever I want?"

"Anything."

"Next time we go to Tokyo."

"Isn't this just perfect!"

Rachel looked again at the stars that hung right above her head.

"I haven't seen so many stars in years," he chortled.

I have. I just didn't have to sleep on the ground in order to do it.

He reached out his arm and pulled her closer. "Penny for your thoughts."

"You wouldn't want this thought for a million dollars, R.J."

"Didn't I find all the rocks before we rolled out your sleeping bag?"

How can I explain in words that he understands? I hate this? This is an utter waste of modern convenience and time? "I'm fine."

"Are you afraid?"

"Of what?"

"Bears, skunks...I don't know..."

"Are you afraid?"

"No."

"You obviously know more about this sort of thing than I do, so if you're not afraid, there's no point in my being afraid, is there?"

R.J. deflated just a little. "Guess not. You just don't seem like you're enjoying it."

Rachel ground her teeth in frustration. "R.J., I just don't see what there *is* to enjoy. Why don't you tell me what you like so much about camping?"

"I don't know, Rach. It's *camping*. You know, wood smoke, s'mores, stars. Finding bits of leaves for the next month in the shirts and pants you wore. Clean, fresh air. The smell of coffee in the morning. Birds singing just for you. The hush of the wind in the trees. It's beautiful here, don't you think?"

R.J. woke up with the heat of the sun on his face. He groaned and put up an arm to shield his eyes before he opened them. He glanced at Rachel's sleeping bag; he was surprised not to see her in it.

"Rach?" he was trying to decide whether or not to be worried.

"I'm right here. I'm fine. You've been so tired, I thought I'd let you sleep."

R.J. sat up. "Rach, where are you?"

"I'm right here!"

He saw a lazy hand rise from an area of meadow grass.

He rolled from the sleeping bag and pushed himself to his feet. Stretching his hands behind him, be began to yawn. Then he saw Rachel.

She was lying in the middle of the grass, looking for all the world as though she were sun bathing in St. Tropez. "Geez, Rachel, put a shirt on!"

"Why? This was a great idea, R.J. I've never been able to get a good tan in the States. They'd throw me in jail for indecent exposure. Besides, who's around to see me except you?"

"Nobody. It's just when I think camping, I think sweaters and flannel shirts."

"First you talk about back to nature and minimalism, and now you demand clothes? You can't have it both ways. I kind of like this."

"It's indecent."

"You like it well enough at home."

"But that's at home!"

Rachel grinned at him.

He blushed.

She lowered her sunglasses and fluttered smoky eyelashes at him. "Are you sure you don't like this? I do."

He threw a shirt at her. "Get dressed. We're going fishing."

What seemed like years later, Rachel found herself sitting on the bank of a small river. Still. They'd been there for two hours. She swatted at a mosquito. "Bloodsuckers!"

"You didn't put on perfume, did you?"

"Of course."

"Most people put on bug repellant in the wilderness, not bug attractant."

"Are you saying what works for you works for mosquitoes?"

He sent her a lopsided smile. "Maybe."

"Did we forget to send the invitation out to the fish?"

"No. Sometimes it's just like this. They're not biting because they're not hungry."

"Just like they weren't hungry in November in Montana. I don't think fish are ever hungry. And how long is it going to take to decide to pack up and go back to camp?"

"It depends. Aren't you having fun?"

"Describe how fishing could be fun, and I'll let you know."

"It's relaxing, Rach. You can sit in the sun and watch the river go by and think."

"And what are you thinking?"

"How lucky I am to have you as my wife."

Rachel smiled and then leaned over to kiss him.

"And if we don't catch a fish, what are we going to eat for dinner?"

Rachel sat on her hands and swung her feet over the bank. "I did happen to sneak a jar of caviar and a half bottle of champagne into my backpack."

R.J. wrinkled his nose. "Caviar. Actually, I've never tasted caviar before. It's fish eggs, right?"

"Right."

"What's it taste like?"

Rachel slid him a look beneath her eyelashes. "Fish."

They ended up eating the caviar that night, though R.J. had a little trouble at first.

"It just doesn't seem right. It's like eating ball bearings or something."

"Think of it as miniature black grapes."

R.J. sniffed at the cracker delicately. "No good. Smells too much like fish."

"Then pretend they're tiny miniature fish." Rachel was determined not to let him ruin her good time.

R.J. closed his eyes, took a bite, chewed twice and gallantly swallowed. After a moment, his eyes popped open in surprise. "Hey. That wasn't bad!"

As the sun dipped below the tree line, twilight unfurled itself on the forest. It was accompanied but a sudden flit-flitting among the branches. Rachel caught a silhouette of something skimming around the trees. "Birds?"

"They're bats."

"Bats!" She ducked her head and tucked it into her sweater.

"Bats eat bugs that hang out by the branches. It's an alliteration of *b*s." He laughed and put an arm around her. "Relax. Unless you have 20 eyes and four or five wings, they're not interested. Look. I'll build a fire. It'll keep them away. Want to help me?"

Rachel gathered as many small twigs as she could find while R.J. broke up several bigger branches. He built a small pyramid on a base of dried leaves. Then he took a lighter from his pocket and lit the bottom of the pile. Taking off his baseball cap, he used it to fan the flame until it jumped to the bigger pieces.

Then he sat down by their sleeping bags and pulled Rachel into his arms. "We should sing."

"We should sing?" She echoed his words as if he were crazy.

"Yeah. Don't you know any campfire songs?"

"No."

"Weren't you in Girl Scouts?"

"No. Weren't you in Boy Scouts?"

"Of course. I'm an Eagle Scout."

"Well, then you sing the campfire songs."

"Okay." He launched into a jaunty rendition of "Do Your Ears Hang Low" that had Rachel disbelieving hers.

"What are you singing?"

"Here. I'll teach it to you." He sang it several times but was unsuccessful in convincing her to join in.

"I'll teach you another one. All you have to do is repeat after me, okay? The littlest worm."

Rachel frowned at him.

"Bat got your tongue?" He jabbed her with an elbow. "The littlest worm."

"The littlest worm," she sang.

"I ever saw."

"I ever saw."

"Got stuck inside."

"Got stuck inside."

"My soda straw."

"That's gross."

R.J. ran through his entire repertoire of classic camp songs. He taught her the ceremonial Hokey Pokey dance by the campfire before they laughed themselves to the ground and sprawled onto the sleeping bags. R.J. poked at the fire with a stick to scatter the dying embers. Then he cupped her face in his hands and kissed her.

"Are you having fun yet?"

She kissed him back. "Yes." She smiled with glowing eyes.

"Okay. There's one last song you have to learn. It's the 'Go to Sleep and Shut Up' song."

"No more songs."

"This one's easy. Once you learn the first verse you'll know all the rest. Ready?"

Rachel sighed. "Ready."

"Ninety-nine bottles of beer on the wall, ninety-nine bottles of beer..."

They got to 82 bottles of beer before their words garbled off and they fell asleep.

Rachel and R.J. returned from vacation dirty but relaxed. The first thing Rachel did was check her fax machine and her voice mail, and then she made a list of the things she needed to do during the coming week. One of the first was to make her donation to the silent auction.

She had a nice bottle of Bordeaux from 1961. A Château Cos d'Estournel. Her grandfather had insisted that it was even better than Lafite Rothschild. Of course, if you were striving to impress, nothing could beat a Rothschild. But if you simply wanted to enjoy a great wine, nothing could beat an Estournel. It was valued at $2000. Buying a bottle that old was always a risk; it was entirely possible that it had already turned to vinegar. But Rachel had ensured its proper storage. It had hardly been moved since it had been purchased, 43 years earlier. It could easily be worth an entire quarter of tuition at the local community college. Besides, she would still have three whole cases for herself.

She finished the list in her leather portfolio, and then she closed it and walked toward their bedroom. She paused in the doorway, looked around, and smiled. She loved this room. The walls were painted the clearest pale moon blue and the windows were hung with dark midnight blue velvet curtains that dropped into pools on the floor. The bateau bed, the dressers, and the armoire were made from highly polished sleek mahogany, and the bedspread and other upholsteries were deep plum velvet. She knew it was the fashion to make a master bedroom into a multipurpose room with a desk for writing, chairs for lounging, and even tables for taking coffee or tea. But in her opinion, a bedroom should be dedicated to sleeping. And this room evoked twilight. The soft, heavy fabrics were reminiscent of the numbing blanket that sleep brought when it came. And, of course, the entire setting was luxuriously sensuous.

This room was her bower. It was the place where night and day blurred with wakefulness and sleep, reality and dream.

She had always known how to create moods, but sexy was new for her. She'd discovered a whole new world of feeling when she'd married R.J. Discovered that the knowing, sophisticated image she'd tried to create for herself was as far from the reality of sex as a sunflower was from the sun itself. Sex wasn't aloof or emotionless or elegant. It wasn't playacting; it didn't demand worship. It was giving and receiving and natural. And when she gave herself to R.J., somehow she always ended up finding herself.

She shed her clothes and then ran her fingers through the tangles in her hair. She laughed out loud when she heard R.J. singing the little worm song in the shower. She decided to join him.

At the next food committee meeting, Anne passed around a copy of the letter she had drafted. A list of addresses was attached to the back.

"How many companies are there?" Karen asked.

"About 40. A lot more than I thought there would be. That was a good idea, Rachel."

Rachel shrugged off the compliment. It was just standard business practice. General knowledge. "I think this is good," she finally said after reading and rereading it. She would have been convinced. In fact, she already was. "How do they get sent out?"

"We'll give a disk to the OSC secretary, and she'll take care of printing and mailing them," Beth explained.

"So now what?" Anne asked.

Beth smiled. "We wait."

Talk turned to other things before they left.

"What do people wear to this thing?" Anne asked Beth.

"Oh, I don't know. It's dressy. Floor-length or a nice cocktail-type dress."

Karen paled. She had absolutely nothing that fit that description. Maybe she wouldn't go. Thirty dollars was a lot to pay for dinner, and Kevin wouldn't be back from Iraq by then anyway.

Anne nodded. She had several dresses from her sorority days that were classic enough to still be in style.

"And the guys?" Rachel asked. Maybe she would need to have a tux made for R.J.

"They'll wear their mess dress." Beth thought that would have been fairly clear.

"What's that?"

"The Air Force version of the tuxedo. You know. Dark blue. Waist-length jacket. Bow tie."

"Oh. Well then, good." Less to worry about that way. And he shouldn't complain about dressing up if it were an actual uniform, although he probably would anyway. Just on principle.

"It's too bad we don't have a dress closet like at the sorority," Anne said with regret.

"What's a dress closet?" asked Karen.

"Ours was a big walk-in where everybody stored their formals. There had to have been at least 40 in there. Once you'd worn yours to a dance, you wouldn't want to wear it again for a while. But you could always look through the closet and ask to borrow someone else's."

"And they'd let you?" said Karen. If she had a new formal dress, she didn't know if she'd be able to get up the courage to wear it, let alone lend it.

"Sure," said Anne.

"But, what if someone spilled something on it?" Karen could hardly trust herself not to do that with her own things.

"There's always dry-cleaning. Usually you'd have it dry-cleaned before you put it back. There was only one time I lent mine that it didn't turn out all right. It came back with huge pit stains." Anne shrugged. "It happens."

Anne heard her own words and looked around at her friends. She suddenly realized that she must sound as much of a snob as Rachel sometimes did.

People just didn't understand sororities. A number of people at her church back home thought she donated her soul to Satan when she'd decided to join one. As if it were as bad as living in downtown Sodom or Gomorrah. Sororities picked their members, it was true. But they just did, in an organized fashion, what people did every day. She could point to cliques or floors in dorms that had a definite personality and always did things together. It was human nature to gravitate toward people who were like you. And with a sorority, there was a sphere of influence of sixty to a hundred people. People you lived with and saw every day.

"What better witness of a Christian lifestyle?" she would ask those church people. They thought it was shameful to live among women who drank and partied and slept around. But not all of the sorority members did that, and those who did didn't do it all the time. And besides, *those* were the very kind of people who needed Christ, not the people who already knew Him.

The church members who had questioned her choice of sorority had also originally questioned her choice of the University of Washington. *A secular university; what could she be thinking?*

She could still hear the astonishment in their voices. What she had been thinking was, *If God can't exist in real-life, rubber-meets-the-road situations, then he's not really God, and he hasn't changed my life.* She shook her head. She got frustrated just thinking about it. At least her parents had supported both choices.

"All I have are skirts and blouses," Karen was saying.

"I have lots of things you could borrow," said Rachel, making up her mind to be helpful. Though Karen was lanky and Rachel was curvy, something should work. Visualizing her closet, Rachel could already think of several possibilities.

Chapter 21

That Sunday, Karen woke with a start. She'd fallen asleep thinking that there was something she'd forgotten to do. And her mind had refused to let her sleep soundly because of it. She stretched. Opened her eyes.

Remembered what it was: She was supposed to have made something sweet to bring to church. She closed her eyes and smothered her head with her pillow. How could she have forgotten? She'd only done it every Sunday since Kevin had been gone.

She removed the pillow and lay motionless on the bed, staring at the ceiling. Her week had been one long blur of activity that had begun and would end at the church. It felt as though she had just left there, and now, in two short hours, she would be there again. She searched her mind for something she could make quickly.

Brownies?

No, she had no eggs.

Chocolate chip cookie bars?

Same problem. No eggs.

Well, she couldn't just buy something!

Why not?

Nobody buys baked goods. Everybody makes them. It would be shameful.

Why? They always taste better, anyway.

Karen let her gaze wander around the room. It was true. Store-bought usually did taste better.

"Darn it!" she said out loud as she sat up. "I'm buying. I don't care!" Then she marched into the bathroom to take a shower.

Karen felt nervous all through church. She looked around at the members with suspicious eyes. Who would be the first to notice? Because it would be noticed. You couldn't just buy something from a store and pass it off as your own. Unless you were lucky. *Please, God,* she prayed, knowing even as she said the words that she couldn't ask God for help when she was shirking her duties.

After service, everyone congregated around several tables filled with sweets and punch.

One of the older women picked up one of Karen's cupcakes and took a bite. "Mmm. Did you bake these, Karen?"

"No. I bought them," she heard herself say. Why couldn't she just lie like normal people? She could feel the eyes of the other women boring into her, could just imagine what they were thinking. *We all have children, but we find time to bake for church. You don't even have a husband right now, let alone a single child. What's wrong with you?*

"My oven's broken." The words leaped from her mouth before she could stop them. Her eyes widened. She *could* lie!

All the women were suddenly clucking sympathetically. "Oh, that's terrible!"

"I don't know how you can survive."

"I hope you've called someone to fix it."

"I have," she heard herself lie. *Again!* "But who works on Saturday?" The conversations around her returned to normal.

The next food committee meeting was looked forward to with both anticipation and dread. Everyone was anxious to hear who had responded to Anne's letter, but they were also afraid that no one had.

"Well," Anne said, drawing a sheaf of papers from her bag with a flourish. "Drumroll, please. I date stamped these letters so that we would know who responded first to our letter of solicitation.

"Three stores volunteered to supply our appetizer. Two stores volunteered to supply our main course, and four bakeries volunteered for dessert. How about that?" she asked, grinning.

Beth clapped her hands.

"So, what I was thinking we should do is to accept the first letter for each course. We can write two different thank-yous: one to the companies we'll accept and the other to the companies we'll have to say no to."

"Do you mind if I draft the thanks-but-no letter?" Rachel asked. There was an art to doing that sort of thing. And if done correctly, they might have even more people to turn down next year.

Beth was the first to respond. The more everyone else did, the less she would have to do. "Please. Be my guest."

Karen tested the bath water to make sure it wasn't too hot. Her foot looked leprous white under the water. She spun it around to check the temperature.

A little too cold.

She adjusted the faucet and then slunk into the water, sighing with pleasure. She had needed this bath all week, but she hadn't had time until now. She was completely worn out driving back and forth to church every day, trying to complete all the tasks they had demanded of her.

Isn't life made for more than just trying to be perfect? When do I get a break? When to I get to let up and just enjoy it? Does it never end?

She sunk deeper into the water.

I am tired of church. I am tired of God. I am tired of church people, always calling, always making demands. I help everyone else. I listen to everyone else. When is someone going to listen to me? Kevin doesn't want to hear it. All those church ladies don't want to hear it. I'm going to ask you, God: What have I done not to deserve a baby? What have I done that half the women in the church didn't think of doing? How come if you have so many spirit children waiting to be born, you won't give me just one?

"Hi...Rachel?" asked a hesitant voice.

"Yes, this is Rachel," she answered, tapping a foot on the driveway.

"Hi, Rachel. This is Karen."

"Hi, Karen."

"Hi. I was wondering if I could ask you something...?"

"Yes?"

"Not right now, I mean, but could we meet? Somewhere?"

Rachel looked down the lawn and saw the roof of the postal truck glide away through the trees down by the road. "Yes. When?"

"This afternoon."

"This afternoon I can't. But I could meet tomorrow. When would be good for you?" asked Rachel into the cell phone as she walked down the long driveway to the mailbox.

"Whenever is good for you. After lunch?"

"Why don't we meet before lunch?" she asked, pausing to sniff a blossoming rose and wave to the gardener.

"I wouldn't want you to have to come all the way into town. Is there any place between town and you?"

"About 15 miles of beach," she responded, pulling her mail from the mailbox.

"Oh. That's right. I forgot."

Rachel began to flip through the mail, tallying the work that lay before her by the return addresses on the envelopes. "Listen, can we make it for lunch instead?"

"Twelve thirty?"

"Good. Twelve thirty. I'll meet you at that pavilion out by West Beach. Do you know it?"

"I'm sure I can find it."

"I'll bring some picnic things. We can just eat lunch there. Have some wine."

"Well...I don't drink wine."

"Beer then."

"Um..."

"Coke."

"I don't drink Coke either."

Rachel rolled her eyes as she walked back up the driveway. "How about this. You bring what you want to drink, and I'll bring everything else."

"Okay."

"See you then." Rachel walked into the house and went straight into her office.

The machine in the corner of the room was spitting out paper. Unconcerned, she gathered it together and bunched it on her desk. Then she took a pair of glasses from a thin desk drawer, put them on, and went to work.

Karen spent her day nervously wandering around the house. She'd flipped through TV channels after she'd finished talking with Rachel, but there wasn't anything on she felt like watching. She watered the ivy Anne had given her. Watered the hanging plants outside. Then she went upstairs and sat on the bed for a while, looking around the bedroom at the collected detritus of their lives. A couple stuffed animals Kevin had given her. She picked them up and looked at them. She supposed they were cute, but stuffed animals had never been her thing.

It's the thought that counts.

The picture on the wall stopped her wandering eyes. It portrayed a place she'd never visited. Some beach along the Pacific Coast was what its former owner had explained at the garage sale. She studied it for a while and then decided she didn't really like it. At the time of purchase, she'd just wanted something cheap to hang on the wall.

She fingered the quilt on the bed. Her mother had made it. A wedding gift. She could hear her mother's smiling voice, "Your favorite colors, pinks and greens." It hadn't seemed important then to remind her that those were a younger sister's favorites.

The thought. It's the thought that counts.

She sighed and stood up. There was already dust on the bookshelf. There was always dust on the bookshelf. The wood was dark, almost black. She preferred lighter-colored stains, but she remembered how thankful they'd been when a friend of Kevin's parents had given it to them. She went to the hall closet to find a rag to chase the dust away. Her eyes were greeted with a rainbow of colors. None of the towel or sheet sets matched each other. They were wedding gifts. Karen suspected they'd come from a discount linen shop not far from the town her parents lived in. She ran a hand down the tidy stacks.

They're nice and thick.

A tear slipped down her cheek. She pushed it away, but another took its place.

"I'm happy here. I have a husband. He has a good job. We live close to the beach. We have a nice place to live," she said firmly, out loud. But her screaming thoughts quickly drowned the sound of her voice.

Who are you kidding? You hate your life. Look at it. Look at those stuffed animals, the quilt, and the bookshelf. These towels! None of these are what you would have picked. Go ahead—say it—you hate this life. You hate all of it. You hate not being able to choose. But you can't. You're trapped. You're trapped living the life other people think you should live.

Karen was waiting at the pavilion the next day when Rachel arrived. She was sitting at a picnic table reading a book about LDS history that she hoped would help her teach Sunday school. She shivered and buttoned up her cardigan another button.

Rachel swung a picnic basket onto the table. "Hi." Her eyes looked at Karen's over the top of large dark sunglasses. She released the basket and pushed the glasses onto her forehead. "Aren't you hot? It must be almost 80 today." Rachel swept a hand over the wood bench before she sat down. She'd hate to get her skirt dirty.

"Not really. It's cool here in the shade." Karen closed the book. "Thanks for coming."

"You're welcome. You hungry?"

Karen nodded.

Rachel flipped open the top of the basket and began to pull out the contents. Baguette. Cheese. Ham. A meat-loaf looking sort of thing. Small pickles. Wine. "So, you don't drink wine. Your religion?"

Karen nodded. "No alcohol or caffeine."

"That's a shame," Rachel said as she distributed napkins and utensils. "In a lot of countries, and especially back in history, it was safer to drink wine than water. Funny how the modern world has made us so self-righteous."

They ate in amiable silence until Rachel had finished. Karen was still picking at her food, taking crisp pieces of baguette and tearing it into tiny pieces before eating it.

"You look like a bird," Rachel observed. "They're always tearing at small pieces of food, making them even tinier."

Karen smiled and made herself eat the rest of the food on her plate.

Rachel swirled her glass of wine around and then finished it. She set it down on the table. "What's up?"

Karen looked at Rachel and tried to think of how to put into words what she wanted. *I don't want to be me? I want a new life?* What she settled on was, "I want a new image."

"New image. What image do you want?"

Karen gazed at her friend. She looked perfectly cool and collected in a white tank top and bright yellow skirt. How could she begin to understand what Karen was feeling? Tears rose to her eyes, and before she could help herself she said vehemently, "Not what I am right now."

Rachel lit a cigarette and took a drag. "Well, that leaves us lots of room to work with."

"I was thinking that maybe you could take me to where you get your clothes. I know it would be expensive," she said hurriedly, "but maybe I would only need a few things."

"I do all my shopping in Paris. Besides, you wouldn't want to dress like me."

Wouldn't I?

"You wouldn't be yourself then; you'd just be a copy of me." She took off her sunglasses and placed them on the table between them. "Tell me this, when I look at the new Karen, what do you want me to be able to see?"

"Like how?"

"When I look at you and I say, Wow! She must be...what? Fill in the blank."

Karen thought about it. For a long time. Then she gave up. "I don't know, Rachel. All I know is that I don't want to be me anymore."

"Karen, I can help with clothes. I can help with hair, but you have to promise me something."

"What?"

"You have to promise me that you'll help with you. Otherwise, you'll be the same person you are right now dressed up in someone else's clothes."

"I'll try."

Rachel gave her a long look.

"I'll do it. I just don't know how."

"Start with you. What makes you happy? What makes you angry? What colors do you like? What music makes you want to dance? It's not that difficult."

It is when you've always let someone else make those decisions. "What should I do?"

"Let's start with finding out what you like. Where do you usually shop for clothes?"

"I don't. Shop. I make most of them. I sew."

"Oh. How does that work?"

"You go to the fabric store, find a pattern you like, and then buy the material to make it."

"Is there a fabric store in town?"

"On Bayview Road."

"Let's go."

"I had planned, actually, on buying the new clothes. Not sewing them."

"I know. That's what you said. What I want you to do is show me what kinds of styles you like."

"Oh. Well, usually I sew Simplicity or McCall's."

"I'm more interested in what kinds of lines you like. What sort of shapes. Fitted, body skimming. That sort of thing."

"I don't really know."

"We'll figure it out." She laid a hand on her friend's arm. "Don't worry."

They packed up the picnic and sprinkled the bread crumbs on the sand for the birds. The midday sun was blinding. And it was only May.

Karen led the way in her car from the beach to the fabric store.

As Karen parked her car, she saw that Rachel had pulled her

convertible into the furthest spot from the store. She shut the door and waited for Rachel to join her.

"There are plenty of spots over here in the shade," Karen said.

"I know. I'd rather park the Alfa where it won't be dinged by anyone."

That was a new concept to Karen.

They walked together into the store. Karen breathed in the smell of new material. It always gave her a thrill to think of all the material wrapped around the bolts, waiting to be made into something.

"I really don't know what I like," she confessed as they walked to the pattern area at the back of the store.

"That's why I'm going to watch you while you look."

"Oh," she said uncertainly as they sat down in front of the pattern books.

"Karen, I want to know what *you* like. I already know what I like. And it's not important what your mother likes or even what Kevin likes. Just point out to me the things that catch your eye. It'll be like a game."

"Here goes," said Karen, opening a book.

For a while, Karen picked out styles that were geared toward Rachel's taste. But then she seemed to forget Rachel was there and the real Karen began to emerge. And she should have been born in the 1950s. The looks she chose were pencil-thin slacks and fitted tops. Simple, clean lines. Classic American styles.

After Karen had finished the fifth and final pattern book, she looked at Rachel expectantly.

"Now we look at fabrics," Rachel ordered

At first as they walked back through the store, Karen stopped to look at everything, but it soon became apparent that she preferred dark, bright colors. Rachel approved. Karen's pale skin and dark hair needed those shades so they could work together. And her blue eyes needed the brightness in tone to sparkle.

After they finished with the fabrics, they drove farther down the street to the mall to go shopping. The moment they walked into the department store, Karen started looking at price tags. She couldn't help herself. She and Kevin were so used to saving for all the nonexistent children they were supposed to have that comparison shopping was second nature.

"I could never bring myself to pay this much for this," she whispered to Rachel, holding out the sleeve of a plain white shirt.

"You're paying for quality, Karen. And style."

"But I could make it for a quarter of the cost."

"You said you didn't want to sew. You insisted that you wanted to buy."

"I know, but…"

"Okay," Rachel said, sighing. "Pretend that you have absolutely no money at all and what you're doing here is picking what you'd buy if you *did* have the money."

It went easier after that, and Karen finally went into the dressing room with an armful of clothes.

Five minutes later she came out in a tight-fitting outfit. Rachel shook her head.

"But the color's good," Karen protested. "I think."

"Would you wear it?"

Karen tilted her head.

"Out in public?"

"I like it…"

"No. I'm not letting you buy something you won't wear."

"But *you'd* wear it."

It was true. Rachel would. "I like my body. Go and try on the next one."

Karen pondered Rachel's words in the dressing room. She looked at herself in the mirror. Did she like her body? She looked at her abdomen. It was flatter than Rachel's. She looked at her breasts. They were smaller. Her hips were slender. She still needed to lose some weight. She pinched at the skin around her waist and then suddenly blushed, realizing she was staring at herself.

In a mirror.

She quickly changed into the next outfit. Rachel was right. She didn't like her body.

They left the store each carrying a bag. Karen was exerting an almost superhuman effort trying not to remember what she'd paid for everything. Kevin was going to kill her.

They strolled through the mall.

"I've always wanted to have hair like this," said Karen, looking at a picture in the window of a hair salon.

"So get a perm," suggested Rachel.

"I don't know," said Karen. "I've always felt as if that would be cheating. If God had wanted me to have curly hair, he would have given it to me."

"If you don't like it, let it grow out and then cut it off."

"You think?"

"There's no other way to get this," she said, indicating Karen's long, limp hair, "to look like that," she said, pointing to the precisely waved hair in the picture.

"It probably wouldn't look right."

"I guess you'll never know."

Karen wavered only a moment before making up her mind. "I'll do it."

Two hours later, she stepped out of the salon looking like a thirties glamour girl. She put a hand up to touch her new chin-length waves. "It feels so light. I can't believe it!"

Rachel smiled at her delight. The look suited her and it lifted her whole face.

The next transformation was in the arena of cosmetics. Makeup doesn't do much for women who have an inner glow of their own, but at this stage in Karen's self-esteem, cosmetics could do a lot.

"I think that's way too dark," Karen cautioned the saleswoman as she reached to apply Bordeaux-colored lipstick to her lips.

"Trust her," Rachel ordered.

Karen closed her eyes and tilted her lips forward. She didn't want to watch the conversion into Frankenstein's bride.

When she finally opened them, she was astonished by the person she saw in the mirror. "I look like an old-time movie star! I'll never be able to do this by myself."

"Of course you will. You're going to take it all off," Rachel ordered, taking a cotton ball from the saleswoman and handing it to Karen, "and then you're going to put it all back on."

They emerged from the mall at 7:00, Karen tired but elated. A billboard in the parking lot in front of them captivated her attention. "I could never look like that. Especially in a bikini."

"Of course you couldn't," Rachel agreed.

Karen looked at her.

"Statistically speaking, fashion models are aberrations. The majority of women are not that tall, the majority of women do not have flat hips, the majority of women cannot possibly maintain any sort of good health with a body weight that low. Usually that sort of deviation from the norm is called freakish. These women ought to be in circus shows. Instead, we've let them be exalted and label them beautiful. I hope you never do look like that. It wouldn't be natural. In fact, you need to put on some weight. You look like a cadaver walking around."

Karen was shocked. She had never had anyone tell her that before. It couldn't be true. In fact, she needed to lose a few more pounds. She put it out of her mind.

Since R.J. was TDY, Rachel invited Karen over for dinner.

They relaxed at a table by the pool; the sound of gurgling water was soothing. Rachel kicked off her shoes, so Karen did the same.

Rachel's cook came out and placed a plate of bruschetta and some wine before them.

Rachel spoke a few words to him in Italian before letting him return to the kitchen. "He'll bring some water for you."

Karen smiled her thanks. She hadn't realized until then how hungry and thirsty she was.

"So," Rachel asked, "what are you living for?"

"What do you mean?"

"What is it that makes you get up every day? Is it your religion? Does it promise you something that makes life worth living?"

"In a way. The church says that after we die, we get to be in charge of our planets…with our families. Like Jesus is in charge of this one."

"If I were you, then I'd just shoot myself right now."

"Why?" asked Karen with horror.

"There's no way I'd want to be in charge of a whole entire planet. I make a promise to myself every day that I'm going to resign from being the master of the universe. I just don't need the stress."

"But then you'll be a slave, serving other people for eternity."

"You said it's the same thing after we die as what Jesus has set up here?"

"Yes."

"Well, I'm satisfied with my life on Earth. Pretty much. And I know I'm not in charge of this planet. So, if what you say is true, then I'm his slave."

"Yes."

"I'd take my job over his job any day. Any day in the next life too. You know what the problem is with your religion? No incentives." She took a sip of wine. "What happens to people like me who don't believe here on Earth?"

"After you die, you have another chance to change."

"There's a second chance? I can do anything I want down here knowing there'll be an option to become a Mormon after I die?"

Karen didn't like the sound of how she phrased it, but it was basically true. That's why LDS baptized the dead. So they could join them in heaven. "Yes."

"Like I said. No incentive. I'm surprised you have so many people in your church."

"Why?"

"There's no incentive to try to be good if you get second chances, is there?"

CHAPTER 22

⁓

Anne was dressed for the auction and ready to go, but she lacked luster. She had wandered into the bathroom and was staring at herself in the mirror, tilting her head back and forth and examining herself. Who was the person staring back at her?

"What's wrong?" Will finally asked. "You haven't been yourself lately." He wrapped an arm around her and nuzzled her neck. "You aren't pregnant, are you?"

"No!" That was the furthest thing from her mind. She turned to face him and detached his arm. "Will, I've never really felt 'black' the way I do here."

"You're Anne."

"That's what I always thought, but down here it's different."

"You know I love you."

"I know. But people are different here. You can't have any idea what it is to be black in America. Almost everywhere you go, you're different from most of the other people you see and live near. Twenty-four hours a day. In Seattle, most of the time I felt that I stood out, more than I do here anyway, but I didn't feel any animosity about it. When we were dating, people stared at us."

"I know. I remember. I was there."

"But they didn't do it out of mean-spiritedness or hatred. It was more like seeing something unexpected. They looked and then they looked away. But here, haven't you felt it? Haven't you felt girls look at you when you're by yourself, and then see them turn away in disgust when they see me come up and kiss you? And black people look at me as though I'm a traitor or something."

"But it doesn't matter what they think. The important thing is what we think."

"I always thought so too. I thought that all the mean racist stuff was mostly from the Dark Ages. I thought the Southern racist thing had been dealt with. But it's different here. Seattle was so politically correct, and I guess I thought it would be the same here. I'll always be black and different; I've gotten used to that. But now I feel like the person I always thought I was isn't the real me. I feel like I've become a person I never knew before. Will, I want *me* back."

Rachel and R.J. were some of the first to arrive at the auction. Rachel felt responsible for the evening, and besides, she wanted to keep track of the bidding on her bottle. It was the same motivation she had for watching a stock. She was curious to see how much return there would be on her family's investment.

Her dress was a soft citron green. She hadn't liked the color when she'd first seen it, but she'd tried it on and the designer had been right. It lit up her face like a spotlight. Rachel had thighs which bulged too much in front to make a true sheath or column-style dress possible. But this Carlo Malucci gown wrapped her slender form without revealing her defects. It's the reason why the designer was her favorite. A slightly draped deep V-neck tied at each shoulder and then plunged straight down to her waist in back. The bias cut skirt tapered up to an empire waist. Her matching shoes had Louis XIV heels with sparkling diamante buckles. Her hair hung the way it always did, although at the moment, one side was tucked behind a diamond-studded ear.

They met up with Anne and Will in the hallway. She was wearing a petal pink georgette column dress with a modest knee-high slit in the front and intricate seed pearl beading along the bottom. She had a chiffon scarf thrown around her neck. Simple and uncomplicated, it suited her.

Rachel studied her friend. She looked off balance this evening and slightly self-conscious. It wasn't like Anne. She had always given off the impression of self-confidence and assurance.

Rachel's brows knit together.

Beth and Marc joined the two couples shortly afterward. Beth's soft baby blue dress accented her personality. Her knee length spaghetti-strapped gown had a closely fitted bodice and a wide blush pink sash tied it off in back. Under the sash, the short blue skirt shot out at a nearly forty-five-degree angle and was supported by a net underskirt.

"That is so cute!" Anne commented.

"I thought it would be fun." Beth's eyes were dancing. "I always wanted a fancy dress. At the academy we had lots of dances, but I always wore my mess dress. So—" she shrugged, but it was plain to see that she appreciated the compliment. "Where is Karen?" she asked. They all felt protective of Karen since Kevin had gone; he wasn't due back for another two weeks.

"I haven't seen her," Rachel commented as she led the way down the hall. She was anxious to begin looking at the auction tables.

In fact, Karen was having a hard time convincing herself that she looked nice. She kept tugging at the material of the dress, trying to make it stand away from her body. "This fits like skin!" She definitely couldn't wear it outside the house. What had she been thinking?

Rachel had sworn it looked wonderful.

Her hair swung into her eyes and she pushed it away. That was the trouble with shorter hair. It always seemed to be where she didn't want it.

She looked at herself in the mirror again and then looked away. At first Rachel had wanted her to try on a clingy halter-style dress. It would never have worked with the LDS garments Karen had to wear, so she convinced Rachel that she didn't want her shoulders showing. Actually, she'd tried to convince Rachel that she didn't want any of her body showing, but Rachel had just laughed at her. "I don't know why you're so careful about what you eat if you don't dress to show off your body."

There was nothing Karen could say to logic like that.

And just look at what she'd ended up with! She frowned at her reflection in the mirror. The dress was almost entirely chiffon. It was a two-piece gown. The first and longest piece was a simple black chiffon under dress with a scooped neck. The short sleeves were lined with white silk. The second piece was a strapless black chiffon bodice that fit over the top and covered the scooped neckline slightly. It was made of swaths of chiffon which were tightly ruched on both sides and stopped at mid-thigh to let the under dress' skirt flow freely. That was how Karen had been able to keep her undergarments hidden and Rachel had been able to convince her to wear it.

"It's too tight!" Karen had complained to Rachel.

"Can you breathe?" she'd asked.

"Yes."

"Can you sit down?"

"Yes."

"Then it's not too tight."

Karen looked at herself and almost started to cry, but she remembered she had mascara on. It would run if she cried, and then she'd have to start all over again.

She allowed herself one more glance in the mirror. At least her hair and makeup looked good.

Rachel spied her bottle on a table near the wall. It was in the proper position, supported in a holder with the neck of the bottle tilted down. She and R.J. made their way slowly, pausing to stop and look at various vacation packages, national league sports paraphernalia, and gift baskets. Finally, they stopped in front of Rachel's bottle.

"Take a look at this!" R.J. chortled. "This bottle is supposed to be worth $200!"

"What?" Rachel was sure she hadn't understood him correctly.

"Two hundred dollars!"

"That can't be right!"

"That's what it says. Who's going to pay that kind of money for something that disappears after you drink it?"

"That can't be right!" Rachel picked up the card. But, sure enough, it read $200 instead of $2000.

R.J. had picked up the bottle and was turning it around and upside down trying to figure out how something could be that expensive. "Hey, Rach. I think I'd rather pay that kind of money to try to get the vacation package to Alaska back there."

Rachel was staring at him in horror. "Put that down right now, R.J.!"

He was so startled he almost dropped it.

"I'm just looking at it, that's all." He was miffed by her sudden scolding.

"If you keep jiggling it around like that, it's going to turn to vinegar!" She took the bottle from his hands and placed it gently back into the stand. "Stay right here. And don't let anyone touch the bottle. I have to get this price corrected!"

She walked as fast as her dress would allow, looking for Becky, the auction coordinator. She finally found her talking to the event manager.

Rachel rarely ever broke into conversations; she considered it rude. But this was not a time to be picky about etiquette. "Becky! I need you to make a correction to this card."

Becky took the card from Rachel's hand and looked at it. "I remember this one. It came in for two thousand dollars, but I knew it was a typo so I corrected it…didn't I?" She flipped the card over, looking for the error. "This is the right card, isn't it?"

"No. The bottle really is worth two thousand dollars. You've got to find someone to change it!"

"Oh my gosh! Don't let anyone touch it!" Becky took off at a run to find some correction fluid and a pen to correct the mistake.

They found R.J. still standing beside the table, arms crossed like a bodyguard.

"Are you sure it's supposed to be for this much?" Becky asked. She still doubted that a bottle of wine could be worth $2000.

"I'm positive!"

"Okay. I doubt anyone will pay it, though."

Rachel clenched her teeth. Of course no one would pay that much. But her father had purchased it for $40 a bottle in 1964. The point was to make a profit. And if people saw that it was worth $2000, then they would be willing to bid more than if they thought it were worth only $200. It was human psychology. And in any case, it was all for a good cause.

Her bottle rescued, Rachel hooked a hand around R.J.'s arm, took a deep breath, and smiled pleasantly at him. "What were you saying about a trip to Alaska?"

Anne didn't recognize Karen at all. She probably wouldn't have recognized her even on Kevin's arm. Beth didn't recognize her, either. Somehow the black dress made her complexion turn from pasty-white to alabaster. It evened out her skin tone, made her eyes sparkle, and her hair shine. She looked, in fact, rather striking.

"Karen!" Beth cried when she finally realized who was in front of her. "I can't believe it! You look incredible."

"Thanks," Karen muttered. She was still convinced that the dress was too clingy and that everyone could see how fat she was.

"I agree." Anne looked closely at Karen. "You look incredible. When did you have your hair cut?"

"Last week. Rachel and I went shopping."

Beth's eyebrows rose. She must have dropped a bundle.

"I feel like everyone's staring at me." Karen glanced around, looking self-conscious and a bit paranoid.

"Of course they are. You look beautiful!" Beth hugged her warmly. "I'm glad you came."

Karen was embarrassed by the attention, but she smiled anyway.

Dinner turned out to be as wonderful as it had sounded when they planned it. The champagne was a nice touch, even though nobody knew who P. Smith Incorporated was. R.J. proposed a toast anyway.

"To P. Smith Incorporated, whoever they may be. Thanks for the great champagne!"

"Here, here."

Mrs. Pritchard even stood at the head table after dinner to recognize the food committee for their wonderful good taste.

The results of the silent auction were awaited with nervous anticipation. Just before the closing of the auction period, the room had turned into a flurry of people running to top a bid, one last time, on an item they had their hearts set on.

"Item number 56, to General Pritchard. Two hundred and fifty dollars." Rachel could hardly contain a smile. Her wine had brought 30 dollars more than she thought it would!

"Item number 58, to Captain Hawthorne, 40 dollars." Rachel turned to see what R.J. had bought, but he had already gone to collect it. The group around the table strained to see him as he walked back to his seat.

He proudly unfurled a Canucks hockey jersey. "They're the best," he said simply, with a big smile.

Beth leaned over the table to speak to Rachel. "I talked to the OSC treasurer. She said the auction was a hit this year. They turned down at least 20 couples that wanted tickets. Putting a limit on it was a great idea, Rachel."

"I'll bet they'll be able to sell at least 460 tickets next year," she said, pausing to look around the room. It was already bursting at the seams with tables. "Or actually, they could keep the limit at 400 and increase the price to $40. I have an idea people would still be willing to pay it."

At the last OSC meeting of the year, the results of the year's funds drive for scholarships were announced: nearly $23,000. It more than doubled the amount of the year before and meant that none of the scholarship applicants would be turned down.

"It has been a pleasure to work with all of you this year. I want to thank every one of you for your help and support," Mrs. Pritchard said. "This has been one of my favorite of the general's assignments, and most of that has to do with this OSC. It goes without saying that this amazing amount of money could not have been raised without your participation. My best wishes to all of you for a safe and happy summer. A fond farewell to those who are departing Bullard for their next assignment. The general and I will be leaving soon too. I know you'll give Mrs. Thompson the same welcome you gave me. If your committee hasn't turned in its after action report for Mrs. Thompson's briefing book, please make sure you do so."

Anne jabbed Beth in the ribs with an elbow as the meeting broke up. "What's an 'after action report'?"

"Don't worry about it. I'll take care of it."

"I can't believe it's summer already." Just a short year ago, she had been planning her graduation and wedding.

"Again," said Karen. She had barely made it through the last one alive, it had been so hot. Her entire goal the previous summer was to move as quickly as possible between air-conditioned locations. From the house to the car to the store or building. It used to be that she avoided parking under trees because of all the bird-droppings a car could catch. Now she understood the value of a shadow.

Beth loved summer. She worshiped the sun and loved to feel the rays soak through her skin and into her bones. They'd already bought a wading pool for the twins. She couldn't wait to fill it up.

Rachel adored the summer season, although she didn't appreciate the way people at Bullard refused to use it. The Italians and Spanish were people who saw value in the heat of the summer sun. They worked in the morning and took a two-hour nap in the middle of the day. Then they revived and worked until the evening. There was strength to be gained in the sultry solitude of retreat. There was sensual pleasure in being able to hide from the heat of the day. She couldn't stand how people here barreled through the long days as if there weren't any change in weather or the climate. By denying this fact, they refused to find its utility. She had been thinking she'd just go to Europe if it bothered her too much.

Rachel and Beth left shortly after the end of the meeting. Rachel was heading to New York that afternoon, and Beth needed to pick up her twins.

"We need to make sure we get together this summer," Beth said on parting. "Or at least before OSC starts up again next fall."

Only Anne and Karen were left in a rapidly emptying room. "I worked through lunch a couple days this week to have enough time for today. I don't feel like going back yet. Do you want to have lunch? My treat?"

It sounded good to Karen.

They went next door to the O Club restaurant.

Anne looked at the menu and had made a choice in a moment.

Karen scanned the menu obsessively. She couldn't decide. "I wish I could eat something and just enjoy it, but I can't. It's either good for me or bad for me. I should either eat it or I shouldn't. And if I shouldn't and I do, then I can't eat something else. It's like a never-ending war."

"You're not anorexic, are you?" Anne had suspected since she'd known Karen that she had an eating problem. She'd had lots of experience spotting the signs.

"No, of course not. I eat. But I haven't eaten any fat or grease in over five years. I can't even eat a hamburger. My stomach cramps so badly, I have to run for the bathroom."

"How can you live that way?"

"We don't go out to eat. I cook our food. I don't use butter or oil. You just figure it out. There's nonfat everything now."

"But what does Kevin think?"

"He doesn't know."

"Karen, it's not a sin to eat."

"I know. I said that I eat."

"But you're restricting yourself."

Karen shrugged.

"You've done something wrong that you feel like you need to compensate for."

"What are you talking about?"

"Whatever it is that you feel like you have to make up for. Classic case in my sorority. One of my good friends started the anorexia thing after she and her boyfriend started sleeping together. It violated her beliefs, and yet she wasn't strong enough to stop. So she stopped herself from doing something else."

"Eating." Karen was staring into the space behind Anne's left shoulder. "She stopped eating."

Anne gripped Karen's hand. "What's going on?"

Karen took a deep breath and then decided to tell her the whole story. "I was afraid I was pregnant almost the whole time Kevin and I were dating," she said quietly. "He was my first boyfriend."

CHAPTER 23

⌒

*I*t had all happened so fast. She'd always taken for granted the frenzy to marry that had guided her life. Everyone got married as soon as possible. And preferably to a guy who had received his temple endowments. Usually before leaving to go on a two-year mission. There were ways to tell without asking. Men who had received their endowments were allowed to wear the temple garments. All a girl had to do was brush against a man's thigh. If you felt the garments, chances were he'd gone and come back. You talked to him. If you didn't feel them, you kept on walking. The guys never seemed to mind. They were proud of having served the church.

If they could wear their garments on the outside, I'm sure they would.

She remembered the night she met Kevin. It was at Wilkinson Student Center, where everyone studied and socialized.

She'd been walking past the tables. She hadn't meant to touch him, but she'd tripped on the leg of a chair and found herself planted on his lap, embarrassed. In an effort to get up, she'd pressed a hand on his thigh to push herself away. *He's been* she thought quickly before taking her hand away. But he'd caught her hand and kept it.

"I'm Kevin Bannister."

"Karen Austin. I'm really sorry."

"That's okay. Are you a freshman?"

She nodded. "Are you?"

"Yes." He looked older than she did, but he'd probably already gone on his mission. He ought to be two years older than the average freshman. "What classes are you taking?"

They found out they had two of their classes together. Calculus and English.

"Maybe I'll see you tomorrow," Kevin said when Karen had insisted she needed to go back to her dorm.

"Maybe," she replied, but she hoped not. *What an embarrassing way to meet someone.*

In fact, he slipped into the empty desk beside her the next day, just before math class started.

"Hi." He flashed a smile at her.

She blushed.

She took notes throughout the lecture. He made her too nervous to do anything else. She kept seeing his hand in her peripheral vision. It was covered with golden hair. His nails were clean and precisely trimmed.

Write.

She felt overwhelmed at the end of the class and closed her notebook, quietly shaking her head.

"Didn't follow?" Kevin asked from the desk beside her.

"Pardon me?"

"It just looked like you were drowning."

"Am I ever," she said with a smile that contradicted her watery blue eyes.

"Do you need some help? We could meet and go over the homework together."

"You wouldn't mind?"

"How about in Wilkinson? Near where you fell for me last night?"

Karen couldn't keep herself from blushing. *Jerk.* She almost decided to refuse.

"I'm sorry," he said, grabbing her hand. "That was a lousy thing to say. Let's meet on the *opposite* side of the room from there at 7:30."

"I'll see if I can make it," she said, taking her hand from his.

The need for help finally trumped preservation of her pride. Even so, she made sure it was 7:50 before she walked into the building. He was already there, working hard on homework. He didn't even see her until she said hello.

"Hi," he said, grinning. "I wasn't sure if you'd come. Wouldn't have blamed you if you hadn't."

She sat down at the table across from him. "I need help."

"Let's see what we can do."

They went over her notes from class.

"Did you write down *everything* the professor said?" he finally asked in amazement.

Karen blushed. "If I don't understand it, then I don't know what's important and what's not."

He explained the concepts until she felt she could work through the problems.

"Do you want to finish them before you go? That way you'll know if you've got it or not."

She looked at her watch. It was 9:30. She preferred to do them back in her room so she wouldn't have such a late walk home.

"I'll walk you back. Don't worry about it."

She worked through the problems. It was 10:30 before she was done. "I think they're right," she announced.

"The answers are in the back of the book."

"I know."

"Didn't you look?"

"No. It feels too much like cheating."

"Well, it isn't. It doesn't tell you how to *do* the problems, but at least if you look, you'll know whether you've got the right answers."

"Oh." She considered his philosophy. "I guess you're right," she said, flipping through the pages.

She had done most of them correctly, and that was good enough for her. She shut the book.

He looked up from his chemistry book. "I have a problem set to do. I'm almost done. Do you mind staying another 20 minutes? Then I'll walk you back?"

"That's fine," she said, trying to swallow a yawn.

She watched his blond head bend over his book. She closed her books, collected her papers, and returned everything to her backpack. Hoisted it to the table in front of her. Then she remembered about germs. Her mother never let her put purses or book bags on the kitchen table. She could even hear her voice, *They'll spread germs.* She quickly lowered the backpack to her lap, looking around the room. There was still a handful of scattered students, heads bent over their books. She yawned and rested her head on the table.

"Karen? Karen?" She heard the voice in her dream. It was far away and she didn't want to listen to it.

"Karen!"

She opened her eyes. She was still in Wilkinson. It was Kevin's voice she'd heard.

"Karen."

She closed her mouth and licked her lips. She'd drooled, she knew she had.

Great.

She carefully put her hand underneath her mouth before she lifted her head.

Please, God, may I not have snored.

"Karen? Are you ready to go?"

"Sorry I fell asleep."

"That's okay. Are you ready?"

He left her at the front door of the dorm. "See you tomorrow, Karen."

She simply waved. She was too tired to say anything.

He sat beside her in class again the next day.

"Hi."

"Hi. Thanks again for helping me last night."

"No problem, but I might ask you to return the favor. I think I need some help with English. That poem we're reading?"

Karen nodded.

"My copy must be different because I don't see *where* the professor pulled all that stuff from yesterday."

"Symbolism. I guess you have to know a little something about mythology."

"Besides the guy who carries a thunderbolt—"

"Zeus."

"Yeah. Besides him, I know absolutely nothing."

"You didn't study it in middle school?"

"Well, yeah, but none of it's true, so…?" He shrugged. "I guess it didn't stick much."

"We can go over it tonight."

"I can't tonight, I have to work. How about tomorrow?"

They arranged to meet in Wilkinson again.

Between Karen's deficiencies in calculus and Kevin's weakness in English, the study sessions became a regular habit. They alternated homework with conversation.

"What are you majoring in?" Karen asked one night.

"Civ E. Civil Engineering. Building roads and bridges. That kind of thing."

"How many kinds of engineering are there? I've never figured that out."

"Oh, there's lots. Mechanical, computer, aeronautical, and electrical, to name a few."

"Not interested in mechanics or planes?"

"Not really."

"Why not electrical?"

He smiled. "EE? There's two *E*s in geek too…"

She laughed. "I never heard that before."

"It's pretty much true. And what is it, O Karen Austin of alabaster complexion, that *you* are studying?"

She blushed. "Nursing."

"Really?"

"Yes. I've always wanted to be a nurse. Ever since I was little."

"I can see you as a nurse."

"Really?"

"Really."

"Do you ever think about graduation?" she asked another night.

"It's too far off to think about. I get discouraged."

"What do you want to do after graduation?"

"Get married. Have kids. How about you?"

She blushed. "I meant as far as a *job*."

"Oh. I was thinking about joining the Air Force."

"Really?"

"Yeah. They send some college graduates to officer training school for 12 weeks, then they're commissioned as lieutenants."

"But can't you go through ROTC or something now?"

"AFROTC. I could. I already tried, but they wouldn't give me a scholarship. At least not this year, and I needed money for tuition now…It's only my mom and me. When Dad divorced her, he left her with all kinds of debt."

"I'm sorry. So you have to work instead."

"Yeah, but it's no big deal. I've noticed you don't work. Do you have a scholarship?"

"Yes," she said, biting her lip.

"That's great! It must make life a lot easier."

"I suppose," she said, turning back to her books. She'd been her class valedictorian. BYU wasn't that expensive for LDS members, and she'd had no problems obtaining a church endorsement from her bishop, but they were still giving her a free ride.

After delivering Karen to the dorm one night halfway through the semester, Kevin stopped her from leaving him.

"Could I kiss you?" he asked softly, his hand tightening around her arm.

"What?"

"Could I kiss you?"

She was glad it was dark because she was blushing furiously. "Kevin," she said, looking at the ground, "I've never kissed anyone before. I don't know how," she admitted. "I would like for you to kiss me. But I can't. Kiss," she finished, backing away from him. "Goodnight."

She replayed the conversation in her mind so many times in bed that it became a nightmare. *Why does everything I do or say around him have to be so humiliating?*

The memory of the night before was waiting for her when she woke up the next day. *I can't go to class this morning. I can't bear to see him. But I can't bear not to see him.*

"Hi," he said as she slipped into the desk beside him. "You're late. For you, anyway."

It was true. Karen was usually in class at least five minutes before the professor started lecturing. She shrugged. As she began to take notes, she shook her hair over her face. She didn't want to see any of him. And she didn't want him to look at her.

Class was over sooner than she would have liked for it to be.

"Hey," Kevin said, using his pen to push aside her hair. "Class is over. Do you want to study tonight?"

"You don't have to work?"

"No," he said, tucking her wall of auburn hair behind her ear for her. He bent down to pick up his backpack. After shoving his books into it, he placed it on her desk. "See you tonight?" he asked.

She nodded.

She studied in fits and starts, sneaking looks at his lips. She wondered what they'd be like to kiss.

"Ready?"

"Hmm?"

"Are you ready to go?"

"Already?"

"I didn't have much homework tonight."

They gathered their books and left Wilkinson. It was starting to snow.

"Only another month and a half," he commented.

"The semester's gone by fast," she replied.

"Faster than I wanted it to."

"The calculus midterm's going to be tough."

"You'll do fine. Really. You've worked through the tough spots."

"I guess I have. It's been nice of you to help me."

"The pleasure's been all mine," he said, grinning. He had such nice even white teeth.

They had reached her dorm.

"The snow's falling fast," Karen said. "Be careful on your way back. Could be slippery."

"You've got a snowflake."

"Where?"

He pointed to his forehead and motioned her closer. He bent and kissed her there. "Got it."

"Thanks," she murmured.

"You've got another one," he said, catching her hand.

"Where?" she asked, watching his eyes.

He pointed to his cheek and then bent and kissed her there. "Got it."

His hand tightened on hers. "And another one."

"Where?" She was mesmerized by the movement of his mouth.

"Right here," he said, tracing her lips with a finger.

He bent down. "Got it," he said after a long minute.

He opened the front door to his uncle's apartment a week later and ushered Karen inside. "Make yourself at home. Maybe a change in scenery will be good for our brain cells. My uncle's gone for the next two months. I'm checking up on the house for him once or twice a week."

They both decided to study at the dining room table.

Karen studied until she was too tired to think. Her watch read 10:00, but it felt as if it was 2:00. "I can't study anymore."

Kevin looked up from his book. "Are you sure?"

"I can hardly keep my eyes open."

"I just have one more chapter I want to take notes on. Do you mind staying just a little bit longer? Go ahead and stretch out on my uncle's bed. I'll wake you up when I'm done."

She curled up and was asleep within minutes. She woke to him kissing her. She wound her arms around his neck. The more they kissed, the more awake and alive she felt.

Stop. Stop kissing and go home.

"We should go, Kevin. We really should."

"Not yet."

"We need to. We really do."

"We don't have to."

"We should."

They never made it past the point of should.

The morning after, she couldn't believe what she'd done. They were kissing and then…they were done. She didn't know how it had happened.

Yes, you do know. You know in painstaking detail exactly what happened. It made her skin numb just to think about it. *You have a midterm today. Just don't think about it until tonight. You'll talk to him tonight and you'll deal with it then.*

Tonight.

She didn't see Kevin until later that afternoon. Not until after she'd bombed her calculus midterm.

"Karen!" He'd waved her down happily from across the street.

She waved back. *Be normal.* A fluttering in her stomach betrayed her.

He waited until the cars had passed before running across the street to join her.

"Do you want to study at my uncle's tonight?" he asked, bending to kiss her.

She turned her head away. "Kevin, what happened last night can't happen again. I mean it, okay? What if someone finds out? What if my church endorsement is withdrawn? They'll disenroll me—and you!"

"It's okay. No one knows. And they're not going to find out. I promise. I'm sorry." He took her hand. "Karen, in spite of what you might think, I didn't mean for that to happen. I really didn't. I wish there was some way I could undo it, but…I'm sorry."

"Sorry" doesn't return what he took…but you didn't try to stop him.

She felt like screaming. She felt like doing it again. "I know you are, but it's not happening anymore."

"Okay. I promise," he said in all sincerity.

In spite of Karen's best intentions, it did happen again. With increasing frequency. They would never have slept together in the dorms. It was too risky; too many people would have been willing to report them. But the availability of the apartment was too tempting.

It was the middle of winter semester when she finally had to start listening to what her body was telling her. She walked three miles from campus in order to buy a pregnancy test where no one could recognize her.

She cried when she saw the results.

"Kevin, I need to say something," she said that night. She bit her lip trying to keep the tears from coming.

"I know. We need to talk. You've said it before and I've agreed. I try not to touch you, but I'm just not strong enough. And when we start to kiss…"

"Kevin?"

"Yes?"

"I'm pregnant."

"We'll get married," he said without hesitation.

He'd said the words she was longing to hear, but as soon as she heard them she became insecure. She'd never know whether he'd intended to ask her to marry him or not. She'd never know whether he really truly loved her.

He moved to kiss her, but she pushed him away. She didn't feel like kissing anymore.

CHAPTER 24

J still don't know about this," Kevin was saying as they rode the
bus from school to Karen's hometown.

"Well, what else can we do?"

"They're going to know. We should just tell them."

"They're not going to know."

"Parents always seem to know."

*Just pretend that you're in love with me, and then they won't suspect
anything!* "I've told them I've been studying with you. It's not like I
haven't mentioned you before. We'll just tell them we can't wait to get
married." *Which is true.*

"Should I ask your father if I can marry you? Should we just say
we're engaged? What's the best way to do it?"

Not this way. "We'll just tell them first thing and get it over with."

"We need to talk, Karen." He was trying to take her hand.

"I have to go to the bathroom." She bolted from her seat and ran
down the aisle to the bathroom. It wasn't the cleanest or most wonderful-
smelling place in the whole world, but it was a place where she could cry.
Her sobs came from deep inside. They made ugly, wrenching sounds.

Afterward she splashed water on her face and then patted it dry
with a paper towel. She looked at herself in the mirror. *You are going to
make the best of this. You will never give Kevin a reason to be sorry that he
married you.*

She took a deep breath, unlocked the door, and went back to her
seat.

"Are you all right?"

"I'm fine," she said, smiling in spite of her red-rimmed eyes. She
kissed his cheek. "Sorry."

"That's okay. I was just going to say that we need to talk about this," he continued in a low tone. He took her hand and then leaned toward her so that he had room to reach into his jacket pocket. He straightened. "Karen? Will you marry me?" he asked, slipping a ring onto her finger. It was a slender gold engagement ring with only the smallest sliver of a diamond in the center. But as she looked at it, she saw hope.

"Yes," she smiled. Tears sprung to her eyes, and she gritted her teeth. She didn't want to cry anymore.

"Mom? Dad?"

"Karen?" came the cry from inside the house.

"Come on," she said, tugging on Kevin's hand. "It sounds like she's in the kitchen."

They walked past stairs that climbed to the second floor. Down a dim hall that served as a family portrait gallery. They emerged into the brightness of the kitchen. It glowed yellow in the afternoon sun. The frilly dotted swiss curtains over the sink had been pushed to one side. The window was open for ventilation. The dense chill that poured in only succeeded in spreading the smell of cinnamon and cloves further through the house.

"Karen? Is that you?"

"It's me, Mom."

"Karen! Let me just put down this pie," said her mother, reaching to hug her. "It's good to see you." Mrs. Austin's cheeks were flushed with exertion. Her sweatshirt was dusted with flour.

"Thanks, Mom. I want you to meet Kevin. Kevin, this is my mom."

"Hello, Mrs. Austin," Kevin said, shaking her hand.

"It's nice to meet you."

"Mom, is Dad here?"

"He will be later. He had to run some errands."

"I wanted to tell you something, but you have to promise to keep it a secret until I can tell Dad. Kevin and I—" Karen began.

Kevin grabbed her hand and squeezed it. "We're engaged," he finished.

"Let's see!" exclaimed her mother, reaching for her hand, looking for a ring.

Mr. Austin was a harder sell. "And you want to get married *when?*" He pulled the lever on his reclining chair, lurching to an upright position while the springs groaned in protest.

"We were hoping over spring break, sir," replied Kevin. He was sitting, ruler straight, on the very edge of a rose-colored sofa.

Mr. Austin sighed. "You're a freshman too?"

Kevin nodded.

"You couldn't wait a few more years? So Karen could finish school?"

"I want her to keep going, sir. We'll apply for married student housing. I've already got a job. We'll make it."

"What is it that you're studying?"

"Civil engineering."

"Karen, will you promise me that you'll finish your studies?"

"I will." *Maybe not in the next four years, but I will at some point.*

"Spring break, huh? Can we put a wedding together in a month and a half?"

They could. They did.

It came together easily. Karen's older sister had married three years before; the dress could be rehemmed for Karen. They could have the reception in the afternoon so they wouldn't have to serve much food.

"Just cake and punch," her mom said with relief. "And I can make the cake."

"Thanks, Mom."

"How about the dress? Do you want to try it on?"

Not really.

"It's upstairs. Will you excuse us, Kevin?"

"Sure. No problem."

"He seems like a nice person, Karen," said her mother, rummaging through a closet.

"He is, Mom."

"How did you meet?"

"We have English and calculus together. He helps me with calculus; I help him with English."

"Sounds like a good arrangement."

"It's worked out so far."

"Here, take your sweater off. You can leave your jeans on. We'll just slip this over your head. It should fit just about right. You and Irene are close to the same size."

Karen struggled with the dress. At first, she couldn't find the armholes. Then she couldn't get it on over her head. She turned, finally, to look at herself in the mirror. The skirt was a cascade of tight ruffles, the sleeves long to hide the sleeves of the garments she would soon have the privilege of wearing. Pointed at the wrists with puffs at the shoulders. It wasn't the dress she would have chosen. But then, she didn't have the luxury of being choosy.

The weekend passed quickly. Mrs. Austin was wreathed in radiant smiles of happiness. Mr. Austin sent Karen and Kevin puzzled glances. He didn't know. Not exactly. But if he thought about it hard enough, he might be able to guess.

A week later, Karen's world crumbled. Again.

She sat looking at her stained panties in disbelief. *This can't be happening. I'm supposed to be pregnant.*

"I was just late," she told Kevin later, with shame. "I wasn't pregnant. Just late." She couldn't look at him. She didn't want to see the relief that she knew would be in his eyes.

Hearing no reply, she turned away from him. "So, we don't have to get married anymore," she said in a statement of the obvious. She struggled with the ring, trying to get it off her finger.

"But what about the test?"

"Tests are wrong sometimes." The ring wouldn't come off.

Seeing her shaking shoulders, he walked over and embraced her. "Would you still want to marry me anyway?" he whispered into her hair.

She turned and nodded miserably as he gathered her against his chest.

"But he loves you, Karen. You can't doubt that," Anne said. She had seen them together. It was obvious that he adored her. "This isn't the nineteenth century. He's not obligated to marry the girlfriend he sleeps with. It's not like you held a shotgun to his head. Especially after you told him you weren't pregnant. He could have easily dropped you. He'd have been a weasel, but he wouldn't have been the first guy to do it."

"But why else would he have married me?"

"Because he loves you."

"Does he?"

"Karen, let's assume the answer is yes. In that case, you have to forgive him. Leave it in the past. You're not the first person in the world to have premarital sex. And you can't keep on punishing yourself."

"But I kept sinning the same sin. And I've never stopped. Kevin and I never stopped sleeping together before we were married."

"I agree that it was the wrong thing to do at the time, but you're married now."

"No. I mean I never truly repented. If I had, I would have stopped. But I kept doing it. If I had truly been righteous, I wouldn't have allowed it to happen."

"And not eating is going to fix that?"

"No, but—"

"Karen, you're human. You messed up. All of us do. It's not like your entire life is screwed up now."

"I can't afford to mess up. And neither can Kevin. Trust me. God forgives, but if you sin the same sin again, it's added back into your sins. As if God never forgave it. And the only way not to sin again is to come to true repentance. And that means to abhor what you did. And I could never do that."

"Karen, when God forgives, it's forgiven. Forever. As many times as we ask him to forgive us. Even if it's for the same thing. Of course, you hope that you can open your heart to God so that he can help you repent. Truly. But God is mercy. And love."

"You don't get it. You just don't understand God, Anne."

"Maybe not, but not eating isn't going to make up for anything. The only thing you're doing is hurting your body."

Karen drew a deep breath and then dropped her bomb. "I'm thinking of leaving him."

Anne felt her jaw drop, but she couldn't do anything to stop it.

"I mean, I'm not actually planning to," Karen retracted. "Just considering it."

"How long have you been thinking about it?"

"Since he left on TDY."

"My dad always says, 'Stand in front of a door long enough and it's sure to open.'"

"Sometimes I wish I could start my whole life over. Everything's just so messy."

"Everybody's life seems messy."

"Not like mine. I just want it to be plain. Simple. I wish it were just me. But it's never been just me. Before Kevin, there was the church, and before the church, there was my family. I've never been just me. And I don't know who I'd be without everyone telling me who I am."

Anne talked to Will about her conversation with Karen while they walked along the beach that night. They strolled until they got to "their" lifeguard chair. Anne climbed up first and then gave a hand to Will.

Arms wrapped around each other's waist, they watched the waves roll in and then retreat.

The sun began a dive toward the horizon, trailing veils of rose and orange.

"Karen's thinking of getting a divorce. And I don't know what to say to her."

"How do you feel about it?" Will asked.

Anne wrinkled her nose. "Here's how I'm supposed to feel: I'm supposed to be in moral anguish at the thought of Karen getting a divorce."

"And?"

"And I'm not. My brain is telling me to tell her it's a terrible idea, while my heart is jumping up and down. If she divorces him, maybe she'll be able to consider God without any outside interference. You know how it's been. We'll talk about God and Christianity, and it seems like she thinks about what we're saying, but the next time we see her, it's like starting our conversations all over again. I think thoughts of Kevin and her church erase everything I say. So maybe if she left him…I mean, wouldn't that outweigh the evils of divorce?"

Will shrugged.

"I've got to say something!"

"Why?"

"Because I want to. She's just so…" Anne scanned the horizon searching for the word. "Lost."

"If you could say anything you wanted, what would it be?"

"There's more. There's a bigger God out there beyond that beautiful sky. A God that makes sense. A God you can think about without him falling apart."

"But?"

"But all my life I've been told that divorce is wrong."

"And you think that in this particular situation, it's right?"

"I don't know what to think. I'm afraid if she stays with him, she'll put God back on the shelf."

"There's something in the Bible about this. About when a woman becomes a Christian, she's supposed to stay with her husband and show him by example what it means to be a Christian."

"I'd buy that if she were a Christian. But she's not. And I don't think she'll have the strength to become one if she stays with him."

Anne looked at the clock. Only 2:35. Five minutes later than the last time she'd looked. *Come on, clock. Go!*

Anne found her job depressingly undemanding. She answered the phone. She took messages. She filed. And once in a great while, she made copies. If it were a really extraordinary day, she got to un-jam the copy machine or pour more toner into it.

And sometimes the things that she did do were things that other people ought to have done anyway.

Mr. Trumble often asked her to telephone someone for him or look up a phone number. Half the time when she telephoned on his behalf to set up an appointment or to give his response to something, people asked for information that only he would have and she wound up transferring the call to him anyway. And why should she look up a phone number in the phone book when he could just as easily do the same thing? She would fume for a while, but then she would remember that it was making time go faster and she would resolve to deal with it.

At times she thought she would go insane from lack of mental stimulation. She walked into Nita's room now and then just to look out the window at all the people driving by on the street below. She always wondered what they were doing. Where were they going? Why weren't they working? How could she get a job like theirs?

The good thing was, she got to learn about local government. It also gave her an understanding of what a master's in public administration was about. And it gave her firsthand experience in how difficult human resource management theory was to implement. It took a lot of work, from the top down, to manage effectively. And if the people at the top weren't willing to change their behavior, you could bet that the people down at the bottom never would, either.

People, she decided, are fundamentally lazy. They do enough to get by. And faced with a choice of doing something new that required a change in behavior or sticking with the old, unless there was a good incentive, the old nearly always won.

Especially discouraging to her was the city's evaluation system. In theory, each employee was evaluated yearly and rated on work-related skills. In practice, the personnel department had to hound each supervisor for the evaluations. They were always turned in late. And supervisors who complained all year about an employee's work performance nearly always gave that employee satisfactory or above-satisfactory ratings. And then they wondered why the employee couldn't be fired.

Anne had spent a whole semester on evaluations and performance. It was such an easy principle: give an employee feedback, point out what needs to be worked on, and then reevaluate at the next rating session. It wasn't difficult, and it provided a long-term record of work performance. But people were uncomfortable in judging someone else's performance.

She heard a piece of paper get sucked into the fax machine, so she rose from the desk to see what was coming through. She picked it up as soon as it was done and immediately recognized the format. It was a hurricane-tracking chart. They'd been receiving them since hurricane season had started on June 1. This particular one was spinning in the ocean near Puerto Rico.

Those poor people had had enough hurricanes to last a lifetime.

She'd never live on a Caribbean island.

Too risky; hurricanes blew through all the time.

Liffsbury hadn't been hit for 30 years. She crossed her fingers and hoped it would be at least three before they saw another. That way she and Will would have moved on to their next assignment.

The phone rang right on time, and Karen picked it up quickly. "Hello?"

"Hi." It was a bad connection. Kevin's voice sounded as remote as a robot's.

"How are things?"

"About the same. Still sunny. Still hot. Still lots of sand. I'm ready, more than ready, to come home. I miss you."

Her cheeks flushed at the sound of longing in his voice. "It's only one more week."

"I know. But you can only go to the gym and work out so many times a day. Some of the guys are talking about building a golf course out here. I'm so sick of this godforsaken place."

"Kevin?" He usually sounded so upbeat and positive.

Halfway across the world, in a camp set up in the middle of the sand, Kevin leaned his head against the phone and closed his eyes. He could see Karen so clearly he wanted to reach out and grab hold of her.

"Kevin?"

"I'm here. I just want to be home. With you. The way we were before."

Karen pulled at a strand of her short wavy hair. Things weren't the way they were before. She didn't like things the way they were before. But it wasn't fair to tell him that now. They could straighten everything out once he got home. "I love you."

"Are you sure?"

She was shocked. "Of course I love you."

She heard him let out a deep breath. "I'm sorry. Things just seem so different out here when you look at sand all day, every day. I'm sorry. I love you."

"Only one more week."

"Only one more week." There was a pause and she heard him mumble something, and then his voice came back strong over the phone. "I have to go. There are other guys here who want to talk to their wives too. I'll try to call once more before I come back. Bye. I love you." He hung up before she could answer.

Are you sure?

His words haunted her, echoing in the silent house. How could he know what she'd been thinking?

She felt like a traitor.

Rachel picked up the phone after the fourth ring.

"Rachel, this is Anne. I need a favor."

"Sure. But I'm not giving up smoking. R.J.'s been harping on me for the last month."

Anne smiled. "The city's evacuating the beach—"

"What for?"

"The hurricane."

"What hurricane?"

"There's one out in the ocean, and it may turn our direction later this afternoon."

"Oh." Rachel walked over to her computer and brought up a weather site on the internet.

"Anyway, they're telling us all to leave. Could I stay with you? It'll probably just be for tonight. I doubt it'll come our way."

"Not a problem. If I don't answer the door, just come in. I'll be out by the pool."

"Thanks."

Anne hung up the phone and then turned to look around the condo. She picked up her keys and purse and almost walked out the door, but then she thought better of it. She set them down and walked upstairs. Stared out the window at the ocean in front of her. It didn't look any different. Maybe a little more calm than normal. Hard to believe that anyone was worried about a hurricane. But Mr. Trumble had insisted that she go home, pack her things, and find somewhere else to stay. And that was in the morning. This afternoon, after the city council had agreed to evacuate the beach, he had practically forced her out the door. She'd volunteered to stay and help staff the emergency services control center. She knew that city staff would set up operations to monitor the storm. He'd absolutely refused, swore that she wasn't essential, and looked as if he was going to escort her down to her car. He even offered her his own guest room.

Anne searched the sky. There were a few clouds, but not many. Will was TDY; he'd left just that morning. She'd have to call him tonight from Rachel's. She slipped the paper with his phone and room numbers on it into her pocket. Then she went and stood in the middle of her living room.

If a hurricane does come through, what would I have wished I had taken from here? Pictures. Our wedding album.

She collected their photo albums and put them in a pile.

What else? Wedding dress? Why not.

She went downstairs and pulled it out from the back of the closet.

Clothes. If there is a hurricane and I can't get back for a couple days, I'll need a change of clothes. Underwear. Socks. Shoes.

She riffled through her closet. Pulled out her drawers. Chose her favorite things.

And Will!

She did the same for him.

Anything else? Jewelry.

She put her jewelry box on top of the growing pile.

She tried to remember the disaster clips she'd seen on the Weather Channel. The aftermaths of hurricanes. *What happens after? Power outages. Food shortages. I need to make sure I fill up the gas tank.*

She went back upstairs and opened the refrigerator. There wasn't anything there she couldn't stand to lose. The freezer was another matter. She lugged the ice chest in from the garage and emptied the contents of the freezer into it, hoping Rachel would have room for it.

What else have I forgotten? Flashlights and candles.

Is this all that's important? She looked around her.

Bible.

She added it to the pile.

Guess that's it.

She took the piles from upstairs and downstairs and loaded them into the car. She closed the door and locked it behind her, and then drove off the beach. There were already sheriff's deputies stationed on the corners of the main intersections. Cold fingers of fear touched her. She glanced in her rearview mirror. The ocean was smooth like glass.

There's no way a hurricane's heading this direction.

When she reached Rachel's house, Beth and her boys were there playing on the front lawn.

"Hey! What are you guys doing here?" Anne called as she climbed out of her car.

"Rachel called and asked us to come. I hadn't even heard about the hurricane. I haven't had time to watch TV. Marc's TDY to a conference."

"Is Karen coming too?"

"She's staying on base. They have shelters set up."

"Help me?" Anne asked. She gave Beth a couple suitcases to carry, and then she followed her with photo albums balanced on top of the ice chest.

Rachel met them at the doorstep and led them upstairs to a guest room. "Hope you don't mind modern." It was the only room in Rachel's house with white walls, but it was punctuated by several floor to ceiling canvasses of the kind Anne didn't even pretend to understand.

"It's fine. Thanks. The hurricane will probably pass us by, but I guess it's better to be safe than sorry." Anne set down her load and then went downstairs to find a TV. Rachel switched it to the Weather Channel and the three of them stood in front of it, listening to a forecaster with a dour face predicting a category five.

"A five!" Beth cried, "I didn't even know the scale went up to five."

"What's five mean?" asked Rachel. She was fighting the urge for a cigarette.

Anne undertook the explanation. "Three means a big storm surge. With lots of damage to everything along the shore. A four will cause major damage to everything along the coast and even some destruction inland. Do you remember Hurricane Andrew down at Homestead? Listen to me, you guys. After the storm, there was no town left."

"And that was a five ?"

"No. That was a four. Five is…" There were no words to describe it.

"What can we do?" asked Beth.

"Okay. First, we need to store potable water. We'll fill the bathtubs. How many do you have, Rachel?"

"Three."

"Good. Fill them all. Do you have any big containers? Pots? Anything?"

"I don't know. We'll have to ask Paolo."

Rachel explained to the cook what they needed, and Beth and Anne searched through the cupboards, pulling out containers of various sizes.

"Take these to the bathroom and fill them with water too," she said to Rachel.

"Now what?" asked Beth.

"Where are the twins?"

"I left them playing in the living room."

"We need to get them into a room where there are no windows and no walls with outside exposure." Anne thanked God that she had actually read all the hurricane-preparedness literature the city had published that spring.

"But the hurricane's not supposed to hit for another couple hours."

"Tornadoes. Hurricanes always spawn tornadoes. And you can never tell when they'll start."

They sequestered the twins in the long hallway in the middle of the first floor of the house. It was the only area that satisfied Anne's requirements.

"Rachel, can you ask Paolo to cook?" Anne asked.

"Of course."

"Tell him that we might be without power for a few days, so he should cook while he can. Anything he can think of."

Rachel left the room and returned several minutes later to perch on the sofa. She chewed the inside of her cheek. "So what do we do for the next three hours? Wait for it to come get us?"

"No." Anne pulled Rachel to her feet. "We're going to make sure it doesn't get us."

CHAPTER 25

~

Anne went out the front door and began to walk around the house.

Rachel followed in bare feet. "What are you doing?"

"Looking for anything that can become airborne. If it does, it'll become a bullet. When Hurricane Camille hit Alabama, it drove pine needles through wood fences as though they were nails."

"Oh, God," Rachel breathed, looking at the slender evergreens that surrounded her house.

"It'll be okay. Go get your keys and pull your car into the garage."

Anne collected pots of flowers from around the yard with the idea of putting them into the garage with the car. Then she walked to the back of the house and groaned. Rachel had two full sets of patio furniture, miscellaneous benches, and a BBQ positioned around the fringes of the pool.

Rachel, having parked the car, came around the house to find Anne still staring helplessly at the backyard.

"I guess we just move what we can," Anne finally decided.

Together, lifting and at times pushing and pulling, Rachel and Anne were able to move the furniture into the garage. The wind was getting stronger and beginning to buffet the surrounding forest. With the last chair moved, Rachel leaned against her car with a huff. "This thing had just better come. I'd hate to have done all of that for nothing."

Anne looked at the house with sudden interest. "Are those shutters?" she asked, pointing to metal panels that were almost hidden in the window wells.

"Yes. Imported from France."

"Great!" Anne had been worried about the number of windows in the house, but she'd had no idea what to do about them. "We need to close them."

Rachel and Anne raced from room to room, prying the shutters from their positions and fighting to latch them closed.

"These are terrific," Anne said after they had closed the last one. The house was dark. Daylight seeped in only through small slits in the metal. They backtracked, turning lights on as they went.

"I bought them because I thought they would protect the house when we're gone. It never occurred to me that they would be useful in a hurricane."

"I feel much safer now."

Rachel smiled a half smile. "Me too."

"It's hard to tell how much longer we'll have power. Do you have a radio?" asked Anne, turning to Rachel.

"In the living room with the stereo."

"One that's battery operated?"

"I don't know. Maybe R.J. does. Somewhere."

"Where? Think, Rachel."

"In the garage with his camping gear?"

"I'll go look. While I'm gone, find some matches, candles, and flashlights."

"Anything else?"

"We have everything important away from the windows. We have water. We have food. Paolo's set?"

Rachel nodded.

"Then we wait."

Several minutes later, the phone rang. Rachel answered. "R.J.!"

"I know I told you we'd be back tonight, but with the hurricane, we can't fly. They're afraid for the planes."

"I understand. It's not a problem."

"Are you all right?" He swore into the phone. "I wish I could be with you, but they won't let me leave. From what we hear, it's going to be a direct hit."

"I'm fine. Anne and Beth are here with me. Paolo's cooked enough for a month. We have plenty of water. We'll be fine. We're nowhere near the ocean."

"I know, but the wind."

"We'll be fine." Rachel said it more for herself than for R.J. Everyone was so frightened that it was beginning to scare her.

They talked for a few more minutes, and then Rachel hung up.

Anne asked if she could call Will.

Rachel handed the phone to her.

Anne glanced at her watch. It was only 4:00 in Denver. He was probably still in meetings. She dialed the hotel and asked for his room number. She let it ring seven times before she hung up and redialed.

"May I leave a message for Will Bradley?"

"Yes, ma'am."

She hadn't given any thought to what she should say. *Hurricane coming. I love you?* "This message is important. Do you have a way to make sure he'll get it?"

"We'll place it in his room if you'd like."

"Please. Just say, 'Hurricane heading toward Bullard. Went to stay with Rachel.'" She gave Rachel's phone number and asked the clerk to repeat it. Then she hung up.

"Beth? Do you need to call Marc?"

"Already did from home."

Beth stayed with the twins and Shelby in the hallway while Anne and Rachel perched on the sofa in front of the TV.

"This is a weatherman's dream," Rachel commented. "There's a natural disaster happening, one that can be predicted, and everyone is hanging on every word he's saying. He's a god."

"And he just said that landfall's in fifteen minutes."

The lights flickered. Once. Twice. Anne and Rachel watched as the TV fizzed and the picture faded away.

"Here she comes," said Anne, tugging on Rachel's arm. "Let's go." They both hurried to the hallway and were soon joined by Paolo.

Four hours earlier, Karen and everyone else from the base housing areas had been gathered into shelters on base. The occupants of Karen's street and the one behind it were placed in a riot-proof sixties-era building made of reinforced concrete. It was a squat, square structure with few windows. They too were sitting in an interior hallway.

A truck had driven through the streets, blaring instructions from a megaphone. Karen had followed them as well as she could, taking her plants inside, pushing furniture away from the windows and packing a suitcase with a couple days' worth of clothing. She took some clothes for Kevin just in case something happened to the house, and added a pillow and a sleeping bag. Then she'd pulled her car into the carport and walked to the designated area to wait for the base bus.

Now she was sitting on her pillow, staring at the concrete blocks in the wall opposite her. The building seemed, for a moment, to compress. Along the hallway, heads lifted. People looked at each other with concern. Then there was a sudden easing of air, and everyone relaxed.

Karen could feel a slight draft running along the hallway. She tucked her legs underneath her and began to unroll her sleeping bag. She had a need to feel something comforting around her body.

The designated monitor, a captain who worked in the building, walked the length of the hallway, stopping at each of the children to smile or say a few words. They were oblivious to the hurricane. Most of the parents had brought a few books or toys to keep their children occupied. One mother was singing to her toddler, trying to get him to sleep.

A sudden crash brought everyone to attention. There was a whistling through the corridor, and a sudden wind raced through the hall, clutching at their ankles.

Karen tried to burrow into her sleeping bag and squeezed her eyes shut. *What if I die?*

Shelby began to whine. Beth petted her pumpkin-colored head. Suddenly she stood and started barking. "Shelby!" said Beth, tugging on her collar. "I'm sorry, you guys," she apologized. "Maybe it's the change in the air pressure. Shelby!" The dog refused to stop. She barked for over two minutes and then quit as suddenly as she'd begun. Flopped on the floor panting.

At first the wind was stealthy, like an army scout. It slunk around the house with a hiss, reconnoitering. Then it charged upon them suddenly, pushing with force, to find weak spots in the structure. First it tried the windows, rattling the shutters with vehemence. Then it retreated, allowing the house to relax, to let down its guard. But it returned, pouring itself behind the shutters in an attempt to push them away from the house.

The shutters held and the wind dropped its game. But then it regrouped and rushed at the door, pushing leaves under it, sending them fluttering to the floor in the foyer, as if to say, "I can't see you, but I know you're in there." Then all of a sudden it was at the roof, trying and prying. First in one direction, and then another. And those pointed advances were just the beginning.

The hurricane followed in force, as if unleashed. No longer did the wind pummel them in bursts. It came in an onslaught, with brutal force and unleashed fury. It came at the windows, doors, and roof in unison. In a fully coordinated attack. And where the precursor, gusting winds were alarming, the hurricane was terrifying. It was a horrible symphony constructed around an ominous, incessant, underlying roar. The melody was composed of a thousand shattering, splintering, cracking, snapping things.

No matter what anyone said, the only truly safe place in a hurricane was underground. Exactly where they weren't.

In a sudden silence, they could hear the house groan and crack. When the next gust hit, the entire house shuddered. They could feel tremors run through the walls. Rachel casually repositioned herself so she wouldn't be able to feel them. "Coke? Sprite? Anyone?" She asked, lifting the lid of the cooler.

The twins were the only ones who took her up on her offer.

The storm had turned the sky dark, and the hallway had grown even more dim. Dim and stuffy.

"You think of wind and rain in a hurricane, but you don't expect it to be so hot and muggy!" commented Beth, stroking damp tendrils from one of the twin's head.

Shelby lifted her head, listening for a long moment. Then she replaced it carefully on her paws with a heavy sigh.

"I wish she could tell us what she hears," Anne said.

"I'm glad she can't! I don't want to know about what I can't see." Beth was terrified. Of the wind. Of tornadoes. Of the thousands of objects that were now flying through the air. She strained her ears, listening for the sound of a freight train. For the rumbling sound that signaled the approach of a tornado.

Was that one?

Her eyes darted left trying to see beyond the walls of the hallway.

Or was that one?

Her eyes darted right as her arms tightened around the twins. She closed her eyes, trying to filter the sound of the storm from the more ominous snappings and moanings that would accompany a tornado. But the problem was, she didn't know what a freight train sounded like.

On base, the monitor's walkie-talkie crackled. The captain walked to the end of the hall and held it up to his ear, trying to conjure words from the hiss and fuzz. He turned up the volume. Struck it with the heel of his hand several times. The static changed pitch. Stopped. Then words materialized. The state policemen and sheriff's deputies had just been recalled. They were told to round up everyone still on the roads and take them to one of the high school shelters that had been opened. Then they were to report back to the crisis center and wait out the storm. It was too dangerous to be out in the open. For the next four hours, not even a fire truck or an ambulance would be allowed to venture out. At the first gust of wind they'd be flipped like a hamburger.

Everyone was on their own.

Shelby sat up again and began to growl, low in her throat, looking toward the door.

The friends looked at each other, alarmed.

The twins began to cry.

Beth took Andy in her arms and tried to soothe him.

Paolo tucked Josh into his side and started making funny faces at him, trying to make him laugh.

Anne drew her knees up to her chest and looped her arms around them. She dropped her forehead onto her arms and closed her eyes. She tried not to think of the pictures she'd seen of Hurricane Andrew. Of plywood driven straight through tree trunks or of blocks of houses that looked like a giant's game of pick up sticks. She tried not to think that she might die. But the fact was that she might. By taking shelter at Rachel's house, she had removed herself from the hazards of a tidal wave-like storm surge, but she had also placed herself in the middle of a forest. On some of the highest ground in the county. She might as well have painted a big X on her chest.

She'd thought she would have all the time in the world. Time to spend with Will. Time to start a career. Time to figure out what kind of person she was. But maybe all of her time was gone.

Maybe she'd already gotten all she would ever have. A year of marriage. A secretary's job and mixed feelings about the color of her skin.

The year with Will had been incredible. The job, not so incredible. But what else could she have done? What other option had there been? Stay at home? And do what? Read? Do crosswords?

And what about their next assignment? Would it be the same thing again? Sending out résumés by the dozens, waiting by the phone for interviews that never materialized? Probably. She was never going to have a high-powered job in human resources because she'd never be able to get an entry-level position or she'd never be able to stay in one location long enough to work her way up the career ladder.

Maybe a secretary was all she'd ever be. Anne Bradley. A black secretary married to a white guy. She couldn't change the color of her skin, she couldn't change her job. She couldn't change anything but her attitude.

She raised her head from her arms, looked around at her friends, and began to smile. She'd never have chosen these people as friends—Super Mom and Super Snob—yet they were the first people she'd call, the first people she *had* called, when she needed help.

She dropped her knees and straightened her legs, glanced over at Beth, and saw one of the twins smile at her. Her eyes lifted up toward his mother.

Beth's eyes were closed, and she had leaned her head back against the wall. A sheen of sweat glistened on her forehead.

Anne glanced at Rachel and saw her lift a hand toward her mouth and begin to chew on a fingernail.

They're scared too. Maybe they aren't so different from me.

Anne cleared her throat. "Look at us. Look at our lives. We're a living rebuke to the women's movement. One career given up to have children," she said nodding at Beth. "One career shipwrecked before it got started," she said, referring to herself. "And one person with no career at all," she inclined her head, mistakenly, toward Rachel.

"It's the military," Beth said, not even bothering to open her eyes.

"Do you think? Really? Or does the military just collect wives like us?" Anne had been wondering about that for a long time. Maybe her friends back in Seattle had been right. Maybe "military wife" was a career. And maybe not having a real career was part of the military wife career.

Rachel said nothing, just kept chewing on her fingernails. When she was finished with one, she went to the next.

Anne jabbed Beth with an elbow and nodded toward Rachel.

"So tell us how you met R.J. Did he seduce you with wine and roses?" asked Beth, trying to keep Rachel's mind off what was happening.

"No." She didn't look up from her fingernails. "I'd never been in a position to say yes before, so when I met R.J., I didn't know what to do. I was afraid to say yes." She put her finger back to her mouth.

"Really?" said Anne with surprise. She figured Rachel would have had a whole string of discarded lovers lighting up her past.

"I was a virgin when I married R.J."

They had spent their honeymoon night together in a castle along the Rhine River in Germany. Rachel had appeared from the bathroom in a long white gossamer robe, cigarette in hand. She looked at R.J. across the wide expanse of the bed.

He stared back at her with such intensity that it was unnerving. How come she'd never noticed before that he had a faint five o'clock shadow?

Crossing her arms in front of her, she cleared her throat and asked, "What do we do?"

"What do you mean?"

"What I mean is what I said." She uncrossed her arms and then crossed them again. She didn't know what to do with herself. "What do we do?"

"You weren't lying when you said you weren't that kind of girl?" Unbelievable. R.J. looked at her with new eyes.

"I don't lie." Then she tilted her head and added, "Usually."

"Come here," he ordered, patting the space beside him.

She came, climbing up into the old-fashioned bed. It was hung with curtains to keep out drafts. She fussed with them for a minute, drawing them closed. Crossing her legs and leaning against the ornately carved backboard, she sat beside him. "My grandfather used to say I intimidated men. I never cared before. I never minded. He was right, I suppose. He usually was. But maybe it's a good thing."

As she'd been talking, R.J. had taken the cigarette from her hand and reached across her lap to crush it into an ashtray. "Shut up and kiss me."

"I was too." Anne had always been proud of that fact. But what if Will had been in Seattle during their engagement? Her virginity was probably better explained by their geographical separation than by her high moral standards.

"Shhh!" Beth said, turning the radio up. "They're talking about the beach."

"...and we have a caller with us from the beach. Where are you calling from?"

"From the Seaspray."

"Why are you still there?"

"I was here for Hannah in '74. This is my home, you know? If it takes out the Seaspray, then I'm going too."

"And what's it look like out there."

"Well, there's some awful big waves. Beach chairs floating around."

"What floor are you on?"

"Tenth."

"Are the waves up to the first floor yet?"

"Over the first floor! Next building down's a three-story. It's floating…"

"Oh, Anne," Beth whispered. She clutched her friend's hand.

Anne squeezed it and tried to smile. "It's okay. Remember, I brought what I thought was important. Besides, I always said it never quite felt like home."

At the shelter on base, there was another crash and the wind rushing through the hall gathered strength.

A baby began to cry.

"It's okay, people," the captain called. "Just a couple of windows blown in. The structure is still sound. We're not going anywhere." *Unless a tornado hits us.*

The woman next to Karen got up from the floor and took tentative steps down the hall. Then she began to run toward the stairwell.

"Ma'am!" the captain called.

"Let me out of here! I'm claustrophobic. I have to get out!"

The woman's son still sat on the floor beside Karen. He looked up at her with big brown eyes.

She placed an arm around him and his arms shot around her waist.

The captain ran down the hall, chasing the woman. He wasn't worried about her getting out; the doors had been boarded up. But he couldn't have people flipping out all over the place. It was bad for morale.

"I can't stand it! I can't stand it!" They all heard the shouts floating up from the stairwell. "I'm going to die." She shrieked. "I can't stay here. I'm going to die."

"What's your name?" Karen asked the little boy.

"Peter."

"How old are you, Peter?"

He detached his arms from her and held up four fingers.

"Do you go to school?"

He nodded. "Is my mommy going to die?"

"Of course not."

His lips curled up and he leaned against her.

I don't want to die, either. I haven't even figured out who I am yet, let alone lived a life I've dreamed of.

"What if we all die?" Rachel asked, peering through the darkness.

"Then let's hope it's quick," Beth answered. "I've always been afraid of dying."

"But everyone dies. How can you live if you're afraid of dying?"

"I just try not to think about it."

"But that's being afraid of living. Life is change."

"I know."

"How can you be afraid of both living and dying?"

"I don't know. Just drop it. I need to do a better job at living before I think about dying." She kissed Andy on the head and buried her face in his hair.

"Amen," Anne said. "Last year, I was graduating and determined to have this great career. And here I am, at Bullard. A secretary." Anne paused and thought a minute. "You know, I am so tired of apologizing for my job. I've wasted so much time trying to fight it instead of just accepting it and getting on with things. I'm a secretary. So what?"

Beth gave Andy another squeeze. "I've been wasting time too. I've felt so guilty since—" How could she explain feeling guilty for staying at home with her sons? She couldn't even explain it to herself. One of the reasons she'd resigned her commission was because she had thought she'd feel guilty if she kept on working. She settled on the easiest explanation. "Things haven't been that great between Marc and me lately."

"Why?"

"Because when the twins were born, we had a big talk about who was going to get out to take care of them. We finally decided on me. I not only hate not working, but if I had stayed in, I'd probably have gotten promoted. Marc might not. So now we have the two worst possible scenarios. In living color."

"You can't have known either of those things when you got out."

"I do know that I would have gotten promoted."

"Well, let me tell you something," Rachel cut in. "I can't die."

She was so certain about it that Anne had to ask. "Why not?"

"Because I'm pregnant—" Her words were cut short by a horrible grind and screech. And then the roof peeled away from the house.

Two more hours of grueling hurricane passed and then, suddenly, the world went quiet. In Rachel's house, the friends lifted weary heads, wondering for a moment what had changed.

"It's over—?" Rachel said, jumping up.

"No." Anne tugged her hand and pulled her back down. "It's just the eye. We'll have silence for fifteen minutes, and then it starts all over again. Except the wind will be blowing in the opposite direction." She didn't say it, but this was the most dangerous part of the storm. Trees and objects that had been fatigued by two hours of wind from one direction were likely to snap or blow away when they were surprised by winds coming from the opposite direction. Now was the time to resist temptation and stay inside undercover.

Paolo crossed himself and began muttering in Italian.

"What's he saying?" Beth asked.

"He says he's going back to Italy as soon as this thing is over. They don't have hurricanes in Italy."

On base, the wind ceased roaming the hallway. Some people, like Karen, noticed and looked toward the captain.

"Just the eye." He tried to smile, but he was tired. "It's half over."

Peter was sleeping quietly on Karen's lap. His mother had returned to her place beside Karen, but she had her arms looped around drawn up knees and she was rocking back and forth. Karen had given up trying to speak to her.

Her thoughts turned to Kevin. She tried to picture him objectively, as if he belonged to someone else. Conjured up his face from memory, examined it from every angle. If she detached from the church, would he still have a place in her life? And if she didn't want the church, did that mean she didn't want him?

The winds never picked up in ferocity and after about an hour, they tapered off. Anne decided to open a shutter and take a look. Rachel helped her unlatch the French windows, and then clear the leaves and twigs that had been caught in the shutters' slits.

"It looks like someone pointed a leaf blower at the window," Rachel muttered. What a mess.

They finally got the shutters open and they folded them back to reveal an angry-looking gray sky, sodden with clouds. It was still muggy.

"There's your roof." It was sitting in the middle of the front lawn.

"Maybe they can salvage some of it." Rachel was trying with all her strength to look on the bright side. "Let's see what's left of the beach." She led Anne upstairs.

"It looks okay up here," Anne said with surprise. She surveyed the ceiling for water damage. "The attic must be strong."

They walked into Rachel's bedroom, opened a window, unlatched the shutters, and folded them open.

Rachel found her binoculars. She handed them to Anne.

"It looks fine," said Anne, her hopes rising. "The beach looks fine."

"Let me see," said Rachel, holding out a hand for the binoculars. She looked for a long while, sweeping the binoculars up and down the shore. "Anne," she finally said in a queer voice, "there used to be condos out there."

CHAPTER 26

*H*urricane Daniela had stalled just before landfall and had lost some of her strength offshore. She had registered category four winds when she hit Liffsbury. By the time the eye came ashore, the winds had become disorganized and the hurricane had fallen apart. Everyone applauded that great fortune.

Although gas station canopies had been crumpled and thrown onto the ground, and although several electrical towers had been crushed by the storm, the damage was not as great as had been expected.

Unfortunately, destruction on the coastline numbered in the billions of dollars. All of the resort hotels, all of the posh condominiums and beach houses were gone. Even the scenic highway that followed the coastline had been washed away. And the destruction had been complete and total. It would take years for the dunes to rebuild themselves. And no one could predict how long it would take for tourists to come back.

The following day Anne phoned her office with Rachel's cell phone. Nita told her the city's plans for beach residents. Advised her not to attempt to go back to the beach.

"There's really no way to even get onto the beach, you know. There isn't even a beach anymore."

It was incomprehensible. The "beach" had been a full ten blocks of condominiums and hotels.

"You mean the road's washed out?"

"I mean it just plain isn't there, Anne. I'm sorry."

"How—" Anne had trouble organizing her thoughts. "How am I going to get my mail?"

"We're setting something up at the post office. You'll need to bring ID, but you'll be able to pick up all your mail there. Just take a few days for yourself, okay? Mr. Trumble said he didn't want to see you back here before next week. Just let us know what we can do to help."

The phone began ringing the moment Anne set it down. She picked it up.

"Hello?"

"Anne?" It was Will.

She began crying as soon as she heard his voice. She handed the phone to Rachel because she couldn't talk.

"Will? This is Rachel. She's fine. She really is. But I don't think there's anything left of your place."

"I saw it on the news. They said the whole beach had been wiped out. Can I talk to her?"

Rachel handed the phone back to Anne. She took it.

"Are you okay? You're all I care about. Who gives a hairy hump about all our stuff? It wasn't even really ours to begin with."

Anne stopped crying and started sniffling. "I'm fine. The roof blew off Rachel's place, but the house itself is solid. And I have our golf clubs. They were in the trunk. At least we can still play golf."

"I'm coming back tomorrow. I changed my ticket."

"You didn't have to. There's nothing you can do."

"I wanted to."

"I'll pick you up if I can. I don't know what the storm damage is like around here. It's back in the woods quite a ways."

"I know. I'll call you when I get into the airport...if the phone works."

Rachel took the phone when Anne was done. She suspected the batteries were getting low and she needed to arrange for someone to mend her roof.

"Conrad? It's me."

"*Chérie.* How are you? Are you safe?"

"Yes, but the roof blew off. I'm on the cell phone and the batteries are dying. I need a generator, someone to put the roof back on, and someone to redo the cupola and the conservatory. You have a plan of the house."

"I do. Did you tell him?"

"Tell who, what?"

"R.J."

Not now. She couldn't handle this right now. "I just found out myself and I was hardly going to tell him in the middle of a hurricane. Can you get me what I need?"

"Of course."

"You'll want to fly everything in by helicopter. I don't know what the roads are like."

"*C'est parti.*"

Conrad's workers came to the rescue the next morning. The helicopter landed on the front lawn, next to the roof, and emptied out tools, supplies, and men. Rachel had to do some fast-talking to keep Paolo from jumping into it and flying out of town.

The first thing they did was hook up the generator. That started the water and sewer pumps as well as the electricity.

Anne decided to brave the roads and see if she could get to the airport.

"At least let me send René with a chain saw," Rachel begged. "He can clear the road for you."

Anne looked dubiously at the Canadian Rachel had imported to help put her house back together, but she accepted the offer and drove off through the woods.

Beth had decided to see if Anne could get through before she piled the twins into the car and tried to go home. She'd been in contact with Marc the previous evening. He wasn't able to return home until the end of the week anyway. Rachel had offered to let them stay until then, and Beth was inclined to accept.

Karen returned home to find things exactly the way she had left them. A tree from across the street had fallen into the yard, but it hadn't hit anything. She moved the furniture back into position. Hung her plants back on the porch. She picked life up right where she'd left off. And Kevin would be home at the end of the week.

When Beth went home later that week, she found several broken windows in their house. She laid towels over the still-damp carpets. Besides that, there was no damage. She got the glass cleaned up just before it was time to strap the twins in the car to get Marc.

He burst into the airport terminal and searched through the crowd in panic, relaxing only after he saw her. She saw tears glint in his eyes before she was engulfed in his hug.

"If anything had happened to you…" He squeezed her so tight she couldn't breathe. She clung to him with all her strength.

"It's okay. We're fine. The house is fine. Even Shelby is fine."

With that, he released her and picked up the twins, balancing them on his hips. "And how about you two?"

"Daddy want to play?" Josh asked.

Karen also went to the airport that Saturday, but she went to the military side of the runway. Kevin's 120-day deployment had stretched to 180 days. Six months. His plane arrived five hours after Marc's. She went an hour early just in case the plane was early. It was actually half an hour late. So she had plenty of time to think of what to say to him. Plenty of time to wonder what he'd think of her new look.

Like me. Please like me. Let him like me.

She was nervous about introducing Kevin to the new Karen.

She saw him walk off the plane and search the crowd that had been allowed to gather at the edge of the flight line. Once, twice his eyes scanned the area.

Most of the families were already welcoming their mothers and fathers home.

Then Kevin glanced at her. His eyes bounced off her face. Bounced back. His eyebrows grasped at each other as he mouthed her name, questioning.

She smiled. And a moment later she was engulfed in his arms. She hugged him back and then loosened her arms. But he wasn't letting go. "Kevin?"

"I'm breathing you."

"You're what?"

"Breathing you," he repeated into her neck. "At night, sometimes, for just a second, I would smell you, and then you'd be gone."

"Kevin, I don't think anyone else is breathing their wife," Karen whispered, her eyes watching the reunions going on around her.

"I don't care. I have the most wonderful wife in the world, and I'm going to smell her if I want to." His nose was ruffling through her hair now. "You don't know how good you smell."

"Like how?"

"Like you. You could make a perfume out of it," he said, finally releasing her.

"And call it what? Karen's smell?" she smiled at him.

"You look fabulous, Karen."

"Do you think so?"

"Yes, I do."

"Thanks," she said softly, her eyes starting to water.

"Could I kiss you?"

"Yes."

"I mean really kiss you," he said stepping closer and picking her up in his arms.

"So, are you glad to have me back?" Kevin asked later that night while they were lying in bed.

"Yes." She laid her head on his chest, grabbed his hand, and played with it. Things had been much simpler in her mind when he had been away, but she'd only just discovered that they hadn't been complete. She might be frustrated with her life, but she loved her husband.

"And why would that be?"

"I've missed you."

"I missed you." He ran a hand through her hair. "I like it this way."

"Have I changed?"

"On the outside," he said smiling, "but on the inside, you're still the same old Karen."

She felt her heart sink as she clenched her teeth together, trying not to cry. "I'm not. I'm not the same old me. I don't want to be me."

"Okay. You're not. You've changed inside and out."

"Kevin, listen, this is important," Karen ordered, sitting up and turning on a lamp.

"Karen, it's midnight."

"While you were gone, I did a lot of thinking. A lot of soul-searching about me. Who I am and what I believe. All my life I've let everyone else define me. My parents told me what my religion was. They told me what to believe in. And I never thought about it. Never even checked to see whether it made sense. Why am I condemned if I can't have kids? God gave me this body—why should he punish me for something he did?"

Kevin sat up, fully engaged now. His eternal future was at stake.

"And the mark of Cain? And Joseph Smith?"

"Karen, stop it. You're talking like an apostate. Who have you been talking to?"

"Is it so hard to believe that I could have thought these things up by myself?"

He captured her body and pulled her back down into bed, toward him. Held her close until he felt her relax. She lay against him, lulled by the sound of his heartbeat, feeling guilty for causing an argument his first night back.

"Karen, I was thinking maybe we should go to a fertility clinic. Maybe that would help."

She began to turn away from him, but then she sat back up in bed and faced him.

"Over my dead body, Kevin. I will never go to a fertility clinic. Do you know why? Because if God is who you say he is, then my purpose on earth is to have children for him. And that's it. It's the only reason I exist. The only thing I know is this: My not getting pregnant has nothing to do with me and everything to do with him. It's not my problem; it's his problem. He's the one who needs to fix it."

"You just have to believe. You have to have faith. Don't give up. We have to hang in there."

"I'm tired of having faith. I want to have answers. I want reasons. I'm tired of thinking I'm not good enough. I am good enough. As good as the next person. The problem is not with me. It's with God. And next time you talk to him, you can tell him that."

"We have to have kids."

"Don't you think I don't know that? I don't understand a god who would require me to have children and then not give me the ability to do it. Why should I worship a god like that?"

"Are you saying you want to leave the church?"

"No. I don't know what I want. Just something different."

"Yeah? Well, it's going to have to include me. Our marriage was sealed in the temple, remember?"

How could she forget? Just the thought of the interview with the bishop to determine her purity made her hot with shame. She had thought she could lie about the nature of her relationship with Kevin. And she had tried. But her blushes had always betrayed her. And the bishop wasn't content with a simple, general answer. He asked her pointed, detailed questions that no one should have had to answer. Afterward, she had hated Kevin for what she'd had to say.

In the end, of course, she was accepted into the temple. At the time she had thought, and had been obliged to tell the bishop, that she was pregnant. And while it wasn't the best situation to be in, it wasn't terrible news, either. Their marriage had been sealed in the temple. They were stuck together, for better or worse, for all eternity.

"Kevin, does it really matter? To achieve the celestial you also have to obey all the commands. And not sin. We sinned. Together. A lot. We've already lost it."

"We're married now. It doesn't matter."

"What if it does?"

It took a long time for either of them to fall asleep.

It was midweek before Beth remembered what Rachel had said before her roof had been blown off: Rachel was pregnant. Beth decided to call the others to come over and celebrate that Saturday. Anne agreed to bring Rachel without letting on why.

That turned out to be a problem. Anne and Will had been able to lease a small vacation rental out in the hills near Rachel's house. So it should have been easy for Anne to get Rachel out of the house. But Rachel didn't want to go anywhere.

"We just thought it would be nice to see each other after the hurricane. Make sure everyone's doing all right."

"Everyone's fine. And I have work to do."

"There's always time for work."

"Not my work. It has to get done today. And I have the contractors to supervise."

"We don't have to stay for long."

"I can't go. I'm sorry."

Anne finally had to tell her. "Rachel, this is for you. Beth wanted to have everyone over to celebrate the baby."

"What baby?"

"*Your* baby! You're pregnant, aren't you?"

"Yes. But I have other things on my mind right now." Her company was in the last stages of a bid for a buyout. They were waiting for her recommendation.

"Just one hour. I'm not taking no for an answer."

When Rachel and Anne showed up at Beth's, they didn't look to be in the best of moods.

Karen had never liked black and navy blue together, but Rachel's black palazzo pants and navy halter top looked perfect. Rachel sat down at the table without a word, her cherry-red lips pressed together.

"Anything wrong?" Karen asked.

"I'm pregnant."

"We know. It's wonderful news!"

"No, it's not. I've never wanted children. I'm mean and selfish, and I know if I have children they'll turn out just like me."

"But there's R.J. The baby will be half his," Karen said. "Does he know yet? He must be excited."

"No. He doesn't know. I don't even know where he is, and no one can say for sure when he'll be coming back! I've spent more time *away* from him than I have *with* him since we've been married." She had opened her purse and was fumbling for what everyone knew would be a cigarette.

As she flicked her lighter, Beth laid a hand on her arm. "If you really are pregnant, you probably don't want to smoke."

That's when Rachel finally burst into tears.

They convinced her to call the clinic on base.

"Appointments desk, Sergeant Horn speaking."

"I need to make an appointment," Rachel spoke into the phone.

"Active-duty military or dependent?"

"*In*dependent. We have separate checking accounts."

"Ha-ha. Active-duty military or dependent."

"*Independent.* Separate credit cards too."

"Ma'am, are you married to an active-duty military person?"

"I guess. He's TDY right now."

"Then as far as the Air Force is concerned, you're a dependent."

She made an appointment with a doctor for the following Tuesday.

CHAPTER 27

*don't understand it!" Rachel yelled. "I don't mind you flying God knows where every other week. I never even ask where you're going. But this is different! A year? And I can't even come with you? Just tell them no. You've done enough flying. It's not like you have to volunteer." She threw herself on the fainting couch in the bedroom. She was in tears.

"Flying an AC-130 is not a game I play, Rachel." R.J. stood across the room shouting at her. "I volunteered the day I got commissioned. If there's a war and they call my name, I'm in. I fight."

"So the only thing I get to do is say goodbye? And right before Christmas?"

"You could kiss me too. And anyway, it hasn't been decided yet. I'll know by September."

"But war is barbaric. It's obsolete. Things can be talked over; treaties can be made. America's greatest power is commerce and free trade, not bombs and missiles!"

"And when that doesn't work, there's the military."

"War is nationalism gone crazy. Nothing is worth that price."

R.J. flushed and his nostrils flared. "War is what I train every day of my life for and pray to God every night never happens. The only thing worse than war is living a life full of nothing worth dying for. When I say 'I love you,' I'm saying I'm willing to die for you. And by being in the Air Force, I'm saying that I'm willing to die for the rest of America too. I know there are people who aren't worth the price of my life. I know that there are people who would run to the end of the earth to escape a draft, and I'm willing to fight to preserve their right and your right to disagree with me. But don't *ever* say that nothing is worth the price of war. The price of war created the foundation of our entire society."

She watched his Adam's apple convulse in a neck gone red from anger. "I know this marriage has not been what you expected. But, until tonight, it had been beyond my wildest dreams."

As he began to walk from the room, Rachel started to protest, but he stopped her, raising a finger and pointing it at her. "Don't ask me to become less of a man for you."

She had never heard him speak in a voice so terrible, and she had never felt such contempt from him.

How could she take back words she should never have even thought? He was right. December was a long way off, and his squadron might not even be called to go. But it was his first night back from wherever he had been for the past two weeks. And it was also the night she was going to tell him about the baby. And then he'd ruined it all with his news.

Rachel crumpled on the couch and began to cry. How could things have gone so wrong?

R.J. didn't come back that night. Rachel woke in the morning on the couch, exactly where she had been when he left. She rose and went into the bathroom. She pulled a comb through her hair and then put on the first clothes she saw. She was due to meet with Beth, Anne, and Karen at Bozo's for lunch.

They were all waiting for her when she walked in 15 minutes late. Her shirt was a sober gray, and she looked just as wan.

"Rachel, are you okay?" Beth asked.

"Fine." Her voice was so dull, it was like hearing it from beyond the grave.

"Is R.J. all right?" Anne praised God, yet again, that Will wasn't a pilot.

"I have no idea."

"Did you guys have a fight?" Karen asked. She could sympathize.

"No. I just put into question his entire ethical code and way of life." She shivered. "I think he truly hates me."

Beth had a premonition. "What did you say?"

"Basically that nothing was worth the price of war and how could he morally justify fighting if he was ever asked to." She looked as if she would have liked to cry, but her face was brittle. And there were no tears.

Beth understood. Deciding to go to USAFA had been a no-brainer. She'd had no fears of being able to measure up physically; she'd always done well in sports and intramurals. Receiving the appointment was an honor; very few people have the chance to attend a military academy. There had been no question in her mind about accepting it. The questions hadn't started then.

The questions had started after she'd graduated. After they'd married. She would read the newspaper, turn on the television, and realize that the majority of what she saw and read didn't match her own ideals. She saw that money, power, and influence were valued above loyalty, dedication, and honor. She read that patriotism could be bought and sold for the Olympic Games just as easily as it could be in a black-market arms deal.

She didn't mind that she was making at least $15,000 less than she would be in the private sector. She didn't even mind that most Americans never gave a thought to the men and women who serve in the armed forces. What she did mind was how many people scorned her for it or failed to appreciate the sacrifice.

People like her guaranteed the liberties of Americans. And most of the time, they did it quietly without asking for any recognition. All she really wanted was the knowledge that Americans were grateful for it; and the knowledge that, if ever asked, they would do the same for her.

Increasingly, she didn't think that was true.

Beth herself didn't know why she had continued to serve. She wasn't a pilot; she didn't engage in combat. She would probably never see a battlefield. But there was something in her that said the service demanded by her country was worth the sacrifice.

To her, the flag meant something. She could never wear it printed on a T-shirt or stamped on a swimsuit. Would never sign one like a yearbook; never make one into a costume. The flag was a symbol of her deepest loyalties.

She would never get rich in the military, but she could serve knowing that she was working for the good of something bigger than herself. And when she thought about it long enough, it frightened her that more Americans weren't willing to do the same.

And lately she wondered if it had been worth it, given that her loyalty to the American public would never be honored or returned.

"Did he leave you?" Anne could hardly bear to ask the question.

Rachel looked at them for the first time since she'd arrived. "I think he might have. I think I screwed it up completely. I don't know what to do."

One lone tear trickled down her nose and onto the table.

She glanced away from them in shame and quickly wiped the tear with a sleeve. She started to speak again, but the words dissolved into a sob. When she caught her breath, she managed to say, "I think I destroyed the only real thing I ever had."

Beth put a comforting arm around her.

"The whole time I was thinking how lucky he was to have married me, and now I know that I never even deserved to know him, let alone be married to him. I was playing at being married. How could I do that to him? How could he ever have loved me?"

"Do you still love him?" Anne was sure she knew the answer.

"Yes."

"Then get him back."

"I don't deserve him, Anne. I don't even deserve to live on the same planet with him. I'm going back to New York."

"I don't think you should."

"Why not, Karen? You haven't seen the way he hates me."

"But he used to love you."

"He didn't even know me when we married. The longer we were together, the worse I became for him."

Karen couldn't believe that. She'd seen them together. "Did he say that?"

Rachel broke down again. "No. He said it had been beyond his wildest dreams. Until I said what I did. Why can't I take those stupid words and stuff them back down my throat?"

Rachel's friends buoyed her, encouraged her, and sent her back home with hope. They planned to meet again at Bozo's one last time the following week, before they dispersed for summer vacations.

Rachel expected that R.J. would come back to the house. He'd have to in order to get ready for his next deployment. And when he did, she would do just about anything to keep him from leaving her.

There was only one problem with her plans: He never came home.

By the time Anne got to Bozo's the next week, Karen and Beth were already there. "Sorry I'm late! The phone rang just before I walked out the door. And of course, it was my favorite city citizen."

"Which one?"

"The one who always calls to complain. About everything: traffic lights, potholes, the budget…And then she'll want me to take a multi-paragraph message for the city manager and repeat it back to her word-for-word when she's done dictating. So that made Will late—we had to drop my car off for a tune-up. He'll be back to pick me up in—" she glanced at her watch and frowned, "in 45 minutes. Where's Rachel?"

Beth shrugged.

"Maybe she's just running late." Karen was always willing to give anyone the benefit of doubt.

Anne glanced at her watch. "Half an hour late? Even that's a little much for Rachel."

The waitress brought Beth's burger and fries and Karen's salad. She paused just long enough to take Anne's order before threading her way through the tables back to the kitchen.

Fifteen minutes later, when Anne's turkey sandwich appeared, Rachel still wasn't there.

"I'm calling her. She should have been here by now. Even if the only thing she ever orders is a vanilla shake." Anne picked up a potato chip and ate it while she fished her phone out of her purse.

"Rachel?"

"Hmm?"

"Rachel? Are you okay?"

"Fine…I'm fine."

"You don't sound fine." In fact, she sounded as if she were detached from reality, her thoughts a million miles away from her voice.

What sounded like a yawn was beamed up to a satellite and sent back into the cellular network. "…sorry."

"Are you sick?"

"No."

"Then why did you miss lunch today?"

"What lunch?"

"Our lunch. The last one before summer."

"Was that today? What day is today?"

"Are you at home, Rachel?"

"Yes."

"Don't go anywhere. I'm getting Will and we're coming right over."

Rachel hung up her cell phone and then opened her eyes. The room glowed with sunlight that had infiltrated the curtains. She began to stretch, straightening a leg into the air-conditioned room. Then she remembered. R.J. was gone; he'd left her. She pulled her foot back under the cover, slowly pulled herself into a ball and willed herself to fall back asleep.

Half an hour later, Will tugged at the doorbell a third time. "I just don't think she's home, Anne."

"She's here." Her lips were drawn together in a grim line. "She said she was home."

"But isn't she from New York? Maybe she meant there when she said home."

"If she weren't going to be in town for our lunch date, she would have told us." Anne took off on a trot around the side of the house.

Will yelled after her. "If she's not answering, there's not much we can do." He gave one more tug on the bell for good measure and went to find his wife.

He found her on the patio, in front of the French doors that led into the conservatory. She was in the middle of a conversation with Paolo.

He was gesticulating wildly. *"No disturba signora."*

"I need to talk to Rachel."

"La signora dorme." Paolo closed his eyes and rested his chin on folded hands to illustrate. He shook a finger at her. *"No disturba."*

Anne threw her hands up in the air and turned to Will. "He's not going to be any help. Let's just go find her."

"Are you sure this is the right thing to do?"

"You can wait out here if you want, but I'm going inside." He watched her weave between the plants before the jungle swallowed her.

The cook was wringing his hands and muttering what Will imagined were dire curses against the person who dared to disturb his employer's rest.

Anne slowly pushed down on the bedroom door's handle and opened the door. She sighed in relief at the forlorn bundle of humanity that slept at the extreme left edge of the bed. Then she tiptoed nearer and knelt beside Rachel's sleeping form.

She reached out one hand to stroke Rachel's tumbled hair and the other to clasp her friend's hand. "Rachel?"

Her friend didn't move.

Anne pushed the hair away from Rachel's eyes and squeezed her hand. "Rachel."

One eye slit open. "R.J.?"

"No. We wanted to make sure you were okay."

Her eye closed and if it were possible, she seemed to burrow herself into an even tighter ball. "I'm fine. Let me sleep."

"It's two o'clock in the afternoon, Rach."

"It's called trauma. I've been traumatized...R.J. left me. He never came back."

"R.J. never came back? How long have you been like this?"

"I don't know."

"And you've been hiding in bed since then? That's the way to make a man feel terrible for leaving: Let your hair get greasy and your pits get smelly. What you've got is not called trauma, it's called feeling sorry for yourself."

"I am not."

"You are too." Anne grasped the corner of the down comforter and sheet that covered her friend and stripped it from the bed. "Time to get up."

"I need sleep."

"You need action."

"I'm cold."

"Then get up and get dressed."

"You're heartless."

"I'm not heartless; I'm ruthless." Anne moved toward the window closest to the bed and whipped away the drape. She moved to the remaining windows and did the same. Then she plopped onto a period fainting couch, crossed her arms under her head, and stretched out. "This couch is pretty comfy." Anne swung her tennis shoe-clad feet onto it and rolled onto her side, propping her head up with her hand.

"It's an antique. Get your feet off of it."

"Can't be worth that much."

"Sixty thousand dollars. Horsehair cushions. Mint condition. One of a kind."

"Well, you'd think a fainting couch could handle a full faint."

Rachel rolled out of her fetal position and sat up in bed. "R.J. left me. He doesn't care about me."

"So you don't care about him anymore?"

Rachel raised purple shadowed eyes to meet hers. "No."

"You liar," Anne taunted. She willed Rachel to react. *Come on. Don't let me down. Start to fight for him.*

"I am not a liar and I don't care what you think. The truth is, he doesn't love me anymore."

"That's not what I asked. I asked if *you* still loved *him*."

Rachel sunk back down into the bed and turned her back on Anne. "No," was her muffled reply.

"Oh." Anne waited a full five minutes by her runner's watch to let

Rachel think about what she'd said. "Pity the poor man whose own wife won't try to win him back."

"He said he didn't want me." Rachel shot away from the bed like a Fury. "What am I supposed to do?" she yelled.

Anne got up and marched close to her. She looked Rachel in the eye. "Either grow up or get out of R.J.'s life. The Air Force doesn't need wives like you," she sneered. Then she stalked from the room.

"Get out of my house!" Rachel screamed behind her. "Go away!"

Anne walked down the long staircase shaking her head. She considered herself a pretty good judge of character, but this time, she'd been way off base. About both of them.

"Did you find her?" Will was relieved to see Anne come through the French doors. He'd had enough of the cook's moaning and sighing.

"Yes. And Miss Silver Spoon is not in today. She's a snot-nosed brat. And that's the best thing I have to say about her."

Anne was silent as they drove back to her office.

CHAPTER 28

～

*A*nne had just finished organizing the computer files when the
door opened. She looked up to see a delegation of people
flood the office. Her eyes sought the refuge of Nita's office.
The door was shut. She glanced at her watch. Nita still had 20 minutes
of her lunch left. She sighed a small sigh as her eyes searched for the
leader of the group. It turned out not to be the largest, the tallest, or
the loudest man among them. It was the shortest man with the least
amount of hair that detached himself from the rest and folded his hands
in front of him. "Judge Peary."

"I'm sorry," Anne answered. "There's no Judge Peary in this office.
You might try the courthouse. Next building on the left."

"No. *I'm* Judge Peary."

"I'm sorry." Anne heard herself apologize for the second time.

"That's all right. I'm here to see Mr. Trumble."

"Was he expecting you?" asked Anne with a sinking feeling, looking
past the judge and counting his companions. There were 12.

"No."

Anne felt her shoulders relax. Good. Then she hadn't forgotten to
pass a meeting to Nita for Mr. Trumble's calendar.

"But surely," the judge was saying, "a public servant wouldn't pass
up the opportunity to meet face-to-face with his public." His eyes
challenged Anne to refuse his request.

"He's not here."

"Oh, really? Well, it's two o'clock. Tell me, when does he find time
to work?"

In reality, Mr. Trumble had already had some rather strenuous and
tedious dealings with his public earlier in the day. At the moment, he
was taking a well-deserved late lunch. But as Anne looked at the judge

and his motley crew of companions, she decided she wasn't about to tell him that. "Actually, Mr. Trumble is quite concerned at the moment with his mother. She's getting older, you know…"

Anne was gratified to see the judge's eyes dodge sheepishly at the carpet.

"May I leave a message for him?"

"Yes. I wanted to speak at the city council meeting tomorrow."

"Requests to speak at the meetings are only accepted until close of business on Tuesday, so I can't schedule you for this week. How about next?"

"I need to speak this week."

"Then you'll need to ask Mr. Trumble about that personally. I'm not authorized to make exceptions."

"But it's for the good of your people."

"What do you mean by 'my people'?"

"The downtrodden and the oppressed. We're all in this together. United we stand."

"I don't have any relatives in this part of the country."

"But you have plenty of sisters and brothers."

"Amen," said one of the judge's contingent.

"You're one of us. We're with you."

"You're talking about the color of my skin?" It was hard for Anne to decipher exactly what the judge was trying to tell her. The delegation was made up of a mix of colors and races.

"We got to stick together."

"Let me tell you something, Judge Peary: I'm not playing. My parents warned me about people like you. Of any color. So why don't you just tell me what you want and I'll tell you if I can do it."

The smile slid right off the judge's face. "There's a contract that's been awarded. Brother Miller here made a bid on it," the judge said, indicating the man who stepped forward. "And he didn't get it. We feel he wasn't given fair consideration, and we want copies of the minutes of the meeting where the bid was given."

"What was the contract for?"

"Ambulance services."

"Then that would have been awarded at the last meeting. But the city clerk makes those records available. You'll have to ask at their office if the minutes from that meeting are complete," explained Anne, reaching for a small sticky note. She wrote the date of the previous meeting and handed it to the judge. "Ask for the minutes of this meeting."

The judge was still staring at the sticky note when the door to the office opened and Mr. Trumble walked in.

"Mr. Trumble!" exclaimed the judge. "Just the man we were looking for."

"What can I do for you?" he asked, making not the smallest attempt to move toward his office. He didn't, Anne noticed, even invite the group to sit down in the reception area.

"I was just talking with your girl. There's been a mistake. Not that we're upset or anything," said the judge, turning slightly in Anne's direction. "See, we called last week to speak at tomorrow's meeting, and we came here today to see what time the meeting started. She said she forgot to put us on."

"That's not true," said Anne in a voice that was much calmer than it should have been. "Not five minutes ago I told you that I could put you on next week's agenda, but that you'd have to ask Mr. Trumble to make an exception for this week's."

"Maybe she just forgot our conversation last week," the judge said, referring to Anne but looking at the city manager.

"In this conversation we had last week," said Anne, "did I say I would leave a note for Mr. Trumble?"

"Yes," said the judge smiling and winking at her. "Yes, you did."

"Well, then, fortunately my message book has carbon copies. What day was it that you said you called?" asked Anne, ready to flip through her message record.

The judge swallowed hard. "I don't really remember."

"That's okay. It'll only take a minute to look."

The judge took a handkerchief out of his suit jacket and mopped his brow while Anne searched her phone message book.

"You won't believe this, Judge Peary, but I don't have a record of your call."

Mr. Trumble cleared his throat. "I believe we can put you gentlemen on next week's agenda, first thing."

"That'll be fine," said the judge.

Anne would never have believed that 13 people could empty a room so quickly.

"You've just made an enemy for life," Mr. Trumble said as he sat on one of the couches.

"Well, I'd hate to have to call him my friend. Is Judge Peary really a judge?"

"Not in this city."

"Didn't think so."

After Anne had gone, Rachel sat up in bed and threw off the covers. Her friend's words had shaken her more than she cared to admit. She wished she had someone she could ask for advice. As she mulled over her options, her grandfather's voice spoke to her as if he were sitting right beside her.

What is the first rule of business?

She could see the stern lines engraved in his forehead and the twinkle in his eyes that had always been reserved just for her. *Never lay more on the table than your adversary does. Never give away anything that someone else will pay for. But he left me. I don't owe him anything. He owes me. Nobody leaves Rachel Porter-Smith. If I knew that he loved me, even a little...but I don't. And apparently he doesn't.*

She could see her grandfather frown as if he knew she was playing games with him.

Then what is the second rule of business?

Always be realistic about yourself and your market position. Do I love him? Yes. Then who has the position of strength? R.J. Because I would kill myself if he never knew that.

What is the third rule of business?

Always know how far you are willing to go to be competitive. What am I prepared to do to get R.J. back? Anything.

What is the fourth rule of business?

Always know the resources you have at your disposal. What are my strengths? Money. My family name. Publicity. It comes down to the same thing it always does: the power to influence opinion. The power to influence R.J.

And if you follow the Four Golden Rules, what happens?

You win every time.

Wrong. You are proactive, not reactive.

Which would have been something if she hadn't had nothing. Her strengths were useless unless she could find out where R.J. was. Until then, none of her assets could be put into play.

The first thing Rachel had to do was tell his parents. She sat in front of the keyboard R.J. used to talk to them. How did it work?

She pushed a promising looking button.

Nothing.

He'd showed her several times, but she'd never really watched.

She pushed another button.

Absolutely nothing.

The third button provoked a reaction. Lights began to blink and a dial tone began. It sounded like a fax machine. And then the window lit up as words appeared. "Hawthorne residence. May I help you?"

Rachel stared at the words.

"Hello?"

She looked down at the keyboard and began to type, and then she realized she didn't know what to say. *Hello, it's your daughter-in-law. Your son left me last week. Do you know where he is? Hope you had a great weekend.*

"Hello?"

The connection was broken and the screen went blank as Rachel folded in on herself and began to weep. *I can't do this.*

She allowed herself the luxury of crying for several minutes before she drew a deep breath, wiped the tears from her eyes, and stood up.

"Hi! What's for dinner?" Marc asked as the door between the house and the garage slammed shut.

Shelby bounced over to him to be petted. Her stub of a tail looked as if it would fly off her body at any moment.

Marc bent to rub her head and then gave her a pat on the butt. It sent her scurrying into the living room, waiting for him to play tug-of-war with her.

"I have no idea. What do *you* feel like eating?" Beth snapped. Her thoughts had been on Rachel and the strain she knew her friend must be feeling. Anne had told her R.J. had never returned.

"I don't know. Anything." Marc unbuttoned his shirt as he disappeared down the hall into the bedroom.

"I don't have a recipe for Anything," Beth muttered. "How come I'm always the one who has to decide what all of us get to eat? How come you guys can't decide?"

The twins stopped banging pots, and two small faces looked up at hers.

"What would we eat if it were up to you?" Beth spied something shiny wrapped in Andy's tight fist. She pried it out and dried the drool from it on her jeans. "Paper clips, huh? Guess we better go with what I had in mind."

"Hey! Can I help you in there?" Marc's voiced floated into the kitchen.

"No. I'm fine." Beth jumped back from the sink as water sloshed onto her pink polo shirt. No big deal. It would air dry in about two minutes.

"How about the twins?"

"They're quite happy banging the pots together." She dried her hands on her faded jeans shorts.

"You sure they're not bothering you?"

Beth looked down at her two terrors. She'd nearly tripped over them ten times. "No. I'm fine."

"Okay. Just yell if you need anything. Tell me what needs to be done."

I am so tired of yelling. Just look around and figure out something to do. Iron. Vacuum. Straighten the bookshelves again. Just do something! How did I get to be the maid in this marriage? And the mother and the chef!

"Hey—I was thinking we should get your racquetball racquet re-strung."

She nudged Shelby under the behind with a foot to get her to move. "I never play anymore."

"Because your racquet's messed up."

"Because I don't have time."

"But you love racquetball."

She ripped the pots away from the twins.

Their faces crumpled. They started to howl.

She grabbed their forearms and yanked them to their feet. "Stop it. Stop! For two seconds just be good. Can you do that?"

"Beth?" Marc was suddenly beside her. His hands closed over her own. "Stop. Let go. You're going to hurt them."

Rachel was beyond feeling depressed. Beyond feeling helpless. Beyond feeling lost. Now she was just plain mad. It had been two weeks since R.J. had gone. And he hadn't even bothered to contact her. So much for courtesy. If she'd planned on walking out on him, the least she would have done is left a contact number or a forwarding address.

She would have tried his cell phone, except that he refused to carry one. It was lying on his dresser, right where he'd left it when he walked out.

She had asked discreet questions where she could, but soon discovered that he hadn't left any trails. He hadn't used a credit card, hadn't used his passport, hadn't accessed his bank account. He couldn't have done a better job at disappearing if he'd tried. It was as if he'd vanished.

Although she'd thought about contacting his squadron commander, she hadn't done it. Not yet. Being laughed at by a lieutenant colonel with the call sign of "Tarzan" was just what she didn't need at this moment.

She'd also thought about contacting Conrad, but she just couldn't bring herself to do it. Couldn't quite admit that she'd apparently failed at the only thing she'd ever tried to do all by herself. She might be a wunderkind when it came to business, but at marriage she was a dismal failure.

She just wished her heart shared the sentiments of her brain. Because in spite of everything she told herself, and in spite of R.J.'s behavior, she still cried in her bed in the stillness of the night. And she knew that although R.J. was the one who had left, it was her words that had driven him out the door.

CHAPTER 29

~

*R*achel woke up abruptly without knowing why, but she was undeniably awake. She rolled over onto her side and stared into the dark. R.J.'s voice haunted her, an echo from the past.

"What if the sky is not the limit, Rach? What if there's something out there?"

What if there's something out there? What if there's something beyond the sky?

She'd never needed God before. Money and power had been able to give her anything, everything, she'd ever wanted. Until now, she had only needed herself. She didn't feel right about asking God for something. How would she feel if a stranger suddenly approached her to ask a huge and inconvenient favor? But for R.J., who had professed a certain basic belief in him, perhaps God might listen.

How do people talk to God?

She supposed it must be like arranging a business deal. After all, if you asked for something big, you'd have to give something to him in return. But what could God want that, if he really were God, he didn't already have?

That was the problem. For any kind of business, you had to know whom you were dealing with. Otherwise, you might obligate yourself to something you could never do. She knew absolutely nothing about God, so she was operating at a distinct disadvantage. What motivated him?

If R.J. had been asking questions about God, perhaps he'd already been doing some research on it.

She threw off the covers and jumped to her feet. Wrapping her robe around herself, she went downstairs to the library. Maybe R.J. had a Bible.

She looked for ten minutes, up and down the shelves, until she found one. It was in a plain black cover, but it had his name stamped on the bottom right corner. She ran a finger across the gold script. *Richard Jarrett Hawthorne.*

She flipped through it. Noticed an underlined section.

"Those who hope in the LORD will renew their strength. They will soar on wings like eagles; they will run and not grow weary, they will walk and not be faint" (Isaiah 40:31).

"But how do I know I can trust you, God?" Rachel heard herself ask.

She shook her head and closed the book. She started to put it back on the shelf, but then she noticed a bookmark in it. She pulled the book open with a finger. Maybe this would tell her what God wanted.

Again, a paragraph was underlined. "Without faith it is impossible to please God, because anyone who comes to him must believe that he exists and that he rewards those who earnestly seek him" (Hebrews 11:6).

What does God want? He wants my faith at a minimum. He wants me to seek him.

God, that takes time. I don't have time. I want R.J. back now. I'll write you a check. I'll write you into my will. But I don't have time.

She skimmed through the chapter surrounding the underlined paragraph. It talked about people she didn't know, but it also talked about God doing amazing things. It looked as though those things only happened because the people had faith.

What gives a person faith like that?

She kept reading on into the next chapter.

"Let us fix our eyes on Jesus, the author and perfecter of our faith... Make every effort to live in peace with all men and to be holy; without holiness no one will see the Lord" (Hebrews 12:2,14).

Okay, what have I got? Without faith it's impossible to please God. God wants faith. Fix our eyes on Jesus, the author and perfecter of our faith. Faith needs Jesus to complete it. Without holiness no one will see the Lord.

"Faith and Jesus I can do something about, but holiness?" she muttered to herself. "I'm a pretty good person, but I'm definitely not holy."

She remembered seeing something else about holiness in the chapter. "God disciplines us for our good, that we may share in his holiness" (Hebrews 12:10).

So why would God discipline people? Because they do the wrong things.
"Endure hardship as discipline; God is treating you as sons" (Hebrews 12:7). No. She'd gotten it backward.

God wasn't disciplining because they'd done the wrong things, He was disciplining so they'd do the right things. Like being disciplined in school or sports.

"But God disciplines us..."
He trains us.
"...for our good, that we may share in his holiness."

Rachel closed the book and sat down on the floor. She cradled it in her lap. *So it's talking about obedience. God disciplines us. He trains us. Why? So we can share his holiness.*

Okay, God. So I have to obey you, and you take care of the holiness. So, what do you want? Faith, which needs Jesus, and holiness, which needs obedience.

It still didn't sound right. What God wanted was individual commitment. That wasn't something she could do for R.J.

Without faith it's impossible to please God. Without holiness no one will see the Lord.

All right, God. I'm at the table. This is the deal.

Number one. I assume that there is something beyond the sky.

Number two. I commit to working on the faith and the holiness stipulations, taking into account that they require some knowledge of Jesus and some knowledge of what your rules are.

Number three. To complete the requirements stipulated in number two, I will read this book. I take no responsibility for acquiring knowledge from materials that I do not know exist.

But that still doesn't do anything for R.J.

Number four. I have the aforementioned faith that you can return R.J. to me.

Number five. Keeping in mind R.J.'s professed interest in you, when he is returned to me, I will tell him what I've figured out about you.

Number six. I will start on the faith and holiness stipulations as soon as possible, but the understanding between us is clear that this takes time.

She didn't bother putting in a cancellation clause, because she didn't have any other options. Her money and family name and connections couldn't do anything to get him back. This God was her only hope.

She leaned her head back against the bookshelf and heaved a heavy sigh. Then she looked at the plain black book lying in her lap. She turned to the bookmark and pulled it out, deciding to start at the beginning of the section. Hebrews, chapter 1.

Do you see me, God? Look, I'm starting.

Karen paused as she walked down the medicine aisle in the commissary. The laxatives caught her eye. *Just in case. You never know when they might come in handy.* She took a box and threw it into the shopping cart without even slowing down.

Later that afternoon she opened the medicine cabinet and toyed with the box of laxatives she'd placed there. She pushed her hair behind an ear as she read the label.

Just one can't hurt. I ate way too much today. I hardly ever do; I don't know what happened. This will make me feel better. Just today. I'll never do it again.

She took the box out and opened it up, peeled the foil away from one of the pills, and shook it from the plastic. Filling a glass with water, she popped the pill into her mouth. And then she caught a glimpse of herself in the mirror.

She stared back.

Trembled. She spit the pill into the sink and rinsed it down the drain with her glass of water. Then she threw the box into the trash and sat down on the toilet. She was shaking now with the realization of what she had almost done, of what she had almost become.

This is beyond my control. This is way out of hand. I'm scaring myself. I need help.

She decided to talk to someone. She called for an appointment at the practice of a psychologist from the church and got one for the next day at ten.

She listened with sympathy as Karen spilled out her story, patting her hand now and then with compassion. Then, as Karen wound down, the psychologist began to speak.

"I know that many people struggle with eating disorders. Especially in the last few years, but I have to tell you, I've eaten three square meals every day of my life, and I've never had a problem. Why don't you start with that?"

Karen began to protest.

The psychologist waved her off. "I know young girls insist they aren't hungry for breakfast, but breakfast is the most important meal. Start eating, and the problem will fix itself. And of course, read your Bible and pray. Once you make things right with God, the eating will fall back into place. Just trust Heavenly Father, okay? Now, take a few deep breaths, visualize yourself eating, and then stop and pick up something on your way home. And eat it! Get yourself something nice, like an ice cream sundae."

Karen could only stare at the psychologist with dazed eyes. She'd come for help, and what she'd received was a scolding. She'd poured out her heart only to hear that she wasn't living life the right way, that she wasn't good enough.

She already knew that!

What she needed was some help in stopping. In fixing the trouble that she'd started. Because the hole she'd dug herself into wasn't something she could haul herself out of.

It was too big and too deep.

"Is this the city manager's office?"

"Yes, ma'am," Anne answered.

"I want to talk to somebody about a complaint."

"Yes, ma'am."

"I purchased a brand-new home just four months ago, and now I'm bailing it out. The foundation is completely under water. The sewer system in our neighborhood isn't working properly!"

"Ma'am, the city doesn't have an organized sewer or water runoff system. The contractor who built your house is responsible for the drainage."

"But the house has been flooded since yesterday!"

"I know, Ma'am, but the city only considers standing water a problem if it doesn't disappear after 72 hours." Anne instinctively cringed as she said this, because she knew what the response would be.

The woman swore into the phone.

"What you need to do is prosecute your contractor." The woman hung up on Anne as she said this.

"Nita?" Anne yelled into the other room.

"Yes?"

"Why doesn't the city have a runoff water drainage system?"

"We do. All the water eventually runs downhill into the ocean."

Ha-ha. "But why isn't there a sewer system?"

"Choices, sweetie. Beaches and recreation areas are more important. Make sure when you move into a new place that you look at it right after it's rained."

Thanks for the tip.

CHAPTER 30

~~

*K*evin, I need to have a job."

He rolled over and groaned. Pulled a pillow over his head. They'd been having a nice Sunday-afternoon nap. "We've already talked about this. The best thing to do is to relax."

She took the pillow away and tossed it to the floor. "I've been relaxing for two years. And it's not very relaxing. I need to use my mind. I want to use my degree."

"But we already decided—"

"No, Kevin. You already decided. It was your decision. But this one is going to be my decision. I don't know if I'll ever be able to have children. So as long as I'm not pregnant, I'm going to work. Trying to be stress free for the past seven years hasn't helped me. Maybe work will."

"But your callings at the church—"

Karen smiled. "Don't you find it rather strange that the callings all came after you left for Iraq?"

"No. God knew you had extra time."

"I don't think so, Kevin. And I don't think it's fair for the church to demand so much of its members. I am exhausted. I have nothing left to give. I'm not going to do it anymore."

"You just can't quit."

"Why not?"

"Because...what will everyone think?"

"I'm tired of caring what everyone will think. I've spent my whole life worried about what everyone will think. I think the most important people in our lives are you and me. What do you think?"

"I just want us to be a happy family..."

"You wanted to say a happy family with kids, didn't you?"

Kevin looked at her. He didn't have to agree. She read the truth in his eyes.

She took his hand. "Kevin, I've turned myself inside out trying to get pregnant. I've cut my soul out and given it to God. And, apparently, he doesn't care."

"You just have to trust him."

"I do. I'm trusting that, right now, he doesn't want me to have kids. So, fine. I'm not going to spend any more time worrying or feeling guilty over it. I want to start living the life that I want, not the life that the church tells me I should want. I'm tired of feeling like a second-class citizen."

Kevin looked at her as if he was seeing her for the first time.

"I know this doesn't fit with the picture of a good LDS wife. If you want a divorce, I understand." There. She'd said it. Now it was his choice.

"Are you saying that you're leaving the church?"

"I don't think so. I'm just not completely convinced anymore that God is out there. That there's anything at all beyond the sky but stars. I don't mind going with you. I'm just not going to play the perfect wife and mother game anymore." She threw off the covers and swung her legs onto the floor.

He grabbed her hand as she tried to leave the bed. "Karen, I've told you a thousand times I'm sorry for what we did before we were married. I take all the responsibility for it. If I could undo it, I would."

She sat on the edge of the bed, surprised at his honesty. She decided to be honest in return. "Why do you love me?"

"I don't know. Honest to God, Karen. I don't know why I love you. But I do. Otherwise, how could I put up with this? If I didn't love you, I would have left months ago." He dropped her hand. There wasn't anything else he could say. If she couldn't see it, there was nothing else he could do to show her. Maybe she wanted him to leave. Maybe the problem wasn't him loving her. Maybe the problem was her loving him. He lifted weary eyes to face Karen and found her kneeling before him.

"You love me." Karen's eyes were lit with wonder. "You love me!" She was smiling in spite of the tears that were streaming down her face. "Why do you put up with me?"

"No more questions," Kevin groaned as he engulfed her in a hug and pulled her onto the bed.

Kevin's hands caressed her back gently in massaging circles. They slowly moved down and around toward her abdomen. She turned in his arms to face him.

He was suddenly gripping her hard by her shoulders.

"You never let me touch you there."

"Where?"

"Here."

She flinched and tried to turn away as he settled his hand on her stomach.

"Why?"

"Because I pooch out there."

"All normal women do. And you have less than anyone I've seen around here."

"Really?"

"You should look at people next time you're in town. Besides, I love you. All of you. And I love to touch you. Even here. This is you."

They made love. Right there. In broad daylight.

"Rachel?" R.J.'s shout reverberated through the house. "Rach?"

It was the moment Rachel had been praying for and the moment she'd been dreading. R.J. was back, but was he planning to stay around, or was he going to serve her with divorce papers? And how would she ever tell him about the baby? She pushed her chair back from her desk. Took a deep breath. Rose to her feet.

R.J.'s head poked around the door frame. "Hey!" He strode to her side and wrapped her in a bear hug, and then he kissed her on a mouth gone slack with astonishment. "I thought I'd never make it back!" He slumped into the chair in front of her desk and bent to unlace his combat boots. "First the mission gets delayed, and then the plane breaks down. Then the bad guys hightail it away and we had to wait until...well..." he cleared his throat, "you know. So, did you miss me?"

"Miss you...?" Rachel felt for the chair behind her knees and sat down in it with a thud. "Where exactly have you been?"

His boots finally off, R.J. straightened. Sighed. "You know I can't tell you that, Rachel. I've been flying. That's all I can ever say."

"Flying."

"In my plane."

"Your plane. You've been flying in your plane."

"Yeah." He looked at her. Saw the confusion in her eyes. "Didn't they give you my note?"

"Who?"

"The squadron."

"No."

"No one told you?"

Rachel shook her head, sure that if she tried to speak she'd end up crying. Or laughing.

"So where did you think I was?"

"Gone."

"Gone where?"

"Gone. I thought you'd left me."

"Left you? Like…left you? Why would you think that?"

"We fought."

"The night I left?" He reached a hand up to scratch his head. "Yeah. I know. Sorry about that. I was really angry. But I still shouldn't have stomped out like that. I drove around for a while before going out to the squadron. Bummed around. I'd decided to head back here when there was a situation and we were alerted to fly a mission. I mean, they would have called me, but I was already there. So I got my bags out of the pickup and hopped in the plane. It wasn't supposed to be for very long, but things happened and I wasn't…I couldn't call. Sorry."

Rachel still didn't know whether to laugh or cry. So she did both.

"You really thought I'd left you?"

Rachel nodded. Then she decided. She began to sob.

Marc muted the TV and cocked his head to listen. He thought he'd heard the twins. They'd been in bed for more than an hour, but that had never stopped them from staying up before. He listened another moment, and then he decided to check on them.

He walked down the hall and stood at the door of their room until he could identify the individual sounds of their breathing. Then he decided to get a drink. As he approached the kitchen and saw the light on, he remembered Beth was there. His step slowed as he realized that it mattered. It wasn't so long ago that knowing she was near would have made him hurry to her side. Now, he'd just as soon keep his distance; he never knew what sort of mood she'd be in. Except to know that she was never in The Mood.

He propped an elbow against the entry to the kitchen and watched her.

She was working on her scrapbooks.

She was always working on something. Like a windup toy, it seemed that from the moment she left bed in the morning she was in perpetual motion, running from task to task, always stressed because she never had time to get everything done. But when they closed the bedroom door at night, just at the point when they finally had time to talk, to catch up on each other's day, she stopped. She fell into bed, rolled away from him, and that was it.

They used to spend hours talking and laughing, playing racquetball or running, or just...doing nothing. And now there was always something.

"Stop it, Beth. Just stop it!"

Beth lifted her head from the scrapbooks she was making. One for each of the boys. She was six months behind. "Stop what?"

"This. All of this...this stuff! The house doesn't have to be perfectly clean all the time. The shirts don't have to be starched. And why are you so obsessed with the scrapbooks? You don't have to be the world's best mother. You only have to be their mother...and I wish you'd be my wife too."

Beth stood, her cheeks flaming. "You don't understand," she mumbled as she left the room "You just don't understand."

"Then tell me!" he yelled after her.

He sat at the table, frustrated and mad at himself. Things hadn't seemed right between them for a long time. It had been forever since he'd heard his wife laugh, really laugh, out loud. An eternity since they'd made love.

He flipped through the scrapbook she had left behind. He had to admit she'd done a wonderful job. Each page was color-coordinated. Each page had a different theme. He left the kitchen, turning out the lights, and wandered into the dark family room. He didn't want to go to bed because he knew what would be waiting for him.

With a heavy sigh, he tossed himself on the couch and ran his hands through his hair, pausing halfway to swear. He kicked a foot against the arm of the couch for good measure. "I'm such a jerk," he muttered.

A low moan drew his attention to a dark corner of the room. The one between the TV and the armchair. Beth was hunched there with her back against the wall, arms crossed tightly against her stomach.

He was beside her in an instant. As he put a hand to her shoulder, he heard a cry of almost inhuman pain. He sat down next to her and pulled her over to his lap. Then she threw her arms around his neck and sobbed into his chest.

He let her cry, wondering if he should do or say something. But he remembered what his mother once told him. She'd warned him Beth would probably cry sometimes. And it could be about something, or it could be about nothing, but the best thing he could do was just be there. So he held her tight until her sobs had turned to sniffles.

"Do you want to talk yet?" he asked

She shook her head.

"Well, then, do you mind if I do?"

She shook her head.

"I'm sorry, Beth. I don't even know what to say except that the capacity to be a big jerk comes with the male chromosome."

He felt one of her hands unclasp from the other. It began to play with his chest hairs. His heart lifted. So she must not hate him. It was a start. "You have to tell me when I start doing jerky things, okay?"

She nodded.

"That way I don't get out of hand." He paused. "But I don't think that all of this has to do with me...does it?"

Beth closed her eyes and shook her head. He could feel her eyelashes flip against his chest.

"Can you tell me?" he asked tilting her head so he could see her eyes.

"I don't know how to be a mother, Marc."

"Sure you do. You're doing a great job."

"But I don't know that. There aren't any SOS courses on this. There aren't any primary objectives. I don't get any evaluation reports. I'm making it up as I go along, and I'm flying by the seat of my pants."

"That's okay."

"But I hate it. I've never felt so incompetent in my life. That's why the scrapbooks are so important. I do a good job at them. Everything turns out looking good. And then," her voice started to quaver, "and then you accused me of being obsessed with them." She started to cry again.

"Oh, Beth. I'm so sorry." He was close to tears now too. He hadn't known. He kissed her forehead.

"I hate my life. Every day is more miserable than the one before. The only happy thought I have is, 'Well, at least I'm not like my mother. At least I'm alive.' I can't do this. There's no structure. There's no one to talk to. And whenever I try with you, I just feel so guilty."

"Why?"

"Because you love the twins so much and I wish they'd never been born," she ended with a sob. "I'm such a horrible person. I resent it that they can't have conversations with me. I resent it that I quit work for them. I want my life back."

"So are you telling me I need to lock up all the knives?"

"No," she sniffed, offended.

"You're not on the verge of drowning them?"

"No," she sighed. "But the first thing I think when I hear them cry in the morning is, 'Shoot, they're already awake.'"

"So why do you keep being their mommy?"

"They're my kids."

"Duty."

"I have to. Who else will take care of them?"

"You remember your first year at the academy? How much you hated it? How much you loathed it?"

She nodded.

"Why'd you come back the second year? You didn't have to."

"I promised myself I'd do it. I wasn't going to give up. I'd already made it through the hardest part."

"And what'd you think of the underclassmen when you were an upperclassman?"

She rolled her eyes.

"So why'd you keep training them?"

"Because I knew they'd be real cadets after it was over."

"Beth, listen to me. The hardest part is over. The twins are almost three years old now. This is when it starts to be rewarding. They'll be talking in real sentences soon. They'll start to become real little people. In a couple years, you'll be proud of the little monsters. And they'll be proud that you're their mommy. What was the cadet motto at the academy?"

"I don't know." Beth wasn't in a mood to be reasonable.

"Of course you don't. It's because you didn't do it, you knucklehead. The motto was 'Cooperate to Graduate.' The idea was that for everyone to survive, everyone had to pitch in to help. There weren't supposed to be any Lone Rangers."

"Oh."

"I don't want you to be a Lone Ranger in this family. I've never wanted you to be one. But, Beth, you have to learn to ask for help. I can't help you if I don't know what you need. Understand?"

"Yes."

"I think we should get someone to help you."

She was shaking her head by the time he finished speaking. "It would cost too much."

"Beth, you are priceless. You own my heart. I want to take care of you, and at this point in time, taking care of you involves getting someone to help you."

"It's too expensive."

"Have you looked into it?"

"No."

"We'll find a way to do it, okay?"

Beth looked at him with shimmering eyes.

"And if you want to, you should find a job."

"I wouldn't know the first thing about how to get one."

"Are you a good engineer?"

"I'm a darn good engineer."

"Well, there's always a job for a good engineer."

"I've been thinking…" Beth couldn't bring herself to say it. She didn't know how it would sound out loud.

Marc pulled her close. "What?" The word was spoken softly into her ear.

"I've been thinking about rejoining the Air Force. Asking for my commission back."

Although Beth couldn't see him, Marc was smiling. "Can't get enough of that uniform?"

"I miss it."

"Really?"

"Really." She sighed and snuggled closer.

"Then let's start asking some questions. But in the meantime, I think you should put the twins in a play group or day care a couple days a week."

"I don't know…the Child Development Center is probably already full by now. Maybe in the fall."

"I think you should do it now. I'll ask around at work tomorrow and see if I can find out the names of any places."

"But the money…"

"It doesn't matter." He kissed the top of her head. "You need some time to be you. To kick back and have some fun."

She was silent for a moment. "Fun. Fun sounds good. But I'm a modern woman," she smiled into his chest. "And I'm into immediate gratification—"

She'd meant to proposition him, but she wasn't able to get out another word. She was being thoroughly kissed by a man who was thrilled to have his wife back.

CHAPTER 31

⌐

*R*achel woke with a start. She'd had a nightmare. R.J. was gone. She put out a hand toward him, not sure if she was awake or asleep. Not sure if she'd find him there or not.

Her hand touched a real arm. She gave it a pinch just to make sure.

"Ow!" R.J. rolled over and glared at her. "What did you do that for?"

"I just wanted to be sure that you were there," she was staring at him, unblinking, through the dark.

"Rach?"

"What?"

"I'm here. I'm not going anywhere." He reached a hand out to smooth the hair from her face.

And she remembered what it was. God. She shot up from the bed, feeling foolish that she hadn't remembered before now.

"R.J., I have to tell you something. I'll be right back."

"Where are you going?" she heard him call as she ran down the stairs.

"I'll be right back."

R.J. threw his hands up into the air and then flopped over onto his stomach. He would probably never understand her, but God knew how much he loved her.

She was back in a minute, breathing heavily with exertion.

He reached out toward a table lamp and turned on the light. "You should be more careful with yourself." He sat up and slid an arm around her. He still couldn't believe she was pregnant. That was going to take some getting used to.

She set a book down in front of them and flipped it open.

296

"Wait a second." He reached for the book and turned it over to look at the cover. "This is my Bible."

"I know. I found it while you were gone."

He put a hand to her back. "And now I'm here."

"I know. It's because I made a deal with God. And a deal is a deal. He gave you back, and now I have to tell you about him."

"Now?"

"Now."

The next afternoon, Beth was dreaming her favorite dream again. She was back in uniform. Back in her job. It was as though she were looking over her own shoulder. She saw herself answer her own phone, pick up a pen, and take a message. Her desk was in complete order. There was a picture of the twins at one corner, a picture of Marc at the other. She looked good. She looked in control.

She woke at the sound of a cry from the crib. Running, she nearly tripped over the toy truck that lay in the middle of the hall. Stepped on a toy carpenter's bench instead.

"Ouch!" she grabbed her foot and rubbed her arch.

The cry came again.

She opened the door and tiptoed to a crib.

Andy was dreaming. Small hands twitching, mouth groping for some unknown food. Fortunately he hadn't wakened Josh.

Beth closed the door and returned to the living room. Her eyes took in the laundry basket, overflowing with clothes to iron. The toy chest, hemorrhaging an assorted collection of stuffed animals, cars, and books. The dirty lunch dishes sitting on the coffee table. She closed her eyes, wishing she could summon that uniformed in-control woman to come and help her. She opened her eyes. Everything was still there. Waiting.

"Move with a purpose," she mumbled as she stacked the dishes and took them into the kitchen.

She had just crammed all the toys back into their chest when she heard telling murmurs from the twins' bedroom.

When she peeked her head into the room, she saw them facing each other in their cribs, hands wrapped around the slats. They were carrying on a conversation in what she called "twin talk," a language that loosely resembled English. They looked happy, so she left them where they were and began to tackle the ironing. She preferred to do it when the twins were contained so that they couldn't accidentally pull the iron down on themselves.

I need church.

The thought came unbidden. She put down the iron to contemplate it because it sounded like a good idea. She'd have to talk to Marc about it.

Beth had almost fallen asleep that night when she remembered her vow. She rolled onto her elbow and ran a caressing hand across her husband's shoulder. "Can I ask you something?"

He caught her hand and folded it into his chest, drawing her near against his back. "Anything."

"Did you go to chapel your freshman year?"

"Of course."

"Do you remember why you went?"

He rolled over onto his back so he could look at her. "Sure—it was the only place where they couldn't get to you. They couldn't tell you to drop to the floor and give them twenty pushups. You didn't have to salute anyone. For one blissful hour, you could be you. It was a haven. It was heaven."

"I need that again, Marc. I need to go to church. I need to have one hour a week where everything is black and white and clear as water. I need to know that there's a big guy up there who has everything figured out."

He lifted a hand to cup her cheek. "Why? Are you afraid of dying?"

"No. It's not that...it's more like I'm afraid of living."

"Where do you want to go?"

"I don't know. I'll find someplace. You don't have to come if you don't want to."

"I'll go. It's not like I don't believe in God. It'll be good for the boys." He rolled back over onto his side.

Beth slipped an arm underneath his and gave him a hug. "Thanks." *Okay, God. I'm back online.*

The next evening, Anne drove to the O Club on Friday to meet Will. It was a CGO meeting day, so everyone would be there. She shook off tension from the phone call she'd received just before leaving the office.

"I want to report something," the man had said.

"I can take a message."

"There's a contractor working on a housing project in the north end of town, and he's not building to code."

"What's the contractor's name? I can send an inspector out."

"I can't tell you his name. Then he'd know who I am."

"Maybe you could tell me what street the house is on."

"No, then you'll know who I am."

"Perhaps if you told me what the problem is, we could look for it that way."

"Then you'll know who I am."

"Is this a prank call?"

"No. I'm just tired of him getting away with things like this."

"Like what!"

At first the whole thing had given her the creeps. As if there were some huge conspiracy in town. But the drive to base had given her perspective, and as she replayed the conversation, she began to laugh. She smiled now as she thought of it.

She looked in the meeting room first, but everyone from the CGO meeting was already gone. As she retraced her steps and walked back toward the bar, she ran into Karen. "What are you doing here?"

"Picking up Kevin. He was at the meeting. How are things for you guys? Have you found a place yet?"

"No, but we have the lease through Christmas. How are things for you guys?" asked Anne, in hopes that Karen would read into the innocent phrase all the hundred questions she really wanted to ask.

Karen blushed. "Everything's fine. It's been wonderful since he's been back."

Anne searched Karen's eyes and saw nothing but happiness there. "I'm glad for you."

"I thought a lot about what you said. About God. About religion. I talked about it to Kevin too. He admits that the Book of Mormon doesn't make sense all the time, but he says it's a question of faith. And of believing..." her words tapered off as she looked at her friend. "I don't know what to think. I know what I'm supposed to believe, but if I think about it too much, it doesn't hold together. I read the Bible you gave me before Kevin got home. And I want to believe it. I really do. It makes sense."

She broke off and looked around the room. Then she resumed in a lower voice. "But I can't. If I believe, then I'll lose everything I have. Kevin. My family. They won't understand. And I'll be worse than a nonperson. I won't be able to go to my sister's wedding. Won't be able to see my nieces and nephews baptized. Their lives will go on without me.

I'll be the strange aunt. The one who left the church. The one it's not safe to talk to. My faith is me, and I don't know who I am without it."

"But that means you're choosing a lie over what you know to be the truth," Anne protested.

"It's not a lie. Not really. I can be a social Mormon without believing in the theology. That won't hurt anyone. I'll just have to pray that your God will understand."

"Just make me a promise. Don't give up on God yet. Please, don't. And always remember that he'll never give up on you."

Anne found Will sitting at a table with a couple she didn't know.

He stood and pulled out a chair when he saw Anne threading her way through the tables.

"Anne, I want you to meet Major Peterson and his wife, Lisa. They just moved here from Wright-Patterson Air Force Base in Ohio."

"Hello, sir." Anne smiled and shook the major's hand and then his wife's. "How do you both like it here?"

"The weather's gorgeous. Will said you moved here right after your wedding. It must have been like a one-year honeymoon. This is paradise."

Paradise? A one-year honeymoon? After one hurricane, one near-divorce, and one near-conversion...I can survive anything! Anne looked at Will. Smiled. "It's as close as it gets."

"Will had just started telling me that you work in town. What do you do?"

"I'm a secretary."

GLOSSARY

AAFES—Army and Air Force Exchange Services. Their mission is to provide quality merchandise and services of necessity and convenience to authorized customers at uniformly low prices.

AWOL—Absent Without Leave. According to Air Force Instruction (AFI) 36-2911, an unauthorized absence starts when a member is absent from where he or she is ordered or otherwise required to be present.

BX—Base Exchange. Operated by AAFES, these "department stores" are present on every base.

CGO—Company Grade Officer. This group of officers is comprised of those holding the ranks of second and first lieutenant, and captain.

CGOC—Company Grade Officers Council. This is the organization comprised of those holding the ranks of Company Grade Officers. It allows CGOs to interact with other military professionals and peers. It also provides opportunities for leadership both on base and in the community.

Commissary—The Defense Commissary Agency (DeCA) operates commissaries worldwide to provide authorized patrons with a safe and secure place in which to buy groceries. Items may be purchased at cost plus a small surcharge.

DG—Distinguished Graduate. This designation may be earned in many Air Force education programs. Traditionally, it referred to the top 10 percent of a graduating class; this is still the case at USAFA. This designation appears in personnel records and is viewed favorably by promotion boards.

DP—Definitely Promote. This is one of three boxes that can be checked on an OPR. The other two are "Promote" and "Do Not Promote."

FGO—Field Grade Officer. This group of officers is comprised of those holding the ranks of major, lieutenant colonel, and colonel.

Full bird—This refers to someone holding the rank of colonel. Colonels are designated by the insignia of a silver eagle on their uniforms, while lieutenant colonels are designated by a silver oak leaf, and majors by a gold oak leaf. Lieutenant colonels are normally addressed as "colonel" in informal situations. Referring to someone as a "full bird" identifies them as a true colonel.

LDS—Latter-day Saint. Used when referring to The Church of Jesus Christ of Latter-day Saints or a member of the Mormon church.

Orders—the actual form authorizing a PCS.

OPR—Officer Performance Report. This is the document through which an officer receives an annual evaluation.

OSC—Officers' Spouses' Club.

Pac-10—Pacific-10. This athletic conference comprises the following universities: University of Arizona, Arizona University, University of California, Stanford University, UCLA, University of Southern California, University of Oregon, Oregon State University, University of Washington, and Washington State University.

PCS—Permanent Change in Station. Someone PCSing is moving to a new assignment.

POA—Plan of Attack.

Rank—Enlisted rank in the U.S. Air Force follows this progression: airman basic, airman, airman first class, senior airman, staff sergeant, technical sergeant, master sergeant, senior master sergeant, chief master sergeant, chief master sergeant of the Air Force. Officer rank in the U.S. Air Force follows this progression: second lieutenant, first lieutenant, major, lieutenant colonel, colonel, brigadier general, major general, lieutenant general, general.

Readiness bag—A bag filled with essential gear that is kept ready to go at all times; generally carried in the trunk of a service member's private vehicle so they are prepared to deploy at a moment's notice.

SOS—Squadron Officer School. This professional military education course may be attended in residence at Maxwell Air Force Base in Alabama. This school is for those holding the rank of captain. Those not chosen to attend in residence must complete this course by correspondence.

SPO—System Program Office. Working in a SPO may allow engineers the chance to work on a particular aircraft or weapons system in an applied-engineering environment instead of a research-based environment.

TDY—Temporary Change in Duty Station. This is the military equivalent of a business trip.

USAFA—U.S. Air Force Academy. Located in Colorado Springs, Colorado. Established on April 1, 1954, the first graduating class entered in 1955. The first class to receive their entire schooling at the current location was the class of 1962.

About the Author

Siri Mitchell graduated from the University of Washington with a business degree and has worked in all levels of government. As a military spouse, she has lived all over the world, including Paris and Tokyo. With her husband and their little girl, Siri enjoys observing and learning from different cultures. She is fluent in French and currently mastering the skill of sushi making.

If you are interested in contacting Siri, please check out her website at sirimitchell.com.

If you enjoyed
Something Beyond the Sky,
you'll want to read
Siri Mitchell's other novel,
Kissing Adrien.

*"The French are always up for romance, so when
the crowd saw Adrien striding through the Paris airport toward me,
I'm sure they were hoping for a good kiss...
I was too."*

Claire Le Noyer, 29, wants a do-over. She wants the life where she majors in history, not accounting. Where she takes two-hour lunches, not ten minutes in front of her computer. Where her pastor boyfriend treats her like an attractive woman he's deeply in love with, not like a nice pet dog.

But for now she's a Seattle numbers-cruncher with a wardrobe from REI sent to fashionable Paris to check out an apartment left to her parents by a mysterious cousin. When her childhood crush—handsome, pleasure-loving, and very French Adrien—introduces Claire to the City of Lights, béarnaise sauce, and kisses in very public places, Claire cautiously begins to embrace another way of living.

Who would have guessed Adrien would also introduce her to the bigger questions she must answer...Who is her one true love? And will she ever learn to enjoy the life God has placed right in front of her?

A fresh, funny novel of faith and joie de vivre—and what happens when they meet.

"A sheer delight! Smart, funny, romantic,
and intelligent. Loved it! *C'est magnifique!*"
LAURA JENSEN WALKER, author of *Dreaming in Black & White*

"Enchanting! Siri Mitchell weaves an irresistible tale. *Merci beaucoup!*"
GINGER GARRETT, author of *Chosen: The Lost Diaries of Queen Esther*

Harvest House Publishers
For the Best in Inspirational Fiction

Mindy Starns Clark
THE MILLION DOLLAR MYSTERIES
SERIES
A Penny for Your Thoughts
Don't Take Any Wooden Nickels
Dime a Dozen
A Quarter for a Kiss
The Buck Stops Here

SMART CHICK MYSTERY SERIES
The Trouble with Tulip

Roxanne Henke
COMING HOME TO
BREWSTER SERIES
After Anne
Finding Ruth
Becoming Olivia
Always Jan

Sally John
THE OTHER WAY HOME SERIES
A Journey by Chance
After All These Years
Just to See You Smile
The Winding Road Home

IN A HEARTBEAT SERIES
In a Heartbeat
Flash Point
Moment of Truth

Hope Lyda
Hip to Be Square

Susan Meissner
Why the Sky is Blue

A Window to the World
Remedy for Regret

Siri Mitchell
Kissing Adrien

Debra White Smith
THE AUSTEN SERIES
First Impressions
Reason and Romance
Central Park
Northpointe Chalet
Amanda

Lori Wick
THE TUDOR MILLS TRILOGY
Moonlight on the Millpond
Just Above a Whisper

THE ENGLISH GARDEN SERIES
The Proposal
The Rescue
The Visitor
The Pursuit

THE YELLOW ROSE TRILOGY
Every Little Thing About You
A Texas Sky
City Girl

CONTEMPORARY FICTION
Bamboo & Lace
Beyond the Picket Fence
Every Storm
Pretense
The Princess
Sophie's Heart